double or Quits!

RACHEL RILEY'S year of
(almost) taking control

D1434072

Also by Joanna Nadin

My Double Life
Double Trouble

Joanna Nadin

2 books in 1

double or Quits!

RACHEL RILEY'S year of (almost) taking control

OXFORD
UNIVERSITY PRESS

OXFORD
UNIVERSITY PRESS

Great Clarendon Street, Oxford OX2 6DP

Oxford University Press is a department of the University of Oxford.
It furthers the University's objective of excellence in research, scholarship,
and education by publishing worldwide in

Oxford   New York

Auckland   Cape Town   Dar es Salaam   Hong Kong   Karachi
Kuala Lumpur   Madrid   Melbourne   Mexico City   Nairobi
New Delhi   Shanghai   Taipei   Toronto

With offices in

Argentina   Austria   Brazil   Chile   Czech Republic   France   Greece
Guatemala   Hungary   Italy   Japan   Poland   Portugal   Singapore
South Korea   Switzerland   Thailand   Turkey   Ukraine   Vietnam

Oxford is a registered trade mark of Oxford University Press
in the UK and in certain other countries

'Back to Life' first published 2009
'The Facts of Life' first published 2010

First published in this edition 2011

British Library Cataloguing in Publication Data
Data available

ISBN: 978-0-19-279266-2

1 3 5 7 9 10 8 6 4 2

Printed in Great Britain

Paper used in the production of this book is a natural,
recyclable product made from wood grown in sustainable forests.
The manufacturing process conforms to the environmental
regulations of the country of origin.

Contents

back to life

Rachel Riley (sort of) seizes the day

Tuesday 1

New Year's Day

1 p.m.

This is utterly the worst start to a New Year ever.

How things change. This time, last January, I was nestled in warm cocoon of love with Braintree College rock god and potential ONE Justin Statham. Whereas today am alone in non-cocoon-like John-Lewis-decorated bedroom, with borderline hangover. Is not even warm as dog has eaten radiator knob and heating is stuck in off position. It is utter metaphor for life. Am wretched outcast like Joan of Arc. Or Amy Winehouse.

It is all so-called best friend Scarlet's fault. As usual. She has, yet again, snogged the object of my desire. This time it is potential future first-ever black Prime Minister Hilary Nuamah. It is an utter betrayal, not just of me, but of our anti-snogging sisterhood pact of abstinence thing. Which would have said last night only was so in shock immediately downed several glasses of punch. Then, fuelled by experimental vodka and eggnog mix, had brilliant idea of going to Justin's house for midnight kiss. But, when I got to the mock-tudor mansion, I could clearly see him grappling Sophie Microwave Muffins Jacobs against the mock mahogany DVD shelving unit, underneath the mock mistletoe, so had utterly missed boat again. So, drowned sorrow immediately in five Marks & Spencer cherry liqueur chocolates, which brought along for energy-giving purposes (no Kendal mint cake to be found), then had next brilliant idea to go back to party to snog Jack, Scarlet's brother, who have kissed previously to some effect (admittedly onstage in questionable production of *Bugsy Malone*, and in dare during mind-slippage episode at Glastonbury, but there was definite frisson, and even thought was possibly the ONE for a while). But when I threw arms around him and said, 'You may kiss me now, Jack Stone,' he did not seem too excited at all. In fact, his exact words were, 'You've been at bloody Justin's, haven't you. I am sick to death of being your sloppy seconds, Riley.' Or words to that effect, as memory may be slightly impaired by alcohol intake. Anyway, outcome is same, i.e. the sisterhood, and my love life, are in tatters. Plus had to watch Scarlet entwined with Hilary in the seventies wicker loveswing thing until Sad Ed offered to walk me home out of pity.

On plus side, am not the only one livid about Scarlet and Hilary. Mum is equally incensed. It is not because she favours him as potential lover for me, it is because he was supposed to repatriate her moronic parents to St Slaughter this morning but, as yet, he has failed to reappear from Scarlet's house. She has just been in to demand that *a)* I stop malingering in bed; *b)* I call Scarlet and tell her to send Hilary home as Grandpa Clegg and Dad are locked in a no-win situation over something to do with Andy Murray's hair; and *c)* I take dog for walk as he and Bruce (offspring of dog, now owned by Cleggs) have combined to form one giant

idiotic canine force and are taking it in turns to disgrace themselves on the dining room table. It is official. My life is pants.

2 p.m.

Have called Scarlet to demand *a*) repatriation of Hilary to 24 Summerdale Road, and *b*) to know why she was snogging him last night when she was: *subclause i*) signed up to anti-snogging pact; and *subclause ii*) fully aware that I was, in fact, in love with him.

She said, *a*) no, he is spending the day in bed being nursed by her and Suzy following potential concussion due to the loveswing falling off the ceiling hook; *b*) *i*) whatever, and *ii*) I had told her I was not interested in him one bit so it is my fault for not being honest about my feelings, in fact.

I said, *a*) that will not go down well with Janet Riley i.e. my mum; and *b*) that's such a lie, you boyfriend-stealing, pact-breaking vampire.

So Scarlet said, *a*) tell Janet to take a chill pill; *b*) *i*) check your diary, you moron, and *ii*) I am not a Goth any more, I am semi-emo, how many times?

So hung up as there is no way can tell Mum to take pills of any kind, let alone chill ones (she is still reeling from the day I experimented with calling her 'Janet'). Plus all the subclauses and degrees of emo-ness were getting confusing. But have checked diary and Scarlet is totally right. I did say I was utterly not into him. Which is very annoying as now cannot officially hate her. Even though she is traitor. Am going round Sad Ed's. He will cheer me up. Or will at least be more depressed than me, which is always heartening. Will take dog. Its absence will appease Mum for the non-return of Hilary.

4 p.m.
Am back earlier than intended due to dog not fully appreciating Sad Ed's mum's many and varied Aled Jones icons. It is now being comforted on sofa by James and a box of Elizabeth Shaw mints. Mrs Thomas is on her own sofa being comforted by Mr Thomas and a CD of 'Walking in the Air'.

On plus side, at least I still have Sad Ed for company in my tortured solitude. He had also broken pact and snogged Melody Bean (apprentice witch, owner of tarantula called Arthur, obsessed with Sad Ed) but is now utterly regretting it. Not only will he have annoying Melody stalking him around John Major High for months, but he says his mojo appears to have been lost somewhere between Hallowe'en and Christmas. Apparently the snog failed to cause any trouser-area stirrings.

He is blaming the sisterhood for depleting his masculinity and says we need to burn all Wicca-related paraphernalia in a ritual sacrifice. Have agreed. It is utterly the way forward. Am going to make it one of my New Year resolutions. Along with following progessive, prosnogging promises:

8

1. Tell the truth at all times. If had not lied about Hilary it might well be my lips he was glued to now instead of Scarlet's treacherous ones.
2. *Carpe diem*, i.e. seize the day! Which means utter experimenting as far as snogging is concerned. Am never going to find the ONE if just keep having accidental liaisons with Jack or ill-advised flirtations with Justin. The ONE is out there somewhere. Maybe even right under my nose. I just need to be open-minded. And open-armed. And possibly open-mouthed.
3. Find someone to return Sad Ed's mojo to its rightful state. His depression is off the scale when he is not getting some. Plus now he does not even have the option of untimely death, having spectacularly failed to drown himself in the shopping-trolley-clogged 'River' Slade last year.
4. Pass all AS level levels. Especially Philosophy as it is completely the subject of generally day-seizing experimental types. In fact might even have started new philosophical theory without knowing it!
5. Get new diary. Charlie and Lola may be ironic but have had to staple several sheets of A4 paper to page already in order to fit more than three words in the allotted space. Plus it was purchased by Scarlet and is therefore contaminated with betrayal.

Life, as they say, is what you make it. And am definitely,

no doubt about it, going to make mine fabulous. Starting now.

. . . .

Wednesday 2

9 a.m.
Hurrah, it is Day One of my new, forward-thinking, truth-telling, love-embracing life. Will start by being honest with all family members.

9.30 a.m.
Am back in room. And not through choice. It is for telling Grandpa Clegg that he is deluded, prejudiced, and smells of athlete's foot powder. It is good job they are going home today as it is quite hard to be honest with Cleggs without referring to them as smelly, racist, or mad. Also Dad not amused as named and shamed him for bringing Cadbury's Roses into house (substandard chocolates, and not to be purchased under any circumstances) when he had blamed Clive and Marjory. Am now political prisoner, like Nelson Mandela, incarcerated for speaking the truth. Hurrah! Am going to phone Scarlet immediately to highlight my philosophical left-wing credentials. And also invite her to the ritual burning of all sisterhood paraphernalia tomorrow.

10 a.m.
Scarlet says I am not like Nelson Mandela and there is

nothing philosophical or edgy about telling Mum that Dad prefers Praline Moments to Quality Street Green Triangles (superior in every way, for reasons known only to Mum). Nor have I started a new philosophy by seizing the day or experimenting snog-wise etc. Apparently liberals are always doing that. Plus she has declined the invitation to the ritual burning of Wicca/sisterhood para-phernalia. She says Suzy is using the cauldron (i.e. the Nigella soup pot) to make parsnip soup, plus burning is environmentally unfriendly and the excess CO_2 could melt too much polar ice cap and drown half of Alaska. This is a lie. It is nothing to do with meltwater, it is because she is ashamed of being the one who ended the dream. That is why she is not coming to wave the Cleggs off on their return to St Slaughter in the environmentally friendly Nissan Micra either. I said she had no need to be embarrassed about her relationship with Hilary, even if it is based on lies and deceit. She said *au contraire*, she is proud of her relationship, but does not want Granny Clegg attacking her with her loaded Spar bags. She has a point.

11 a.m.
The Cleggs have finally left the environs of Saffron Walden taking Hilary and the perpetual smell of Fray Bentos with them. Mum has opened all windows and turned the Glade plug-ins on to full. Even the dog is relieved. It was being upstaged by Bruce in the hairy,

moronic stakes and has now been restored to its rightful position. It is currently licking the carpet in celebration.

The departure did not go completely smoothly though. Scarlet was right about the Spar bags because, when Hilary finally arrived, unshaven and with telltale scratch marks on upper chest, Granny Clegg smacked him round the leg with a particularly heavy one. I pointed out that it was potential racial harassment and/or employee abuse but she says it is not that he is black, it is that he has betrayed me, and her, for a commie. (She means Scarlet, who is not a commie. She is a social Marxist. Apparently they are entirely different.) I was worried she might decide to sack Hilary but she says she is going to keep him on so she can wheedle sordid details out of him and pass them on to me. I said if I wanted sordid details, which I do not, I could just ask Scarlet, but Granny Clegg says she cannot be trusted not to put a New Labour spin on everything. This is true. She has learned from the best, i.e. Suzy, who worships at the altar of Alastair Campbell. Anyway Granny Clegg cannot afford to sack him, as her new non-fortune-telling hip is still settling in and Grandpa Clegg is still weakened from his appendix operation and cannot bend down to restock the freezer with Viennetta on his own.

Before he went, Hilary asked if he could speak to me in private (i.e. the garage, the only room not infested by Cleggs or Mum and her all-seeing eye (aka James)) to say he was sorry if there was any misunderstanding about his

intentions, which were entirely honourable, that I was in no way a lesser person than Scarlet, just that their hearts both beat to the same tune (i.e. the 'Red Flag' and/or 'A New England') and that, if it was any consolation, he would always think of me as a sister. Annoyingly was duty-bound (or resolution-bound) to tell truth so said his Facebook poking was entirely misleading, that I knew as many Billy Bragg songs as Scarlet, and that no, it was no consolation at all, as it was bad enough being a sister to James, who makes the mathletes look edgy. Luckily at that point Dad came in to find Bruce (consuming bottle of ant powder) and Hilary escaped before I could maim him with a Swingball racket. I pity him now though. He has seven hours confined in a small space with the Cleggs who will witter non-stop on their preferred topics—is Stonehenge 'real' (no idea); is Bruce better than the dog (no, equally mental); and aren't the Exeter services amazing (no, unless you come from Cornwall). Whereas I am in 24 Summerdale Road, which is Clegg-free and peaceful at last. Just the 'click click' of James Googling frenetically, the 'psshhht' of Mum Cillit Banging the suspicious ring off the bath, and the 'tap, clonk, "bugger"' of Dad trying to putt practice balls into an Ovaltine jar and hitting the DVD player instead. The sweet sound of normality.

Also have new diary. James agreed to swap as he got three: This Day in History, Cats and Kittens, and bog standard WHSmith desk. I went for the WHSmith one as do not like whimsical kittens (have inherited fear of them from Mum) nor do I want such gems as *Today in 1872 Brigham Young was arrested for having 25 wives* clogging up my philosophical thoughts. James is pleased with the transaction as says he can sell the Charlie and Lola one to an impressionable Year 2 for £3 or a term's supply of first break biscuits. (He is becoming well-versed in the ways of a playground gangster. Mum is right, the sooner he is away from St Regina's menace Keanu O'Grady and lackadaisical headteacher 'Nige' the better. She is counting down the days until his secondary place offer comes through and she can purchase his St Gregory's Girls uniform.) Anyway, point is, am only two days into the New Year and it is one resolution down already. Maybe will find love of life tomorrow and will seize day and embrace him with immediate snog. Hurrah!

Thursday 3

Did not find love of life. In fact only saw two men who are not related to me. Sad Ed for ritual sisterhood burning, and former Criminal and Retard Mark Lambert (now of BTEC bricklaying fame) going in to Thin Kylie's house for a booty call, and there is no way he is my ONE. He has a Nike tick shaved into his head.

Sad Ed says I need to be patient and that love will manifest itself when I am ready. I said I am ready and, if waiting patiently was the answer, why was he so desperate to find his missing mojo that he would resort to

asking to borrow James's talking Nicola doll (fortunately deceased following extended stay in dog's intestines)? He said he did not want it for pornographic purposes, he wanted to burn it as part of the ritual as she symbolizes all that is wrong with sisterhoods (synchronized outfits, questionable hairdos, backstabbing friends). This is a lie. I clicked his internet history and he has been on the official Girls Aloud website seven times today trying to arouse himself. Obviously to no avail as he is still utterly miserable. He says he will not find inner peace until he can 'stand to attention'.

5 p.m.
Oh God. Have just had thought. What if Sad Ed is ONE after all? Should I have embraced him over the dying embers of our melted Wicca wands (broken light sabre and electric fly swat)? Maybe it is not plastic Nicola he needs. Maybe I am the one to stir his mojo. We have snogged before, after all. And even though earth did definitely not move, did not vomit either. Plus would kill two resolutions with one stone. Ooh, maybe will try it tomorrow. Yes. Will seize day and experiment with Sad Ed. Hurrah!

. . . .

Friday 4
9 a.m.
Today is crucial day as may well discover I have been

living several doors away from potential ONE all along, and also that I am the answer to Sad Ed's missing mojo. Am wearing carefully calculated Sad Ed arousal outfit. It is combination of Tuesday's psycho/emo look and border-line homoerotica, i.e. excess lipstick, fishnet tights, and a Morrissey T-shirt that he left behind at Scarlet's once. One of them is bound to turn him on.

9.30 a.m.

Mum has sent me back upstairs to change. She says there is no way any daughter of hers is going out dressed like Scarlet. It is not the lipstick. It is the Morrissey T-shirt. Which says 'Meat is Murder'. She does not want Marjory next door thinking she condones militant vegetarianism in any way. On plus side have already done another res-olution, i.e. was totally honest, i.e. when she said 'Where do you think you are going looking like that?' I said, 'To seduce Sad Ed.' Clearly she thinks this is either sarcasm or an impossibility as she has not batted an eyelid at my Mickey Mouse T-shirt which is age eight so very tight and bust-revealing. Anyway, have Morrissey T-shirt in bag to put on when am out of her jurisdiction and am off to seize day and fulfil several of my resolutions and Sad Ed's desires!

1 p.m.

Or not. Apparently I am in no way the answer to Sad Ed's mojo issues. Sight of Morrissey T-shirt just made him all wistful about Tuesday because apparently she wore it the first time they did 'It'. I offered to talk in American accent and show him my bra (now 34B, official measurement) but he said he was dead, heart-wise and penis-wise, and nothing would revive him. He says he is thinking about becoming a famous celibate instead like the Pope or Stephen Fry and channel his energies into his artistic leanings instead. I said that was an excellent idea, even though he has no discernable cre-ative talent unless you count being able to draw the Powerpuff Girls.

Anyway, left him to it and am back home, having fulfilled no resolutions or desires whatsoever. Am some-what relieved though as finding out Sad Ed is your ONE is total double-edged sword, i.e. like discovering you are related to someone famous and it turns out to be Anthea Turner. Maybe will focus on Resolution Number 4 and read some Nietzsche instead. He is totally pro-tragedy and will no doubt find inspiration in his wise thoughts.

4 p.m.
Cannot understand a word of it. Am going to watch *Mary Poppins* with dog instead. It is strangely fond of Dick Van Dyke and licks telly whenever he comes onscreen and does unfathomable accent (Dick Van Dyke, not dog. Dog cannot speak. Obviously).

17

Saturday 5

8 a.m.

Was looking forward to day of forward thinking but sadly the coalface (or tofu-face, i.e. Nuts In May healthfood outlet i.e. my Saturday job) beckons. It is a shame did not make resolution to give up work but sadly still have shackles of third-world-scale debt around legs, i.e. owe Mum £78. Am going to make New Year resolutions amendment i.e.:

6. Do not fritter away money I do not have by breaking fake babies, using Dad's mobile to phone two-timing rock gods from overseas, or going to waterlogged music festivals where end up snogging best friend's brother and weeing in a Pringles tube.

6 p.m.

Work was as awful as anticipated. Not only has Mr Goldstein (proprietor of Nuts In May, beard, hunchback) made a resolution to change in-store music from CDs of our choice (eclectic mixes of ambient sound, as created by Sad Ed) to CDs of his choice (not-at-all ambient Beverley Sisters), but ailment-ridden Rosamund has made resolution to visit her equally ailment-riddled parents in Wales more often, which meant that Jack was in today. Normally this would be a positive thing, because Jack does not flinch from the till of death, plus he is much better at playing Who'd You Rather? than Rosamund (who has no TV and does not read magazines so is limited to

18

'celebrities' like Hugo Thorndyke MP (Con) or Prince Charles). But today he was clearly still sulking at being last in line in my ill-thought-out New Year's Eve snog list. I said I had turned over a new leaf and this year I am being honest with myself and others and am not going to not snog someone if I feel like it (I think that is right). But he said I would not know the truth if it smacked me in the face with a wet kipper and that I am emotionally illiterate. I said that was ridiculous as I got nine GCSEs and am well-known for my literacy skills (enforced by Mum). He said case proven and went off to unbox the ayurvedic toothpaste. Am more determined than ever to snog random people now. And as soon as one of them stirs my mojo, I will tell them immediately. I will hide from true love no longer. That will show him how emotionally literate I am.

. . . .

Sunday 6

Hurrah, have been dealt a last minute reprieve from Mum's Sunday-morning conversational French lessons (imposed following my illicit switching from French (real subject) to Politics (made-up subject) A level). It is all thanks to the *Sunday Times* pasting news of the Norovirus vomiting bug stalking hospital wards and classrooms on today's front cover. It has sent Mum into a frenzy of anti-bug precautions in the run up to school tomorrow. She is at Waitrose with James bulk purchasing anti-bacterial wipes and probiotic yoghurt drinks—hygiene takes precedence over a rounded language education any day.

Am quite looking forward to school, vomit-strewn corridors or not. At least it will be replete with people to potentially seize day with. Am running short on options in environs of Summerdale Road. The only passing males are Clive, Thin Kylie's stepdad Terry, and Rory De'Ath (aka 'the grim reaper') at Number 12, who is in Year Eight and called Rory, both of which are grounds for avoidance.

. . . .

Monday 7
Back to school.

This is typical. I finally get to be in Sixth Form, i.e. with all its accompanying kudos of ditching regulation kilt and blazer in favour of own wardrobe of utterly vintage outfits, when school is overtaken with *St Trinian's* madness, and uniform, albeit a slutty, miniature version, is suddenly de rigueur. Even the goths are hitching up their voluminous black skirts and revealing pasty legs and suspenders. As is Scarlet. I said was outraged as *a*) I did not know she had kept her kilt, and *b*) this kind of fashion-following would never have happened in the days of Trevor and if she is trying to please Hilary she is mistaken as he is not interested in *Grazia*, he is more of an *Economist* man. She said, *a*) Suzy kept it in case she ever has another baby (she is getting broody—it is the threat of

Jack leaving home); *b*) it is not fashion following, it is fashion-forward, do I not watch Gok? And *c*) *au contraire*, *Grazia* is compulsory Labour Party reading to know what the masses are thinking and she is just trying to connect with the potential electorate at an early age so she cannot be accused of bandwagon jumping later in life when she is Education Secretary. She is mental. Hilary is obviously brainwashing her. Or she is blinded by love. I don't know which is worse. Anyway, told her about my truth-telling, day-seizing, love-embracing new lifestyle. She said, 'It will end in tears. And Levonelle.' Which thought sounded nice until got James to Google it and it turns out it is the morning after pill. Anyway, she is wrong, being experimental does not mean doing 'It' with everyone. That is province of Fat Kylie and she is far from philosophical. In contrast, will just do kissing and possibly read poetry to each other. It is utterly French.

Asked Mum if she had kept my kilt when I got home. She said James had borrowed it. Asked James why he had borrowed it and where it was now. He said he had worn it during Ghost Hustlers' hunt for the Hounds of Hell down Battleditch Lane and it is in a recycling plant somewhere as it got soiled when a hound (Fat Kylie's poodle Tupac, so quite hellish) jumped on him and knocked him into a pile of poo. Will just have to improvise. There is bound to be enough uniform in the house. Mum thinks it is the answer to all of society's ills and would be happy if everyone had to wear it throughout

21

life. She would do well as headmistress. Or prison guard. Or fascist dictator.

. . . .

Tuesday 8
8.30 a.m.

Am totally *St Trinian's*-ed up. Am wearing very short skirt (aka Thin Kylie's old boob tube), one of James's school shirts (i.e. too small so buttons cannot feasibly be done up at all), Dad's knee-length fishing socks and golf club tie. Look definitely borderline slutty, though possibly with a hint of insane bag lady. Outfit did not go down too well at Shreddies table, i.e. James said, 'Good God, is that what teenagers are wearing these days?' And Dad said, 'Don't get anything sticky on that tie, I've got a crunch four-ball with Wainwright coming up.' But luckily the gatekeeper, i.e. Mum, was otherwise engaged untangling dog from the banisters so managed to escape without a thorough vetting. Will be utterly star of saggy sofa, beating Scarlet and her run-of-mill regulation kilt version. Am totally Alexa Chung uber-fashion forward model type, and she is Coleen Rooney, i.e. mere follower.

4 p.m.

Am not Alexa Chung. Or even Coleen Rooney. Cannot keep up with this fashion-forward thing. Already the look has progressed to involve ironic straw boaters and

22

prefect badges. Saggy sofa was awash with 'Head Girls' and 'Team Captains'. Scarlet even had Suzy's old 'Milk Monitor' lapel pin. I pointed out that all this trend-following was compromising her semi-emo ideals and what had happened to the old, stand-out-from-the-crowd, bat-embracing Scarlet but she said gothness is totally passé now that entire lower school thinks they are being clever and interesting by dressing like corpses. She cited the fact that Goth Corner Mark II in the upper school canteen has swollen to three tables, forcing the mathletes to move to the 'lurgy' table (with Nigel Moore who has impetigo (not potato blight as widely rumoured)). She is right, there are minigoths every-where. Trevor Pledger (head goth, owner of vegetarian leather coat, ex-boyfriend of Scarlet) is like Pied Piper, i.e. swarms of becaped wannabes follow him wherever he goes and guard him outside the toilet like gargoyles. Scarlet says the adoration is not healthy and is giving him 'bad batitude'. She is right. He actually thinks he has vampiric powers now. I have seen him trying to fly off the top of the bike shed roof.

. . . .

Wednesday 9

Have given up on *St Trinian's* look and am going to go back to vintage. Will say it is fashion fast-forward, i.e. at some point is bound to be back in vogue and will be leader of pack.

4 p.m.

Vintage look definite improvement. That tie was hazard in canteen, i.e. it kept hovering dangerously near vats of baked beans (vegetable of the day). Jack agrees. At least I think he does. He said, 'Thank God someone has the courage not to follow the herd.' Did not say it was because could not keep up.

4.15 p.m.

Ooh. Though probably should have under terms of being honest resolution. Yes. Will definitely have to try harder tomorrow. Especially as stance totally backed by brainy philosopher Immanuel Kant who said we have categorical duty to tell truth regardless of consequences. And he was from Enlightenment, so must be right.

. . . .

Thursday 10

Truth telling not as easy as it sounds. In theory, honesty should be refreshing and empowering. In reality just annoys people and is potentially disaster-causing, e.g. was quietly minding own business at fruit and nut dispensing machine, purchasing yoghurt-dusted blueberries with Scarlet, when Melody Bean appeared from behind machine in disturbing manner and asked me whether Sad Ed had said anything about her since their liaison on New Year's Eve. I said yes, in fact he had: he said the snog was a colossal mistake and that he didn't fancy her at

24

all and his lack of penis movement only confirmed this sorry fact. At which point she burst into tears and had to be taken to school secretary Mrs Leech (bad hair, too much face powder, biscuit habit) for reviving Peak Freans, and Scarlet thwacked me round head with a packet of Bombay mix, causing me to choke on blueberry. Plus, then Scarlet told Sad Ed and he rushed to comfort Melody and is now officially going out with her out of guilt even though she is utterly non-mojo-arousing. I bet God didn't envisage this sort of trouble when he wrote the commandments. He should have thought ahead and added some subclauses. And Kant should have known better as well. No wonder he was celibate.

. . . .

Friday 11

Ha. Have had truth revelation in philosophy. It turns out that Kant is possibly wrong and not at all enlightened and that honesty is NOT always the best policy. Apparently there is opposing opinion that ends justify means, i.e. only tell the truth if it is in the interests of all concerned. DO NOT tell the truth if it is going to annoy someone and get you thwacked for your efforts. It is called consequentialism and am definitely following doctrine from now on. Why did they not teach us about this on Wednesday? May well write to Gordon Brown to demand radical rethink of AS level syllabus to ensure mix-ups like this cannot occur.

Anyway, have had resolution rethink and will limit truth-telling imperative to matters of the heart, i.e. when have found ONE and have to tell them before Scarlet pounces. Or when have not found ONE and want them to go away before do purple sick on them (to avoid future Kyle O'Grady incidents).

· ·

Saturday 12

6 p.m.

Oh my God. 24 Summerdale Road is awash with honesty issues. It is not James, who is the usual perpetrator of cover-ups, mostly to do with the dog. It is habitually truth-telling Colin Riley, i.e. Dad. He has been caught speeding on the B1383 Saffron Walden to Stansted Mountfitchet road. Mum is livid. It is not the law-breaking (though she is a stickler for limits, and only does ten miles an hour in heavily populated areas), it is fact that he tried to disguise it with web of deceit, i.e. when a suspicious envelope from Essex police arrived this morning he claimed it was a letter warning them about potential burglars operating in the area. But Mum, whose motto is 'trust no one', and is au fait with all burgling habits (they are concentrating on Seven Devils Lane at moment, home of pint-sized eighties pop star Nik Kershaw and someone who once played for Leyton Orient), dug it out from under his tax returns and found the evidence in black and white, i.e. a blurry photo

of the Passat going past the Elsenham turn-off, not just at speed, but slightly over the white line, thus breaking several rules at once. She is jubilant about one part though. The police have given Dad the option of a fine and three points on his licence or going on a refresher driving course, which is with none other than Mike Wandering Hands Majors, former instructor and admirer of Janet Riley, and sworn enemy of Dad. Dad begged to get the points but Mum has filled in the driving course request and has sent James to post it before Dad can interfere.

Also there is a new 'member of staff' at Nuts In May. It is not replacement for Rosamund, she is back from Wales, complete with new ailment, i.e. glue ear. It is a new non-death-inducing till. Mr Goldstein has finally bowed to demands and invested in fully digital twenty-first-century version. Apparently Mrs Goldstein got little finger trapped in till of death on Wednesday and had to be rescued by fire brigade, which was straw that broke camel's back (or hunchback) and no one argues with Mrs Goldstein, she makes Mum look ineffectual. Anyway, new till is lovely and shiny. But no one knows how to use it and we keep getting random numbers on display so have resorted to improvising with calculator and emergency drawer release button for moment until Rosamund goes on training course. On that point, till of death actually improvement as, though it was life-threatening, at least it was self-explanatory.

6 p.m.

Have called Sad Ed to see if he wants to come over but Mrs Thomas says he went straight to Melody's after trolley-herding duty. He is mad. He is wasting perfectly good moping time with someone who, even if she did stir his mojo, could not actually do anything with it as she is only fifteen and therefore illegal. He should be honest with his feelings like me. It is the route to happiness and fulfilment.

8 p.m.

Or possibly to being in on own on Saturday night watching *Casualty* with dog. Scarlet is too busy superpoking Hilary across the internet ether and even James has an engagement—he is going round Mad Harry's to blow stuff up. Life post-sisterhood is somewhat less edgy than I imagined.

. . . .

Sunday 13

10 a.m.

Something odd is afoot at 24 Summerdale Road. It started at breakfast when Mum announced that Conversational French would be cancelled for the foreseeable future as she had a timetable clash with another more pressing engagement. But what could be more pressing in her eyes than conjugating *nettoyer* now that vomiting bug seems to have been successfully avoided? (Am on four Yakults a

day to build up defences. Have so many good bacteria in stomach think can actually feel them crawling.) And now, have just seen her go into dining room, aka Dad's office, wearing rubber gloves and cycle helmet. Hope it is not weird sexual role-play activity with Dad aimed at reviving love life. Had enough of that when Grandpa Riley and Treena were living here. Only Baby Jesus has to suffer that hoo-ha now. And he is easily distracted with Wotsits and Nickelodeon.

10.10 a.m.
It is not sexual. Have just seen James enter dining room armed with a notebook, several felt pens, and a USB cable.

1 p.m.
Aha! Have discovered secret activity. Not by cunning deduction, admittedly, but by more traditional method of bursting into dining room demanding to know what is going on. It is computer lessons with James! Mum is overcoming her greatest fear (bar terrorists, all-you-can-eat salad bars, and Austrian blinds) and learning to surf the web. It is one of her New Year resolutions. (The others are: eat more fish and find a new hobby to do with Dad in bid to rekindle recently strained relationship (due to stresses caused by constant presence over festive period of non-festive Cleggs). Apparently Dad has complained that any new activity would cut into his precious golf time but she said that is the point and got all

thin-lipped so Dad agreed.) I said this did not explain the helmet and gloves, unless their new hobby is bike maintenance. But she says it is protective wear to stop her skull and fingers getting permeated by the WiFi signal during her lesson and frying her nervous system. I pointed out that we did not, in fact, have broadband, we had chuggingly slow dial-up, which actually made cranking noises, but she said, not any more, she gave James the go-ahead last week to sign up to the twenty-first century (following strict criteria set by the *Which Guide to the Internet*) and we are now 'cooking on gas'. I am not sure I like this wise-talking technology-embracing version of my mother. It is disturbing the natural order of things. What if she gets hooked on online gambling and neglects her cleaning schedule? Although it is more likely she will only use it to log into Mumsnet and swap tips on stain removing and fussy eaters (she has conquered James's fruit/meat aversion by cunning use of pork and apple sausages). Said what about online perverts and hackers trying to steal her identity/millions but Mum says she has made James put up seven firewalls. Then before could question further, Dad came in and suggested she take a break from her lesson to prepare a nutritious family meal. Mum agreed. Not because she is subservient non-feminist type who cannot allow man to do cooking, but because if she does allow man, i.e. Dad, to do cooking it will involve beans on toast and the smoke alarm going off several times. James was glad of the

diversion. It is because Mum is not a model pupil. Apparently she says 'Why' more than Baby Jesus, and yelps with fear every time he minimizes a page in case it is lost in the ether. But James says this is a normal reaction for an old person and it will improve with time. Asked him what he was getting out of this arrangement. He said quality time with a parent. He is idiot. Or, more probably, liar.

. . . .

Monday 14

8 a.m.
It is two weeks since New Year and demise of anti-sex sisterhood and I have still not snogged anyone in experimental fashion or otherwise seized day, so am going to rectify immediately and seize Monday by embracing first male I can lure onto saggy sofa, regardless of musical preferences, fashion choice, or GCSE qualifications. (Though am sticking to common room as then I can at least rule out anyone underage as only fully-fledged A level students allowed into vicinity.)

4 p.m.
Oh God. And BTECers. Have done something awful. Have snogged Davey MacDonald, former: ballerina, Criminal and Retard, and ex-boyfriend of Thin Kylie. It is all fault of Mark Lambert who had partially exploded a Pot Noodle in the microwave so the BTECers were out

of their designated area and colonizing the saggy sofa. And basically it was him or Fat Kylie. Was going to back out but Sad Ed was invigilating and said seizing day did not include humming and ha-ing because someone is wearing fake Kappa tracksuit. Anyway, did utterly French batting of eyelids but he just said, 'Got something in your eye, Riley?' So upped the ante with some bosom heaving (learned from Suzy, though her bosoms substantially more heavable) but that just made him back away and fall off arm of saggy sofa onto sticky carpet so just straddled him on ground and kissed him before he could crawl to safety under the 'coffee' table. And before Jack hauled me off and asked what the hell was I doing sexually harassing someone with catalogued 'special needs' in that area (he has habit of getting thing out in lessons). Jack pointed out I could be imprisoned, or at least given detention and made to wash up the communal mugs for a week. I said obviously I was seizing the day, which, as a devotee of all things literary and rock star-ish, he should be all in favour of. And also breaking down the barriers between academia and proletariat, which, as devotee of all things left-wing and pro-masses, he should be all in favour of. He rolled eyes and said, 'Jesus, Riley. At least pick on someone you actually fancy. Or who fancies you.' I said, 'Like who?' He said, 'Beats me.' Am undeterred though. Will try again tomorrow. Maybe.

Tuesday 15

Have had seventeen offers of sofa snogging including four Year Sevens and, surprisingly, Davey MacDonald (clearly Jack was wrong and he was not unwilling victim in proceedings). My snogging skills are more potent than I thought. Have declined all though. Not sure that reputation as school slut was what had in mind when drawing up this resolution. Am going to have rethink and possibly restrict seizing day to situations that have definite potential ONE possibilities to them. Have told Sad Ed to put rumour out that yesterday was momentary lapse of reason brought about by overdose of non-drowsy Benylin, so all actions were under influence of drugs. That will sort things out.

On plus side, Mum has found Dad a new hobby to sway him away from golf. It is morris dancing. Clive does it. Dad has been sent next door to be fitted for leg bells. He is not pleased. I said it was hardly an activity they could share but Mum said *au contraire*, she and Marjory will be able to laugh from the sidelines quite effectively. I said didn't she mean 'cheer'? She said she knew exactly what she meant. She is still sulking about the speeding cover-up. James is trying to get in on the morris action too. He has demanded to be the mascot. It is because he is also looking for a new hobby now that ghostbusting has been added to Mum's ever-increasing list of banned activities. (She says she is sick of having to remove 'ectoplasm' (variously soup, dog vomit, and Badedas bubble bath)

33

from the Hoover bag.) But Mum says he will have to look elsewhere as the job has gone to a sheep called Donald. James is not best pleased. It is the first time he has been out-nerded by a ruminant.

. . . .

Wednesday 16
8.30 a.m.
Have got strange text from someone called Mac offering to 'do me' for 'an eighth'. Must have wrong number. Probably for Fat Kylie who has similar number. Am frequently getting calls for her from her many brothers, several of whom seem to be called Liam.

4 p.m.
Was not wrong number. Was result of Sad Ed's rubbish attempt at quashing slut rumours. Apparently now entire school is labouring under misapprehension that am drug addict who will do anything for a hit. Four Year Nines have tried to sell me Nurofen Plus, common room dealer Reuben Tull (enormous hair, staring eyes, entire Pink Floyd back catalogue) said I could have some 'herb' on a try-before-you-buy basis (and do not think he means marjoram), and cannot go down D Corridor (i.e. Criminals and Retards) without hearing muted strains of 'Pusher Man'—which is quite witty for class whose activity is usually limited to raffia and Biff and Chip. Even Jack is joining in. He deliberately put 'Love is the Drug' on

stereo when walked into common room after double philosophy. He claims he is going through a Roxy Music
phase but it is lie. I know for fact he thinks Bryan Ferry is
an effete Tory.

5 p.m.
It gets worse. One of the Liams has just been round to
offer me Ritalin. Luckily Mum was busy on Which.com in
her helmet and rubber gloves and James answered door.
As soon as he saw it was an O'Grady he got Mum's
weapon of choice from windowsill, i.e. Raid Fly Spray,
and temporarily blinded him. He says he is thinking of
becoming a young super-hero as his new hobby. I said,
what, 'Hobbit Man'? He gave me withering look and said,
no, 'Brains Boy'. Then he accused me of being ungrateful
and said I could deal with my own drug-pushing door-
stepping menaces next time. Said sorry as do not think
can deal with entire O'Grady horde on own. Some of
them are deadly. Especially the girls.

Thursday 17
Sad Ed asked me if it was true that I was in the market for
a speedball. I said, who told him that? He said Melody
Bean. I said *a)* I don't even know what a speedball is; *b)*
no, you idiot, can you not even recognize your own
shoddy rumour?; and *c)* why are you still with Melody
Bean when you don't even like her? He said, *a)* it is a

combination of heroin and cocaine and is what led to untimely deaths of both John Belushi and River Phoenix (he has been trying to procure one for several years); *b*) sorry; and *c*) every time he tries to break up with her she starts crying and it panics him so he snogs her to shut her up. We are both victims of our twisted ideals. It is utterly Chekhovian. Possibly. Have not actually read Chekhov but is bound to be complicated.

· ·

Friday 18

A strange thing has occurred. Grandpa Clegg and Dad have found something in common. It is road impediments. Grandpa Clegg rang to moan about potential tolls on the A30 during tourist season. He says the government is trying to price him out of his car and on to a rusty old bicycle. Mum pointed out that he hates tourists and does not own a car, let alone a bicycle, so he is utterly unaffected. But Grandpa was not swayed and demanded to speak to the man of the house. Mum gave the phone to James but apparently he meant Dad, i.e. someone who is not on Mum's side in all matters, particularly those concerning cleaning and laws. Then they spent forty minutes bonding over speed cameras and road humps and their mutual love of right-wing motoring 'journalist' Jeremy Clarkson. Mum is outraged. She is very much anti Jeremy Clarkson, due to his flagrant disregard for the highway code, women, and rules pertaining to tucking your shirt

in when you have paunch. Plus he ruins her potential holy trinity of BBC-based Jeremys, also involving Vine and Paxman. I predict a chorus of disapproval at tomorrow's morris dancing debut (two o'clock outside the town hall, in honour of ancient East Anglian festival 'Plough Monday', now moved to Saturday for myriads of reasons mostly to do with annual leave and parking).

. . . .

Saturday 19
8 a.m.
Thank God have got day in confines of Nuts In May selling fungal paté and fake bacon so that do not have to be linked in any way with abomination that is Dad in his morris dancing outfit. He looks like a madman and jingles wherever he goes, which is distressing the dog no end. It is cowering behind the sofa, and am minded to join it. Have begged Dad not to appear in public but he says he is proud to be upholding Essex tradition. He will be pargetting next. Or roof thatching. It is utterly appalling.

6 p.m.
Dad's morris dancing did not go completely to plan. Apparently there was some sort of choreography issue and Dad waved his hanky when he should have been crossing sticks and got jabbed in the eye by Clive. So he jabbed Clive back which initiated some sort of mini morris men riot and the end result was seven black eyes (two

37

of them Dad's), three broken sticks, and an arrest (Mark Lambert, who is not morris man, but general hooligan who was passing by and joined in for fun). To make matters worse, Mum made James bring Dad to Nuts In May for a sit down while she got the Fiesta from Waitrose car park so now all and sundry (well, hippies and vegetarians anyway) know that am related to village idiot.

On plus side, Dad is giving up the dancing. Even Mum agrees it was possibly a bad idea. She says the all-male atmosphere only breeds violence, and that he needs to do something transgender, i.e. mixed sex, not changing sex, as pointed out to Dad when he had panic that she wanted him to have bits removed à la dog, to curb his fighting spirit. James is disappointed. He is quite taken with the whole morris experience. It is the bells and mysterious and ancient manoeuvres. He is doubly determined to be the mascot now and pointed out that at least he is unlikely to poo outside Halifax, unlike Donald. But Mum still said no. She says he is too easily led and fears he will be caught up in the mania.

* *

Sunday 20

I miss sisterhood. Even though it was utterly restrictive snog-wise, at least it meant there was always someone to hang out with at weekends. Now Sad Ed is busy fending off Melody Bean and Scarlet is busy un-fending long-distance left-wing love Hilary. She says it utterly does

not affect her friendship with me and that their phone conversations are entirely political not pants-based. But this is lie. Have witnessed her in 'political' conversation and all that ranting about David Cameron has weird and worrying effect on her. Anyway, instead am spending Sunday on godmother duty, i.e. counselling Baby Jesus in ways of righteousness. Am not actually going to church as it is too fraught with potential danger (requirement to be quiet and generally not draw on hymn books or drink font water). So am going to take advantage of his love of television and use it to subliminally send pro-God/good behaviour message. Have lined up *Sound of Music*, *Jesus Christ Superstar*, and *The Jazz Singer* (do not want to limit him, religion-wise). James (the godfather, though not in horse-head-in-bed insane Italian way) is in agreement with method. He says it is well-practised propaganda tool and am following in footsteps of evil geniuses like Hitler, Peter Mandelson, and Pringles crisps (it is true, once you pop you can't stop). Not sure this is good thing. But is nice being political genius, even evil one, and will possibly win me marks with Mr Slatter (beard, Fair Isle jumper, history of failing miserably in council elections) who, so far, has been utterly disappointed with my A level potential (it is not my fault that my political education up to this point has been Scarlet's rantings and Grandpa Clegg's biography of Thatcher (he has not read it, he just likes everyone to know where his loyalties lie)).

4 p.m.

Mum has ended evil genius subliminal pro-God screening session prematurely. It is not Baby Jesus. He loved the dancing nuns. As did James, who, worryingly, knows all the words to every song and gave simultaneous performance dressed in blue bed sheet. It is dog. It cannot cope with surround sound yodelling and had 'episode', i.e. insane barking fit, ending with consumption of furniture. Dad was disappointed though. It is because he thinks he is Captain Von Trapp, i.e. distant and brooding but potential musical genius. He says he could have been John Barrowman (assume he means leading man, not gay with scary hair and rictus grin) if he had not met Mum at accountancy college. Asked Mum if this was true. She said he can do a passable 'Edelweiss' but that any pretensions to West End possibilities are ill-founded and that in fact she is one with musical talent. James has suggested a sing-off at 7 p.m. but both have declined. They claim they have no need to prove their abilities. But I fear this is not the end of it. Mum is planning something, I can tell. Clearly she will not be outdone hygienically or musically.

Monday 21

Reputation as vintage version of Fat Kylie (i.e. snogs anyone, but in better clothes) is still hovering over me like giant bat. Breaktimes are fraught with hordes of lower

school boys begging me to kiss them. In stark contrast to Jack who has taken to falling on knees and begging me not to kiss him whenever he sees me, in what he thinks is hilarious ironic manner. It is not. Anyway I said 'as if' then pointed out that being experimental was, in fact, utterly tragic and poetical and am like Byron and Pete Doherty rolled into one. He said, 'Whatever. It's tragic, that's for sure.' Which is excellent as tragedy is utter plus in life.

At least philosophy rises above the tabloid obsessions of the masses to deal with more important questions. Like who is God. Majority conclusion is that God is all knowing, all powerful, and all good. Minority opinions include Sad Ed (God is dead); Scarlet (we should place faith in politics and not a fictitious creation designed to lull working classes into compliance, whose powers appear to be mostly limited to party tricks like making the face of his son appear in a slice of Nimble toast. Whereas Gordon Brown has the ability to change the entire tax system, if he wants); and Reuben Tull (the supreme being is a dog-headed lizard with lasers for eyes).

I said party tricks were just God's way of proving he exists (have no idea why took God's side, maybe it is responsibility of moral education of Baby Jesus). But Scarlet said if an all-powerful God did exist he wouldn't waste his time on being an invisible Derren Brown, he would banish all evil from world and the fact that he hasn't proves he is made up. So I pointed out that *a*)

41

without evil there would be no saints or miracles, and a world without tragedy would be like 24 Summerdale Road everywhere and that *b*) she had fallen prey to patriarchal stereotypes and several times assumed God was a he. At which point Scarlet had panic attack and had to breathe into paper bag (former home of Reuben's 'stash', resulting in her passing out and being carried to Mrs Leech for Tango and bourbons).

. . . .

Tuesday 22
4 p.m.

Do not need God anyway, as have Mum and James who are all-knowing and all-powerful, i.e. there is nothing that escapes their watchful gaze, and eventual punishment. Got home from school and Mum demanded to know if I was addicted to sex and 'injecting Ecstasy'. Apparently my reputation has seeped down to St Regina's and several Year Sixes are begging their parents to change their secondary choices so they can be tutored in the ways of love by me. Keanu has already offered James £10 and a fake driving licence for lessons, and he is only seven. Told Mum that it is all a colossal mix-up and that was just trying to have positive outlook on life and seize day etc., etc. She said if I seize the day again I will be home schooled before I can say crack marijuana.

Weirdly for someone so puritanical Mum absolutely does not believe in God. She just embraces the restrictive

and guilt-inducing elements of organized religion. James on other hand has eyes firmly on prize. He says believing is the only option because, if God does exist, at least he will go to heaven. Said this was hedging his bets and not at all pious or religious. James then had panic that God will see through his cunning ruse so he said he is going to be good anyway, not for payback, and then he will be in for sure. So pointed out that this was even more cunning and duplicitous so James now in religious meltdown in room trying to find a way to guarantee everlasting life.

6 p.m.
James says he has got it. He is going to embrace all religions, then one of the gods will take pity on him. Said this was hedging bets on Las Vegas scale and there was no way God was going to fall for that one. He is back in room.

7 p.m.
James is out of room. He is going for Seventh Day Adventism because they are glad to take anybody and will overlook his reasons. Said this was as bad as the time he turned to Islam because he thought their God was scarier plus they had prayer mats. He is back in room.

8 p.m.
James has decided any god worth hanging out with for

43

eternity should be glad of his supreme brain in heaven and so he is just going to wait for one of them to come to him. And in the meantime he is going to carry on following the ways of the Ninja. And the Jedi. And the Hobbit. He is idiot.

. . . .

Wednesday 23

Mum is combining her two New Year resolutions in one forward-thinking activity, i.e. she is surfing web (in regulation cycling helmet and rubber gloves) to find a new hobby for her and Dad (with James's assistance, of course; she is still trying to master shift key and scroll function). Is shame she did not think to consume fishfingers at same time so could have had resolution hat trick. Anyway, so far she has bookmarked pages for the Saffron Walden Historical Society and Friends of the Saffron Walden Museum. She will have hard job persuading Dad to take up either of these. He is rubbish at history (although not on scale of Cleggs who think that the Roundheads were some genetically mutated 'little people') and does not like museum due to 'funny smell'. Pointed out she could just take up golf and be done with it but she says that's what he wants her to do and she is not going to give him the satisfaction. She is wrong. Dad does not want Mum anywhere near the golf club. He says it is sacred time—free from all rules pertaining to spillage and saying 'bugger'. Though it is riddled with

ones pertaining to footwear and trouser length so do not see the gain frankly.

. . . .

Thursday 24

James says he has found his new hobby. And possibly his new religion too. It is crap TV game show *Gladiators*. He and Mad Harry are going to apply. He says it is like getting paid to be a superhero. They have already chosen their names: Gazelle (James, no idea) and Sabre (Mad Harry, as in light, not toothed-tiger, apparently). Pointed out that it was a battle of bodies not brains and that neither he nor Mad Harry had the physique of Adonis (Greek God, not Education Minister, who is more Andrew than Adonis i.e. bald and weedy). Plus, as usual, they are several years under age. James is undeterred. He says spending the next seven and a bit years cultivating the body of a steroid-obsessed pinhead is a small price to pay. He is starting with push-ups and all-protein diet. It is good job he did not put down John Major High as his secondary school of choice. He would not last five minutes with all his many nerdisms and obsessions.

6 p.m.

All-protein diet abandoned due to enforced vegetable eating, as dictated by Mum. She says there is no way she is just cooking him eight sausages for tea, it will bung him up and cost a fortune. Plus she is sick of him trying to copy whatever Keanu does (he has not told her the precise reasons for his new diet, he is simply allowing her to assume it is the devilment of an O'Grady). They compromised on two and a half sausages, peas (for brain power), and mash (for gladiatorial energy). Push-ups not going too well either. He managed one. Think allowing dog to sit on his back for extra challenge was mistake.

. . . .

Friday 25

Granny Clegg rang after school to update me on all things Hilary. I said I was utterly not interested in his life as was moving on, love-wise. Granny said good, as he is definitely in love with Scarlet, and she is backing him. I said she was a turncoat but she said, 'You can't argue with the spirits.' Apparently Maureen Penrice from the Spar is 'blessed with a fifth sense' and has declared that they are a match made in heaven. Plus Russell Grant (Granny Clegg's favourite fat gay astrologer) says their star signs are totally aligned at the moment. I asked how come she and Maureen knew so much about Scarlet. She says Hilary has told her everything and he is like the grandson she never had. Pointed out *a*) she was supposed to be boycotting Hilary for betraying me, and *b*) she did in fact have two grandsons—James and Boaz (God-bothering offspring of Aunty Joyless). She said, *a*) she did, for half an hour, but he has such nice teeth it is hard to be cross

46

with him, and *b*) they do not count. It is because James baffles her with his encyclopaedic knowledge and Boaz just baffles her.

Am now feeling utterly despondent again. I know am being modern and progressive etc., (in non-sluttish way and only in circumstances where Mum cannot find out) but part of me wishes was in Maureen-blessed relationship with utter soulmate person, like Hilary and Scarlet. Especially as he was in fact my utter soulmate person until Scarlet showed up and out-left-winged me on all fronts. Is not that cannot be complete person without boyfriend to justify existence (illegal in Scarlet's eyes). Just that snogging is nice and weekends are boring.

Saturday 26

Dean 'the dwarf' Denley is back at work. To be fair had not noticed he was missing from his meat-mincing position. But apparently he has been off with measles for three weeks (victim of hippy-perpetrated MMR 'scandal', according to Mum, who thinks we should be vaccinated on yearly basis for all diseases including bird flu) and under strict quarantine. Although not that strict, as clearly the saggy-sofa snogging/drugs episode had slipped past security. He said, 'I heard you were going through a bad time. It happens to all of us in the music business.' (He is not actually in music business now that the Back Doors have disbanded, and nor am I since got sacked as Justin's

47

groupie, but he is right that we are creative etc.) I said, 'It wasn't drugs, it's an experimental thing. Like Jim Morrison, you know.' He said, 'I do. And any time you want to experiment, you know where to find me.' Then Mr Goddard shouted at him to get back to the sausages so he had to climb on his box and ram several pounds of pork down the chute. Which sort of ruined the moment.

6 p.m.
Not that there was a moment. Although am glad that at least he understands my quest for snogging freedom. Even so, will not take him up on invitation. Am not that desperate.

7 p.m.
Yet.

. . . .

Sunday 27
8 a.m.
Scarlet has just rung. Which is unprecedented as usually she does not emerge from her bat cave until after T4. Thought it must be her new emo-ish tendencies allowing her to embrace daylight a bit more but apparently it is because she has not been to bed yet. She has been up all night watching the South Carolina caucus on CNN. I said I thought caucus was something out of *Alice in Wonderland* involving a dodo and liquorice comfits. But she rolled her

eyes (I can sense this even over the airwaves) and said, 'It is in fact a state-wide poll in America to decide who is going to be the candidate for the actual Presidential election.' (Which is possibly another reason why Hilary is going out with Scarlet not me as she does not suffer these habitual mix-ups between fact and fiction.) Anyway, she says we are at the dawn of a new non-racist age because gangly black democrat Barack Obama has finally won one. I said it must have been a hard decision for her, between Hillary (Clinton, with two lls, as opposed to Nuamah, with one l and a penis), i.e. a woman, and a black man (Scarlet is so pro-positive sex discrimination she believes you should always vote for the woman, even if they have no qualifications, or are mental or dead). She said it was a tug of love for feminists everywhere, but that Barack understands our plight, and is an honorary woman. Plus she thinks Hillary (two lls) might in fact be in possession of penis as she has very deep voice and fondness for trouser suits. And Bill is scared of her. Anyway, am invited round for celebratory hummus and olives later with Bob and Suzy.

9 a.m.
Have ingenious plan to fulfil resolution number 3, i.e. locate Sad Ed's missing mojo. Will take him to hummus and olives Obama caucus victory party and casually let slip to Suzy that he is having penis problems. (Obviously will not mention this to Sad Ed. He will not come if he

thinks Scarlet's sexpert mum is going to interfere with him with her plethora of manuals and technical terms for genitals.) Hurrah. Am brilliant friend.

4 p.m.

Sad Ed not entirely in agreement with 'brilliant friend' title. He says he feels utterly raped by Suzy and her demands to see the evidence. I said I had suffered indignities of my own, i.e. Jack giving me bag of liquorice comfits for the 'caucus party'. (I said it was an easy mistake to make, and at least it showed I had wide knowledge of literature. He said, 'And I suppose thinking the Dalai Lama is a sacred camel makes you a genius then.' How was I to know that it is actually old man, not woolly animal?) Plus Suzy said she was proud of me and my completely Marianne Faithfull approach to love, i.e. not very faithful at all. Sad Ed said I should be grateful for the compliment and at least I have not been sent home with 'Get Sweaty With Suzy' DVD. But do not think compliment from woman who has discussed Jeffrey Archer's willy on prime-time telly is really very poetic.

. . . .

Monday 28

Scarlet is jubilant again. This time it is Hilary (one l, penis). He has been accepted by Cambridge University. All he has to do is get three Ds. I said if that is the grade requirement, then I may well apply. She said don't be

ridiculous, they only give low offers to geniuses with outstanding extra-curricular records. Again I said I should apply. She said if you even get past the interview, which given your recent llama/lama mix-up is unlikely, then they will offer you at least four As. Said she was being rather harsh for a best friend. She says it is utterly kind to tell the truth now so I am not disappointed next year. Plus I am the one who kept banging on about honesty. She is right. I think. It is in interest of all parties so conforms to Kantian and consequentialist doctrine. Anyway, asked her if Jack had heard as well but she said she didn't know as Jack is spending day looking around his back-up university (Hull, i.e. only need three Ds even if non-genius) and she would have intercepted post except that, when she left, postman (and notorious gossip) Beefy Clarke was too busy embroiled in a conversation with Edna the non-Filipina Labour-friendly cleaner about Mr Costain at Number 13 and his red gas bill to hand over the post. I said it was risky leaving Edna alone with the post as she has been known to store it for several months in random places according to her crap and frequently changing household management regimes (as witnessed by my own confession to Jack two years ago, when mistakenly thought was in love with him, which got 'lost' on top of the fridge). But Scarlet said Suzy has imposed a new rule, i.e. 'Immediately on receiving post place it on kitchen table in full visibility, and away from any water or incendiary objects'.

Anyway, Scarlet is utterly jubilant about Hilary defying his background education-wise. Pointed out that Mrs Nuamah had studied law at Oxford and Mr Nuamah had got a double first in politics and dentistry from Cambridge. She said she meant being born in Wales and raised in Cornwall.

Tuesday 29

Hurrah, Hilary is not the only victor in defying his humble roots to enter the playground of the upper classes (i.e. Cambridge). Jack got in as well. Although he is not that humble as Bob drives Volvo and they have never eaten anything with Findus on the label. Anyway, clearly Edna is abiding by Suzy's post diktat because Scarlet brought the letter in to show us. He has to get four As. I said that was unfair as Hilary only had to get Ds and was possibly reversely racist. She said that reversely was a made-up word and anyway it is nothing to do with colour, it is more that Hilary touched on gene splicing, patient confidentiality, and the ethics of circumcision in his interview, whereas Jack spent all of it wittering about whether Billy Bragg deserved a Nobel Peace Prize for contributions to 'agitpop'.

Anyway it is utterly brilliant and wanted to congratulate him but he is still on his way back from Hull, which is hundreds of miles away, possibly in different time zone, so had to text him instead. Said DON'T

WORRY ABT HILARY GETTING BETTER OFFER. U STILL
V BRAINY. X

7 p.m.
Just got text back. Clearly he has entered earth's atmosphere from the galaxy of the north-east. It said THXX.
He is clearly a man of few words. And too many Xs.
Which does not bode well for someone who wants to
be simultaneous Foreign Secretary and Mercury Prize
winner as he is going to have to spend entire life on
Newsnight getting grilling from Paxo, or on *Never Mind
the Buzzcocks* making jokes about knobs with Phil Jupitus
and that goblin one that looks like our road sweeper
Mollo.

. . . .

Wednesday 30
A university-related bombshell has been dropped on the
Stone household. It is that Jack thinks he might actually
prefer Hull to Cambridge. He says the politics course is
second to none, halls are cheaper, and it is the seat of
anti-slavery, i.e. William Wilberforce is from there. Plus
there are fewer rugby shirts and pashminas by volume.
Bob is delighted with his pro-Northern/pro-working-
class/pro-fish stance (he is related to a crabber from
Grimsby). Suzy on other hand is going mental with
premature empty nest syndrome. She says at least if
he was at Cambridge she could pop in whenever she

fancied with a lentil bake and free condoms. Scarlet says Suzy is more adamant than ever that she wants another baby. She has bought ten ovulation kits and Bob is on twenty-four-hour call for insemination duty the minute her eggs are released. Asked Scarlet if she minded having a baby brother or sister, as it would make her the disadvantaged and syndrome-ridden 'middle child'. She said *au contraire*, middle children are in fact utterly brilliant, look at Madonna and John F. Kennedy, and she is all for it. Did not mention other notorious middle children Bill Gates, Princess Diana, or Mark Lambert as do not want to worry her unduly. Suzy will never get pregnant—she is away filming half the week, plus all the drugs in the eighties must have messed with her ovaries.

Mum is in agreement with Suzy as well. It is not middle children, or the empty nest thing. It is that only bad things come out of Hull in her eyes, i.e. Fat Boy Slim and John Prescott (just Fat Boy). Mentioned William Wilberforce but she said even he opted for Cambridge University.

Thursday 31

12 noon

Have just seen Sad Ed coming out of the lower school toilets looking ecstatic. Think Suzy's DVD must have done the trick and his mojo is found, and possibly in overdrive.

12.30 noon

Was not mojo-related. Was that Mark Lambert had managed to utilize his BTEC skills and brick in one of the Year Sevens while they were having a pre-lunch poo (speed not quality of wall being aim of game—he actually has certificate for being fastest cementer in North Essex). Mr Wilmott has ordered him to knock the wall down immediately but Mark Lambert pointed out that the wall would thus collapse inwards, possibly injuring Bryce West (pooing Year Seven) and that in fact it would be better if Bryce knocked wall down from his side (which is quite brainy for someone who only got one GCSE). Except that Bryce did not have sledgehammer on his side of door so had to knock wall down with Power Rangers pencil tin. Sad Ed had gone in to cheer him on.

Friday 1

9 a.m.

Dad is in vile mood. It is because he got his letter confirming his date with destiny, aka Mike Wandering Hands and his refresher driving course. Mum has already warned him not to even think about feigning illness. She is investing in a tamperproof digital thermometer to catch out any fakery.

6 p.m.

Hurrah. The sisterhood is back on. Temporarily. Admittedly it is only due to fact that Suzy is ovulating so Scarlet is avoiding the house at all costs, and Melody keeps trying to touch Sad Ed 'down there' so he is avoiding her at all costs. And there will be no Wicca spells or anti-snogging pacts of any kind. But nevertheless, it is utterly excellent as cannot spend another Friday night watching *A Question of Sport* with dog or watching Mum negotiate the interwebnet in her helmet outfit.

10 p.m.

Sisterhood evening a partial success. On plus side, we have solved Sad Ed's Melody sex dilemma. I said the trouser groping was usually a cause for celebration. He said *au contraire*, the lack of response is embarrassing. So I said he should tell her about the celibacy thing. He says he has but she just sees it as a challenge. So Scarlet (in controversial pro-God/anti-honesty move) said he should

59

say he has seen the light and is going to wait until he is married before having sex. I said in fact he had already had sex (i.e. with Tuesday) but Scarlet said he can be revirginized, she saw it on Channel 5. Sad Ed has agreed it is the only way forward. He is going to get a Jonas Brothers-style chastity ring for full effect.

On downside, Thin Kylie also came over. It was not to partake in general discussion on Sad Ed's penis. It was to invite me to her birthday party tomorrow. Declined on grounds that cannot desert friends in hour of need, and Scarlet refuses to cross threshold of anyone who wears fur (Cherie has coat made of rabbits, or possibly guinea pigs). And Sad Ed is barred from Thin Kylie's for various misdemeanours, e.g. being fat, possibly gay, and once wearing tea cosy on head in Badly Drawn Boy phase. But Scarlet said Suzy is away filming tomorrow so she will be back home discussing the religious right with Hilary. And Sad Ed said he will be at Melody's discussing the religious wrong, i.e. not having sex until married. So ended up agreeing to go, as long as no one tried to sell me drugs or make me snog anyone under the age of sixteen. She said most of the O'Gradys are on electric tag curfew, so I should be fine. Asked if there was a theme. She said, 'Like, duh, get drunk.' Scarlet said, 'How imaginative.' Kylie said, 'Why, what do you do at your parties? Talk about the news?' Scarlet said, 'Yes.' Kylie said, 'Bloody lezzer.'

At least the theme is honest. Though am not entirely

sure why she wants me to go. Maybe her and Fat Kylie
have fallen out again. Though saw them on wall sucking
Chupa Chups earlier (i.e. nicotine replacement therapy).
Or maybe she is trying to matchmake me. Oooh. Perhaps
she has a cousin who is overcoming his chav roots with
poetic or literary talent. Like The Streets. Or maybe actually is The Streets! Hurrah. Maybe will meet my ONE
tomorrow after all and marry controversial musical
genius!

11 p.m.
As long as it is not Donkey Dawson with the saveloy-
resembling penis. I don't care if he is a legend. I am
utterly vegetarian when it comes to those things.

. . . .

Saturday 2
11.30 p.m.
I was right about Thin Kylie. But it was not potentially
poetic cousin The Streets (her cousins were there, but
they are called Dane and Casey and spent most of evening setting light to stuff, including selves at one point.
Which is not at all poetic) or Donkey Dawson and his
frankfurter-shaped appendage. It was Davey MacDonald,
my saggy sofa snogging victim! Apparently he is completely smitten and gave Kylie a six-pack of Smirnoff
Ice to invite me. So had to spend three hours hiding
behind Fat Kylie as protection (Davey is scared of her

after she decked 'Big' Jim behind the bins, aka Rat Corner). Which was fine when Fat Kylie was just main-lining Bacardi Breezer, but not so good when Mr Whippy was exploring her Nobbly Bobblys. Plus then I had to compromise my own security due to fact that had been drinking Diet Coke as contraceptive measure (i.e. there is no way would snog a chav when sober) and bladder finally threatened to give way and had to let go of Fat Kylie in order to go to loo (she refused to come with me on 'lezzer' grounds). But Davey MacDonald saw me and cornered me on landing. He said 'I'm, like, glad you came, Rachel.' So I knew he was desperate as *a*) he called me Rachel and *b*) he used the correct tense. So he is obviously trying really hard to better himself. And then had revelation and realized it was all utterly Lady Chatterley. And he is underprivileged but gorgeous proletariat gamekeeper Mellors. But then a bit of wee actually started to come out so had to run to loo before moment ruined by me peeing all over the peach shagpile. Which is not at all Ladylike. (Not even Lady Chatterley. Who did all sorts of kinky stuff, according to Scarlet.)

But once safely on toilet and relieved of gallon of Diet Coke wee, remembered that Mellors was master of love, i.e. schooled in the sexual arts. Not rat boy who gets thing out in language lab. Luckily when opened bathroom door Mr Whippy had got in way of Casey and his trigger-happy lighter and he was claiming that his 99 had been singed,

and Davey too distracted by potential penis-related chav fighting to see me escape.

Got home to find Dad was still up watching *Top Gear* repeats on BBC3. I said if Mum caught him he would be for it, given her aversion to Jeremy Clarkson (now grouped with Kyle, in her 'evil Jeremys' subsection). But he said Mum had taken a herbal Nytol to counteract her computer-related jittering and staring eyes and was out for the count. And anyway he was getting tips for his refresher course. Which is great as long as Mike Wandering Hands wants him to drive a Sherman tank over a caravan, beat Ewan McGregor around Silverstone in a Robin Reliant, or fly a Harrier Jump Jet.

. . . .

Sunday 3
11.30 a.m.
Mum is incensed with anti-binge drinking fervour. It is the *Times*'s fault for reporting the dangers of passive drinking. I said surely it was impossible, as you cannot get drunk from sniffing Taboo and black, just mildly nauseated. But she says it is the ensuing violence in pubs, and even a minute amount can affect anyone within a ten-mile radius with devastating consequences. She has a point. Last night I only had Diet Coke and ended up with a twisted ankle (in escape to freedom tripped over Fiddy (yappy miniature Pinscher, former lover of dog, passed out in hallway from drinking Crème de Menthe)) and

four burn holes in my T-shirt (Dane). Anyway, it has sent Mum over the edge in her anti-alcohol stance. She is writing to Mr Wilmott to demand that he include an anti-binge drinking lecture on his citizenship syllabus. She thinks he will be sympathetic given that his sister weirdy Edie is a recovering alcoholic. She will be disappointed. Binge-drinking is endemic at John Major High. Half the staff start the day with an Anadin and soon-to-be-broken vows never to touch the bottle again. Mr Vaughan (chief drinker) says it is due to the pressures of endless paperwork and SATs. It is more the pressure of having his supersized nipples illegally groped by Sophie Jacobs. Anyway, then Dad said what about passive drug-taking, i.e. he was suffering from shout-induced earache due to her being grouchy from the herbal Nytol last night. At which point had to leave the table as not-at-all passive violence threatened to break out over the coarse-cut marmalade. Luckily they have gone out now. Treena is doing Sunday lunch. James and I are excused on the grounds our immune systems are not as well-developed as Mum's and Dad's.

1 p.m.
Oooh. Doorbell. Maybe it is Sad Ed come to update me on his fake religious anti-sex ploy.

2 p.m.
Was not Sad Ed. Was Mellors. Aka Davey MacDonald! He

is not giving up in his pursuit of across-class love. (Or 'pervy nerd sex' according to Thin Kylie.) He said, 'Can I, like, have a word?' I said, 'OK.' He said, 'So, do you, like, want to go out, like, somewhere?' I said, 'Um.' Which admittedly is not very articulate but was transfixed by his many gold earrings, and slightly confused by all the 'likes'. Then he said, 'It's like, I like you, like.' At which point, temporarily lost all track of what he was saying. Luckily James was on hand to translate and said, 'Unbelievable. Billy Elliot is asking you out.' So I said, 'Um. I'll think about it. I'll call you.' And then shut door before he could do any more 'liking'. Which I know is utter cop-out. Especially as do not actually have his number. Though could probably get from Thin Kylie for a packet of B&H. But am now utterly torn. On the one hand, he would be utter experiment in Lady Chatterley across-the-divide love. But on the other hand he is flashing rat boy. This is how Princess Diana must have felt when deciding whether or not to snog son of grocer, and wearer of criminal leather jackets, Dodi Al Fayed.

At least James is happy. It is the closest he has been to the 'criminal fraternity' and he is mental with potential ASBO excitement. He says it is lucky that Mum is out but that he will be monitoring all my movements from now on and any breaches will be reported to the authorities, (i.e. Mum).

Monday 4

Mind has been temporarily swayed from Davey MacDonald conundrum by incredible news that Sad Ed is now ENGAGED! TO BE MARRIED! Apparently he popped the question during T4 yesterday. Although was not actual popping of question. More begging by Melody Bean following disclosure of his no sex before marriage rule. He is now utterly inconsolable. Pointed out that, on plus side, at least he is safe from her gropings until she turns sixteen. But he says that only gives him two months' grace. So said he could always actually tell her the truth, i.e. that not only does he not want to marry her, but that he never wanted to go out with her in the first place, it was a total sympathy thing and that in fact she physically repels him. He said, 'Yeah, right.' So said, 'How are you going to get out of it then?' He said he is going back to his depressives' favourite get-out clause, i.e. untimely death. He says by this time next year he will be but a postscript in history. He is overegging it. He will be lucky to get two lines in the *Walden Chronicle*.

. . . .

Tuesday 5

Shrove Tuesday i.e. Pancake Day

Not only is today Shrove Tuesday but is also apparently something called Super Tuesday. Which is very important politics-wise in America. (Although does not contain pancakes or indeed food of any sort and is mostly about voting so does not sound that super to me.) Anyway, I know this because Scarlet is in complete overdrive and is in two-way communication with Hilary at all times via text. They are all worked up over whether Barack or Hillary (two ls, no definite penis) will win California, New York, and Utah. I said no one in their right minds would want to win Utah as it is full of morons, as she had pointed out only last week. But Scarlet said, 'Mormons, you moron. God, you are so politically smalltown.' She is right. This only highlights further why she is with left-wing Hilary and I am being pursued by no-wing Davey. How utterly ironic. And crap.

5 p.m.
Although maybe Davey MacDonald is actually potentially political. He could be like trade union leader for bricklayers or something.

5.30 p.m.
Except have just remembered he once tried to join BNP.

6 p.m.
Although admittedly it was so he could get cheap Fred Perry shirts off someone called Wiggy.

6.30 p.m.
No, that is still not good enough. Ignorance is no excuse. Look at the Cleggs.

Wednesday 6

Sad Ed is still engaged, i.e. he has neither told the truth, nor managed to kill himself in the last forty-eight hours, despite several attempts at the latter, including binge drinking water to burst his brain. Apparently all that happened is that he had to go to the loo seven times in music and has been referred to the nurse (aka school secretary Mrs Leech) with possible diabetes. Apparently his weight and excess sugar consumption are also key indicators. Asked him if he had broken the happy news to Mrs Thomas yet (wedding, not diabetes). He said no as she will probably encourage it. He is wrong. She is dead set on him marrying female version of Aled Jones, i.e. Welsh and chaste. Not sex-mad Goth from Bird's Farm estate. Plus he is mad if he thinks he can keep it a secret. Melody has already signed up four minigoths as bridesmaids.

. . . .

Thursday 7

Went round Scarlet's for tea after school with Sad Ed. She and Hilary are all texted out after Super Tuesday and she said she needed the company of those with simpler intellectual needs. I said in fact my brain was a hotbed of conflicting intellectual thoughts, mostly brought on by this afternoon's philosophical discussion/row, i.e. what would heaven be like? (Probably not swirly marshmallow paradise, where everyone has rocket packs and X-ray vision as imagined by Reuben Tull.) Sad Ed just shrugged. He is glad to be anywhere that Melody isn't. All the wedding talk is wearing him down. Sad Ed says she is going for a *Corpse Bride* theme, with a black dress and raven-feather fascinator thing. I said is economical as she can wear it to his funeral instead. He said, 'God willing.' He is utterly determined. Am actually worried he might succeed this time. He says he is like Odysseus—trapped between two evils (i.e. the whirlpool of death and six-headed monster). Scarlet said he is not trapped by any evils, more caught up in his own web of idiotic deceit and cowardice.

Anyway, tea was utter disaster due to Edna's steam cleaning all kitchen cupboards without bothering to empty them first and all labels falling off tins. So now all food consumption is utter lottery, i.e. what Scarlet thought was asparagus soup followed by Ambrosia rice pudding (retro food of proletariat and therefore de rigueur in Labour households) turned out to be cannellini beans and condensed milk. Suzy does not mind. She says it is waste not, want not and refused to throw it away due to all the children starving in Africa. Scarlet said she would rather starve along with them. So Sad Ed had both tins. He said he quite liked it. Either he has killed his taste buds with too many Nice 'n' Spicy Nik Naks or it is a lie and he is hoping it is a fatal combination. Me and Scarlet had a bowl of cornflakes instead. Is nutritionally equivalent of cardboard, but at least is edible.

Friday 8

The cannellini beans/condensed milk was not fatal. Though was not without serious side-effects. Sad Ed is very much alive and smelling. He has been banned from the common room and is in quarantine in a language lab until he is fresh again. This could be weeks. Sad Ed says he welcomes the solitude because *a*) Melody cannot find him, and *b*) Leonard Cohen, patron saint of depressive types, is playing Glastonbury, so nothing can dampen his good mood, ironically. Scarlet says she is boycotting Glastonbury. It is not Leonard Cohen. Or controversial rap star Jay-Z. She says she is suffering festival fatigue. There are too many pretenders out there now and the spirit of free love is being watered down with Boden wellies and private portaloos. She is right. I will boycott it too. Though more because do not want to repeat last year's Jack weirdness. Or wee in Pringles tube.

Saturday 9

Oh my God. Got visited by both Dean Denley and Davey MacDonald at work today. Am complete man magnet. Or rather midget and mentalist magnet. But, none the less, is progression on last year's drought. Dean came over in his meat-spattered apron (possibly actually white coat from dressing-up doctor kit, as has stethoscope drawn on pocket) to ask if I wanted to go to see someone called Bingo Bob play tonight at the Lord Butler Leisure Centre

(Jockey Wilson Suite). Said no thanks, as do not like country and western. Said is not country and western, is death metal from Billericay. But luckily, before he could use his powers of persuasion, Mr Goldstein demanded he remove himself from premises as pork traces were offending the vegans, not to mention his own Jewish sensibilities. Then, five minutes later, Davey MacDonald came in, not in meat-spattered apron, but in blue nylon Puma, which is possibly equally offensive, to ask if I wanted to watch Darryl Stamp beat up Ricky Stuart later. Also said no. On so many grounds cannot begin to name them. He seemed genuinely sad. Maybe he is actually sensitive under his mask of thuggishness. He could be potential rough diamond.

8 p.m.
Oh my GOD, he is Heathcliff. And I am spoilt rich girl Cathy. Who will ignore true love of gypsy type and marry for money and end up miserable. It is utter revelation. Think Davey MacDonald may well be ONE after all. Will phone Scarlet and Sad Ed for second opinion.

9 p.m.
Scarlet and Sad Ed not available due to various political/bridal commitments so forced to ask James. He says Davey MacDonald not Heathcliff but run-of-mill Whiteshot Estate pikey and that if he catches any more hints of me pursuing ASBO love he will be forced to

intervene. I said that was rich coming from someone who consorted with an O'Grady on a regular basis. He said he does not actually like Keanu. It is purely a means of avoiding getting beaten up and is more in the tradition of Guy Ritchie squiring Vinnie Jones. And yes he actually used word squiring.

· ·

Sunday 10

11 a.m.

Hurrah, no French again. It is because Mum and James are gloved and helmeted up and busy researching gladiatorial skills on the computer. Mum does not know about James's TV ambitions. She thinks it is because he is doing ancient Rome at school. He is not. Nige thinks it is too bloodthirsty. They are doing grow your own crocus instead.

3 p.m.

James has fallen at first gladiatorial hurdle, i.e. fighting wild beasts. In absence of lions, he tried to wrestle with dog, causing surfeit of howling and scuff marks on lino. He has been sent to his room to think about the perils of aggression. The dog is on the sofa with a rich tea and a smug expression. It is not often that it is at the centre of a kerfuffle and is identified as victim rather than perpetrator of crime. Have told James he should rethink his hobby and find one that utilizes the skills he does have, as opposed to ones he has no hope of acquiring. But he said he is not a quitter and that, like phoenix, he will rise again, stronger and more powerful from the ashes of today's defeat. In fact is thinking of changing name from Gazelle to Phoenix. Am not sure which is worse.

Anyway, more importantly, have made decision to stop obsessing about the ONE. (Following extensive reading of Treena's copy of *Glamour* which she left here yesterday and which have rescued from recycling. Though have disguised inside *Accountancy Today* to avoid shouting from Mum.) Think maybe there is no Mr Right. Just Mr Right Now. Instead will have series of interesting lovers and will grow as person from each liaison in manner of Sienna Miller. (Though will not snog Rhys Ifans as he just looks dirty.)

Monday 11

Saw Davey MacDonald at school today, seeing how many times he could headbutt wall before wall collapsing/him passing out. All signs point to James being right. He is not Heathcliff. He is moron. Think will focus on seizing Dean Denley. It will be experiment in cross-height love. Which is almost Romeo and Juliet-like, if you think about it. We will both grow as people from liaison. Which would be excellent, in his case.

Also, am not going to tea at Scarlet's again. Had tinned tomatoes and custard today. Suzy is embracing the new

73

regime as an experiment in culinary taste and an exercise in using up all the stuff from the back of the cupboard. Bob, Scarlet, and Jack are not so forward-thinking. They are mostly existing on hummus and cereal.

Tuesday 12

Am thinking philosophy possibly bad choice for AS level. Apparently there are NO right answers, there is only opinion. Which is why Mum does not agree with it, due to potential for free thought/getting marked wrong. James on other hand appears to be embracing it. It is his vast cavern of brain which welcomes subject in which there are endless answers to everything. He has read all my Kant ('too obvious') and is on Descartes now. There is no way he is not going to get into St Gregory's. He is freakishly geeky. Although he says he may not actually be attending secondary school at all as he is still aiming to fulfil his gladiatorial ambition. He is hoping to also incorporate philosophy. He says it will make him mentally superior and physically unbeatable. It will not. It will make him look like weirdo he is and he will still get hammering. He can't even outwit dog at moment.

Wednesday 13

It is Valentine's Day tomorrow and in new experimental Mr Right Now style, am going to send several cards. It is

James's idea. He says I need to cast my net wide to ensure a good catch. He sends at least ten every year. Pointed out that he didn't actually have girlfriend so results do not bear out theory but he said, 'That's what you think.' Oh God. Think James might actually be stud nerd at St Regina's. Anyway, have drawn up shortlist and am sending them to Dean, Davey, and Reuben Tull. It is all-embracing group, to show am not in any way anti-chav and that can also overlook height issues and beliefs in laser-eyed dogs. Was going to send one to Jack as well. But *a*) Stones do not 'do' Valentine's Day due to it being made up. And *b*) he has made his views on me utterly clear, i.e. I am not snogging material any more. Which is sort of a shame. As he is utterly good at snogging. But he is not Mr Right Now. He is Mr Back Then. And he can't be only one in world to stir my (girl) mojo.

5 p.m.
Can he?

7 p.m.
Dad is not so excited. It is not the worry about Valentine's Day (he gets Mum the same thing every year, i.e. pre-approved box of Green and Blacks chocolate miniatures and card with Tate print on). It is that tomorrow is his refresher driving course, i.e. he is being forced to spend most romantic day in calendar with Mike Wandering

Hands Majors, aka Mum's not-so-secret admirer. He says he would rather swim naked in Grafton Centre fountain. James said Mad Harry once did that. Does not bear thinking about.

10 p.m.
Have added Justin to Valentine's list. To show that do not bear grudge and also because snogging your ex is also utterly allowed in the rules according to *Glamour*. Have borrowed emergency spare card from James. Has geek-theme, i.e. picture of embracing chess pieces, but he will think it is ironic. Possibly. Am not signing them anyway so is untraceable.

10.30 p.m.
Though what is point of sending them if no one knows who they are from? It is utter Catch 22.

10.40 p.m.
Will just put mysterious 'R' inside. Am like Zorro.

. . . .

Thursday 14
Valentine's Day
It has been an excellent Valentine's Day, card-wise, i.e. got fourteen. In fact is best haul since Year Two when Mrs Bunnet forced everyone to make cards for everyone else in fit of inclusiveness. Not sure they are all genuine

declarations of love. In fact think several are left over from 'do anything for drugs' rumours. But it beats James who only got eight. He is not too disappointed as he sent eleven, which means he is only £3.30 down overall. On the down-side, think my mysterious Zorro-style 'R' may be confused with both Ramona Fork in Year Eleven and recipient of one of my cards, drug baron Reuben Tull. Who spent two hours drawling on about how he must have been in an alternative reality last night because he sent a card to himself. He was not in alternative reality. He was just stoned. As usual. Also have no idea who mine are from. Except one, which is definitely Davey MacDonald's as, in true Retard and Criminal tradition, he had signed it. Sadly none of them are in Justin's illegible scrawl. But do not care about provenance as am not limiting myself to one man. Am embracing love itself today, in spirit of experimentation and general day seizing. (Though purely in philosophical sense. Am not Leanne Jones.)

In contrast Dad has utterly not embraced the spirit of anything. It is because he spent six hours driving around the Hockley one-way system with Mike Wandering Hands. Mum went to invigilate. Dad accused her of only going to ogle Mike but she said she went to ensure fair play and value for money. It is a good job she did. Clearly Mike Majors is no admirer of Mr Clarkson either as he told Dad off forty-seven times and said it is a wonder he is still alive or has a licence at all, and is a good job he has a role model to observe in Mum. At that point apparently Dad performed an illegal U-turn and emergency stop and stormed out of car. He only returned because Mum threatened him with divorce, or being transported everywhere in her Fiesta if he didn't. (He said he doesn't know which would be worse.)

James pointed out that, on the plus side, it is the last Dad will ever have to see of Mike. And now he knows what speed limit on motorway is (i.e. not 99mph, as previously thought). Mum agreed. Plus she distracted him with her Valentine's surprise. It was not heart-shaped cake or new underwear. Thank God. It is news of their new hobby and is guaranteed to cement their love, i.e. Saffron Walden Amateur Operatics Society. They are auditioning for major roles in this year's production of *Grease*. It is Marjory's idea. She has been banging on about it ever since she and Clive got to be backing dancers in *Chicago*. Which is horrendous thought. Also, am not entirely sure it will cement love as actors are always philandering, especially amateur ones. And fear a repeat of the whole Captain Von Trapp sing-off hoo-ha. But at least it means they are out of the house every Sunday afternoon for the foreseeable future. Plus they have a whole new social calendar, starting with a 'meet and greet' tomorrow night at the Seven Devils Lane home of perpetual lead actress (and ferocious lady golf captain) Margot Gyp.

Friday 15

Hurrah. Today was last day of school for a week. Can rest brain from complicated A level thought for seven days of hanging around town, hanging out watching crap telly, or hanging from Scarlet's loveswing (repaired and re-inforced). Apparently it is actually quite philosophical and experimental to lounge about and watch members of opposite sex, according to French philosophical genius and poet Baudelaire. It is called being a *'flâneur'*. Although admittedly his *flâneur*ing was in Paris and passers-by probably included Simone de Beauvoir lost in poetic thought as opposed to Keanu O'Grady trying to breakdance on head outside the Abbey National. None the less, am starting general air of French loucheness tonight, and taking advantage of Mum and Dad's operatic absence, by watching *À Bout de Souffle* and eating maraschino cherries from the tin with a spoon (donated by Scarlet who was offered them on toast for breakfast).

11 p.m.

Baudelairean evening marred only by dog deciding it doesn't like maraschino cherries after all and hawking one up on sofa (yet it considers cutlery edible). Luckily James is also master of all things stain-related and used Mum's arsenal of equipment to full effect.

Mum and Dad did not enjoy such laid-back evening of entertainment chez Margot Gyp. A spanner has been hurled into their romance-cementing operatic dream. It is

Mike Majors! He has also signed up. Though not to seal love, but more probably to engage in extra-curricular hand-wandering. Anyway he and Margot did an impromptu rendition of 'Summer Lovin'' and according to Mum he has 'quite the voice'. Dad said, 'Yes, if you like the thin, reedy sort.' I predict hoo-ha on a colossal scale come the auditions.

. . . .

Saturday 16
8 a.m.
Have decided to continue air of French loucheness by seizing day with Dean Denley. Will corner him near meat bins on break and experiment, Sienna Miller-style.

6 p.m.
Ick. Have begun and ended brief growing-as-a-person liaison with Dean Denley. I do not care how experimental Sienna Miller is, I bet she never had to lift Jude Law up in order to kiss him. Dean did not seem to mind too much when I apologized and said I was just trying something out and possibly would never do it again. He just said, 'Rock and roll, Riley.' He is clearly under delusions he is fully-fledged music industry tart. When in reality he is undersized meat-mincer with a set of Fisher Price bongos.

No sign of Davey MacDonald on man front. Although maybe he is still trying to read Shakespeare sonnet that

80

wrote inside Valentine's card. I know for fact he struggles with *Floppy the Hero*. Did see Reuben Tull in Waitrose car park at lunchtime though. Unbelievably he is Sad Ed's new trolley-herding apprentice now that Sad Ed has been promoted to chief herder (following Gary Fletcher's suspension for various crimes on freezer aisle). Reuben said, 'Nice smell, Riley,' in appreciative manner then rode off on trolley into darkness of Level One like Dick Turpin on Black Bess. But with enormous afro and singing 'Shine On You Crazy Diamond'. (Would like to say smell was classic Chanel No. 5, but was actually environmentally friendly drain cleaner, which Rosamund spilt on my shoes at tea break.) Told Sad Ed that am utterly amazed at Reuben's appointment and if Waitrose are desperate for workers maybe I should rethink my own employment situation. But Sad Ed said, in fact, Reuben is not last resort, but first choice for job. I said it's hardly rocket science but Ed said *au contraire*, there are several key skills to success, e.g. hair able to withstand extreme weather conditions, and ability to sidestep Year Nine skateboard pests who use spiral exit route for ollying etc. Plus he is happy to talk nonsense all day. This is true. When I left he was wondering aloud whether or not a man will ever be born with wheels instead of feet. Waitrose should start including mandatory drug tests for Saturday boys. May well write to Mr John Lewis to suggest it. Although it is improvement on Gary Fletcher whose topics of conversation were limited to radio-controlled cars and Janine off meat's breasts. Anyway Sad Ed is right. Would look like giant puffball, or Reuben Tull, if my hair was exposed to endless howling wind and damp of car park. And the nylon overall does nothing for complexion.

. . . .

Sunday 17

1 p.m.

Hurrah, Mum and Dad have operatics so can spend entire afternoon in bed in manner of French experimental type. Only dressed and alone. And reading *Penguin Guide to Houses of Parliament* instead of erotica. James is also pleased. He is planning a gladiatorial arena in the bathroom where he will attempt to remain under water for five minutes. Said did not think this was actually a gladiator challenge but he says he has thought about what I said about sticking to what he is good at, and is going to try to rewrite the rules to include his special skills.

1.30 p.m.

Lounging and drowning in bath attempts both banned due to alternative arrangement made by Mum to spend quality time with Baby Jesus, i.e. save him from axis of evil that is Treena and the O'Gradys next door. At least Grandpa is vaguely experimental type, i.e. he is ageing lothario with dandyish style of dress (though not always deliberate). Maybe will actually be quite French after all.

5 p.m.

19 Harvey Road not in any way French. Unless you count bottle of flat Orangina in fridge. Though Grandpa showing signs of being experimental. Had very lengthy discussion with him about benefits of pentapeptides. Thought he may actually be scientific genius for minute but Treena says it is not that. It is that he has been reading all her *Grazia*s and *Heat*s and is now also well-versed in waterproof mascara, St Tropez versus Fake Bake, and Jordan's 'boob nightmare'. Which is weird. Although suppose is good that he is educating himself in ways of modern woman. Is better than Grandpa Clegg who rang up in a panic about free radicals after seeing an Oil of Olay advert. He thought an 'army of Commies' was about to invade and that somehow face cream might save him. He is advertisers' dream, i.e. utter moron.

Attempted to have philosophical discussion about God with Baby Jesus in ongoing religious education role. But he more interested in James's gladiator antics, i.e. trying to catch him in fishing net. Although on plus side Jesus already utterly obeying one of ten commandments, and one of my New Year Resolutions, i.e. Thou Shalt Not Lie. He is happy to tell truth at all times, e.g. 'Who did that smell?' Jesus: 'I done it.' Or 'Who ate all the Wagon Wheels?' Jesus: 'Wachel.' Am going to have to overrule pro-God education for anti-Mum education, i.e. he is going to have to toughen up and learn the Riley rules if he, or any of us, are going to survive.

Luckily Mum too preoccupied to do any interrogation of Jesus today. She and Dad are all fired up with operatic potential. They have just a week to prepare for their auditions. Mum is going for Sandy and Dad for Danny Zuko. Have warned them that they should aim lower as *a*) do not want to step on toes of established company members, and *b*) they are not that good, or young. But all pleas have been in vain. Mum says it is high time Margot Gyp made room for new blood. Plus Mike Majors is also going for Danny and Dad says there is no way he is going to let him get his greased lightning anywhere near Mum.

Monday 18
Half term

9 a.m.
Hurrah, it is beginning of week of *flâneur*ing, following yesterday's interruption to play. Am going to start by lying in bed until eleven. Then may go round Sad Ed's for some moping. Then to Scarlet's for some hovering before ending with some idling outside Gayhomes (crap hardware shop, not homosexualist one). Excellent.

9.15 a.m.
Am out of bed. Mum says she does not care how French it is, I am not lounging about festering on laundry day and if I have nothing to do I can test her on lines while

she presoaks the pants. Declined. It is not the pants. It is Mum's version of Sandy. Who seems to have gained implausible Australian accent and insane smile. She has no chance. Will leave her to James.

9.30 a.m.
James also declined. He is devoting half term to gladiating. He is going to Mad Harry's to consume protein for day. Will go to Sad Ed's instead for early moping. He will not mind. Plus even if he still asleep is generally same effect, i.e. pale and quiet with occasional grunt.

9.45 a.m.
Sad Ed not in. He has gone to Cambridge with Melody to buy clothes, according to Mrs Thomas. This is an utter lie. Sad Ed does not buy clothes. He has had same T-shirts for four years. It is cover-up for illicit wedding activity. He has probably gone to choose his hypothetical tuxedo. Will go to Scarlet's instead for hovering.

10.30 a.m.
Scarlet not in. Apparently Suzy drove her to Cornwall yesterday to reunite her with left-wing love Hilary. Jack said I could come in and hover anyway but said hovering not same when no one else to moan at T4 with. So he said could just come in and have brunch (banned in our house for being *a*) American, *b*) a made-up word, and *c*) usurping elevenses in popularity). Was hesitant, as did not want to end up with vichysoisse instead of baked

beans but it turns out Edna's tin regime has been abolished. It is because Bob opened up Kitekat and said was last straw. Edna said she ate cat food in the war and was grateful. But Bob said if he can't eat filet mignon he is hardly going to chow down on scrag end and eyeballs. All tins have been donated to Pink Geranium Sheltered Housing (old people will eat anything as long as it is mushy, even cat food) and so had full (vegetarian) English breakfast brunch-style meal. Which was revelation as Jack is first man have met who can cook. Grandpas Clegg and Riley do not cook on principle (it is women's work, along with household cleaning, and purchasing of pants), and Dad does not cook on grounds that Mum gets too shouty when he does. Also Jack is only man whose breakfast conversation is not limited to tax (Dad), Ninja Turtles (James), or groaning (Sad Ed). Was tempted to ask if could stay for lunch too but remembered had *flâneur*ing to do in town. Jack says am welcome back any time though. Which is excellent as apparently he can also do Eggs Benedict (also banned chez Riley due to Hollandaise sauce being chief perpetrator of food poisoning, according to *Which* magazine). Plus we have nice time when we are not busy being all minty with each other about ONE issues. Experimentation is definitely way forward.

4 p.m.
Though do not think *flâneur*ing in town is. No one lost in poetic thought, only usual mental trances. Plus got

questioned as to reasons for lurking on bench by PC Doone, Marjory PI, and James (on shopping trip with Mad Harry and Mrs Mad Harry to buy fun fur for gladiator outfits).

. . . .

Tuesday 19

11 a.m.

Oh God. Have just witnessed horrendous sight. It is James and Mad Harry in furry leopard pants. Cannot believe Mum is not stopping them. It is operatics. It has taken over her life already. She is neglecting her child-rearing duties in favour of singing about someone called Sandra Dee who is 'lousy with virginity'. Cannot watch either display any longer. Am going round Sad Ed's. And if he not in will just sit in darkened corner of Waitrose car park. Reuben Tull may be stoned and think God is a futuristic Alsatian but he is marginally less disturbing.

4 p.m.

Was right about Sad Ed. He spent four hours trying to squeeze into a wedding suit in Moss Bros. Asked what he had gone for. He said his choice was limited due to his 'unique build', i.e. shortness and roundness, and he is going for pale blue and ruffles. He says it is exactly like the one Jamie Oliver wore when he married Jools. Said it sounds more like one Elton John wore when he married David Furnish and that pale colours will only accentuate

87

his 'unique build'. Then he accused me of being unsupportive. At which point accused him of being idiot as he is not getting married in a baby blue suit or any suit for that matter as wedding is giant charade.

Spent rest of day reading *An Introduction to the European Union*. Which is not experimental, but is partly French, and at least does not feature schoolboys in fur pants or forty-somethings pretending to be lovestruck sixteen year olds.

. . . .

Wednesday 20

Thank God. James and Mad Harry have given up on being gladiators for time being. It is partially due to pant irritation (fake fur has brought Mad Harry out in genital rash) and partially due to total lack of gladiatorial powers. James says he is going to stick to philosophy for a bit. He is confident of being on par with Derrida by end of year.

. . . .

Thursday 21

Went round Jack's again today for brunch (scrambled eggs with parsley garnish). Asked how Scarlet was getting on in Cornwall, spiritual home of UKIP and all things backward. He said she is having excellent time and she and Hilary are busy converting the Cleggs to the cause. Said that was waste of time. Jack said they have given up on Grandpa Clegg who, according to Hilary, is unreconstructed Thatcherite with Powellian ambitions (personally thought he was just moany old racist). But that they are making progress with Granny Clegg. Apparently Scarlet says she has been repressed by Grandpa Clegg's patriarchal regime and that she may look like a weak old lady, but that under the housecoat lurks the beating heart of a true suffragette. Said she is wrong and all that lurks under the housecoat is a saggy woman with a Viennetta habit. Which made Jack laugh. Although was not actually meant as joke. Is true.

Did not do any *flâneur*ing. Watched *Ugly Betty* repeats with Jack instead. Which is almost the same. Why oh why can I not meet someone like Henry, i.e. brainy, yet surprisingly good looking and with nice chest?

. . . .

Friday 22

Have discovered reason for mysterious lack of Davey MacDonald activity. He is in Formentera with the rest of the MacDonalds. I got a postcard this morning. It says:

> Deer Rach
> Its well hot. Dad burned his nippel so bad a bit fell off. Wicked.
> Wish you was here,
> Davey ☺

I can safely say I do not share his sentiment, i.e. I

do not wish I was anywhere near Formentera, or the sight of his dad's 'nippel' scab. James has issued another ASBO-love warning. He tried to take it to higher authority but luckily higher authority too busy lip-synching to Olivia Newton John in mirror. I hope Dad is not this bad at work and neglecting his crucial paperclip stock-taking or whatever it is that he actually does in favour of doing Danny Zuko impressions at the water cooler. The shame.

6 p.m.
Apparently Dad is as bad. Mr Wainwright has threatened to promote Malcolm from IT above him if he doesn't stop knee skidding along the nylon carpet.

. . . .

Saturday 23
Still struggling at work with till of confusion. It has taken to using Hong Kong dollars instead of pounds. Rosamund says it has bad 'chi' and is going to burn a healing candle over it on Monday.

More worryingly, tomorrow is the big day, i.e. Saffron Walden amateur operatic audition madness. Mum and Dad did a full dress rehearsal before *Doctor Who* in front of specially invited audience, i.e. me, James, dog, and Riley senior household (i.e. Grandpa and Baby Jesus. Treena would have come but was down Queen Lizzie with her cousin Donna who is 'double mental'). Was awful. Is not

the singing, which is actually passable. Is horrendous attempts at being American teenagers, which is excruciating. Had to overrule honesty resolution when Mum asked for 'constructive criticism' (she does not mean constructive criticism, she means be nice). Said was truly groundbreaking. Baby Jesus and dog not so good at constructive criticism and sobbed/howled throughout proceedings. Grandpa Riley conveniently stunned into silence. Only person who actually enjoyed it was James who danced in the aisles (aka in between John Lewis nesting tables) in 'Greased Lightning', and actually shed tears during 'Hopelessly Devoted to You'. He has offered himself up as their manager to take them to new heights of stardom.

. . . .

Sunday 24

10 a.m.
Have gone back to bed. Is not French-style lounging. Is to escape audition madness downstairs. James is shouting 'fantastic fantastic fantastic' in demented John Barrowman fashion as Dad and Mum (in leather jackets, presumably left over from Clive and Marjory's bondage backing dancer *Chicago* stint) jive around the sofa singing 'I got chills'.

5 p.m.
Mum and Dad are back and are in vile moods. It is not

that they were awful (although Dad was, according to Mum, and Mum was, according to Dad) it is that Margot Gyp has fielded a ringer, i.e. she has persuaded Saffron Walden's only celebrity, i.e. the not-so-famous McGann brother, to try out. And if he is Danny, he will make sure Margot is Sandy, as he has been on waiting list at golf club for a year and it will seal the deal for membership. Dad says the dream is over. Personally do not think it ever really began. James Barrowman, on other hand, says he must never lose sight of his ambition and that a bit part in *Emmerdale* cannot compete with Dad's raw unschooled talent (it can). Anyway, it is all tenterhooks until next Sunday when the winners are announced. On plus side at least there will be no more horrendous 'wella wella wella uh'-ing for at least a week.

Monday 25
Back to school

Am actually looking forward to school. It will be excellent for *flâneur*ing. Can just stand at nut dispensing machine in black vintage dress looking coquettish. Though not exactly sure what coquettish means. (Should probably have kept to French A level instead of politics. Politics not all cracked up to be. Seem to spend most of time trying to fathom point of Europe.) Will be enigmatic instead, i.e. look bored.

4 p.m.
Gave up on being coquettish at nut machine. Potential men too busy bulk purchasing Bombay Mix to respond to enigmatic antics. Scarlet said did not look enigmatic anyway, just looked retarded. Which is possibly why Mark Lambert offered me one of his 'tasty nuts'. As if I'd fall for that. Said hello to Davey MacDonald. But did not thank for card. Am still disturbed by scabby nipple image.

Scarlet is still insisting that Granny Clegg is not mental or bigoted by nature but is in fact a political powerhouse waiting to burst out of her elasticated trousers. Apparently she and Hilary went round several times last week (officially to restock Fray Bentos and unblock toilet, and unofficially to debrainwash her) and are slowly breaking through the layers of conservatism that have built up over the years from repeated exposure to Grandpa Clegg and the *Daily Mail*. Scarlet says I will be surprised at the new woman I see next time I visit St Slaughter. I doubt it. She will still have polyester slippers and tendency to say 'hooge'.

5 p.m.
Oh my God. Granny Clegg just rang to demand that Mum start boycotting the Jade Garden Chinese Restaurant in protest at Chinese occupation of Tibet. She says the Beijing Olympics is an historic opportunity to put the plight of the Tibetan people on the world stage. Scarlet

was right after all! Two weeks ago she thought Tibet was in Wales. I bet Grandpa Clegg is going mental. Although he probably supports the boycott. Not because he is sympathetic to Tibet, but because he is anti all foreign food. Anyway Mum has agreed.

7 p.m.

Oooh. Wonder if can persuade Mum to boycott sadistic dentist Mrs Wong on same grounds.

7.30 p.m.

Mum has declined. I said it was hypocritical to boycott one Chinese outlet and not another but Mum says she is not boycotting the Jade Garden because of Tibet. Or foreign food issues. It is because take-aways are evil, i.e. they are overpriced, trans-fat-ridden, and harbingers of e-coli. Whereas Mrs Wong is just overpriced.

. . . .

Tuesday 26

8.30 a.m.

Grandpa Clegg *is* going mental. He has just rung to demand that Mum has words with Granny Clegg over the arrival of a 'highbrow left-wing rag' at the breakfast table this morning. Mum said there is nothing wrong with the *Guardian*, bar the annoying Berliner size issue, and it might do him good to see other side of story for once. Grandpa said it is not *Guardian*, is *Daily Mirror*

and it has put him right off his Grape Nuts. Mum says she is not interfering in their relationship. The last time she did that was in 1995, over the infamous Judith Chalmers stand-off, and no one spoke to her for a month. Though frankly think that would be a bonus.

. . . .

Wednesday 27
4 p.m.
Philosophy ended in row again today. It is thorny issue of cloning and 'playing God'. Personally am not concerned whether people get to choose sex or hair colour of baby or clone them in their own image. Would mean end to unmanageable frizz etc., etc.

4.30 p.m.
Although possibly Mum would have chosen two Jameses instead of me. Or cloned herself and had a litter of small Mums. Oh God. World would be awful place with endless Cillit Banging or Googling. Am changing opinion. Is utterly allowed in philosophy. James is pro though. It is not that wants to clone self. It is dog. He wants to freeze it when it dies until it can be reincarnated as 'Hyperwolf'—part dog, part robot. Mum has refused. She says it's bad enough when it's alive, she cannot be expected to put up with its hairy expression leering out from the frozen peas when it's dead.

. . . .

Thursday 28

Is Dad's birthday tomorrow. And, as is leap year, is actual official one, i.e. on 29th instead of substandard fake birthday on 28th. But, more interestingly, is day when all women are encouraged to propose to men, in stand against traditional rules of romance. Scarlet says it is media-manufactured nonsense and if she wanted to get married, which she does not, because it is repressive act that only perpetuates antiquated religious and patriarchal mores, she would propose whenever she liked, instead of waiting until GMTV offered her a slot to do it live on telly just because it was 29th. She is right. Anyway have no one to propose to. As usual. Although is excellent seizing day opportunity. Melody Bean should have waited though. She could have got a free bridal makeover thrown in if she'd done it in the studio with Kate Garraway.

. . . .

Friday 29

School is awash with seizing the day and general leap year madness. Thin Kylie has proposed to Mark Lambert and he has said yes! She did it outside the mobile science lab with a glow-in-the-dark ring out of a packet of Coco Pops. They are going to get proper ones from the Argos catalogue later. Scarlet said it is pathetic and will be over by Christmas when he snogs someone else or has fatal minibike crash, and what was wrong with my eyes? Said was despair at futility of it all. But was lie. Was utterly swept away by true chav romance. Sad Ed also happy. Though not at romance. He is just relieved that he has teen wedding rivals. He said Thin Kylie is bound to go for Wayne and Coleen style nuptials, which will detract attention from his and Melody's alternative ceremony. Pointed out there wasn't going to be a ceremony. He said 'Hmmm.' Said what does 'hmmm' mean. He said he thinks it might be easier to just go through with it and then get a divorce on grounds of non-consummation due to missing mojo. He is insane. Then missing mojo will be public, and Mrs Thomas, knowledge, and he could save himself humiliation, shouting, and colossal cost of wedding by just TELLING TRUTH NOW! He said I underestimate Melody's determination. Said I give up. The girl is mad though. Sad Ed is not that much of catch. I have seen his buttocks.

Dad not so seized with leap year madness. Although he is enjoying his heart-rate monitor (James) whilst watching *Lovejoy Christmas Special* DVD (me). Apparently it goes up massively every time Ian McShane appears. It is horror at mullet hairdo. He says he is saving Mum's present, i.e. celebration cake (wholemeal date and seed) for later. He is not. He is going to 'lose' it, i.e. feed it to dog.

march

FURRY
GLADIATOR → PANTS

RESCUE
REMEDY

£20

Saturday 1

St David's Day

Rosamund's candle-burning till chi remedy has failed. Till of confusion now not only unfathomable but has lumps of smelly wax all over it which means drawer now sticks, which means is also now till of death. On plus side, have only two weeks left until am debt-free. Hurrah! So can lavish money on fripperies instead of posting it into Mum's collection tin (WHSmith petty cash tin, locked, with keys stashed in unknown hidey hole) every week.

6 p.m.

Or save sensibly for my pension, as James has suggested.

. . . .

Sunday 2

Mothering Sunday

Mum utterly not excited by Mother's Day gift of packet of halva (on discount from Nuts In May due to partial packet breakage). Is because of operatic anticipation. I pointed out that it does not matter if she fails to be cast as Sandy as the most important role in the world is being a mother, which she already plays to great (and somewhat irritating) effect. James did not agree. He said mother-hood has stifled her ambition and thwarted her destiny and that this is her chance to find herself, and fame. He is still fully of belief that she and Dad are acting dynasty couple like Michael Douglas and Catherine Zeta

Jones. Or Chuckle Brothers. Which will be proven this afternoon.

5 p.m.

Mum and Dad are not acting dynasty. As predicted, main roles went to McGann and Margot Gyp. But is possibly more terrifying. They are Rizzo, the school slut, and hard heart-throb Kenickie. Which is most misled casting ever. Mum had not even seen a willy at age of sixteen, let alone got possibly pregnant by leather-clad stud. Marjory and Clive are the 'kooky' (i.e. fat) pink lady Jan and someone called Eugene. Who does not even get to sing. Which is more sensible all round. Mum is delighted though. She says it will be a real challenge to play the bad girl. Dad is also accepting defeat gracefully. It is not because he is relishing role. It is because Mike Majors is ugly rival gang leader Leo, i.e. not a stud. Pointed out that Leo gets to snog Rizzo. Dad not so graceful now. In fact is mental with Wandering Hands rage. Mum says he will have to rise above it as is only acting and no feelings are involved. Did not mention Jack *Bugsy Malone* stage kiss, when however hard tried not to let feelings get involved, was utterly swoony by end of it. Luckily James interrupted by reminding the Zeta-Jones-Douglases of other impending matter, i.e. secondary school admissions results are released online tomorrow. Mum has got the gloves and helmet out in readiness. She does not want to waste a minute of vital gloating time when James secures his place at St Gregory's

Girls, and future place in history as general boffin type, and Mad Harry ends up at Burger King Sports Academy.

. . . .

Monday 3

Tension at Shreddies table is utterly palpable. Mum is checking clock every few seconds. Although this is point-less as James has forbidden her to go online until he gets home from school so that he can share the joy. He has hidden Marigolds to ensure she does not cheat. Said she was not this het up when I was getting my place. She said James has more sensitive needs. He does not. He is just nerd. He is not worried though and has departed for St Regina's confident in the knowledge that he will be enjoying a state-of-the-art computer lab and hygienic toilet facilities in six months' time. Leaving me to endure germ-harbouring cracked bowls, and a Dell with a stolen shift key.

4 p.m.

The gloves and helmet are on. James is singing the *Star Wars* theme. The dog is jumping around like crazed crea-ture of hell.

4.15 p.m.

Gloves and helmet are off. Dog back under table chewing a shoe. A travesty has occurred. James has failed to secure a place at St Gregory's Girls and has been allocated to substandard, unboffiny John Major High! Mum has already rung the council to point out mistake but Mr Lemon (formerly of housing department, now of education office) said it was actually not mistake and that is all down to catchment area and to please stop shrieking. James has stopped singing *Star Wars* theme, but is not completely despondent. He says his superior intellect will still out, even with broken locust tanks and second-rate teaching. Plus Mad Harry is going too. Mum has vowed to take it to appeal. And, failing that, move to Bishop's Stortford.

5 p.m.
Granny Clegg has rung. She says James's disappointment is inevitable consequence of abolition of grammar schools and catchments are fairest method in ultimately flawed system. Asked if she was reading script provided by Scarlet. She said no, she heard it on Radio 4 this morning! This is unprecedented news. Granny normally only listens to Pirate FM and shipping forecast (does not understand it, thinks it is mystical ancient language, plus it soothes Bruce). Maybe Scarlet was right and she is actually repressed Carla Bruni. Except in body of old woman.

Tuesday 4
8 a.m.
Mum is drawing up her appeal plan with military

104

precision. She has taken SatNav out of car to check exact distance door to door, and is also listing James's many and varied 'special' needs.

8.30 a.m.
Dad has rung to know where SatNav is as he is lost somewhere in Harlow and has been round same roundabout twenty-three times.

4 p.m.
Told Scarlet about James's school results. She asked how he is taking it. I said he is back to philosophical gladiating at moment as fallback in case his education now doomed. Scarlet said he is idiot because reality TV, game shows, and talent contests give the masses false hope that there is an easy way to money and happiness and that education is the only ladder out of poverty. I said except for Paul Potts. And Girls Aloud. And egghead Judith Keppel. So Scarlet thwacked me with a Grizzly Bar.

5 p.m.
She has a point though. James is no Cheryl Cole. He is one of the weirdos they let through just to humiliate them on live TV. And look at Granny Clegg. Prior to power of education she was borderline racist with Fray Bentos habit and now she is potential suffragette. Ooh, have had brainwave. Will elevate Davey MacDonald out of his council house by power of education. After few

months of political awakening he will be utterly Hilaryesque (one l, penis). It is brilliant. He is utter blank canvas, literature- (and most things) wise and I can mould my ideal man. Am like Mary Shelley and he is my Frankenstein's Monster. Hurrah! Will start tomorrow by agreeing to meet him out of school hours. Where no one can see us.

. . . .

Wednesday 5

Have arranged to meet Davey. Is out of school hours, but is very much in public. It is at party at football club hut on Saturday night, to celebrate Thin Kylie and Mark Lambert's engagement. Agreed on grounds that will be dark, and everyone will be drunk, so they will either not see us together, or be too busy trying not to be sick on dance floor to care. Also, have made clear that agreement is not green light to start groping my bra or pants region yet. He will have to pass tests first. He said he definitely does not have chlamydia because Leanne Jones got tested and she is totally clear. I said not that sort of test. Although is reassuring to know his penis is infection-free given that he has been known to wave it around in crowded areas. Though not so reassuring he actually said cholera not chlamydia.

. . . .

Thursday 6

Sad Ed has changed his mind about Britcher/Lambert

106

nuptials being welcome diversion. Melody is determined not to be outdone and is demanding a party of their own. Sad Ed has agreed as long as they don't actually call it engagement party. It is at Melody's on Saturday night. He is begging me and Scarlet to go as reinforcements. Said I had prior engagement at REAL engagement party, i.e. where givers are actually going to wed. He says if that's the way I feel then Scarlet can be best man. Have agreed to make appearance. Do not want to lose potential as best man, even if is only hypothetical. And am not man.

Friday 7

Grandpa Riley has rung and is mad with excitement. He has been watching Crufts and thinks dog may actually not be hairy, valueless mongrel but pedigree Otterhound with star, and money-making, potential. He is booking it in for assessment with Official Otterhound Society (Essex branch) next week. He is making mistake. Dog is not pedigree. Is moronic mix possibly including orang-utan and amoeba.

Saturday 8

6 p.m.

Could not concentrate at work due to impending political education appointment with Davey MacDonald. Not entirely sure that Thin Kylie engagement party is the right setting though—chances of overdosing on bacardi and Hi-Tecs quite high. Rosamund has given me a bottle of herbal Rescue Remedy. Is not actual drug. Is just calming flowers etc. Have to put drop on tongue when am feeling anxious. Have had twenty so far. Thank God arranged to meet Davey at football club. James is already suspicious. He asked why I was going to celebrate such an ill-conceived union, i.e. Thin Kylie and Mark Lambert. Which even if is not divorce statistic in a year, has no hope of producing genetically superior offspring. He is genetics obsessed at moment. It is the dog cloning Hyperwolf thing. He is hoping to develop a method to isolate its eating gene and make a man who can eat an entire fridge. Anyway, said was celebrating seizing of day, not teen marriage per se, and that his attitude on eugenics was bordering on fascism. He said is not. Is just common sense. Did not mention Melody Bean and Sad Ed engagement party. The genetic implications there are quite scary.

12 midnight

Am home. Evening has been education. Though possibly not for Davey MacDonald. Have learnt several things:

   a) Rescue Remedy does not work. Had taken fifty-eight drops by the time I got to the football club and was feeling sicker than when started. Then Davey saw me with pipette thingy in mouth and accused me of being on drugs. I said, *i)* not actual drug is only herbal, and *ii)* I would hardly think he minded. But he said, *i*) is made-up then, and *ii*) he had never done any drugs, not even snorting iron tablets (briefly in vogue amongst more idiotic Criminals and Retards) because what is point when cider is cheaper and legal. Said was not strictly legal as he is only seventeen. He said actually no he is eighteen. Said no he is seventeen. He said no is eighteen as was kept down a year. Said is it dyslexia? He said no, is thickness. Plus the penis-revealing thing.

b) Alcohol does work. Had several halves of Magners, purchased by genuine older man, i.e. Davey, and was instantly calmer. And much better at dancing too.

c) Davey also not approving of teen marriage. I said exactly, as marriage is defunct institution, which is repressive to women, and does not even come with tax advantages any more (cunningly combining Scarlet's and Dad's theories on subject). He said, whatever, she will be bored in a year and trying it on with Liam O'Grady again. Said which one. He said all.

At that point said had to go to other engagement party, which also doomed, but not actually real, so not as bad. He said he would walk me. Said am modern woman and can walk by self thank you very much. He said am girl and can not walk on own unless look like Fat Kylie. Plus he needed to go to offie for fags.

Quite liked caveman approach. Although was worried his penis-revealing antics might rear their ugly head.

Literally. But walk was thankfully penis-free. Said he was welcome to come to party (as would be excellent opportunity to integrate him with best friends and let Scarlet use her powers of political education) but he said he'd rather watch Casey and Dane set fire to football club than goths and fat emos swaying to crap music. And anyway, wasn't Sad Ed gay? Said sadly not, as it would solve several mojo- and marriage-related issues, plus had been hoping for Gay Best Friend for years.

Said goodbye on corner of street. He tried to do kiss but managed to dart head to side so he only got mouthful of hair. He said, 'What's up, Riley, you weren't so shy before.' Said yes but was temporarily overcome with resolution madness and am not ready to seize day, (or Davey), again yet. (May take weeks, or months, before he is fully reborn. Have not even begun to deal with wardrobe issues.)

He has point about hanging out with goths and emos though. Melody Bean's dining room was like crowd scene from Tim Burton movie. But was not there for fun but purely to show face at fake engagement party. So can be fake best man. And pick up pieces when bridegroom admits to all fakeness and bride has meltdown. Though am worried about scale of potential meltdown. Melody Bean is marriage mad. Cannot believe Mr and Mrs Bean do not know what is going on. One of her bedroom walls is covered in cut-outs from *Brides* magazine. Which is only marginally less disturbing than the wall that is covered in Sad Ed cut-outs. Reuben Tull liked it though.

110

He lay on the floor staring at it through a pint glass until he got paranoid that all the Sad Eds were going to attack him and had to be talked down by Scarlet.

Sad Ed is also depressed at the scale of it all. The number of bridesmaids has gone up from four minigoths to twenty-three and Melody is also talking about arriving on the back of the black stallion with all the bridesmaids in a winged chariot. Said they will not fit in. He said that not point. Is that it is getting harder and harder to keep it a secret. Especially as Melody gave his home number to a catering company and they keep ringing to ask if he prefers traditional fruit cake or a chocolate profiterole pyramid. He told his mum it was just random market research calls. It is lucky he is glutton and so is entirely plausible. Asked what he preferred. He said profiteroles.

. . . .

Sunday 9
2 p.m.

Sad Ed has been round all morning. Thought was to spend quality time with best friend (he is my second best friend, but I am his first best friend. Is excellent arrangement. For me anyway) but was only to escape Melody, her twenty-three bridesmaids, and the black stallion dream. He said he would not choose to spend several hours listening to my mother singing about being 'trashy and no-good' unless times were desperate. He is right. Is a horrifying performance. Just hope the director (i.e. Russell Rayner, closet homosexual, golf club resident professional, once in Erasure video) has the talent, and endurance, to deal with her. Though fear not. Performance is only in eight weeks. Anyway, was productive, despite sound of James urging Mum to 'notch it up a level' echoing up the stairs. Told Ed he should suggest to Melody that they elope to Gretna Green instead. Which is like Las Vegas, but in Scotland. Is utterly romantic, money-saving, and, by definition, secret. Sad Ed says am genius. Hurrah!

. . . .

Monday 10

Sad Ed says am not genius. Plan has backfired horribly. Melody has agreed to eloping idea, but, now that no planning of winged chariot or profiterole tower involved, she wants to do it on her birthday, i.e. next month. Have said sorry. But also that is not entirely my fault as am not idiot that agreed to marry her in first place to avoid dealing with missing mojo issue. Have volunteered services as best woman to make up for it. Said, as his first best friend, is least I can do. He said thanks but is not that easy as Scarlet, who is also claiming best friend status, has put herself forward for role. Said it was an outrage as *a*) I am actual best friend, and *b*) Scarlet does not even believe in marriage. He said, *a*) actually we are both equal best friends, and *b*) I said I was anti-marriage too. I said, *a*) that is slight shock and will be revising own friend list

forthwith, and *b*) I was only parroting Scarlet's opinions and actually think marriage is ultimate romantic gesture, especially if also involves suicide à la Romeo and Juliet. He said Oh. Anyway he has gone home to draw up list of my and Scarlet's attributes so he can choose best woman to be best man. Will win obviously.

. . . .

Tuesday 11

8 a.m.

Mum is in bad mood. It is not *Grease*-related for once but is Delia Smith, original domestic goddess (as opposed to pretender Nigella who is just heaving bosoms and flashy gadgets), and her new 'How to Cheat' TV series! Mum, who is anti-cheating at any time says it is a symptom of the decline of the BBC, and society in general. James agrees. He says it is a betrayal and is writing to Mark Thompson (Director General of BBC) and Gordon Brown to complain. Said Gordon probably had more important things to worry about than tinned mince. As do I. Though is not economic decline. Is battle of the best men. Though am confidently expecting to triumph by double English. Will serve Scarlet right for stealing Hilary and forcing me to create my own.

4 p.m.

Am not best man yet. Sad Ed says it is a trickier decision than he thought. I said what is tricky about it? I am reliable, my hair looks good in weddingy up-do, plus am not likely to object at last minute due to militant feminist tendencies. Scarlet said, *au contraire*, she would overcome her desire to stop proceedings because supporting her *best* friend was more important. I said I thought I was her best friend. She said she has reconsidered following the Hilary hoo-ha and anyway she thought Davey MacDonald was my new best friend. Said he is not friend. Is social experiment. And how did she know about him anyway? She said Tracey Hughes (mum answers phone at police station) saw us doing the macarena at Thin Kylie's engagement party. Do not remember that. Must have blocked from memory. Anyway, at that point some of the new but unimproved Criminals and Retards set the fire alarm off (proving that it is genetically inbuilt) so had to shiver on the sheep field for half an hour and was too busy conserving energy to argue. But am now in shock as started week with two best friends and now have potentially none.

. . . .

Wednesday 12

Have made decision to downgrade Scarlet and bump Ed up to first best friend. Now he will have to choose me. Plus have stolen packet of Duchy Chocolate Butterscotch biscuits from cupboard as bribe. They are his favourites but Mrs Thomas does not buy them because Aled prefers macaroons.

114

5 p.m.
Sad Ed not swayed by upgrading or biscuits. Says is still racked by indecision and is like choosing between Morrisey and Leonard Cohen. Plus Mum now in forensic hunt for missing biscuits. I said was dog (habitual biscuit thief) but she says is not dog as he does not like butterscotch (but will eat brillo pad). Said was James. She said he is too short to reach cupboard. Plus he is joining in the hunt. Am not concerned. She will never work it out. Have carefully concealed trail of evidence, i.e. biscuits in Sad Ed's tummy and empty packet in Sad Ed's bag.

Thursday 13
Scarlet trumped the Duchy Chocolate Butterscotch biscuits and brought Sad Ed a dozen homemade Nigella-recipe triple chocolate nut muffins (in contrast to Mum, Suzy is definite fan of heaving bosoms and flash gadgets). Cannot compete with that. Even dog rejected Mum's celebration seed cake. It dropped it on kitchen tile and caused minor cracking. Have resigned self to being second best friend and not at all best woman.

Also Mum still consumed with missing biscuit mystery. Dad is currently suspect Number One. Mum says it is not her he is cheating, it is himself, with his potential cholesterol issues. He says he is cheating nobody and is in fact eschewing all fatty products in bid to lose middle-aged paunch before playing decidedly non-middle-aged

Kenickie. She is not convinced and says he cannot have pudding. Is yoghurt. So no loss.

. . . .

Friday 14

An excellent thing has happened. In fact three excellent things. 1) Am best woman. Thanks to 2) Davey MacDonald, who may well be idiot savant after all as opposed to plain idiot. Bumped into him in oven chip queue at lunch and explained entire best woman hoo-ha and he said why not just have two? Mark Lambert is having Davey and Darryl Stamp. Is stroke of genius! Though possibly not for Mark Lambert—speeches will be potentially horrendous. And 3) We have all agreed to reinstate each other as equal best friends so there is no confusion any more. Is slightly annoying that Scarlet is also best woman. But I get to be ring bearer so am slightly more equal. Ha! Though mainly because Scarlet says she is allergic to any contact with non-precious metals.

On downside, Mum has identified biscuit thief, i.e. me. Was not cunning forensics though. Was Sad Ed, who came round after school and said, 'Got any more of those butterscotch things?' Mum said she cannot afford to lose entire packets in the current economic climate and offered him a digestive or a rich tea finger. He went home for macaroons instead. Have agreed to pay Mum £2.49 to cover cost of biscuits. Which means will not be debt-free

116

until 3 p.m. as opposed to 2 p.m. Is minor setback. Will still be cash rich by end of tomorrow.

· ·

Saturday 15

6 p.m.

Hurrah. Am liquid again (cunning financial speak for having actual money). But debt-free status is not without potential threat. Mr Goldstein (of similar paranoid persuasion as Mum) is also concerned with economic climate and has issued a warning that there may be cutbacks in the coming months if Gordon Brown does not pull his finger out, i.e. compulsory redundancies. Is bound to be me for the chop. Rosamund is older, is not afraid of till, and has vast experience of herbal remedies and health-foods given that she is vegan and ailment-ridden. Plus she does not come back from lunch break with trolley-related injuries to fingers that mean she cannot lug lentil sacks for several hours. Is last time I let Reuben Tull push me down spiral ramp. All drugs have left him with inability to judge distance from wall. Sad Ed is far better herder. He is slower, but does not crash so frequently.

· ·

Sunday 16

10 a.m.

Mum's recession panic is mounting following study of *Times* money section. She says banks are dropping like flies and she is thinking of withdrawing her life savings

117

and keeping them in a shoebox. James has warned her not to regress to Clegg-style money madness. Pointed out that her security arrangements are stricter than Barclays.

2 p.m.

Mum changed mind about shoebox. Is not James's Clegg argument. Is because dog has eaten a twenty pound note that Dad had left out to pay window cleaner. Her window locks and alarms may be state of art but dog is most definitely not. Is complete security threat.

Grandpa, who was round for lunch, said to stop shouting at dog as is harmful to pedigree animals to be treated like ruffians. He is taking it for its Otterhound assessment tomorrow and says he is hopeful dog will be key to surviving downturn as will potentially rake in fortune from shows/stud fees. Mum says it is pointless as even if dog is Otterhound, which it is not, is worthless as *a*) is too disobedient to be in show, and *b*) has had genitals removed so cannot pass on pedigree. Grandpa says if that is case then he may well have grounds to sue Mum for lost sperm.

Did not get involved in absurd sperm wars. There is no point as dog will not pass test. Is not pedigree. Pedigree dogs do not look like Chris Moyles.

. . . .

Monday 17

St Patrick's Day

As predicted, dog is not key to fortune. Otterhound

Society (Essex branch) says it is in no way related to their superior breed as its face is too long, its legs are too short, and it has asymmetrical ears. Grandpa said that is only where Bruce ate a bit of one of them in a fight over a plastic octopus. But they were not moved. Felt bit sorry for dog having to listen to all its faults being listed. Grandpa said it did not mind as it was still chewing the liquorice toffee he gave it to persuade it to get on bus to Chelmsford in first place. Plus it is used to being called variety of insulting names, e.g. hairy idiot, moron, and prize pest, on regular basis.

Tuesday 18

Philosophy today all about moral relativism, i.e. bad things for good ends, e.g. euthanasia. Mum very pro-euthanasia. Think she is keen to dispatch Cleggs asap. Mum not so keen on Reuben Tull's answer to moral right or wrong of achieving ultimate happiness, which was to put mind-altering drugs in the water system. She is pro-fluoride but think she would struggle with Ecstasy on tap. I said was not aiming to achieve ultimate happiness as pain is part of all great literature, e.g. *Wuthering Heights*.

Saw Davey at nut dispensing machine after lesson (not buying nuts, he does not consume healthfood, just watching to see who got the mouldy apple that has been in there for a fortnight. He has 40p on Alan Wong). Asked what he'd been up to. He said, 'Bricks and stuff.' Gordon Brown is wrong. A BTEC is not like three A levels at all. I said I had been discussing whether pain was an essential part of life and literature. He said, 'My mum's got them sort of books.' So maybe is actually not in house full of *Chat* magazine and *Gun Monthly* but library of Brontës and Thomas Hardy.

. . . .

Wednesday 19

9 a.m.

Davey MacDonald not in house full of Brontës. He brought in one of the 'pain' books for me. It is by Marquis de Sade, i.e. is about sex. I said no thanks.

3 p.m.

Scarlet said I should have borrowed book. She says it is eye- and mind-opening and is considered a literary classic. I said, 'Yes, by Suzy,' (who is great fan of 'pain' and all things sex-related). She said in fact by entire forward-thinking world. Have borrowed book after all.

7 p.m.

Mum has confiscated book pending its return to Suzy and said if she finds me reading filth again she will have to consider calling in reinforcements, i.e. Auntie Joyless and her Christian army. I said it is considered a classic by entire forward-thinking world. Mum said not in this

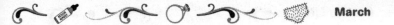

house it is not. Did not tell her it wasn't Suzy's. If she finds out about ASBO love experiment she will possibly implode.

. . . .

Thursday 20

Hurrah it is Good Friday tomorrow, i.e. no school. We are going to see *Juno*, which is compulsory viewing in common room. Admittance to saggy sofa is now strictly for those who can say 'homeskillet' with confidence. Mum is not happy as according to her sources (Marjory) it glorifies teen pregnancy and I will be possibly with child within minutes of watching. As if. There is nothing cool or in any way enviable about being pregnant at school. Look at Emily Reeve. She is still a stone overweight and her nipples will never be the same. Have asked Davey to come. Hopefully tale of geeky but brilliant types will seep into brain and he will be listening to the Moldy Peaches by Saturday instead of 50 Cent.

James not coming to cinema as is a) too young, b) of same mind as Mum concerning teen pregnancy films, and c) on revived gladiatorial duty with Sabre aka Mad Harry. They are going to do muscle building in James's bedroom. Am glad am not in house as is potentially terrifying. Melody Bean is not coming either. Sad Ed says there is no way he is letting her get ideas about babies. Said he was being paranoid as film will not in any way make intelligent teenagers want babies but he is not moved.

He has told her he is spending day writing his vows instead.

. . . .

Friday 21
Good Friday
6 p.m.

Oh my God, I *am* Juno: i.e. cool-talking music buff type. Although obviously am not pregnant. Though think life would be utterly more interesting if were. Even clothes did not look too sacky. In fact Topshop do maternity wear now so would possibly look better pregnant than not as wardrobe currently depleted due to previous debt. Plus washing machine chewed up one of dresses after time Jesus climbed inside to poke Rice Krispies through holes in drum. And Juno is excellent goddess name. Like Venus or Dido. Whereas Rachel is utterly dull. If do get pregnant will call daughter Juno. Or possibly Olympia.

Davey MacDonald not entirely in agreement about seminal nature of film. In fact slept through most of it. Possibly as is first movie he has seen that is not either *a*) cartoon or *b*) involving Steven Segal and enormous weaponry. Plus he was up late last night revving cars on Barry Island. Scarlet not thrilled about his presence. She says he smells of chav, i.e. Burberry Brit. Said that was very non-mass-embracing of her but she says it is not non-mass-embracing just that she is allergic to non-organic perfume. Pointed out that at least he met us at cinema and did not squish into sick-smelling Volvo. Though perhaps would have killed off vomit odour finally. Its persistence is staggering.

Got home to find Gazelle and Sabre (aka James and Mad Harry) on sofa under blanket with cups of Lucozade (and strict instructions not to spill any on floor on pain of death). James said they were merely replacing lost joules from all the muscle-building and under the blanket their biceps were bulging magnificently as we spoke. Did not look in case they were also wearing furry gladiator pants but got truth from Dad who said Harry strained his groin after two lunges and James got bitten when he tried to weightlift the dog. Is lucky Mum was out at Marjory's having a character building Pink Ladies pyjama party (aka thermal nightgown party and no actual slumber involved due to Marjory having the spare room redecorated and a general aversion to zed beds).

7 p.m.
Mum is back from pyjama party. Said it was somewhat early for a hard-drinking hard-smoking girl gang. Mum said Frenchy (aka Mrs Noakes (bad perm, calls trousers 'slacks', works on Waitrose deli counter)) wanted to get home for *Gardener's World*.

. . . .

Saturday 22
Jack was at work today. It is because Rosamund has

gone to Wales for Easter. Not for egg-based celebration but to tend to mother's many ailments. He asked what I thought of *Juno*. Said it was forshizz excellent. He nodded and said, 'So what's with you and Davey MacDonald then? Didn't think it was his type of film. Or that he was your type of boy.' I said *a*) nothing is with me and Davey MacDonald it was just one trip, and *b*) how do you know if it is his type of film, have you even seen it? He said *a*) you also took him to Thin Kylie's party, and *b*) yes I have. So I said *a*) are you keeping tabs on me? *b*) Davey is a sort of social experiment, am trying to create perfect combination of political awareness and brawn, and *c*) what's your favourite line? He said *a*) As if. Scarlet told me, *b*) why can't you just let Davey be Davey? and *c*) where Mac Macguff says, 'Good mood, bad mood, ugly, pretty, handsome, what-have-you. The right person is still going to think the sun shines out of your ass.' Then he went off to stack the glucosamine before could reply.

He is wrong anyway. Cannot let Davey be Davey. Do not fancy him enough in current form. He is completely un-Paulie-like. Plus the best bit is where Juno says, 'Being pregnant makes me pee like Seabiscuit.' Even Davey laughed.

Would be nice to find someone who thought sun shone out of my ass though. Even with my uncontrollable hair and impossible mother.

Sunday 23

Easter Day

10 a.m.

Hurrah, it is Easter Day, i.e. licence to eat cheap chocolate in vast quantities, as opposed to the rest of the year when bars of Green and Blacks are broken into small squares and doled out one at a time like a scene from wartime rationing. And Mum and Dad are at operatics this afternoon so even exhortations to be sensible and save some for tomorrow will be null and void. Plus, after years of experience, can safely say that is better to do all in one go because after a week you cannot face any more hydrogenated fat without feeling sick and so is waste as dog always gets it. Only have three eggs though—from Mum and Dad, James, and Baby Jesus. Granny Clegg obviously too busy listening to Radio 4 and reading *Das Kapital* to go to Trago Mills for cut price sweatshop confectionery.

4 p.m.

Have another egg! Is not from Scarlet (boycotting Easter due to Cadbury's moving factories to Far East) or Sad Ed (ate one he was going to give to me in emergency low-sugar episode during *The Wire* last night). Is from Davey MacDonald. He brought it over after lunch. Luckily Mum and Dad were busy at Rydell High with Marjory PI and James was at Mad Harry's doing a gladiatorial egg challenge. No idea what it involves but suspect they will fail, as usual. Davey was definitely angling to come in. But feared Mum would use spooky sixth sense and sniff out presence of chav somehow, so restricted access to front garden only. He said it was 'well nice'. Compared to his, which is mostly concrete and a bit of leftover car, I suppose it is. But was only small talk as obviously neither of us interested at all in shrubbery or pea gravel. Was delaying tactics for kiss. But did not want to do kiss. On several grounds. Mostly that do not fancy him and am scared mojo will not move. So said had to go and sorry for not getting him an egg then shut door in panic. Experimenting with Mr Right Now is more complicated than thought. Is shame about failed Dean Denley thing. At least he likes The Doors so half the challenge is done.

5 p.m.
As predicted James failed his gladiatorial challenge, i.e. eating fourteen crème eggs and half a giant Toblerone. He has been sick twice and is now in bed. Said did not think chocolate-eating was actual part of TV show. He said it is weight gain programme. Mum's diet is too balanced and he has not bulked up at all since January. Then he had to be sick again. So no bulking up there either. Hope he is better by tomorrow. It is his birthday and he likes to be fighting fit for examination of gifts. Have got him DVD of *Spartacus*, i.e. actual real gladiators, as opposed to idiot eleven year olds in furry pants. Or lycra-clad pinheads on Sky One.

Monday 24
Easter Monday
10 a.m.
James absent from birthday breakfast table (featuring special celebratory real tablecloth, as opposed to usual wipe-clean surface). He has been compromised by yesterday's egg consumption. Though has told Mum it is norovirus. Birthday outing to Mole Hall Wildlife Park to see exciting new exhibit of flamingo postponed until further notice.

2 p.m.
Have delivered invalid's lunch of Marmite on crackers to James. He asked where Mum was. Said she was antibacterially cleaning surfaces to avoid cross-infection.

5 p.m.
James has emerged from sick bed and is on sofa with Dad and dog watching *Spartacus*. Mum has installed precautions including emergency bowl and plastic matting. And she has had three Yakults in last hour. Said James should admit to egg mania and put Mum out of her misery. He said *au contraire*, she lives for hygiene emergencies as it gives her a chance to show off her skills. He is possibly right.

7 p.m.
James revived by gladiating film. Both he and Dad claiming to be Spartacus. Said neither of them looked at all like

Kirk Douglas. James gave me withering look and said am cinematic heathen. Am getting tired of being accused of being emotionally and filmically illiterate etc., etc. Am utterly versed in all matters creative and brain-based. And am right about Spartacus. If anyone is Spartacus, it is dog. It has cleft in chin and absurd hair.

. . . .

Tuesday 25

Saw Davey in common room at lunch today. He was not on saggy sofa (due to refusal to say forshizz every other word), was in kettle corner preparing nutritious meal of microwave cheeseburger. Think possibly losing battle experiment wise.

. . . .

Wednesday 26

4 p.m.

Common room, and country, has gone mad for French first lady Carla Bruni aka Mrs Sarkozy. She is living proof that you can be political, poetic, and look like supermodel. I bet Lembit Opik is kicking himself for not aiming higher and only going for Cheeky Girl. Maybe I am not Juno after all but am destined to be Carla Bruni type, i.e. brainy, with legs to die for, and ability to play more than 'House of Rising Sun' on guitar.

5 p.m.

Although am only 158 centimetres and cannot even

play 'Bobby Shaftoe'. Will stick to Juno. Short, average-looking, and prone to mishap.

5.15 p.m.
Although even she can play guitar. Is obviously essential instrument. Will ask for one immediately.

5.30 p.m.
Mum has refused on grounds still have clarinet gathering dust in cupboard and three recorders in James's bedroom being used for God knows what (answer: pipes of pan during Elvish phase). Said was utterly committed and would not cease practising until had secured record deal à la Kate Nash. She said I said that about the clarinet, and flower pressing, and the majorettes. Which is true. But said was different this time. But Mum says there are to be no new hobbies until economic climate on upturn. Said what about operatics. She said that is different as does not involve purchase of expensive props or costumes. They are all being recycled from *Chicago* and 1996 production of *Showboat* (the mind boggles). Will ask for guitar for birthday instead. Will still be into it in August as is not passing phase but definite commitment.

● ●

Thursday 27
Have gone off guitar. Scarlet says is passé and ukelele is instrument of moment. Do not want to play that as may

be instrument of moment but also is instrument of embarrassment. Look like mental giant holding one of those. Dean Denley could take it up though. On him it would look relatively normal. Whereas he still has to sit on three cushions to do the drums.

Also Granny Clegg has rung. It is Carla Bruni. She is causing hoo-ha in St Slaughter. Not literally. Do not think state visit includes visiting former disused playgrounds and a Spar. Is that Cleggs are split in their support for poetic/political first lady, i.e. Granny Clegg is very much for and Grandpa is against. He is against all things European. And feminist. And all poetry, unless it is of 'hilarious' limerick variety. Granny says she is tiring of his backward attitude and is minded to move into the spare room with Bruce. Mum told her not to overreact and that she has put up with his jingoism, and feet, for fifty years, so a few more won't make a difference. Granny says she is not so sure. But has agreed to wait a week when Carla will be safely out of country and political wives will be back to wearing Hush Puppies and Marks & Spencers instead of Chanel and Louboutins. Plus Hilary is coming to Scarlet's for the holidays so her personal Karl Marx will be off limits. She will be back to the *Daily Mail* and Viennetta in a fortnight.

Am reinspired by Granny Clegg's torment though. If she can be awakened then there is hope for Davey. Will recommence experiment forthwith.

130

Friday 28

Last day of school

But not yet. Davey is going to Sciathos for a week. Why is it that Riley household travel arrangements consist of Cornwall once a year, and that is usually torturous, whereas Britchers, O'Gradys, and MacDonalds of world spend half of lives enjoying exotic foreign climes, e.g. Florida, Bahamas, and Benidorm?

Davey said he would write. Have said do not. Even with Mum busy handjiving all week, James will come down on me like tonne of bricks.

. . . .

Saturday 29

Jack was at work again today. Pointed out to Mr Goldstein that I do not take endless days off to tend to my ailing Welsh mother (although she is so fortified with vitamins and Yakult cannot remember last time she was actually ill). Mr Goldstein said *a*) she not in Wales, she is in Sudbury at Vitamin D conference, and *b*) economic downturn is beyond his control. Jack said is not true. Mr Goldstein says it is, she got the bus at eight this morning. Jack said not the vitamin conference, the belief that he has no ability to sway financial destiny, and is mistake to sack workers as business will be compromised and income will fall even further. In fact what he needs is to raise game. Mr Goldstein said is not a game. Is serious business. And went back to pricing up Buzz Gum.

131

Think my fate as one of jobless millions is sealed. Will start search for alternative employment next week in anticipation of gloom. Is better to resign than be sacked.

. . . .

Sunday 30
Summer Time begins (i.e. clocks go forward)
11 a.m.
Thank God have one less hour of Sunday. Think twenty-four is too much. Already have had to endure Mum and Dad practising Rizzo and Kenickie snogging scene over Fruit 'n' Fibre, and James getting dog to pull him round garden on gladiator chariot, aka Toys 'R' Us plastic sledge. Is house of idiots. Am almost glad to be decamping to Riley senior establishment this afternoon.

4 p.m.
Was right. In surprise reversal of fortunes, Whiteshot Estate in fact far more educational than Summerdale Road for once. Grandpa very au fait with Mr Right Now theory, as has been reading all about it in *Cosmo*. Said did not think Treena got *Cosmo*. He said she doesn't. He has started buying as beauty news is of superior quality to *Glamour*, plus is full of sex. Anyway, Grandpa says am wasting time trying to mould Davey MacDonald. Should just accept him for what he is, i.e. man candy, and use him for his body, like Jennifer Aniston and Vince Vaughn. Said did not like Grandpa using words like 'man

132

candy'. He said 'shag bunny?' Said not to use any words at all.

Grandpa right that Davey MacDonald does in fact have nice body, due to brief and ill-fated stint as ballet dancer. But still do not think want to 'use' it. Am not shallow user. Am more interested in beautiful mind.

4.15 p.m.
In combination with six pack and thighs of steel.

5.15 p.m.
Just hope can find beautiful mind in there somewhere among desire to melt stuff and eat Monster Munch.

. . . .

Monday 31
Like Hilary, now fully installed chez Stone. Had forgotten quite how muscly he is. In brain and body departments. Is utterly depressing that he is Scarlet's man candy. Is not shag bunny, have asked her and she said she is making him wait to test his commitment. Maybe if she makes him wait too long he will seek solace with me. Hurrah! Then will not have to create my own Hilary. Am going over later to discuss division of best woman duties. Will test waters by doing some French lounging. Would be utterly experimental to share boyfriend. Look at Dylan Thomas. He was doing it with Keira Knightley and Sienna Miller.

4 p.m.
Scarlet has instructed me to stop staring at Hilary as makes me look retarded. Plus she says am not Keira or Sienna but am bit-part jealous maid-type who cannot admit is actually better suited to stable boy.

On plus side, best woman duties are as follows: co-ordinate outfits (Scarlet). Check train timetable to Scotland (me). Getting married is cinch. Do not know why people make such a fuss.

Tuesday 1

April Fool's Day

9 a.m.

Awoke to 'hilarious' April Fool breakfast of gruel with suspicious black things on top. Have not eaten. Have gone back to bed until Mum is back from whatever it is she is doing and has shouted at James for meddling where he is not wanted, i.e. food management.

10 a.m.

Was not April Fool. Was new recession-busting regime, as declared by James. There is to be no more luxury muesli or Duchy Originals marmalade. It is health-giving porridge and 'fresh, wild fruits of the forest' (aka some partially defrosted blackberries from the bottom of the freezer) from now on. Said temporary economy drive possibly threatening permanent hygiene drive and they need to think long-term. But James says he has taken over control of the kitchen while Mum concentrates on her glittering stage career. Plus he says if gladiating fails he can be TV chef à la Jamie Oliver instead. He cannot. There is no way anyone would fantasize about him in their kitchen naked. Ick. Have done involuntary shudder at thought. Will escape to Riley senior household to wish Grandpa happy birthday. And avoid potentially minging lunch. James is going food foraging, in hope of unearthing truffles behind compost heap. Will be futile. Only things lurking behind there are slug trap and semi-digested tennis ball.

4 p.m.

Have given Grandpa Riley *Vogue*, *Marie Claire*, and *Chat* as birthday present (emergency purchase from Mr Patel's) so he can learn about peplums, Somalian refugees, and the woman who got anaphylactic shock from her Primark pants. Is essential this season reading. Got home to discover that Mum has regained control of kitchen. She says James is to be admired for his economy-drive skills, but not for his food foraging ones. There are no truffles, and lunch (nettle soup) resulted in borderline hospital emergency after James fell in nettle patch. He is now lying on plastic sheet on bed covered in layer of antihistamine cream, listening to *Harry Potter* CD. We have got liver for tea instead. Which is peasant-like and utterly economical. Plus does not sting.

. . . .

Wednesday 2

9 a.m.

It is utterly depressing. Am sixteen years old and should be at prime of style iconness, i.e. in black lace and Agent Provocateur underwear à la Daisy Lowe. But instead wardrobe consists entirely of M&S pants, grey T-shirts, meat lorry vintage dress, and rejected St Trinian's outfit, i.e. have NOTHING to wear to Sad Ed's wedding. Plus still have no money to buy anything due to frittering last week's wages on Grandpa's glossy magazine habit.

Although, traditionally, groom has to buy best man

138

outfit. Is brilliant plan. Will go to Waitrose and demand money from Sad Ed so do not show him up at altar.

3 p.m.
Sad Ed says there is no way he is footing bill for vintage Chanel dress. Or any dress for that matter. He is saving everything so he can stage his own disappearance after wedding and start a new life as Irish recluse. Or pay someone else to kill him as he is spectacularly rubbish at doing it himself. On plus side, have put name down on list for Saturday job at Waitrose. Is forward thinking back-up move, as advised by mad-eyebrowed Chancellor Alistair Darling, in case Mr Goldstein and his lentil emporium do not weather the economic storm long-term. Although will possibly be offered job within week as there were only two names above mine and one of those was an O'Grady. Plus I saw Reuben Tull crash his trolleys into a blue Lancia. I said that was hardly successful herding but Sad Ed says the Lancia belongs to Cormac Costain who owes Reuben fourteen pounds and an MGMT ticket so it was in fact expert handling as it totally looks like a scrape from the Yaris parked next door and Reuben will be blame-free.

Thursday 3
Thank God James is off food duty and we are back to Cheerios and Shreddies. (Waitrose own brand though, i.e.

practically povvy. Have suggested Mum changes her supermarket of choice to Lidl but she says things are not that desperate yet.) James is still sticking to the gruel and old fruit regime though. He says it is what gave Madonna her muscle definition. Asked where he got that dubious fact. He said Grandpa Riley and his oracle *Grazia*. Am going to Scarlet's in minute for economy drive wardrobe planning. We are going to raid Suzy's vast closet of vintage designer wear. Is utterly brilliant plan as is bound to be full of OTM 1980s finds. (No idea what OTM stands for but Grandpa says is essential fashion speak and has replaced fashion-forward, which is totally last season. But then he also said I should embrace harem pants, which, as any fool knows, are not to be worn if are midget with hips, so am not entirely convinced of his role as withering non-Chinese Gok Wan man.)

4 p.m.
Am still outfit-less. There has been a crime against fashion chez Stone. It turns out that Suzy has been victim of fashion 'gurus' Trinny and Susannah, who took umbrage at her 'hot hippy' look during their turn on her sex sofa and sent a minion round to 'streamline' her wardrobe. All the spangly bust-revealing stuff has been replaced with severe capsule wardrobe more befitting TV star. So we have had rethink and are going shopping in Cambridge next week after I get paid. Scarlet is depressed though. She says Channel 5 fame is messing with Suzy's socialist

140

ideals and she will be joining golf club next. Said that would never happen and suggested a swing in the bat chair and some T4, but not even *Friends* could cheer her up. And was one where Ross bleaches teeth, so things really bad.

· ·

Friday 4

There has been another gladiator-related incident at 24 Summerdale Road. James and Mad Harry are dressed in their leotards and furry pants and have been attacking each other with 'pugil' sticks, i.e brooms with pillows tied around the end. But their aim is less than expert and they have broken a Hobbit figurine and bent Des Lynam's head in a funny angle. Plus the dog is wedged under bed in fear. It sustained no less than three body blows. Although is possibly its own fault for trying to eat pugil stick mid-action. Mum is redoubling her school appeal panic. She says if both menaces end up at John Major it will be all over for James and he will end up in Dartmoor like cousin Leonard (swarthy relative of Grandpa Clegg). Am inspired by Mum (and slightly panicked at hazy memory of cousin Leonard, who ran own father over in tractor) and am redoubling academic and Nuts In May work efforts, i.e. will be so dedicated at lentil-face, Mr Goldstein will offer me extra shifts and management position by end of tomorrow. And when am not triumphing over till of insanity, will study ceaselessly to better chances in life.

141

5 p.m.
After Paul O'Grady show.

. . . .

Saturday 5
8 a.m.
Am fully prepared for new pro-work ethic attitude. Am wearing business-like outfit, i.e. St Trinian's but with minor adjustments, e.g. impenetrable black leggings instead of fishnets. And have prepared list of suggestions to revamp Nuts In May, e.g. on-premises thai massage (luring in demographic currently absent from sesame seed aisle, i.e. meat-consuming and impressionable forty-something men) and, for the women, buy one get one free offers on slow sellers like chemical-free sanitary towels. In fact think am maybe candidate for *The Apprentice*. Alan Sugar would be lucky to have someone with my combination of business acumen and knowledge of nineteenth century literature.

10 a.m.
Have been sacked. Did not even get to tell Mr Goldstein about the genius BOGOF offer as he ordered me into the stockroom the minute I walked in the door. I said I was sorry that the credit crunch was affecting his Fruesli sales but that if he gave me a second chance I would more than prove my £2.85 an hour worth. He said is not crunch, is treachery. Mrs Noakes told Mrs Dyer (unconvincing dye

job, fat feet, smells of Yardley) who told Mrs Goldstein (wife of hunchback, i.e. Esmerelda) that I had begged for a job on the toiletries aisle, i.e. his main competitor, claiming I could not tolerate third world working conditions any longer. Is possibly true did say something like that. But on understanding that was in confidential employment-type meeting. Not engaging in idle banter with badly permed, loose-tongued town gossip. James says I should look on the bright side, i.e. I get to spend quality time in the bosom of loving family. Said Mum and Dad are next door pretending to be sex-mad American teenagers, the dog is fighting a cushion and do not fancy look of James's furry pants either. Although suppose at least will not have to beg for next Saturday off for wedding.

Will go and lie down on bed for bit. And prepare self mentally for arrival of Mum and her shouting. She makes Alan Sugar look meek. Will come up with genius financial recovery plan and baffle her with words like subprime and spreadsheet.

10.15 a.m.
Will just watch bit of T4 first though. Is true there are some advantages to being one of jobless millions.

2 p.m.
Mum not at all happy about sacking. Cousin Leonard mentioned again. Nor is she happy about my brilliant idea

that she pay me to give her private drama lessons. (Was only suggestion had time to think of due to incisive documentary on Justin Timberlake. Did not know he had dad called Randy. Is interesting.) Mum said her talents do not need honing, they are already polished and primed for action. (She is wrong. Her rendition of 'There Are Worse Things I Could Do' is brimming with irony.) Said, on bright side, it meant I could concentrate on my AS levels and earn my fortune in the future with my ability to repeat large swathes of Jane Austen dialogue or name the most marginal constituency in Scotland. She said was not swayed and am being sent out to tramp the streets on Monday begging for work. It is utterly Dickensian. Am Oliver Twist. James has asked to join me but she says child labour is illegal. Notice it does not stop her paying him to comb dog and delimescale bath on weekly basis though.

. . . .

Sunday 6

Went round Scarlet's to mope about being victim of economic crisis. She less than sympathetic. Said not victim of economic crisis but of schoolboy error of saying anything to Mrs Noakes other than 'A pot of olives, please.' Also she and Hilary busy on phone being outraged at Olympic torch being processed around country in flagrant disregard for Chinese crimes against working poor etc. And outraged at Suzy's apparent lack of outrage. Scarlet is right, she has definitely gone off the boil, socialism-wise. She is baby-mad. There are ovulation charts and thermometers all over house. Took my temperature. Was forty-one degrees. Had panic that was going to melt but Jack said was false reading as was using in wrong orifice as is uber-sensitive bottom one. Had bigger panic and washed mouth out with entire bottle of Listerine.

At least Jack understanding about my employment issues. He said it is all utterly anti-workers rights and by the sound of it I could take Mr Goldstein to a tribunal. (He not party to conversation about libellous gossip with Mrs Noakes.) Did not want to disappoint him, left-wing wise, so said to be fair did not like job that much and think will be better off elsewhere in long run. Is very nice of him though. He offered to boycott store and refuse all stand-in shifts from now on. Said did not want him to suffer financially because of my misfortune. (Or idiocy.) Then he said Suzy is on lookout for personal assistant type person if I need extra income. Said is very kind but would possibly prefer to hack up lamb shanks with Dean the Dwarf for seven hours a day than listen to Suzy talk about pelvic floor exercises. He said is fair point. Both he and Scarlet have turned it down already.

7 p.m.
James is in mourning. It is also Olympic torch related. He says Konnie Huq (his all-time favourite *Blue Peter* presenter, also potential future wife (in his dreams)) has

145

lowered herself by carrying the torch and ignoring plight of Tibet. Said was impressed by his new-found politicism. He said it is all thanks to his mystical guru. Asked who mystical guru was. Is Granny Clegg. Mum not so inflamed with mystical guru wisdom. She says it is bad enough having to listen to her talk about the miracle of Blu-Tack let alone the Chinese class system. Had to leave room at that point as this information was relayed to me in absurd accent with much hand-on-hipping and eye-rolling. It turns out that Dad and Mum are following in footsteps of Dustin Hoffman and have taken up method acting. They are trying to stay in character as Rizzo and Kenickie at all times. Is completely unbearable.

. . . .

Monday 7
9 a.m.
Am happy to be sent out on Dickensian job hunt. Trudging the dusty cobbles (aka gum-soiled concrete) will be breeze compared to having to witness Mum 'smoking' cigarette (HB pencil) whilst eating pancake stack (Waitrose drop scones). Said Rizzo would still be in bed now, not, in fact, consuming nicotine or heart-congesting breakfast. But Mum said, 'I gotta get ma jobs done, sweety-pie.' Think she is confusing Rizzo with someone from *Gone with the Wind*, or possibly Peggy Mitchell, but did not risk pointing this out. James is already in his room for suggesting she tones down the make-up.

4 p.m.

Is utterly depressing. Saffron Walden like Poland, i.e. land of no opportunity. No wonder everyone is moving to Sawbridgeworth. Tried at no less than three establishments (Gray Palmer, WHSmith, and Boots—all other shops on proscribed list (mine) due to things like being called Gayhomes or (Mum's) containing too many Kylies). But none are taking on new staff until the Christmas rush, i.e. September. Went back to Waitrose to see if have moved up on waiting list but in fact am two places down. Said that was outrage, but Mrs Noakes said is all utterly fair and merit-based, i.e. Alan Wong has previous experience with fish (he has a tank of piranha—toothy fish favoured by dentists) and Rebecca Hooton is dyslexic, and they are down on their minority quota since Lawrence Gavell (enormous head, no qualifications) left to be beet picker. Am doomed to poverty.

Oooh, am excited now. Poverty is good for literary chances. Will be utterly like J.K. Rowling, i.e. writing by candlelight in scabby café. May well get notebook and sit in Mocha immediately!

5 p.m.

Have remembered still cannot afford wedding outfit. Let alone fritter 70p on skinny mochalatte (i.e. Nescafè and a Cadbury's Highlights mix). Am depressed again.

Tuesday 8

11 a.m.

Hurrah. My Frankenstein's monster (aka Davey aka Hilary to be) is back from his week in Sciathos. He has sent me a text saying to meet him outside Smeg Launderette and Mr Patel's 2 (aka Mrs Patel's) at half one. He has got a present for me. Is probably hideous stuffed donkey or bottle of undrinkable and illegal liquor. Still it is thought that counts and once have schooled him he will be purchasing only Chanel No 5 at Duty Free. Is odd that MacDonalds are not suffering credit crunch issues. Although they are used to shopping in Lidl so it is business as usual. Will not tell Mum where am going. She is busy doing method acting with Jan (i.e. telling Marjory Lakeland catalogue is 'swell') so will not even notice I am missing. And James is round Mad Harry's attempting wall climbing challenge (scaling garage), so am not at risk of capture by their anti-ASBO love patrol.

3 p.m.

Was not hideous stuffed donkey. WAS in fact Chanel No 5. Well, actually Chantel Numero 5, i.e. fake purchased from man with huge moustache on beach, but is a step in right direction none the less. Said thanks and even gave kiss on cheek. Am aiming to move to centre of face, i.e. lips, millimetres at a time so is not too much of shock to system. Did not get to stay long though, despite invite to 'go for a burn in Lambo's wheels'. (Translation: ride recklessly around the estate in Mark Lambert's Toyota, which appears to be held together with No More Nails and parcel tape.) Was because have got text from Scarlet demanding to know whereabouts. Said was on Whiteshot Estate. She said HAVE U BEEN MUGGED? Said NO AM WITH DAVEY. She said IS AS BAD. Then she demanded that I leave environs of Whiteshot Estate and walk forthwith to her house to resolve urgent wedding dispute with Melody (GET ARSE HERE NOW MELODY MENTAL). I then suggested that Jack, Hilary, or Sad Ed could act as negotiator in proceedings (ASK MEN) but apparently Hilary is refusing to be involved on grounds of wedding being non-progressive, Jack is refusing to be involved on grounds of it being non-sane, and Sad Ed is not man due to missing mojo. She did not text this, she rang, as was getting too complicated and threatening to aggravate her text thumb issues. Anyway, apparently Melody wants me and Scarlet to wear same dresses, as her bridesmaids now whittled down to six (which is still too many, but is compromise on twenty-three anyway). But Scarlet says Best Men are superior and outfits must reflect this. Agreed to go round at four as am excellent deal broker. Maybe could be like United Nations ambassador and secure peace in Middle East. Hurrah. Have invited Davey to come with me and get taste of socialist lifestyle. He said would meet me there once has burned up and down the estate a few times.

149

5 p.m.

Did not broker excellent deal. When got there dispute already settled by Scarlet's favoured 'who can shout loudest' method. We are going to Cambridge tomorrow to purchase superior Best Man wear. Pointed out only had seven pounds fifty to name so will not be entirely superior but Davey said, 'I'll borrow it you, I got a monkey for offloading the Kawasaki.' (Translation: I'll lend you the money, I have made £500 for selling on a lime-green motorbike.) Scarlet rolled her eyes and said 'Whatever.' She is only annoyed as Hilary will not buy her clothes as it is too patriarchal. That is problem with socialist love. Whereas sexist ASBO love means I will be able to purchase excellent vintage Best Woman outfit and be better Best Woman. Hurrah.

5.15 p.m.

Although is NOT love. Obviously. Is experiment.

. . . .

Wednesday 9

10 a.m.

Am fully prepared for arduous day of wedding outfit purchasing, i.e. have eaten double Shreddies for energy and have reread *Vogue* to focus mind on prize. Scarlet, Jack, and Hilary are picking me up in the non-sick-smelling car of the people. Said was surprised Hilary has even agreed to accompany us. She says he is only coming so he can acclimatize to seat of learning (St Slaughter to Cambridge could induce massive culture shock due to lack of tractors, rain, and processed foods). And Jack is only coming because the Nissan Micra is leaking black fumes in not at all polar-bear-friendly way and is at fat Len Viceroy's being fixed. He will not let Hilary drive Beetle. He says it requires a special touch. It mostly requires shouting at and thump on dashboard.

Have texted Davey to come too. Is only fair as he is funding purchase. Have not told Scarlet that yet though. Will be excellent surprise. Have not told Mum either. Though not as am preparing it as excellent surprise (it would not be), is because she has gone to Wandlebury Wood with James and the dog to forage for wild herbs. They have taken *Observer Book of Shrubs* to avoid any near-death experiences. I did point out that was not sure Rizzo would go yomping around wood looking for sorrel, i.e. is not wholly in character, but Mum says she going to wear Pink Lady jacket under cagoule.

5 p.m.
Have got outfit. Is utterly vintage-look chiffon tea-dress from Topshop. Am practically Kate Moss! When suck cheeks in and squint at mirror. On downside Scarlet is wearing exactly same. But she had to pay for her own. Whereas mine is token of love. She is not at all happy with Hilary. He got minty with her for going into Topshop in first place due to possible sweatshop/non-organic

151

issues. And then, when we tried dresses on, and did practice Best Woman walk in shoe section, Davey said, 'You look skill, Rach.' Whereas Hilary just shrugged and said, 'True beauty is on the inside.' I think Scarlet is beginning to regret her choice of lover. At least Trevor got swoony over her in her vegetarian leather goth coat. Political prowess is nothing when it comes to raw bat sexuality.

Got home to find James and dog being sick in downstairs toilet and patio respectively. Apparently they both dared question the authority of the *Observer Book of Shrubs*. Asked how this travesty had occurred under beady eye of Mum. James said stiletto heel got stuck in bog. But Mum said Rizzo possibly couldn't even read so was in character at least.

Oooh. Maybe Mum/Rizzo swap is good thing, i.e. Rizzo would embrace Ribena and Wotsits etc. Will just go and ask.

5.15 p.m.
Or not. Apparently even Rizzo understands the perils of chav snacks.

. . . .

Thursday 10
10 a.m.
Have just bumped into Thin Kylie on wall. Was taking dog for walk and not concentrating as wall is usually

danger-free zone at this time of day due to scheduling of Jeremy Kyle/Trisha etc. But apparently their Sky is on blink and Fiddy needed poo. So had to endure sex-related questioning as follows:

KYLIE: 'Are you, like, shagging MacDonald?'

ME: 'No.'

KYLIE: 'You should. He is, like, totally good in bed. His thing is bent though so just keep your eyes shut.'

ME: 'Uh, thanks.'

KYLIE: 'Him and Lambo are over mine later. You have, like, totally got to come, innit. Whippy's bringing his van so we can get 99s for nothing.'

ME: 'Well, I . . . '

KYLIE: 'Nice one.'

ME: 'OK. I have to go now.'

KYLIE: 'How come your dog can shag with no balls?'

ME: (Yanking dog away, who is trying to conjugate with Fiddy, who is mid-poo in gutter) 'No idea.'

Is true. Is complete mystery. Sad Ed has got two and he has no stirrings and the dog is gonad-free and is at Fiddy every chance he gets. Is ironic. Or possibly depressing.

Anyway, more worryingly, am now haunted with hideous images of bent penises, Mr Whippy's 99 cones, and potential chav orgy situations. Oh God. What have let self in for? Experiment is not working at all. Cannot breach two worlds. Is like Elizabeth Bennet trying to go out with Phil Mitchell.

10 p.m.
Thank God. Did not have to do anything untoward with anyone's penis. Although have consumed four 99 whips, which is almost as bad in Mum's book. In fact, evening vaguely amusing, i.e. watched Davey doing some *jetés* as dare across the laminate floor. It is utter shame he got thrown out of Royal Ballet. He is very athletic and almost swan-like in his grace. Although not so much when he skidded on DVD box (*Resident Evil*) and crashed headfirst into display cabinet of glass fawns. Kylie says Cherie will go mental as she has been collecting them out of back of *Mail on Sunday* for months. Personally think he has done Cherie, and world, favour.

Also, have invited Kylies, Mr Whippy, Davey, and Mark Lambert to Sad Ed's secret wedding. Actually is more that they invited selves as Kylie is wedding-mental at moment. Did not explain about missing mojo though. As it is they all think he is gay. His unresponsive penis would seal the deal.

Am totally bridging two worlds after all. And harmoniously integrating them in manner of peacekeeping type. Am like Gandhi. Or Gabriella in *High School Musical*.

10.30 p.m.
Not that have seen *High School Musical*. It is just what have been told.

154

Friday 11

Only one day to go now until joyous union of Melody Rapunzel Bean and Edward Arthur Thomas. Though Sad Ed not at all joyous at moment. He has been lying on my bed emitting low moaning noise for several hours. Did point out to him that there is obvious way out of this mess. Sad Ed said web now too entangled to tell truth. I said not that obvious and, *au contraire*, I meant that Sad Ed could revive his mojo, reverse his 'no sex before marriage' claims, and do it with Melody tonight. He said he had thought of that but not even fantasizing that Melody is actually Susan out of *Neighbours* had any discernible effect on pants area (thank God). Said on plus side he will be unable to consummate marriage so will be null and void anyway. Sad Ed just moaned some more.

7 p.m.

Sad Ed has finally left, resigned to his fate, but slightly more cheerful due to the Duchy Lemon Thin I procured from James's secret stash. (He is also taking advantage of Mum's Rizzo-related lapse in larder security. Not for consuming purposes (he is still on poverty-style porridge diet) but so he can sell them in playground for 10p each. He has amassed 70p so far. Said it was hardly going to solve economic crisis. He said it is just beginning of his fortunes and even Bill Gates started small and he is confidently expecting to rival McVities by the end of the year.) He did not give them up without fight though and demanded to know precise nature of Sad Ed's woes. Said his willy does not work. Just hope James does not offer to 'mesmerize' him into action with his Ninja skills, like he did with bust.

11 p.m.

Scarlet has just texted to ensure that I have done best woman duty and checked trains to Scotland. Said yes. To be fair have not. And not entirely sure where Gretna Green is. But will be simple. Will just buy tickets to Edinburgh and get taxi. Endless military checking spoils atmosphere of romance. I bet Madonna didn't spend hours on phone to Network Rail making sure that she could get a connection to Skibo Castle.

· ·

Saturday 12

9 a.m.

Hurrah. Is brilliant am not working. Especially when have rich admirer to fund wardrobe. Am already wearing dress and hair is in elaborate beehive thing, as styled by Thin Kylie. Though drew line at emergency spray tan and bikini wax. There is no way am letting her turn me into Jodie Marsh again. Also do not want to aggravate Mum further. She already suspicious as to why *a*) Thin Kylie up at 8 a.m., *b*) Thin Kylie invited into bedroom, and *c*) why we wearing 'cocktail outfits'. Told her it is annual sixth form anti-war, save-the-whale, non-alcoholic charity cocktail morning. Is made-up but sounds ridiculous enough to be plausible. James not so easily duped. He eyed me with air of positive mistrust over his gruel. Luckily he is going with Mum, Dad, and Mad Harry to London to see West End version of *Grease* (following educational and tedious tour of no less than four museums) and will not be home until midnight. By which time we will be back from Scotland, Sad Ed will be married, and I will be snogging my home-made Hilary, i.e. Davey MacDonald. Have decided today is day. Admittedly he is still not very progressive. But am imbued with wedding fever and he did look almost Heathcliffish at Kylie's yesterday. If Heathcliff had worn a baseball cap and fake Evisu jeans.

Have pointed out Mum and Dad are mad going to see the professionals though. It can only reveal their own shortcomings. James said, *au contraire*, he is hoping they will be talent spotted during the audience participation bit and asked to join the cast. He is over-optimistic. Or just idiot.

9.30 a.m.

Can see wedding car, aka the non-sick-smelling car of people! Jack is driving me, Scarlet, Hilary, and Sad Ed to station. Davey is going with Kylies in Mr Whippy's van and Melody and bridesmaids are catching Viceroy bus. Hurrah, this is it! In just a few hours Melody Bean will be Mrs Sad Ed. And I will be breaching British class system and engulfed in experimental ASBO love.

1 p.m.

Wedding did not go entirely to plan. Am not in Gretna Green. Am in totally non-Scottish 24 Summerdale Road (unless you count a packet of Highland Shortbread, now in James's biscuit stash). And am not engulfed in love, ASBO or otherwise. Is all fault of James. Although James says is all fault of self and failure to adhere to resolution and be honest about feelings.

Events unfolded as follows:

9.45 a.m.

Non-sick-smelling car of people arrives at Audley End station and decants occupants all attired in full wedding regalia. Bar Hilary who is wearing black shirt and unhappy scowl.

9.55 a.m.

Mr Whippy's van arrives and decants occupants, all attired in full wedding regalia, but also full of Nobbly Bobblys and Reef.

10 a.m.

Sad Ed notes lack of bride, or bridesmaids, or indeed any sign of Len Viceroy's supercoach.

10.30 a.m.

Not-so-super coach arrives, having had to stop three times on Sparrow's Hill to let bride vomit on verge. Was nerves. Not alcohol. Bride demands to see birthday present from groom. Groom admits forgot was birthday in wedding panic.

10.35 a.m.
Bride calls wedding off due to crapness of groom. Groom says 'great'. Bride collapses in heap in car park. Groom has panic and tells her his love is present to her. Bride announces wedding back on. Rachel Riley announces groom is muppet.

10.40 a.m.
Thin Kylie vomits on bonnet of ice cream van. Was not nerves. Was alcohol.

10.45 a.m.
Wedding party agrees is time get show on road and sends travel co-ordinator, i.e. Rachel Riley, to ticket office to buy tickets to Gretna Green.

10.50 a.m.
Rachel Riley returns sans tickets having been informed it will *a*) cost £248 each, and *b*) take nine hours and six changes due to engineering works at Peterborough and Doncaster. Wedding party shouts at travel co-ordinator.

10.55 a.m.
Mr Whippy offers to drive wedding party in van. Wedding party attempts to squeeze in amongst Magnum boxes.

11 a.m.
Wedding party emerges from van with coating of raspberry syrup and scattering of hundreds and thousands. Rachel notes is almost confetti like.

11.05 a.m.
Idiot savant Davey MacDonald says he will commission fat Len Viceroy to drive party to Scotland with his Kawasaki money. Rachel Riley kisses Davey MacDonald on cheek (but at least five millimetres closer to lips than last time).

11.10 a.m.
Wedding party boards supercoach.

11.11 a.m.
Coach does emergency stop due to obstacle. Len Viceroy does emergency swearing. Travel co-ordinator Rachel Riley sent out to investigate nature of obstacle.

11.12 a.m.
Obstacle identified as Mr and Mrs Thomas, aka Sad Ed's mum and dad, lying in road, engaging in last-ditch attempt to pervert course of marriage.

11.13 a.m.
Wedding party unboards coach. Sad Ed attempts to explain self. Mrs Thomas says, 'Aled would be turning in his grave.' Rachel Riley points out Aled Jones not dead.

Mrs Thomas gives Rachel Riley withering look. Rachel Riley vows to keep mouth shut.

11.15 a.m.
Sad Ed demands to know how Mr and Mrs Thomas found out about secret wedding. Mrs Thomas admits to having informer. Sad Ed demands to know identity of informer. James Riley appears from behind ticket machine with red A4 ring binder and Mad Harry.

11.20 a.m.
Rachel Riley demands to know *a*) why he not at home with Rizzo and Kenickie preparing for nerd-a-thon, *b*) whereabouts of Rizzo and Kenickie, and *c*) what is with folder?

11.25 a.m.
James Riley says, *a*) he got lift with Mrs Mad Harry, *b*) they on way right now to catch 12.14 to Liverpool Street, and *c*) is dossier of evidence against Sad Ed and Rachel Riley. Though was only back-up as bet Rachel Riley did not alert marriage authorities in Scotland with official two weeks' notice.

11.30 a.m.
Scarlet demands to know more about marriage authorities and period of notice. James Riley explains Scottish law in mind-boggling detail. Rachel points out that they

didn't show that in *Hollyoaks*. James explains difference between soap operas and real life, i.e. nor do they show pooing due to it not being of dramatic consequence unless is dysentery-related and essential to tropical disease plot.

11.35 a.m.
Melody Bean demands to know nature of dossier of evidence. James unveils transcripts of conversations between Rachel Riley and various other members of wedding party concerning *a*) Sad Ed's missing mojo, *b*) fakeness of wedding, *c*) annoyingness of Melody Bean.

11.37 a.m.
Melody Bean faints and is carried by horde of bridesmaids into Mr Whippy's van for reviving cider barrel lolly.

11.40 a.m.
Davey MacDonald calls James Riley 'nosy little knob' for spying on Rachel Riley. James employs Mum's favoured 'sticks and stones' routine and threatens to reveal Rachel Riley's evil intentions. Rachel Riley threatens James Riley with actual sticks and stones. Davey MacDonald offers James £50 of Kawasaki money to reveal evil intentions. Rachel warns James not to succumb to bribery. James says, 'Needs must in these hard times,' and tells Davey MacDonald that Rachel does not fancy him, he is just pawn in her political game.

11.45 a.m.
Davey MacDonald points out he 'ain't no sodding prawn'. Kylies escort him to Mr Whippy's van, which departs complete with an ice-cream man, four chavs, six brides-maids, and Melody Bean.

11.50 a.m.
Mrs Thomas ushers Sad Ed into Mini Metro. Metro departs with 'Walking in the Air' coming from windows and Sad Ed's rotund face pressed against glass in defeated manner.

12 noon
Jack suggests rest of wedding party also departs before arrival of Rizzo and Kenickie.

12.01 p.m.
James and Mad Harry depart for station shop to spend Kawasaki money on Polos, Quavers, and copies of national rail timetable.

12.05 p.m.
Non-sick-smelling car of people departs for Saffron Walden in silence. Possibly in reverence at dream being over. Possibly because Scarlet not talking to Rachel over train issues, Hilary not talking to Scarlet over non-progressive issues, and Jack not talking to anyone over idiocy issues.

It is all utterly depressing. Am back to where started. And am utterly annoyed with James. Do not know why he persists in gladiator ambition, he is much more suited to being nosy detective type. He has obviously been hiding Ninja-style in nooks and crannies, trying to overhear conversations. Or possibly just listening in on other phone, as learned from Mum in pre-Rizzo days.

Plus it is a waste of my Kate Moss-style best woman dress. Even Jack agrees. When I got out of the car he said, 'Davey was right. You do look skill, Rach.' But is meaningless unless have someone to rip it off me in frenzy of experimental love.

1.30 p.m.
Though at least have house to self. Even dog appears to have been farmed out for day.

1.45 p.m.
Dog not farmed out. Was trapped in airing cupboard. Life is just one endless disappointment. Usually involving dog sick and shouting. At least James has promised not to tell Mum and Dad though. Am not strong enough to endure their wrath at me engineering teen marriage. Or ASBO love. Plus he has not asked for anything in return. Is selfless brother. Am lucky to have him.

Sunday 13

Am still depressed. Is partly Davey MacDonald hoo-ha and partly Rizzo and Kenickie hoo-ha. Mum and Dad are infused with West End musical fever and are in *Grease* overdrive. Have already witnessed full-scale rendition of 'You're the One That I Want' (complete with James as Danny Zuku stand-in and dog as Sandy) and is only nine a.m. Am going over to Sad Ed's. Aled Jones is bearable by comparison.

6 p.m.

Sad Ed not depressed for once. Despite being grounded for two weeks and having Bontempi organ confiscated as punishment for anti-Aled secret wedding plans. Is because, despite humiliation, has had lucky escape from being tabloid fodder. And Melody Bean fodder. Scarlet also there. Though not so philosophical. Apparently Hilary decided she is not the woman he thought she was and has ended their left-wing love affair. He retrieved Nissan Micra from Fat Len and drove back to Cornwall yesterday afternoon, in cloud of anti-polar bear fumes. So she is utterly single too! BUT, in interesting twist, she says is not devastating as Hilary did not stir mojo like Trevor! I said what about het-up phone calls? She says is political talk that is stimulating. Not Hilary. Which is odd, as on paper he is her ideal man but in fact her mojo is far more interested in weedy-armed bat boy. But is too late as he is still going out with minigoth Tamsin Bacon. We have all been in utter denial. It is lucky I did not mould a new Hilary if he is so disappointing mojo-wise.

Mum and Dad are back from operatics and are also visibly disappointed. Is not mojo-related. Do not think they ever had them in first place. Is because Margot Gyp aka Lady Golf Captain aka Sandy and Russell Rayner aka gay golfer aka director did not take on board any of their suggestions for show improvements. James says they will regret refusing to move with times and has offered to set up a rival production, but Mum says she has nothing left to give. Rizzo has drained her emotionally and physically. Thank God. Maybe will be able to eat breakfast without having to pretend am stuck in episode of *Happy Days* from now on.

. . . .

Monday 14
8.30 a.m.
Mum is revived Rizzo-wise and is back with vengeance. She is determined to outshine Margot and prove her mettle as leading lady for next year's production. James says he is delighted she is thinking long-term. Asked what next year's production was. Is *Hair*. Which does not bode well, anything-wise. Thought of Mum and Dad in tie-dye, or worse, nude, singing about the age of Aquarius is terrifying. Thank God am going to school. Will be breeze compared to insanity of 24 Summerdale Road.

166

4 p.m.

School not quiet retreat had hoped for. Am now in unholy trinity of hatred along with Scarlet and Sad Ed. Nowhere is safe. D Corridor is full of armed and dangerous Retards and Criminals, C Corridor is minefield of Melody Bean minions, and canteen out of bounds due to proximity of goth corner. Not even the common room can provide sanctuary. Fat Kylie has warned me if any 'boffins' even put one toe over the boundary of BTEC corner we will be 'totally, like, dead, innit'. Plus now have A levellers on back as well as no one can use CD player or leaky microwave and we have to suffer 50 Cent and smell of idiotic BTEC microwave experiments (oranges, Mars Bars, shoes) all day. I begged for mercy but Thin Kylie says no one messes with their men and I should stick to my own kind. Said I no longer knew what own kind was. She said, 'Knobby weirdos like fat boy' (i.e Sad Ed). Is utterly depressing. Was trying to break down barriers. But walls now even higher. And will possibly be actual walls if Mark Lambert and his BTEC bricklaying skills get their way. Plus am social pariah. Like leper. Or Nigel Moore, who has impetigo (not potato blight). Sad Ed says is small price to pay for freedom. But he has iPod and underactive nasal capacity.

. . . .

Tuesday 15

Saw failed experiment, i.e. Davey, at the nut dispensing

machine today. Tried to hide behind gaggle of maths geeks but they move too quickly and in pack, like cockroaches, so was not at all camouflaging. He said, 'I ain't gonna deck you or nothing, Rach.' Said thanks. I offered to pay him back for best woman dress. Even though have no money and no job. But he said, 'Keep it. Anyway, the Kawasaki was nicked off Ducatti Mick so, like, you owe him not me.' So not only am social pariah, but have been wearing illegally gotten goods. Am utterly gangster's moll. Or ex-moll. Am not telling Mum. Or James. He will only use information to own advantage. It turns out he actually not selfless at all but storing up secret knowledge about failed elopement in order to blackmail me into his gladiatorial idiocy. He has demanded that I join his troupe. He has already got stage name for me. Am Amazon. Said what about Mad Harry? James says he is taking time off duties to recover from pugil-stick inflicted injuries and recoup his strength, and James needs replacement fight companion. Suggested dog (aka Hyperwolf) instead but apparently dog not keen. Plus paws too small to hold pugil-stick. Have given in. But only if can choose own stage name. There is no way I am being named after website. Will possibly be Mantis. Or Black Widow. Which sound sexy as well as menacing.

. . . .

Wednesday 16

Thank God. Mr Vaughan has announced an A level

theatre trip to see *Macbeth*. Have signed up immediately. Am not going to try to transgress any class, social or other barriers ever again. Thin Kylie is right. Need to stick to own kind. Though obviously not 'knobby fat weirdos'. Not that Sad Ed knobby fat weirdo. Though still has man boob issues, i.e fat. And suicidal tendencies, i.e. weird.

5 p.m.
Mum has asked if she can come on theatre trip for inspiration. Have pointed out it is Shakespeare, i.e. not involving any Cadillacs, pyjama parties, or dance-offs. But she says she is thinking of basing 'her Rizzo' on tortured Lady Macbeth. Said trip overbooked already. Do not want Mum infesting coach with her health-giving snacks and cagoule.

. . . .

Thursday 17
When will common room class-war end? Had to endure CD of Wildcats banging on about getting your head in the game nine times during free period. Sophie Microwave Muffins actually had to be taken to Mrs Leech with symptoms of nausea. Is like Middle East. And leaky microwave and CD player are in West Bank. Though at least A levellers still in control of Jerusalem, i.e. saggy sofa. Sad Ed tried to enter Gaza Strip (i.e. stain-ridden blue carpet) to retrieve half a Snickers, but got pelted with

honey-roasted cashews. I bet Jamie Oliver didn't think of potential ammunition issues when he invented nut dispensing machine. Crisps are far less dangerous, missile-wise.

Friday 18

Class war has escalated. Scarlet sneaked into Gaza Strip when BTECers distracted by sheep versus Criminals and Retards hoo-ha on field outside and microwaved their *High School Musical* CD. But then Thin Kylie trumped her with Ministry Of Sound mix, which has a bass line that actually made teeth hurt. Mrs Leech had to come upstairs to common room and threaten to turn electricity off as a piece of plaster fell off ceiling and narrowly missed her head. She not so worried about head though, more concerned at its actual target which was packet of ginger snaps, now irretrievably in state of crumbs. Head boy and girl, i.e. Jack and non-smelly Oona, have said enough is enough and have tabled peace talks on the saggy sofa before registration on Monday. Do not rate their chances though. BTEC 'peace' ambassadors are Fat Kylie and Mark Lambert who employ violence as first, and often only, resort.

Saturday 19

Am inspired by Jack and Oona's historic stand against

oppression (and also sick of being broke) and am going to seize day and demand rise in pocket money from Mum and Dad. £3 a week is utter poverty pay. Cannot even buy *Vogue*. Am like Dickensian workhouse orphan. Although not actual orphan. Or in workhouse. But am poor. Anyway, am confident of success as have special secret weapon. Is James and sidekick Google, who have printed off evidence of national pocket money average, i.e. £6.30 for under-12s (i.e. James) and £9.76 for sixteen year olds, i.e. me. Will be rich beyond compare by this afternoon.

11 a.m.
Had forgotten Mum also now au fait with Google. She immediately donned helmet and rubber gloves and produced conflicting evidence that pocket money dependent on myriad factors including academic background, level of household chores, and average cost of wheat. According to her calculations, am lucky to be getting £3 and any more querying of a) her absolute power, or b) her money management skills will be met with a reduction, and penalties. James asked what penalties might be. Mum said that counted as a) querying absolute power so he is down 20p already. Am going to have to employ Plan B.

11.15 a.m.
Forgot have not got Plan B. Will write one immediately. Once have watched relaxing T4.

1 p.m.
And eaten thrifty lunch of soup and roll.

2 p.m.
And lurked in Waitrose car park with Sad Ed.

4 p.m.
Still have no Plan B. Will do brainstorm with James. He excellent source of scientifically proven ideas.

5 p.m.
James's ideas not so scientifically proven as hoped. List as follows:
1. Become champion gladiator,
2. Revive ancient art of alchemy, i.e. creating gold from base metals,
3. Discover buried treasure.

Pointed out he and Mad Harry tried alchemy before and only succeeded in creating enormous mess. Plus his gladiatorial career showing no signs of moneymaking success at moment. In fact, they are financially out of pocket following purchase of fake fur for pants. He said what about buried treasure? So reminded him of Grandpa Riley's ill-fated phase with the metal detector when he became convinced there was ancient Saxon gold buried under Mum's lupins. All he got was a Norwich Castle Museum badge and a hefty shouting.

5.15 p.m.

Oooh. Have had idea though. Grandpa Riley may be key to restoring Riley fortunes after all. Will offer to revive babysitting career!

6 p.m.

Grandpa not key to restoring fortune. He says the credit crunch is biting hard at the residents of 19 Harvey Road. (It is not the credit crunch. It is his magazine habit.) He pointed out that theoretically, as am godmother, should offer to look after Jesus for nothing but benefit of his moral betterment. Said these were hard times. And also long words for Grandpa. He said is due to *Economist*. Said glad he upgrading from *Chat* magazine. He said he is not, he bought it by mistake because it had Cheryl Cole on the cover (was story about financial planning in music industry, not Ashley Cole betrayal, as he had hoped). Anyway, best he can offer is £1.50 an hour. Have refused. Is worse than Mr Goldstein. Will have to search for other babies. Preferably rich ones. Ooh, maybe the not-so-famous McGann man has some small McGanns that need minding while he is busy being Danny Zuko. Will ask Mum to ask him at operatics tomorrow.

Mum says she is not asking any favours from the entrenched hierarchy. Plus I can barely be trusted not to cause stain-making chaos at 24 Summerdale Road, let alone a celebrity household, which is bound to have ill-advised pale carpets and too much faux suede.

. . . .

Sunday 20

9 a.m.

Thank God is Sunday, i.e. is practically illegal to work. So do not have to feel guilty about being jobless and generally aimless in life.

10 a.m.

James has, yet again, shattered my aimless dreams, i.e. he has reminded me I have gladiator practice this afternoon. Have resigned myself to fate. Though maybe will be champion gladiator after all and make thousands from endorsing cleaning products and questionable convenience foods.

6 p.m.

Am not champion gladiator. Though on plus side, James has also admitted this is case and has excused me from practice in future. He says even Hyperwolf (now official name for dog) has more natural skill than me. Is because I broke shed window with pugil-stick and fell off 'wall of doom' (aka patio surround) nine times.

Also, Dad is in vile mood. It is because Mum and Mike Majors had to rehearse their kissing scene this afternoon. Mum pointed out that the whole purpose of kiss is to

174

make Kenickie jealous so is utterly brilliant acting. Dad says Leo would not have said, 'Thank you, Janet,' afterwards. James asked if was authentic, i.e. did they use tongues. Mum said tongues is unhygienic. So there is still a glimmer of Janet Riley under the chain-smoking Rizzo façade.

7 p.m.
Mum has demanded James stops calling dog 'Hyperwolf'. She says dog confused enough as it is after the Otterhound incident and cannot cope with any more identity issues. Plus it sounds mental.

Monday 21

Is historic (and frankly unbelievable) day in John Major High common room. BTECers and A levellers have signed tentative peace agreement allowing mutual access to West Bank (leaky microwave and CD player). Plus the walls of Jerusalem, i.e. saggy sofa, have been toppled. BTECers get the cushion with the spilt Yazoo and A levellers get the one with Um Bongo. So is utterly fair.

Tuesday 22

Scarlet is inspired by the BTEC/A leveller peace accord in the common room and is determined to take class war one step further (plus she is bored now that she is not consumed with multicultural love). She says she is going to lead boycott of golf club until they reassess their ancient and misogynistic rules that mean women can only tee off on Mondays, Wednesdays, and after two on a Sunday, and are banned from wearing trousers except during particularly inclement weather conditions. She says she is guaranteed success because Suzy came on this morning and baby failure is bound to make her want to throw herself into causes left, right, and centre. And Suzy can use celebrity status to gain publicity. Said not sure publicity will be entirely favourable, given *Walden Chronicle*'s past coverage of Suzy. (e.g. election drug and lesbian in closet scandal. Metaphorical closet. At least think it was. With Suzy, can never be sure.) Scarlet says she is not concerned with tinpot local rags, which all perpetuate the twisted agendas of their small-time small town owners. She is aiming for broadsheets and broad minds, i.e. the front page of the *Guardian*.

. . . .

Wednesday 23

Scarlet's anti-golf club campaign has suffered celebrity endorsement setback. It is Suzy. Apparently her status as non-fertile Myrtle not as invigorating as Scarlet had hoped and she says she not able to actually do any boycotting as will be too busy exploring alternative routes to motherhood. Scarlet pointed out she is already a mother, twice, and maybe she should just get another cat, but

Suzy says she cannot suckle a kitten (not legally anyway) and besides it is her human right to have another baby. Scarlet says she is undeterred and will find other famous and enlightened women to swell the ranks of the masses. Or failing that, just shout louder.

Sad Ed has offered his services to swell ranks. Scarlet pointed out that *a*) he is not famous, except for crap suicide attempt, plus *b*) he has penis so not actually discriminated against. But Sad Ed said *a*) penis malfunctioning so might as well be woman, and *b*) combat trousers and beanie hats are banned from the clubhouse as well so he is discriminated against as an artistic being.

Thursday 24

Have found woman to swell ranks of fight against oppressive golf club. Is Mum! Not so much because is enlightened but is because she is anti Margot Gyp. Scarlet says cameo in local operatics is not quite level of celebrity she was hoping for but I pointed out her excellent credentials fighting the scourge of dog poo. Plus she is wife of club member so she will be whistleblowing insider. Like Russell Crowe fighting the evil tobacco industry.

Scarlet has agreed and is going to write to *Guardian* immediately. Mum is going to be spellchecker. So she is invaluable in several ways.

Friday 25
11 a.m.

There has been a setback in the common room peace accord. It is the appearance of a suspicious spillage on the Um Bongo cushion. Sophie Microwave Muffins has accused Fat Kylie of deliberately soiling our side of the saggy sofa with Cherry Tango. Fat Kylie says it was not her, it was Bat Boy Trevor with his fake blood (i.e. Ribena Strawberry). The maths geeks have biopsied the cushion and taken it to Miss Mustard (lab assistant, not Cluedo character) for further investigation. Until then, the saggy sofa is out of bounds to all sides and we are having to squat on the Gaza Strip, aka blue carpet, which is stained beyond all recognition so no one is claiming it at moment.

2 p.m.

Lab results are in. Stain was neither Cherry Tango nor Ribena Strawberry but had high cranberry content, i.e. was Sophie Microwave Muffins' Ocean Spray anti-cystitis remedy. She has been forced into humiliating climbdown and banned from sofa for a week. The goths are jubilant. They say it is a blow to both the Plastics' domination of the Um Bongo cushion and the BTECers perpetual repression of 'bat people'.

Saw Scarlet get a bit teary during Trevor's speech. I said is it because she is stirred by Trevor but is too proud to seize day and declare undying love. She said no. It

is because a piece of celebratory flying raisin got in her eye. It is a lie. Trevor is her mojo-stirring destiny. She just needs to be honest with her feelings. She has learned nothing from the whole Hilary/wedding/Davey MacDonald debacle.

. . . .

Saturday 26

Bumped into Jack in town today. Was actually in Waitrose car park having utterly philosophical discussion with Sad Ed and Reuben Tull, i.e. 'are goats actually evil?' when Jack beeped horn of non-sick-smelling car of people and offered me a lift home. (He and Edna are job-sharing as Suzy's PA until she finds someone who can fulfil all roles. Jack is doing shopping as Edna cannot be trusted not to purchase Nestlé products or multipacks of pink wafers (rogue biscuit, substandard to HobNobs in every way).

Anyway he has offered me a job. Well, not actual job, as will not get paid, is more work experience. It is to be a life model for his A level art portrait. I said, 'No way, pervy,' but he said I can totally keep my clothes on. It is not about nudity, it is about capturing the essence of the person within. So then I said, 'Why me?' He said, 'I don't know. You're just interesting, Riley.' Which admit was kind of disappointing. Was hoping for, 'Because you are utterly Pre-Raphaelite beauty and I am undone at the sight of you.' But was better than, 'I asked Scarlet and she told me to bog off,' which was expecting. I said I was actually quite busy, timetablewise, what with the golf club campaign and my AS levels, and all my extra-curricular philosophical activity. He said, 'What? Hanging out with the Hair Bear Bunch and talking about farm animals?' Said, 'Actually Reuben is very enlightened when it comes to philosophy, his eyes have been opened to higher plains of experience.' Jack said, 'No they haven't. He's just smoked too much weed again.' Which is possibly true. Then he said, 'Look. It'll only be a couple of hours on a Sunday for the next few weeks. Just think about it.'

So am thinking about it. And think it might actually be quite good. Admittedly Jack is not Lucian Freud. But this is good thing as do not want to end up looking like wonky minger. And being a muse is utterly Kate Mossish. Even if he does not think I am Pre-Raphaelite beauty nor is undone. Though what is undone? Is it magical clothes falling off because someone so mojo-stirring? Is odd.

5 p.m.
Not that want him to be undone.

6 p.m.
Do I? Oooh, what if he is my destiny? Maybe I should do it and seize day (i.e. artistically-charged atmosphere) and see if our clothes magically fall off.

7 p.m.
No. Muses do not actually do it with artists. They are just vessels of endeavour. Or something like that.

8 p.m.
Except Colin Firth was totally in love with Scarlett Johansson. Oh my God. I am the girl with a pearly earring!

8.15 p.m.
Possibly.

. . . .

Sunday 27

Jack has rung to ask if I have given any thought to being life model. I said there were a lot of considerations to weigh up. He said, 'Christ, if it's that hard, I'll ask Oona.' Is clear am not girl with pearly earring at all but just one in list of potential muses. So said yes. Do not want to be out-mused by former smelly bisexual. Am going to start next Sunday. At worst will be cheap Christmas present for Mum and Dad, i.e. portrait of beloved first-born.

6 p.m.
Though by Christmas may well need two portraits. Operatics is not love-inducing activity at all. Got home to find them more divided than ever. Is because not-so-famous McGann has been offered Lenor advert and

Margot is having to emergency recast Danny. Dad says he is in with a chance but only if Mum rethinks her golf club boycott. Mum said she is not rethinking boycott and anyway part will go to Mike Majors who plays off scratch and compères annual salmon sandwich quiz night. Which proves why a golf boycott is necessary. Seized on Mum's zeal and gave her Scarlet's *Guardian* letter for spell checking.

- -

Monday 28

Mum has finished letter. Is not just spell checked but totally rewritten. With fewer uses of word 'hegemony', no swearing, and a lot more punctuation. Will post on way to school. Am sending it to Julie Burchill at *Guardian*, John Kampfner at *Independent*, and Deirdre Roberts at *Chronicle*. Am not telling Scarlet about last one. Is my own completely brilliant plan. Am adding paragraph to point out that is paper's chance to cast off its reputation as reactionary and ineffectual and become forward-thinking paper of the people. Hurrah!

- -

Tuesday 29

James has come home with devastating news from St Regina's. Headmaster Nige has banned the maypole demonstration this year. Partially due to fear of injury risk and partially because it is non-embracing of

Muslims, Hindus, and other minority religions. James pointed out that there are no Hindus at school and only one Muslim, i.e. Mumtaz, and she is thrice area maypole champion. But Nige is unmoved. He says the maypole is staying in the cupboard along with the apple bobbing bowls (drowning potential) and hula hoops (just rubbish), and there will be a non-denominational assembly about rabbits instead. James says it is political correctness gone mad. He is just disappointed because last year Keanu managed to weave Maggot Mason into a multicoloured cocoon and he had to be cut free.

* *

Wednesday 30

There is no sign of any golf club coverage in today's *Guardian* or *Independent*. Mum does not mind. She says she has too many other battles on hands. It is more May Day related hoo-ha. But this time at other end of country, and PC spectrum. It is not to do with non-minority-embracing maypoles. It is to do with annual St Slaughter non-minority-embracing 'Darkie Day' (i.e. ancient racist celebration whereby local types black up faces and chase hobby horse around streets). Granny Clegg is refusing to don the boot polish this year and instead is joining the Nuamahs on their anti-racism reusable carrier bag stall. Grandpa Clegg (who is fan of both racism and non-environmentally friendly Spar bags) rang to demand that

Mum has word with Granny Clegg and remind her who wears the trousers in the Clegg household. He picked wrong day though as Mum was most definitely wearing trousers (non-golf-club-approved Marks & Spencers linen) and told him to belt up. Grandpa Clegg then demanded to speak to Dad but Mum pointed out *a*) he has no jurisdiction in these (or any) matters, and *b*) he was not even wearing trousers as was limbering up for dance practice in bedroom. Grandpa said, 'This family is going to the dogs,' and hung up. He is right about dogs though when it comes to Dad. There is nothing at all progressive about man in pants doing grapevine along landing carpet.

CONDOMS

MACBETH

Thursday 1

9 a.m.

Scarlet is not at all happy at the continuing lack of press coverage of our golf club boycott. She says the broadsheets are missing a trick as the story has all the elements of left-wing front-page news—sexism, sport, children of Channel 5 celebrities with heaving bosoms. I said there was still the front page of the *Walden Chronicle* to hope for. But Scarlet said, *a*) we never sent them a letter, and *b*) anyway only old people and my mum read it, so would be pointless.

4 p.m.

The golf club is in the *Walden Chronicle* after all! Though not on front page but on page 7 between a story on mini roundabouts and an advert for manure. Plus is not exactly pro-boycott coverage was hoping for. Headline is 'Youths Swing Nine Iron at Century of Sporting Tradition'. Which makes it sound as if hoodies are marauding on the course with a set of Pings. Which we are not (although Scarlet had suggested this for publicity stunt). Scarlet is outraged. Reminded her that only old people and my mum read it so is not utterly destroying. But do not think she heard me as she too busy demanding to know who wrote to paper in first place. Said it was habitual *Chronicle* reader Mum. Which is technically true, i.e. she drafted letter. Scarlet said this is last time she does any power sharing with a Lib Dem.

187

Mum is also outraged. As is James. Is not so much coverage, is that paper has misspelt 'rabid' as 'rapid', which makes Margot sound fast (positive), as opposed to mad (negative). Dad is only one who is happy. He says at least there is no evidence of Riley family involvement in the boycott and he will still be in with a chance of getting lead role. He is fooling himself if he thinks that is only barrier to stardom. His lightning is less than greasy.

7 p.m.
Granny Clegg has rung. Apparently Grandpa Clegg has surpassed himself in both his racist tendencies and idiocy. They had run out of shoe polish so he used a can of black Hammerite from the garage. Except it was not washable emulsion. Was permanent gloss. Granny says she has been at him with white spirit but he still looks like a coalman. She is thinking of buying some pink emulsion to try to return him to 'normal'. Mum has begged her not to.

· ·

Friday 2
Mum and Dad are both in vile moods. It is because Dad secretly emailed Margot offering to assist her in fighting the masses but Mum (who now has gatekeeper access to all email accounts) saw the evidence in his outbox and has accused him of undermining her authority.

So Dad accused Mum of undermining his privacy but James accused Dad of undermining Mum's IT education. Left before I got accused of undermining anything. Unlike dog who managed to eat the flashing mouse in all the hoo-ha and got accused of undermining everybody.

Scarlet is still depressed about her failed campaign. I said it was unlike her to give up so easily in the fight against oppression and look at Granny Clegg who is still resolute against the boot polish despite selling no reusable bags and having a husband who looks like a mentalist. But Scarlet said Granny Clegg is still in her political infancy whereas she has been active for sixteen years and is suffering fatigue.

. . . .

Saturday 3

10 a.m.
Scarlet has just rung. She is revived, campaign-wise. It is because she has been talking to Edna about her dead husband Stan who was a flying picket in the miners' strikes. She says we need to set up a picket line in the golf club car park and shame/bully members into submission. Did not ask her about how we are going to fly. Even though wanted to. Air power would be excellent special weapon to befuddle all the Pringle-wearing types. Anyway, whatever it is, we are doing it on Captain's Day, which is crucial golf tournament, like FA cup final.

11 a.m.

Thank God did not ask Scarlet about flying pickets. Flying does not actually mean we have wings. It is something else altogether, according to James. Politics A level definitely paying off, i.e. at least am curbing desire to ask stupid questions!

. . . .

Sunday 4

11 a.m.

Am getting used to life as long-term unemployed, i.e. reading important literature (*Times* Style section) and watching seminal documentaries (Girls Aloud tour secrets). Do not know why anyone moans about it. It is utterly self-improving and enjoyable. Do not even have to put on make-up or wash. So is economic too. Am almost annoyed at effort it will take to walk to Jack's later to be life model. Although at least just have to sit still and can probably also read/watch TV during process.

11.05 a.m.

Have just had thought. Do not want to be immortalized with unfeasibly large hair, no mascara, and stained Brownie T-shirt. Will have to wash after all. And plan wardrobe. This is life-defining moment after all.

11.45 a.m.

Am halfway there, i.e. am clean and hair visibly less

terrifying, but am not dressed. Cannot decide on what look want to go for, i.e. casual top and denim mini, or best woman dress. What if portrait ends up in National Gallery? Do not want hordes of tourists laughing at Mickey Mouse T-shirt, which may be over by next year, or even next week. On other hand, do not want Mum getting minty about picture of me wearing stolen goods. Maybe should have asked Jack to pay for special outfit. And hair products.

12.00 noon
Have gone for holey vintage dress. Is timeless look. And has interesting story attached, i.e. Granny Clegg's sister and the meat lorry. All great art has interesting story involved. Have done full make-up as well. Want to be renowned for Mona Lisa-esque smile, not Grandpa Clegg-esque dark circles. In fact am feeling utterly muse-like. Think Jack will definitely be inspired!

4 p.m.
Jack definitely inspired. Though with few minor adjustments, i.e. less make-up. And more clothing. He said he was hoping for a less formal feel, and it is not about external trappings, but what is inside. Which was possibly nice way of saying 'you look like mad transvestite and will fail exam if paint that' (which is what Scarlet actually said). So ended up in one of his Led Zeppelin T-shirts with limited Touche Eclat and no lipstick. Plus he told me to stop

pulling faces and just be me. Was not pulling faces. Was trying to be Mona Lisa, i.e. enigmatic. And said was worried that if am too much me he will fail as will look like portrait of Robert Plant, who everyone knows is dead and so cannot pose for Annie Leibowitz, let alone art A level. But Jack said to stop being paranoid. Plus Robert Plant not actually dead. Just looks bit like it.

Did not get to read. Tried to but Jack said he did not want copy of *Grazia* in picture. Said he was being snob but he said no, he just cannot do shiny magazine effect very well. Did not watch TV either as was *Will and Grace*-A-Thon and Scarlet's snorting not conducive to atmosphere of contemplative artistic genius. So in end we left den and went up to his bedroom which is TV and Scarlet-free. Although is also sofa-free so had to lie on his bed. But he says it is a classic pose, as is relaxing. Which at first was a bit hard. As was in enemy territory, i.e. boy-smelling bed (in boy-smelling T-shirt). But then Gordon and Tony came in and sat on feet, which was nice and warm and relaxing (cats, not Labour supremos—they would probably just argue about trade deficits which would be utterly non-relaxing, not to mention painful, and surreal). In fact two hours disappeared weirdly quickly. I said I did not mind doing overtime, but Jack said he had drum practice. And, anyway, it is best not to rush these things. Which is true. Although normally he is uber-fast painter like Rolf Harris and can do cartoon dog in less than two minutes. Did not mind though, as all in all was excellent experience and came home feeling utterly Kate Mossish. Am no longer idle unemployed. Am muse. Which is not same thing at all. Is important and potentially fame-making. Look at pearly earring girl.

Dad not so inspired by potential fame. He did not get role of Danny, despite his illicit wooing of Margot. Mike Majors got role. Dad says only consolation is that at least his wandering hands will not be anywhere near Mum now. Mum not so circumspect. It is because PC Doone has been promoted to be gang leader Leo, so she will have to lock tonsils with him now, and he has a moustache and gingivitis. Thank God the show opens on Thursday. By this time next week it will all be just an unhappy memory.

· ·

Monday 5
Bank Holiday

Do not know what is wrong with this family. Bank holidays are meant for legitimate lazing around and snacking, yet have thrice been disturbed and told that if I have nothing better to do then I can usefully take dog for poo/wash Passat/umpire a gladiatorial match. Have declined all. Anyone would think I am unemployed! When in fact am busy being muse. Did point this out to Mum but she said there is nothing muselike about watching *Hollyoaks* repeats and eating Cheerios out of the packet. I bet Mona Lisa did not have to put up with this.

Thank God is double philosophy tomorrow when will be in presence of expanded brains and creative thinking.

. . . .

Tuesday 6

And drug-addled trolley herders.

Lesson was on whether external world is real, e.g.

1. Do objects exist when no one is watching them (yes, duh);
2. How do I know if I am dreaming (because hippo-gryphs are not real and there is no way you are going to fly on one in real life).

But apparently my common sense approach is in minority as Mr Knox says, in fact, instead of saying, 'I can see a desk in front of me,' it is utterly legitimate to say, 'I am having a desk-like visual experience.' So then Reuben Tull spent rest of day in happy trance claiming he was having a school-like visual experience.

Think Mum was right after all. Philosophy is just encouragement to stoners. May well write to Gordon Brown to complain. Or suggest to Mr Wilmott that he restricts intake to those not inclined to believe in mythical beasts. Thank God tomorrow is theatre trip, i.e. utterly highbrow and with no potential for desk-like visual experience nonsense. Plus *Macbeth* is all about powerful and ambitious women, i.e. is utterly feminist.

. . . .

Wednesday 7

Theatre trip was completely brilliant. It was genius political version with Macbeth and Mrs Macbeth wearing Tony and Cherie Blair masks and Gordon Brown as Macduff. Though not sure who funny man with accent and tights was supposed to be. Maybe Harriet Harman. Anyway was utter allegory of self-destruction of New Labour. I bet Scarlet is depressed she chose Economics over drama. Economics is just maths for the overambitious. Plus it is taught by Mr Waiting who has bad ties and distracting mole on nose.

Do not quite see how it is completely feminist though as Mrs Macbeth went mental and died. Plus the witches were wearing corsets. Which got sections of audience all het up. But luckily was sitting next to mojo-less Sad Ed who just sighed wearily and ate another packet of Maltesers.

Anyway, it has set a high standard for theatrical experience this week. I fear Saffron Walden Amateur Operatic Society's *Grease* will find it hard to meet the bar. Especially as their director is not Trevor Nunn type but gay golfer, and their set has been designed by Mrs Noakes.

Thursday 8

Scarlet says *au contraire* Economics is full of drama, intrigue, and back-stabbing. She is kidding herself. Last week they spent two hours on the introduction of the euro.

Got home to find that 24 Summerdale Road had mysteriously transformed into *X-Factor* style boot camp, i.e. Mum and Marjory limbering up on the stair rail in headbands and legwarmers, James issuing military instructions regarding 'jazz hands', and Dad and Clive doing something messy in the bathroom with Brylcream and a tube of Maybelline Dream Matte foundation. Even the dog will be glad when this is all over. It is confused by all the strange goings on. It actually tried to attack Dad and Clive in potential burglar madness when they emerged from 'make-up' with excess of grease, overly brown faces, and madly applied eyeliner. Offered to hose them down but James says under the harsh glare of stage lights they will actually look normal. He is wrong. He might as well put Grandpa Clegg and his Hammerite up there.

. . . .

Friday 9

There is air of dramatic tension over Shreddies table. Mum and Dad are not speaking. Though have ascertained through series of complicated hand gestures and post-it notes that this is to preserve vocal cords rather than due to any Mike Majors or Margot-related hoo-ha last night. James said in fact dress rehearsal went without a hitch, bar Mrs Wong getting left in green room in overture, though this may have been deliberate. And the general feeling amongst the crew is that this is the show to beat all shows, even the infamous 2002 production of *Oklahoma* which included real life cows and a wind machine. Pointed out that James is not, in fact, crew, but he said Barry from Radio Rentals electrocuted himself yesterday and he is now assistant assistant stage manager. He gets to turn on the house lights. Said, 'Dream big.' But do not think he got the *Juno* reference. His cinematic experiences are limited to *Lord of the Rings* and *Finding Nemo*.

Am not going to show tonight though. First nights are notoriously messy. Will wait until show has bedded in, i.e. tomorrow. Plus then if anything goes wrong, it doesn't matter so much as most of audience will be drunk due to happy hour in the Siam Smile (formerly the Dog and Bucket, owned by Les Brewster and former sex worker wife Ying) every Saturday from five (currently on the waiting list for one of Mum's complaint letters due to it *a*) being pro binge drinking, and *b*) lasting two hours so bad maths and a breach of advertising law).

. . . .

Saturday 10
9 a.m.
Mum and Dad are not talking again. Though this time think it is Mike Majors-related rather than vocal cords as Mum has also shouted at dog for trying to sit on washing machine (it likes vibrations). Will ask

assistant assistant stage manager in charge of light switch, i.e. James.

10 a.m.

James said there was a minor incident last night when Dad forgot his lines and Mike Majors had to play two parts, which made him look a bit insane. Mike has told Margot he is sick of 'carrying dead weight' and that if Dad does not shape up in the matinee then maybe his understudy should step in for tonight's crucial performance. Asked who understudy is. It is Mrs Wong. James said there is nothing to worry about as Mum is going to devote morning to rigorous testing. Plus it is utterly normal for creative theatricals to 'run hot'. Said it is something to worry about and show had better be good as Scarlet and Sad Ed are coming tonight and do not want them rolling round aisles in hysterics, which is what usually happens. James said, 'Believe, sister, and you will see the magic.' Am not hoping for magic. Just something that will be able to live down at school. Plus there is the after show party to worry about. If it is anything like our one for *Bugsy Malone* it will be fraught with sexual scandal. Though possibly no one will measure their penis with Mr Wilmott's ruler.

5 p.m.

Grandpa Riley and Jesus have just been round on way

back from matinee. Asked if they had enjoyed it. Grandpa said yes especially the bit where the witch got squashed by a house. Although Jesus got scared when the Oompa Loompa people did their menacing dance. Am now more worried than ever.

6.15 p.m.
Am slightly less worried. It turns out that Grandpa went to see 5th Guides (Baptist) production of *Wizard of Oz* by mistake. He just rang to ask if Mum was OK as she was looking a bit peaky, and possibly short, in the performance. Asked him which role he thought Mum was playing. He said Dorothy. Said no, that would be Lydia Briggs who is eleven. Would have thought the braces and ginger hair gave it away.

Maybe it will all be OK after all. Maybe I am worrying over nothing and Mum and Dad do have talent. Yes, I should have faith in parents. They always have faith in me. Even when I decided wanted to be Darcy Bussell. Actually that's not true. Mum said was waste of money as had two left feet and grace of elephant. But I know deep down she thinks I will triumph one day.

6.30 p.m.
At least she had better do.

12 midnight
I was right the first time. The operatic dream is over,

drowned in the flood of tears, and crushed by the weight of Sad Ed falling off chair in fit of hysterics.

It is totally not Dad's fault though. Mike Majors started it. He was the one who tripped over Dad's blue suede shoes and ended up crashing Greased Lightning (Rory De'Ath's racing car bed) off the front of the stage, sending two pink ladies flying into orchestra pit and injuring Russell Rayner on Moog in process. But James said the worst of it was backstage during the interval when Mike accused Dad of deliberately wearing overlarge footwear to present a tripping hazard. Dad said he was not wearing overlarge shoes, he just has overlarge feet and that if Mike couldn't control a chipboard Chevvy then he was in no state to be in charge of a fleet of Ford Fiestas. James said he is not entirely sure who said what next, but Dad and Mike ended up on floor in horrifying wrestling display and Russell demanded that the understudies get prepped. Except that Mrs Wong was still unconscious from death plunge into orchestra pit and only other person who knew all Kenickie's lines was James. So second half had so many disturbing implications actually had to lock self in toilet, shut eyes and hum quietly to self until show finished. Suspect Mum wishes she could have done same.

Amateur operatics is clearly lethal for mental and actual health. Suspect it is statistically more dangerous than Formula One. On the plus side, the after-show party has been cancelled so at least only one

marriage hangs in the balance at the moment. Thank God the show is over and things can go back to normal tomorrow.

Sunday 11
Whit Sunday
10 a.m.

Hurrah. As predicted was awoken to the nostalgic sound of antibacterial spray being squirted on every available surface. Rizzo has finally left the building. Dad is still not up though. James says he is suffering classic 'after-show comedown'. Asked what symptoms were. He said he is groaning intermittently and bowels are bit dicky. Said it sounds more like classic hangover to me. James said *au contraire*, it is like war vets who still hear the hammering of machine gun fire. Dad's inner brain is probably still resonating to the sound of 'Beauty School Dropout'. Said more like Mum shouting, 'Lift your feet up, Colin.' James then shook head in annoying patronizing manner and said he didn't expect someone like me to understand the delicate mind of a poet. He is a moron. Also evidenced by the announcement that he is giving up on gladiating for good and is going to pursue a career on the stage following last night's public debut. He says he has had a taste of glory and it aroused strange feelings. Oh God. Maybe he has found Sad Ed's mojo.

Anyway, he is wrong about not having delicate mind

of poet. I am utterly fragile. Like Sylvia Plath. Or Amy Winehouse. At least Jack must think so as am off to do more musing this afternoon. Hurrah.

5 p.m.
Have had excellent afternoon of muse activity, i.e. lying on Jack's bed with cats on feet listening to Editors CD. He said he was sorry to have missed the show yesterday. I said not really unless he enjoyed ogling car crash am dram. Anyway it is clear he understands that I am the Riley with creative leanings as then he said I would make an excellent Rizzo. Which is true. I am utterly tortured but witty.

5.15 p.m.
Or maybe he means sluttish and cheap.

Dad was up went I got home. So clearly he not as delicate poet as James assumes. Or else he could no longer bear Mum's moaning. I suggested that maybe it was time he returned to tried and tested methods of obtaining extra curricular enjoyment, i.e. golf. But Mum said there is no way Dad is picking up a four iron again until there has been regime change in the clubhouse so we are back to square one. The only Riley to have enjoyed experience at all is James, who is currently in his bedroom reading John Barrowman's biography aloud to the dog. He is determined to be the youngest boy ever to play Hamlet. I feel sorry for him. It is like ghosthunting, Ninja Turtles,

and gladiating all over again. He is heading for certain disappointment.

Monday 12

Grandpa Clegg has rung to moan. It is not Darkie Day-related. It is Gordon Brown and his decision to withdraw troops from Iraq. Grandpa is not in agreement and wants him to shovel more in instead. Although in bizarre contradiction he said what Britain needs is a good dose of someone like Saddam because at least you know where you are with a dictator. He is mental. Asked him how the gloss paint was. He says he picked most of it during *Heartbeat* but there are persistent patches on his forehead and ears.

Tuesday 13

Granny Clegg has rung to moan. It is not Darkie Day or Gordon Brown. It is Grandpa Clegg. As usual. She says he has signed up to join the Cornish Revolution and is being sworn in at secret ceremony tomorrow. She said she has pointed out to him that Cornwall is economically dependent on the EU and Brussels but he is having none of it and claims the county can just live on ice cream and pasties and does not need anything from a bunch of 'sausage-eating frogs' (assume he thinks Germany and France combined to form gigantic stalking continental

force). Said do not think there is anything to fear as it is just horde of straw-chewing pasty-wavers who will cower at the first sign of opposition from Westminster. She said are you sure? Asked her who else is involved. She said Denzil Junior from the Crazy Car Warehouse (Denzil Senior having choked to death on a sherbet lemon, as predicted by hip of doom) and his friend Pig Gibbons (pork farmer, excess facial hair, smells of slurry). Said point proven.

. . . .

Wednesday 14

Yet another phone call from the realms of idiocy, i.e. St Slaughter. This time it is Grandpa Clegg. Apparently he is now a fully fledged member of 'Trelawney's Army'. Was worried initiation might have involved menacing 'hazing' activity like running naked through streets or drinking pint of sheepdip but apparently Pig Gibbons just made him swear on a copy of *Jamaica Inn* that he would die for his county, and never buy Plymouth Gin (from Devon, so enemy liquor). Asked him when he is going on manoeuvres with rest of battalion. He said they are meeting round Denzil's tomorrow to sing mining songs and eat fairings. I said it did not sound very army-like. Grandpa said on the contrary (he does not say *au contraire* due to *a*) not liking French, and *b*) not speaking any language bar English, and not that very well) it is Cornish fodder for the troops and he is also anticipating getting his first

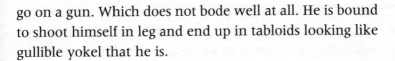

go on a gun. Which does not bode well at all. He is bound to shoot himself in leg and end up in tabloids looking like gullible yokel that he is.

- -

Thursday 15

Thank God. Trelawney's Army does not actually involve any real guns. Unless you count Denzil's anti-pigeon water pistol (£4.99 from Trago Mills). Granny Clegg rang to revel in Grandpa's disappointment. She said he was hoping to be hunting tourists on the moors this afternoon. Instead they just sat around moaning about up-country ways. I said he usually likes nothing better than to moan about foreigners (anyone from over Tamar is foreigner, even Dad). She said it is true, but he has got Magnum madness now. I said Magnum madness is not real, is made up by Walls to sell more ice cream. But she said it is completely real according to Maureen Penrice, whose son is in army, and is not ice-cream-related but is obsession with Clint Eastwood-style weaponry.

Mum is also tetchy. It is not Magnum madness. It is potential irresponsible sex madness. It is because apparently a new anti-sexually transmitted disease drop-in clinic is opening at the back of the Costcutter. I said this was a good thing, given evidence that sex education in schools is not working (widespread belief that can catch syphilis from lower school toilet seats, Primark Donna belief that cannot get pregnant if have sex standing up). But Mum says presence of genitally-compromised people will bring down tone of whole area and house prices will plummet and we will be in grip of recession. Said recession complicated economic phenomenon, according to Scarlet, and not usually caused by sex clinics, but Mum not in agreement. Nor is Marjory next door. She is going to stake it out with her digital camera and photograph all the culprits. (She is back to PI duty after her brief stint as fat pink lady. It is a wonder we survived without her spying services.) I said that was invasion of privacy and would not help in battle against underage sex or gonorrhoea. Mum said it is a small price to pay and anyway the threat of Marjory with a camera is enough to put anyone off sex. Which is true.

Friday 16

The saggy sofa is awash with anti-sex disease drop-in clinic excitement. It is not at potential to be declared disease-free. It is that there are rumours that they hand out free condoms. The maths geeks are already planning a mass 'drop-in' to secure a supply. They are going to sell them in their own anti-sex disease shop (aka the Upper School toilets) for 50p each. The only person who is not excited is Sad Ed of missing mojo fame. He said it is like waving a packet of Starburst at a diabetic.

Saturday 17

Went to see Sad Ed at lunchtime to try to cheer him up about sex clinic menace. But his trolley herding was even more morose than usual. It is because he had a driving lesson last night and Mike Majors is refusing to let him take his test yet. Reuben Tull offered to give him 'something for his nerves'. But according to Mr Wandering Hands, that is not the problem. It is more lack of concentration, inability to find fourth gear, and persistent belief that the kerb is further away than it actually is. He said it is two kicks in two days as being told you are bad at driving is devastating mojo-wise.

The ongoing missing mojo mystery is completely depressing. It is not just Sad Ed who is suffering though, it is Scarlet and me too. This was supposed to be year of seizing day and experimenting love-wise. Instead have just got dumped by future prime minister (Scarlet) and future prison statistic (me). When will we be stirred into love? James says it is all just a matter of oxytocin levels, they have proved it with voles. But voles do not have dress sense or guitar ability to consider. One vole is the same as the next. It is different for living breathing poetic people like me and Scarlet. (Though possibly not for Leanne Jones who is vole-like in her willingness to do it with anyone as long as they have £2.50 and a chart CD. She will be at anti-sex drop-in clinic on weekly basis.)

Sunday 18

And Jack. Have just realized that he has not gone out with anyone since the whole Sophie Microwave Muffins hoo-ha last year. Yet he has excellent dress sense. Plus he can play drums. Will ask him at muse session later what is going on, mojo-wise.

5 p.m.

It is universal affliction! Jack is also mojo-compromised. I asked him why he wasn't going out with anyone and he said none of the girls in his year do it for him. And he isn't going to waste his time with Mrs Wrong. Or try to change them into Mrs Right because that never works. You either love them or you don't, from the very start. Which think was possible dig at Davey MacDonald hoo-ha. But ignored. As, to be fair, he is right. Then he asked if I was doing any more experimenting. Said was concentrating on exams and had no time for affairs of the heart. Or mojo.

Maybe there is something in water after all, as well as fluoride. Though not mind-altering but mojo-altering. Grandpa Riley says in the war the Navy officers put bromide in his tea to keep his mojo down. But it didn't stop him as he only drank liquorice water. He is delusional. He was only seven when World War Two broke out and closest he has been to Navy is pedaloes in Margate.

Monday 19

The saggy sofa is extra saggy under anti-sex disease clinic disappointment. The maths geeks did their mass drop-in at lunchtime and it turns out there is a monthly ration of ten condoms per person. Fat Kylie said it must be 'run by mingers' if they think ten times a month is normal. So clearly there is nothing in the water. At least not in the Whiteshot Estate supply.

Marjory is also disappointed at her sex surveillance. She said most of the customers seemed to be respectable looking young Asians with clipboards, who were probably doing a survey. Did not tell her it was utterly non-respectable maths geeks on mission to flog cut-price condoms to sex-mad Sixth Formers. I said surely she should be jubilant at clean-living Saffron Walden. But James says *au contraire*, Marjory lives for scandal. It is the price you pay for being a private eye: you spend your life trying to eradicate crime and deviant behaviour, but without it your existence is meaningless. Is like Mum and dirt.

Tuesday 20

Marjory is revived and is mad with sex scandal excitement. Apparently four mystery men went into the anti-sex drop-in clinic today. She has photographic evidence and is going to enhance them digitally on the computer later, with the aid of her helmet-wearing assistant Mum.

They are hoping to have positive identifications for the *Walden Chronicle* by tomorrow's print deadline.

<hr>

Wednesday 21

The sex clinic mystery has been solved, and without the aid of Marjory's photofit software. It was not four mystery lotharios with compromised genitals. It was one sex-crazed Mr Whippy and his 99 cone. Fat Kylie was holding court on the Yazoo cushion this morning with story of how Mr Whippy tried to fool authorities with his armoury of disguises (i.e. four different hats). Asked if it had worked. She said no, she thinks his unmistakable aura of sex gave him away. It is more likely the lingering smell of chemical ice cream. And attempts to actually use 'Mr Whippy' as one of his pseudonyms. Scarlet said she thought Fat Kylie's Catholic beliefs forbade her to use contraception. Kylie said it was a tough decision but Dr Braithwaite (huge hands, lazy eye, bottle of whisky in desk drawer) says he is imposing a three-abortion limit due to NHS underfunding. It is not underfunding. It is overshagging. Have told Marjory. She is not bothering to contact *Walden Chronicle*. The whole town is already aware of his sexploits. There are still grainy CCTV videos doing the rounds of him and Leanne Jones on Barry Island, featuring the unforgettable sight of her buttocks glowing eerily in ice cream van headlights.

Thursday 22

Am feeling utterly ravaged by credit crunch. The lack of employment prospects is seriously compromising my potential for day-seizing experimental love (and potential use of anti-sex drop-in clinic), i.e. have no new clothes bar illegal best woman outfit plus hair is in desperate need of cut. Curl volume now reached epic proportions and is complete health hazard, i.e. things get stuck in it, e.g. four locusts, a pencil sharpener, and a Chomp bar (although think some of them possibly inserted by Mark Lambert during assembly). Have begged Mum for funds (i.e. £40) for a restyle at Toni and Guy in Cambridge but she has compromised on £15 for a wet trim at Curl Up 'N' Dye. Said that is not compromise, is punishment, as is where Thin Kylie sweeps up clippings on a Saturday, and she is still minty with me about meddling with Davey so would end up maimed with thinning shears. Or worse. Mum said beggars can't be choosers and said she could always go round edges with the kitchen scissors. Also declined. The last time I let her do this she made me wear salad bowl as guide and ended up looking like lampshade. Though James got worse deal. He opted for a risotto dish and was positively monk-like for several months.

Friday 23

Hurrah, is last day of school. And for once, do not have life-changing exams to revise for. AS levels are not actual exams, according to Dad, but just spurious inventions of government, designed to boost England in OECD rankings. Mum and James, who embrace testing of all kinds, are not in agreement, but they are too busy concentrating on Boffin Boy's upcoming SATs to impose the usual rigid revision timetable. Mum is pinning her appeal hopes on him getting unprecedented 100 per cent and being inundated with requests from head teachers begging her to allow them to accommodate James's freakish brain.

4 p.m.
Am utterly going to revise for exams. Mr Wilmott gave Year Twelve his annual half-term exam rally assembly this morning (i.e. AS levels are not made-up, despite what Mrs Leech says, and should be taken seriously etc.) but, this year, he has added a menacing credit crunch theme, i.e. if you don't pass them, you will be completely at bottom of job queue and could face a lifetime of benefits and misery. He is wrong. Mark Lambert will be at the bottom of the job queue. And Caris Kelp who eats glue. But am worried none the less. Am already struggling to find work, despite having several GCSEs. Though being muse will be excellent on CV. Maybe should let Mrs Noakes in Waitrose know. I could be useful on toiletry aisle as inspiration, look-wise.

Have solved haircut issue though. Mum has found a recession-busting device on the internet that you attach to the Hoover and it gives you an even trim all round. She is mad with excitement as not only is it economical, but it tidies itself up immediately and is therefore her holy grail of gadgets. Said it did not sound too promising, but she says it is infallible, according to Mrs F from Puckeridge. Asked who mysterious Mrs F was. She said is author of glowing online testimonial. I said I hoped Mum's new found internet skills are not compromising her usual rigorous appliance appraisal skills, involving *Which* magazine, and instore testing. But she says it is that or the bowl method. Have agreed to hoover hair. Device is due to arrive tomorrow. So at least will be trimmed in time for portrait sitting. Jack said if hair got any bigger it would compromise Jimi Hendrix poster in background, which is essential part of composition.

. . . .

Saturday 24

10 a.m.

The Hoover device is here! Mum is going to do all of us, including the dog. Have suggested James is guinea pig, as his hair is not essential, muse-wise. He said, *au contraire*, he is minded to grow it and go for a Lee Mead rock opera look. Mum said over her dead body. But she has agreed to let him go after Dad, who is itching to do some putting practice. Mum said she hopes it is just hypothetical and that he is not hoping to put practice into practice. He said, 'Would I lie to you?' Which James then pointed out is, technically, not an answer. But Mum was too busy whirring her Hoover device to get into semantics.

11 a.m.

It works! Dad and James are utterly shorn and do not look either mental or in pain! James said the buzzing was actually quite pleasant and has asked to go again. Mum said no as she needs a tea break before tackling her trick-iest customers, i.e. me and the dog. It is not our fault we are cursed, follicularly.

11.30 a.m.

The dog has been done. It is revelation. Have never seen it look so tidy. Dog is also in shock. It has been staring at self in mirror for several minutes. Is my turn now. Am almost excited. May well take device to school and offer cut price trims on saggy sofa. Will put BTEC hair and beauty, i.e. the Kylies, out of business in a week! Hoover is tidier, quicker, and does not call people 'lezzers'.

12 noon

There has been a Hoover-related hair accident. Am too weak to communicate. Am going to lie down in dark and pray for world to end. Or hair to grow. Very quickly.

1 p.m.

Oh God. World has not ended. And hair is as bad as thought. Have not got even trim. Have weird two centimetre-short patch on back of head and rest of hair is just as absurdly huge as before. It is because hair got clogged in rotor and had to be cut free. Mum has offered to even it up with scissors but said do not want her lack of styling skills near hairdo ever again. She says it is not her fault if the device cannot cope with my level of matting. I said it *is* her fault as mental hair is totally the Clegg gene, look at Grandpa—if he doesn't keep it under a centimetre long he looks like midget Monty Don.

2 p.m.
James has come in with grave look. He says he has dissected Hoover haircut gadget and has evidence he would like to present to all parties.

2.30 p.m.
Mum is jubilant as hair accident not caused by user error or rogue Clegg gene. It was due to sticky substance concealed in hairdo, which James says can only be attributed to negligence on part of haircutee, i.e. me. Asked for sample of sticky substance to identify provenance.

3 p.m.
Ha! I am jubilant as sticky substance proven to be partially cooked sultana from last night's spotted dick, cooked by none other than Mum. So if her suet were not so claggy, sultana would have been sliced like butter by vicious rotor blades.

3.30 p.m.

Have just seen back of head in mirror and am unjubilant. Oh God, is going to ruin already compromised image at school. Plus career as muse. Do not know any muses who have inexplicable baldy bits. Am utterly unfanciable. Jack will never be inspired by me again.

4 p.m.

Not that Jack fancied me.

. . . .

Sunday 25

Am still depressed hair-wise. Plus have barely slept due to recurring dream about being swallowed by a Dyson, driven by dog. Mum says I am overreacting and that patch is only size of a small potato and can be concealed by cunning arrangement of ponytail or plaits. Said patch more size of Granny Smith apple and anyway ponytail would mean Jack having to redo entire portrait. James said is not Granny Smith, is Cox's Pippin-sized, but that if that is all concerned about then am being idiot as patch is at back of head and assume portrait is frontal. Said had had enough of fruit hair madness and fact that bald patch not in picture is not point. I will know it is there and Jack will know it is there and, therefore, I am unmuseworthy.

5 p.m.

Have had weird muse session. On plus side, Jack not at

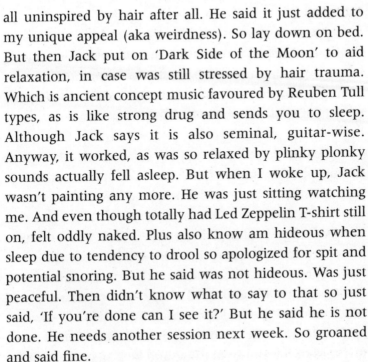

all uninspired by hair after all. He said it just added to my unique appeal (aka weirdness). So lay down on bed. But then Jack put on 'Dark Side of the Moon' to aid relaxation, in case was still stressed by hair trauma. Which is ancient concept music favoured by Reuben Tull types, as is like strong drug and sends you to sleep. Although Jack says it is also seminal, guitar-wise. Anyway, it worked, as was so relaxed by plinky plonky sounds actually fell asleep. But when I woke up, Jack wasn't painting any more. He was just sitting watching me. And even though totally had Led Zeppelin T-shirt still on, felt oddly naked. Plus also know am hideous when sleep due to tendency to drool so apologized for spit and potential snoring. But he said was not hideous. Was just peaceful. Then didn't know what to say to that so just said, 'If you're done can I see it?' But he said he is not done. He needs another session next week. So groaned and said fine.

But the thing is I didn't feel groany. I actually felt pleased. Oh God. Think might fancy Jack again. Am so confused by all day seizing and experimenting can't tell any more.

5.15 p.m.
Have just seen hair in mirror. Am utterly unlovable. Day seizing definitely out until hair grows. Which could be months. If not years.

Monday 26

Spring Bank Holiday

Thank God is half-term so can hide in bedroom revising instead of being object of hilarity in common room for having 'spazzer head'. No wonder Einstein was so brainy with hairdo like that. He had to just sit inside learning, out of harsh glare of world.

James is also holed up in his bunker, though is through choice, rather than due to image issues. (He is permanently nerdy so bad hair would have no effect.) He has drawn up a strict SATs timetable, with scheduled wee breaks and a health-giving snack every forty minutes for optimum brain performance. Asked what the silver stars represented. He said that is scheduled creative time, during which he and Mad Harry will rehearse. I said rehearse what. He said for Beastly Boys. It is his new boy band. He says he is hoping it will revive the ailing fortunes of the House of Riley, and be a stepping stone to his stage career. Like H out of Steps. I said only fortunes that are ailing are mine. Plus H is pants. But James says according to *Financial Times* the office supply sector is suffering in the current anti-waste paper climate, which means Mr Wainwright will be looking at ways to tighten his belt and offload excess baggage. I said Dad is not excess baggage. But James said a computer, or possibly monkey, could do Dad's job and he will struggle to find a new one with his medieval qualifications and then we will have to sell house, but, due to stagnation

218

in the market in Uttlesford, and sex clinic, we will be forced to downsize to a more C2DE community like Harlow, losing our fourth bedroom and the all-essential stormporch. At that point left as was more depressing than an afternoon listening to Leonard Cohen with Sad Ed.

On plus side have spent four hours rereading Nietzsche. On downside, it is still as confusing as it was six months ago.

. . . .

Tuesday 27

Am doing English revision today. It is far less complicated and does not require struggling internally with issues like whether famine is proof that God does not exist, or whether we should put drugs in the water. Will reread *Pride and Prejudice*.

11 a.m.

Or possibly just watch DVD instead (borrowed from Marjory, with strict instructions to keep out of consumption range of dog) as is utterly same thing plus can ogle Colin Firth in wet shirt.

2 p.m.

Oh God, think maybe Jack is Mr Darcy and we are just going round being sarky to each other, oblivious to our overriding mojo attraction.

3 p.m.

No, Jack not Mr Darcy. He does not ever use word 'ardently'. And cannot imagine Colin Firth ever drumming along to 'Teenage Wasteland'.

4 p.m.

He might be Jude the Obscure though. Which means I am cousin Sue. Oh God. English more confusing than philosophy.

5 p.m.

Have just had thought. Maybe I am not anyone. Maybe I am just me. Maybe I need to stop reading too much into novels and just do what Mrs Buttfield tells me, i.e. memorize Brodie's notes. And if that fails, do what Suzy tells me, i.e. write pertinent quotes on thighs.

6 p.m.

No, that is even more depressing. I have to be someone else. Otherwise English Lit, and life, is pointless.

. . . .

Wednesday 28

Is politics revision day. Politics is not fraught with issues of existentialism, or whether or not I am William Pitt or Gladstone. There is no way I am anyone in politics. They are all odd looking and wear criminal outfits.

4 p.m.

Although maybe am suffragette Emmeline Pankhurst. Am totally pro women's rights—look at golf club boycott. Plus she had vast curly hair.

4.15 p.m.

Though probably not with sultana-related bald patch on back of head. Am disguising it with permanent ponytail. No one need know until am fully hirsute again.

. . . .

Thursday 29

Drama day. Cannot revise for drama. Either have talent. Or do not. And I utterly have it, as evidenced by B in my GCSE and standing ovation at end of *Over the Hills* (*Sound of Music*-based school musical involving battle of bands and nuns in lingerie), though that might have been to do with Fat Kylie bursting out of corset. Anyway, am not worried as have definite something. Unlike James. Have just sat through Beastly Boys rehearsal. Is horrifying. Particularly their version of 'I Kissed a Girl'.

Luckily Scarlet interrupted to remind me and Mum that it is golf club boycott day on Saturday. She says half of Walden will be there, as well as potential celebrities to embarrass into action. Asked who. She said the not-so-famous McGann is definitely back from Lenor advert. And there is a chance he might bring the bloke who does the Comfort advert, who also was once on *Strictly Come*

Dancing with Bruce Forsyth, who is celebrity golfing legend! Asked if Suzy would be using her celebrity status (or heaving bosom) to sway them into changing sides but Scarlet says she is apparently otherwise engaged today, probably with a C-list willy. Mum is not joining us either. It is not in any way penis-related. It is because she will be escorting James and Mad Harry to Kart Mania for Maggot Mason's birthday party. I said couldn't Mrs Mad Harry do it. She said Mrs Mad Harry did Keanu's and is still picking gum off the car upholstery so it is only fair. Thank God one of the Riley women has principles and is sticking to them, i.e. me. Treena has no principles. She goes out in leggings.

. . . .

Friday 30

Mum has begged James to give up Beastly Boys. She says she cannot endure any more renditions of 'You Raise Me Up' (featuring Mad Harry lifting James aloft like prize trophy). James has warned her she may regret her lack of faith when we are living on a diet of benefits and transfats on Whiteshot Estate. Mum said there is no way Dad is going to lose his job as he is the only one at Wainwright and Beacham (Hogg has defected to Parker Pens) who knows how coffee machine works. Plus now that he has given up golf, she can reassign his colossal membership fees as emergency credit crunch funds. So in fact we are not on poverty line after all. But we are still not getting any more Duchy Originals Chocolate Butterscotch thingies as they work out at 25p per biscuit whereas digestives are 3p. And rich tea fingers are 1p.

4 p.m.
Oh my God! Dad has not given up golf at all! There are no membership fees to be reassigned because he handed them over to Margot Gyp yesterday, along with his £30 entrance to the Captain's Day cup. Mum is labouring under false illusions. Dad said he only told me because of impending caddy crisis. It is that his usual bag-mule Malcolm has a Star Trek convention in Knutsford so he is caddyless for tomorrow's competition. He has begged me to do it instead. I said, as he knows only too well, I am utter suffragette, i.e. am boycotting golf club due to evil anti-women rules, and will not cross the threshold of the clubhouse, let alone tramp around eighteen holes with a load of ironmongery on my back. Suggested James as alternative. He said he cannot ask James as he cannot be trusted not to tell Mum. So said is true, but my lack of allegiance to Mum is overridden by my political ideals. So Dad said he will pay me £50. Said yes. Scarlet need never know. Will call in sick to boycott and sneak onto fairway via sewage works. Political ideals are all very well if your mum hands out pocket money like sex tips. Mine is repressed in every possible way.

Saturday 31

9 a.m.

Hurrah. The plan is simple. As all brilliant infallible plans are. Mum and James are already safely on their way to endure several hours of madness and e-numbers at Kart Mania. Dad is already warming up on the practice tee. And I will be joining him via the ditch next to the sewage works (aka poo factory) shortly. Then, as soon Dad has sunk his last ball, or whatever it is, will ditch Pings, and hat, and join Scarlet at front for shouty picketing. So in fact am killing two birds with one stone—principles and pocket! Have told Scarlet that am having hair shame crisis and may be late due to having to fashion intricate plait work. She says she understands, and it is a woman's right to feel confident in herself as much as it is to wear hideous golfing trousers and hit balls pointlessly round hillocks. Which is good point. We are possibly fighting for cause we don't actually like. As golf is utterly mental. But all sports are equal in eyes of suffragettes.

9.05 a.m.

Except water polo. Which should not be played under any circumstances.

9.10 a.m.

Or snooker. Which is not even a sport. It is just spotty men in nylon waistcoats playing giant bagatelle. Anyway, point is, plan is excellent. Nothing can go wrong.

224

4 p.m.

Except had not factored in the following crucial circumstances:

1. Keanu would try to off-road his go-kart.
2. Manager of Kart Mania would suspend all preliminary heats whilst Keanu is recaptured (halfway along B1053, where he had stopped at garage for Wall's Feast).
3. Party would be banned from Kart Mania for life, forfeiting the Grand Prix, and buffet luncheon (sausage rolls and Capri-Sun).
4. James would persuade Mum to go to boycott after all (in theory, so she can take political stand, in reality in case midget impresario Louis Walsh shows up to play round with old friend Bruce Forsyth and he can give impromptu performance of 'I Kissed a Girl' and be signed to Sony for a three-album deal).
5. Boycott would get bored with standing around in car park, getting toes run over by Mercedes X-classes, and decide to storm fairways and throw themselves in front of golf buggies, suffragette- (and Mrs Thomas) style.

Was awful. Tried to do Keanu-style getaway by hijacking golf buggy, but was impeded by Sad Ed (on his lunch hour) sprawled in front of me. He claims I tried to kill him. I said he should be grateful as he could be first ever golf-related suicide but he says if he is going to die in car

crash, it had better be à la Marc Bolan, i.e. crashing into a tree in a psychedelic Mini, not squished by a mini milk-float. Plus I had got tyre marks on Waitrose property and might be liable for a fine.

Luckily Scarlet was too horrified at cunning twist in events to shout about my betrayal. It is that Suzy was at golf course after all. But not at boycott. She was in a four-ball with Bob and the Braithwaites from Number 11! Worse, she was wearing unfathomable pink triangle jumper and plus fours. Scarlet went mental and demanded the number for Childline and immediate fostering but Suzy threw herself on ground (now littered with bodies, like some WWI killing field) and begged for mercy. She said she and Bob had only done it for the sake of the family. It turns out Suzy's hot flushes are not valium-related, they are early menopause and she can't have any more babies, so they are going on the adoption register instead and were trying to make themselves look like good parent material. Then Scarlet was racked with remorse, and injustice at world, and said that Suzy and Bob were best Mum and Dad and they do not need golf, because all their special skills mean they are bound to be given babies (am not sure am in agreement with this as do not think ability to perform abortions and knowing location of G spot is necessarily good parenting but did not say anything as did not want to draw attention to self now that Scarlet happier with Suzy). So Suzy flung off her jumper and said she was going back to the right, or

226

left, side of the picket line. As did Bob, and several other golfers including the man from the Comfort advert. Though this was possibly due to fact that Suzy now wearing only plus fours and balconette bra. At which point Margot Gyp went purple and had to be carried to leather banquette in clubhouse for emergency Dubonnet.

Anyway, then everyone decided to give up the peaceful-ish protest and go back to Bob and Suzy's for hummus and olives as golf is ridiculous sport after all and unworthy of attention. They are going to focus on the darts club, which has a topless calendar behind the bar. I would have gone but Scarlet said I needed time to reflect on my Thatcherite self-interest before I am allowed to take a seat at the hummus table again.

Mum did not go either. It is because she has decided to make dramatic Suzy-style U-turn. Though, thank God, this did not involve removing any clothing. It is that she is going to join the golf club. She says on reflection, the clothing rules are sensible and, quite frankly, she does not want to play at the same time as the men because they are loud, smell of too much cologne, and never replace their divots. Dad has begged for alternative punishment but her mind is made up. She is going to be fitted for brogues tomorrow.

So now am back at home listening to Beastly Boys sing 'Holding out for a Hero' for the seventeenth time, have had £50 confiscated by Mum as a lesson in something or other (possibly deception, or bad driving), plus have lingering odour of faeces on shoes due to slight slip along sewage short cut. So all in all, not brilliant day. The only plus point is that Jack was not there to witness it or he would be sacking me as muse for sure. According to Scarlet he was too busy fiddling with his etchings. Think this is literal not metaphor. Although, in that house, anything is possible.

GOLF
CLUB

Sunday 1

Today is my last muse session with Jack, potential rock genius, anti-war foreign secretary, and future Damian Hirst. And am feeling slightly odd, i.e. stomach is bit jumpy again. Think it is because it is utterly the end of an era as exams start tomorrow and then Jack will be leaving in few months for university. It will be weird not having him around. Had not really thought it before as am used to him always lurking in background. But will miss him. And possibly not just as friend. Will put to back of mind though. Must think of art above self and ensure final session is peaceful celebration of painting, which is more important than mojo issues.

5 p.m.

My career as muse is over. Am utterly sad. Plus last session not peaceful celebration of painting. Was fraught with tension. Mostly mine. Think I covered it up OK though. Although Jack not too happy with me lying on hands as made me look a bit like mental patient or corpse. But was essential emergency method to prevent me flinging self at Jack across his gouache board as mojo definitely stirred! Is typical. Mojo is completely out of step with current affairs as is too late now. At least will not have to see him until the end of exams party now so will not be tempted to embarrass self on saggy sofa.

Also am annoyed as Jack will not let me see portrait. He said he needs to do a few finishing touches in private and then I can see it in the end of term exhibition after it has been marked. But think he is lying. More probably, painting is hideous and he is scared I will shout at him and possibly sabotage A level.

Monday 2

Scarlet is also depressed. It is nothing to do with her mis-directed mojo. It is related to issues of democracy. It is because her political ambition has been thwarted twice in the space of two days. Not only is her anti-golf campaign utterly over. (She says it is a voluntary decision not to waste her lobbying energy on pointless ball games. Though is possibly more to do with restriction order ban-ning her or any member of Stone family from within 200 metre radius of clubhouse or fairways.) But now, Mr Wilmott has decided to ban head boy and head girl elec-tions. Instead they will be appointed by powers that be, rather than wasting weeks, and valuable stationery, whipping up the Upper School into election frenzy. Scarlet says he is being utterly fascistic. But he said he is being sensible because the common room is already fac-tionized anyway, and he does not want full-scale conflict breaking out. (Personally I thought the saggy sofa peace accord was holding quite well despite breach last week when Fat Kylie sat on Um Bongo cushion. Is not her fault buttocks spread over two territories though. Actually it is her fault. Due to excess chip consumption. But was not deliberate anti-Jerusalem act.) Plus he says he is tired of candidates offering budget-breaking sweeteners to win votes. He is still trying to fund Oona's free tampons and membership of Greenpeace. Scarlet demanded to know which powers that be, aka evil dictators, were going to make the appointments and on what criteria. He said him and Mrs Leech and they will pick someone with broadly popular appeal, who can unite the A levellers and BTECers. Or at least not drive either side mental. Scarlet said it is utterly against the underdog and we will end up with plastic prom queens instead of dynamic political personalities. Though personally think it is not bad idea as at least it rules out single-issue candidates like maths geeks who wanted calculator ban and compulsory lunchtime chess. Or Scarlet, who was going to enforce toilet paper ration and maximum one flush a day. Is not fair on Big Jim who has been known to block toilet with outgoings.

Tuesday 3

Is historic day, on several counts. Partly because Barack Obama is official democratic candidate for American election. Saggy sofa is mad with multicultural-embracing excitement. I bet Gordon Brown wishes he wasn't so pasty-faced now. Complexion, and greasiness of hair, are not aiding him in his time of trouble.

Also, more importantly, was last ever philosophy

lesson today. Was actually sad as has been enlightening year, in sense that now know that anything goes, philosophy-wise. For example, today discussed whether forgeries were art or mere craft. Thought was obvious, i.e. Tracey Emin = good, Woolworth's poster = bad. BUT it turns out that is possible that a brilliant fake might be just as good as the real thing. After all, who is to judge which has greater artistic value—Boyzone or Westlife. So maybe my Davey MacDonald experiment was not so mad and my fake Hilary would have been as good as the real thing. Except that am clearly not very good forger as end result still resembled joyriding chav. Though was possibly subject matter and should have picked someone who could name three members of cabinet. Or at least knew where Houses of Parliament were.

Maybe I will find another Jack though. Maybe somewhere out there in my future there is another long-haired, drum-playing, political-minded artist, who will make me feel all breathless when he kisses me. Is heartening to know that all is not lost.

. . . .

Wednesday 4

Scarlet is not in agreement about the clever fake thing. She says, however good a copy is, it will never be worth as much as the real thing, look at Pepsi Max and Diet Coke. She is just annoyed because Trevor is still

234

canoodling with Tamsin Bacon, who has modelled her entire life and wardrobe on Scarlet. She says she is the original and best. But think she is overestimating Trevor's discerning taste. He would be happy with anyone with black nail varnish and a plastic bat.

She is revived head girl-wise though. She says she is going to prove herself a friend of all parties, i.e. A levellers and BTECers, so that she will shine out as ideal candidate. Although initial attempts to infiltrate the Yazoo cushion were less than promising, i.e. Thin Kylie who told her to get her 'lezzer arse' off their side before they 'caught gayness'.

Thursday 5

Exam season has begun. Though not mine, thank God. Is James. He is positively mental with SATs anticipation. He is flying in the face of advice from headmaster Nige though, who told Year Six that SATs were not a test of intelligence but of being able to parrot statistics, so not to get worked up at all. Instead he is obeying advice of Mum, who says if he does not excel then he will be joining generations of Rileys in the ranks of the average. I hope she is not including me in that equation. Though possibly is. She still hasn't forgiven me for the nine out of ten I got in spelling in Year Four when I put a silent p in triceratops. Let alone my several Bs at GCSE.

4 p.m.

James is home and is jubilant. He says it was all complete breeze and is confidently expecting offers to roll in from Eton and Rugby within weeks of results being published. He is pest. Now will have to do extra well in AS levels or will be outshone yet again by hobbit-worshipping moron.

. . . .

Friday 6

Granny Clegg has rung. She and Grandpa are at opposite ends of the nylon-carpeted front room again. It is because Grandpa wants to rename their house Pasty Manor in honour of his newfound Cornish Revolution allegiance. Granny says if it is going to get a new name at all it should be Herbert House, in honour of Mr Benson who is sole Labour councillor in Redruth environs. In fairness, either is better than its actual name Belleview, which is misleading as there is no view other than Hester's battery chicken shed/holiday cottage and windswept rec, both of which are less than belle. Mum said not to worry as Grandpa is armchair fascist, i.e. will not actually do anything, just likes ranting about it from comfort of broken Parker Knoll.

. . . .

Saturday 7

Granny Clegg has rung again. She is mad with anti-Grandpa fervour. It is because, in her absence (she was at Trago Mills with Hilary buying cut-price tinned tomatoes), he left the broken Parker Knoll, and he, Denzil, and Pig Gibbons have redecorated the front of the house. Not only has a 'Pasty Manor' sign been nailed to door, but they have painted a Cornish flag on the cladding with what was left of the Hammerite. Asked how Grandpa was looking these days. She says he still has generally dirty look about him, and for some reason his ears are particularly stubborn. Said ears are mirrors of his soul. Granny said she thought that was eyes. I hope not. His eyes have look of murderer. Anyway, Granny says it is war now. And if he is going use underhand and non-democratic tactics, then so is she. Grandpa says as man of house he was merely taking executive decision. But do not think men who wear string vests as outerwear and have Hammerited ears count as executives.

. . . .

Sunday 8

Mum is playing her first round of golf today, after two o'clock, and in approved skirt, gloves, and appalling pastel jumper. Dad says she is mad to be investing in kit before she has even tried the game as she will probably give it up when she realizes she is not going to be Seve Ballesteros, like most amateurs. Mum said *au contraire*, *a*) the jumper is from 1986, *b*) she borrowed gloves from Marjory (though they are not strictly for golf, they are for Jenga), and *c*) she is only playing to improve her fitness and co-ordination skills, and does not have any pretensions to professionalism. This is a lie. Mum does not do anything half-heartedly. Even her washing up is competition standard. Plus she has enlisted James as caddy. Dad says he asked first but James says he will do both, for double pay and injury money. Said that was unfair seeing as Mum and Dad are sharing clubs but James says caddying is one per cent lugging bag and ninety-nine per cent brain power, i.e. being highly tuned to your player and knowing instinctively which club they will need so will be doubly taxing. He is wrong. It is just bag carrying. And possibly argument defusing.

On plus side it means have house to self for afternoon to practise philosophizing for tomorrow's AS exam. Need peace and quiet to ponder questions of existence, and possibility of laser-eyed dogs. Hurrah. Am actually looking forward to revising!

3 p.m.
Revising not as productive as anticipated. Mostly due to presence of non laser-eyed but definitely peace-shattering dog, which decided to take advantage of lack of visible authority and chew a hole in James's beanbag chair. (Formerly quarantined in attic due to potential fire hazard issues, now out of quarantine having being sprayed with flame retardant. Though possibly life-threatening due to hideous chemical content.) Have hoovered up most of beans but bag looking bit deflated so have inserted some of James's old toys inside to bulk it up and

sellotaped hole. He will never notice. Cannot remember last time he played with naked Will Young.

4 p.m.
Mum is back from the fairway and is jubilant. She got two birdies and an eagle. Said did not think point was to brain wildlife but James said is golf jargon and means she is utterly a natural. Dad not so jubilant. He says not only are his peaceful Sundays in the company of men over, but he is also losing authority in the only area in which he could confidently claim to be better than Mum. He says it is all affront to masculinity. I predict mojo issues. Though am hoping Mum and Dad do not actually have sex so will not be in any way marriage threatening. Cannot cope with Cleggs and Rileys on verge of marital breakdown. Is like week's worth of Jeremy Kyle.

5 p.m.
James has sustained a beanbag-related injury. He threw himself backwards on it and got stabbed in the right buttock by Will Young's microphone. He has filed official complaint with Mum about beanbag sabotage. So have filed one back about misuse of furnishings, i.e. that according to her rules, they are to be sat upon only, and under no circumstances to be used as crash mats or climbing frames. We have both been sent to rooms with punishment tea of cheese and crackers. It is utterly unfair. He should know better than to engage in gymnastic leaps

239

inside the house. Plus how am I supposed to excel philo-sophically when have only had Ryvita and Pilgrim's Choice for sustenance.

5.10 p.m.
Though possibly should not have put Will Young inside bag. Is lucky did not also insert Dalek though. The potential of injury by sink plunger attachment is horri-fying.

. . . .

Monday 9
8 a.m.
Am feeling utterly clever and philosophical. In fact, think undernourishment may be useful as am quite floaty-headed and possibly experiencing higher levels of percep-tion. Will skip Cheerios to be sure though, i.e. feed them to dog. Mum will never know.

3 p.m.
Lack of food not quite as genius-inducing as thought. Had dizzy spell in exam hall (aka Mrs Brain's custard and cabbage-scented canteen) and had to go to Mrs Leech for medical attention, i.e. five French fancies and a party ring. Then had complete sugar rush and finished exam in thirty-five minutes instead of allotted two hours. Though is possibly fine and just means have excellent grasp of consequentialism.

3.30 p.m.

Although probably should not have just answered 'yes' to 'Is there always a right answer?' Also, Mum now worried have anorexia due to exam stress. It is because dog coughed up Cheerios on nest of tables during *The Archers*. I said was just first-day nerves and will be consuming hearty breakfast from now on. She says I had better do or she will be booking me in for a session with school psychiatrist (aka Mental Morris) faster than I can purge a digestive.

. . . .

Tuesday 10

8 a.m.

Have eaten health-giving breakfast of Bran Flakes, two pieces of granary toast and Marmite, and banana. So will definitely not faint in politics exam. Though may possibly need to go to loo several times due to extreme fibre content. Is lucky Scarlet not in charge of toilet paper yet.

3 p.m.

Hurrah. Exams are over for this week. And totally excelled self today with brilliant treatise on how rapid reaction force is totally not same as standing army. Think would be excellent politician in fact. Or better, could be celebrity lobbyist like Bono. Scarlet says it is not merely question of being good on paper and that politicians need the three Cs: 'charisma, charm, and connectability'. But that is rubbish. Gordon Brown has none of the above, and Alistair Darling just has mad eyebrows.

. . . .

Wednesday 11

James has come home from school with exciting St Regina's related news. It is the annual Year Six leavers' trip. Headmaster Nige has instigated a change to itinerary, i.e. instead of the usual four days ingesting fried food and then throwing it up on rollercoaster at Butlin's, they will yomp around Epping Forest going 'back to nature'. James is mental with anticipation. It is because he thinks it will be utterly like *I'm a Celebrity* . . . and he will be devouring spiders and wrestling crocodiles to win his dinner. Mum is not so overjoyed. She has reminded him of his phobia of pooing on anything but fully-cleansed and flushing porcelain and says £145 is a lot of money if he is just going to whinge to be picked up after six hours because he needs a number two. But James claims his Ninja brain training and gladiatorial strength has cured him of poo issues and he will embrace portaloos and even holes in the ground and it is complete man-making style challenge. Mum says she will think about it. Frankly think £145 is cheap to have James off your hands for six hours, let alone four days.

. . . .

Thursday 12

There has been more marriage-wrecking madness in St Slaughter. Granny Clegg has had her revenge for the Hammerite Cornish revolution flag. She has 'mutilated Bruce' (according to Grandpa Clegg). Thought this might be some strange celtic ritual like cock-fighting but it turns out she just got him done. Grandpa says she used underhand tactics and 'her and that commie, Chalky' dognapped him. But Granny says, *a*) he is not a commie, *b*) his name is Hilary, and *c*) it is not her fault that Grandpa was down the Farmers Arms with Denzil and Pig Gibbons eating pickled eggs and plotting to take over the world at the time. Grandpa says Hilary has brainwashed her and that a few months ago she couldn't even bear to cut Bruce's toenails in case he yelped and now she is happy to lop off his crown jewels. He has begged Mum to stage an intervention and release her from the cult. Mum says the Labour Party is not a cult and that preventing Bruce perpetuating his idiotic line any further is an act of community-minded charity. And also to stop eating pickled eggs or he will get trapped wind and have to have it manually released like in 1984. All of which are true. But am concerned that Mum is not taking the Cleggs' disharmony seriously enough. I fear Granny has climbed ladder of education and is fast moving out of realms of Grandpa's world of idiocy. She has not bought Fray Bentos for over a fortnight.

Friday 13

8.30 a.m.

Bruce has gone missing. Apparently Granny let him out for a wee during the *Today* programme and he has not been seen since. Grandpa Clegg says he has gone to search for his missing testicles. But Granny Clegg claims mysterious Friday 13th forces may have spirited him away. Which is promising, marriage-wise, as she clearly still has one foot firmly in the realms of mentalism, even if she does listen to John Humphrys.

4 p.m.

Told Sad Ed about Bruce. He says he sympathizes. He has lost its mojo and is clearly wandering through his lonely existence in search of meaning. I said I do not think Bruce thinks that deeply about anything and probably just went after one of Hester's chickens or got shut in the launderette again. But it is sad none the less.

5 p.m.

Bruce is back. He was not chasing poultry. Or getting trapped in industrial washing machine. He was on the 8.35 bus to Bodmin. Granny Clegg demanded to know why Mr Rabbet (bus driver, ferrety face, known as Bugs) had let him on without a ticket, but he said animals ride free on Badgerline. Plus he fancied the company. (Do not blame him. Usual customers make Pig and Denzil look attractive.) Apparently he got off at Somerfield, walked

towards the prison, and was in the queue for the 3.05 return. Maybe the removal of his mojo has allowed rest of brain to expand and he is now genius dog!

. . . .

Saturday 14

Bruce has shut himself in washing machine again. So is not genius. Is just weird. But on plus side, Granny and Grandpa have overcome their political differences and are reunited in relief at return of moronic dog. Mum said let that be end to it all. I hope she is right.

I wish our dog would take to getting the bus for a day out though. All its antics are not at all conducive to revision. This morning it has:

- got its head stuck in a chair,
- eaten four ludo counters and a VAT receipt,
- boil washed Mum's criminal golf jumper.

Latter was possibly act of genius though. It has worked out how to switch on washing machine so it can enjoy endless vibration. Said this to Mum but she says until it can work out the right temperature setting for wool acrylic mix it is banned from operating heavy machinery.

. . . .

Sunday 15

Father's Day

Oh my God. Have just witnessed horrifying scene. It was

James, attempting to demonstrate he is camp-ready by pooing in the back garden. Ploy has not worked. Mum has reached never-before-seen levels of anger and has banned several things including the partial removal of pants anywhere except fully-enclosed designated toilet areas. Poo has been buried under weeping pear and she is now decontaminating area with patented mix of Dettol and bicarbonate of soda. James has been sent to his room to reflect on the meaning of the word civilization. He claims Mum is missing the point and it just proves he is a man. I said I had not seen Dad pooing in the vicinity of the patio anytime recently. Or ever. Thank God.

On plus side, al fresco poo has completely overshadowed Father's Day so have totally got away with credit crunch present of bag of Fox's Glacier Mints and postcard of Nick Faldo.

Monday 16

The house is still in shock at poo incident. Even dog is giving James wide berth. Though do not know why as its displays on the pooing front are hardly civilized. Have pointed out to Mum that revision is suffering due to trauma and that she may need to be lenient when it comes to results time. She said she is not issuing any poo-related amnesties and that if I fail it will be down to my own lackadaisical attitude rather than

James's bottom. Am back in room with annotated *Macbeth*.

⋅ ⋅

Tuesday 17

James is jubilant. It is because Mum has agreed to his school trip after all. I said she should not be swayed by his Neanderthal attempts to weaken her resolve with pooing exhibitions. She says it was not the pooing exhibition, it was the letter home that said if he stayed behind he would have to spend four days being supervised by Mrs Bunnet (64, deaf, moves at pace of compromised tortoise). Mum said last year she forgot entire class on school outing to police station and went home to watch *Diagnosis Murder* and eat flapjack. (Though on plus side, Keanu now knows what it is like to spend several hours in cell.) Mum said is also last hurrah for him and Mad Harry as the appeal is due in two weeks and then they will be separated for ever. Pointed out that they will still live less than half a mile apart and can see each other at weekends. But Mum said he will be moving in higher circles once he is installed at St Gregory's Girls, and Mad Harry will get left behind with the rest of the John Major intake, with any luck. I fear she may have overestimated the appeals process and underestimated the staying power of Beastly Boys.

⋅ ⋅

Wednesday 18

Yet again I am reminded why drama was wise choice over economics. While I will be spending morning discussing excellent and non-taxing issues like Mrs Macbeth and her mentalism, Scarlet will be struggling with utterly taxing problem of tax. Ha.

4 p.m.

Although have had interesting thought which is that, while I may be having more fun, exam-wise, all the economics geeks are having fun money-wise, i.e. the credit crunch does not seem to be affecting their ability to purchase Warhammer crap. Scarlet says it is down to money management skills. Think it also possibly down to their illegal betting ring. They have made £73.50 so far this term on *a*) how old is Mrs Brain (54, not 103, as guessed by Kyle O'Grady), *b*) how many sheep pellets can human consume before being sick (276, as tested by Mark Lambert), and *c*) who will get the mouldy apple in nut dispensing machine? (Was Mr Knox in end. Was act of mercy though to put apple out of misery. It had started dripping on the dried apricots.)

Thursday 19

Hurrah, exams are over. Though am not at all sure excelled self in English. Was not due to inferior brain power. Was distracting activity in exam hall, i.e. presence of Kylies, Fat and Thin, tutting and sighing and consuming Haribo Tangfastics. Do not think am at all in agreement with written tests for BTEC hair and beauty. It is not at all accurate measure of their wet cut skills. Plus they cannot sit still for more than twenty minutes at time. Thank God the bricklayers just get corralled into their cage and timed on their concreting. Mark Lambert is still claiming he is going to transfer to BTEC nursery nursing as soon as Mr Wilmott's teen pregnancy haven, i.e. crèche i.e. former pig pen, is open. I said he could be waiting a long time. But apparently Mr Wilmott has had genius idea to extend skills and beat credit crunch by getting BTEC bricklaying to design and construct it. Mark is fully expecting it to be ready in six weeks. He is mental. Even if it does stay up for more than five minutes, will take years to remove odour of Gloucester Old Spot.

Friday 20

Today was officially the end of school for Upper Sixth and has been marked by annual ceremonious emptying of sacred talismans (i.e. crap) from lockers to make way for next year's wave of saggy sofa wannabes. There was much weeping over Blu-Tacked Green Day posters and gel pens. And this is just tip of iceberg of nostalgia fest because they will all be back for prom in three weeks. Plus there is the last day of school silly string, false fire

alarms, and sheep in places that sheep are not meant to be ritual to endure. Even I was caught up in wave of emotion sweeping over saggy sofa when Duncan Evans put vintage Busted on CD player. Scarlet says I am clinging to rose-tinted view of past like mad World War Two vets who wish Blitz was still on, and it is in fact not sad at all, but day to be embracing future, i.e. chance to lord it over likes of Tamsin Bacon once Scarlet is appointed head girl. I said it was not at all in the bag that she is going to get the job but she says it is a no-brainer. The only other potential prize-winner is Emily Reeve, who has a one year old and cracked nipples holding her back.

Scarlet agrees that head boy is impossible to call though. The maths geeks have no people skills, Reuben Tull is walking advert for rehab, and Sad Ed has no mojo, flabby upper arms, and potential to kill self halfway through term. I said Jack is hard act to follow as is charm-ing, charismatic, and connectable, e.g. brokered Middle East saggy sofa peace deal, proving credentials as future anti-war foreign secretary. Plus he has good arms and mojo. Scarlet said, 'Are you feeling all right, Riley?' Came to senses and said was just caught up in another wave of emotion due to school caretaker Lou polyfilla-ing up hole where Trevor hit head in attempt to avoid getting anti-vampire staked by Mark Lambert last Hallowe'en. Do not want Scarlet thinking want to seize her brother. But it is true about Jack setting high standard. I saw him on the way out, carrying his locker spoils to the non-sick-smelling car of the people. Is historic day, politics-wise. Like when excellently-coiffed Tony Blair left office to make way for Vosene-compromised Gordon Brown.

. . . .

Saturday 21

3 p.m.

There is no way either Sad Ed or Reuben Tull are going to be head boy. Went to see them at lunchtime and they were trying to outwit Pay and Display machine. But, on plus side, have been invited to post-exams party tonight at acropolis (i.e. giant fake Parthenon in country park, and general haunt of tedious stoners). Reuben says everyone is going to be there. I said who is everyone. He said him, Max Calloway in Year Eleven who once saw Jesus's head in his microwave (beardy religious one, not toddler uncle, and under influence of prescription painkillers, not general mentalness like Granny Clegg), and possibly Dean 'the dwarf' Denley, if his hay fever has calmed down and he hasn't passed out on Piriton. Am going. There is nothing else to do except watch James and Mad Harry doing synchronized dancing to Sugababes or listen to Mum and Dad argue about water hazards. Will ask Scarlet to come. And maybe Jack. He does not smoke but is pro-legalization of cannabis (mainly to avoid Suzy or Bob getting criminal record).

12 midnight

Have just got back from party. Was excellent. Max, Sad Ed, Jack, and Scarlet came (pollen count too high for dwarf to vacate concrete-based areas) and Reuben made us all lie on our backs and look at the stars through the roof of the acropolis and think about space and universe and life on other planets. It was best philosophy lesson ever. Am thinking of writing to Mr Knox to demand he adds a practical element to AS level. Although possibly will require protective clothing as bat pooed on Max Calloway's forehead at one point. He said was gift from gods. It was not. Anyway, then Reuben felt inspired to commune with beasts of nature and went to pester cows with Max, Scarlet, and Sad Ed, so was just there next to Jack. And stopped thinking about space and started thinking about life on earth instead and how much weirder it is. And then it just came out. I said, 'I'll miss you, when you go.' But luckily think Jack still mesmerized by space thoughts because he just said, 'What?' So asked if he had decided between Cambridge or Hull yet. He said, 'Depends.' I said, 'On what, your grades?' He said, 'No. On how far away I need to be.' But before could ask what he meant, the cows stampeded (obviously they not in agreement with Reuben about being mystical minotaurs willing to convey him to ABC Barbeque for cheesy chips) so we had to run before they fatally trampled us, which, as James frequently

points out, is cause of 0.05 per cent of deaths in UK every year.

Anyway. Is bit depressing as is utterly clear Jack is moving on and wants to leave Saffron Walden as soon as possible. We are not at all on same wavelength any more. I have missed my seizing chance. Sad Ed also very quiet on way home. Maybe he is having internal wranglings over his missing mojo. Or most likely he drank too much of Reuben's 'magic' cider and was having paranoid thoughts about the cows again.

· ·

Sunday 22
10 a.m.
Oh my God. Sad Ed has just rung with astonishing news. It is his mojo. It has finally returned. He is coming over after *Hollyoaks* omnibus to reveal details. Oooh. Maybe mojo was stirred by Reuben or Max Calloway and he is homosexualist after all! That would explain every-thing—the lack of interest in Melody, the love of Morrissey, the encyclopaedic knowledge of *Gossip Girl*. Hurrah! Have finally got gay best friend. Was worried would have to procure one at university and that supply might not meet demand as everyone will want one by then.

2 p.m.
News is even more shocking than anticipated. On

downside have not acquired gay best friend. BUT it turns out that Sad Ed's mojo was stirred by none other than other best friend Scarlet! Apparently she was so overcome by fear at Reuben astride marauding cow that she threw herself into his flabby upper arms for comfort. I asked if there was snogging. He said no, but the contact caused massive pant area upheaval. Asked how she did not notice, or is mojo in fact very small. He said is not in fact very small, but that he pretended needed a wee and then hid behind bush and thought about Aled Jones very hard. He has demanded advice. I said I was in no position to give out advice as my mojo has also been stirred by a member of Stone family, i.e. Jack. Sad Ed said that was hardly news. I said was utterly news as had confessed it to no one except him. He said it is blindingly obvious to everyone except, apparently, me. And possibly Jack. And, thank God, Scarlet, who is too busy being stirred by weedy bat boy to see what is going on under nose.

So Sad Ed happy at return of mojo but more depressed than ever as cannot use it. He says it is like being given a limited edition twelve inch of 'Sheila take a Bow' and being told cannot play it under any circumstances. Oh God, our mojos are stirred by people who are wrong wrong wrong. We are doomed to life in a Brontë novel.

3 p.m.
Or are we? Maybe we are just fighting the truth. Maybe

our mojos are more attuned than our brains and we are actually right for each other. Will ask Sad Ed tomorrow. Will not disturb him again now as he says he needs to test mojo out to full extent of capabilities and have worrying suspicion what that might involve.

. . . .

Monday 23

Have talked to Sad Ed about theory and suggested it might be good idea to seize day after all. Sad Ed says he not really seizing type but said he does not actually need to be dynamic, he just needs to be honest. Have suggested that he corners Scarlet in conducive atmosphere of free love and abandonment, i.e. Glastonbury! He pointed out that he did not get tickets after all as he was too depressed by fake wedding and thought presence of Cohen (Leonard, not Seth) might send him over edge. Said thought that was what he wanted. He said if he going to die in untimely fashion, he is not doing it in field of 100,000 sweaty campers waving glowsticks and drinking Fosters. It is undignified. Plus police would probably miss point and declare it accidental death by misadventure instead of tragic cry-for-help suicide. Said 'whatever' and there are still tickets left due to crapness of *a*) weather, and *b*) line up, so to pull himself together. He is going to ask Scarlet tomorrow. On the condition that I am also honest with Jack about my stirrings. Have agreed. Have nothing to lose.

5 p.m.
Except possibly pride, reputation, and happiness.

. . . .

Tuesday 24

Scarlet has refused to go to Glastonbury. She says any time off school at this point could seriously compromise her battle to be head girl. I said *au contraire*, her absence would only remind us all what we were missing, and common room will descend into anarchy, and then, when she returns, she can restore harmony and win hearts and minds of Mrs Leech and Mr Wilmott. She says she will think about it.

5 p.m.
Scarlet has thought about it and is still refusing to go to Glastonbury. She says she is suspicious as to *a*) Sad Ed's unprecedented proactiveness, and *b*) my motives and that maybe Sad Ed is my henchman and is whisking her away because I am hoping to be crowned head girl and will actually undermine her and spread vicious rumours about her political capabilities. Said I would rather chew tinfoil than try to keep the Um Bongo and Yazoo cushions free from cross-contamination, and that Sad Ed is just keen to mingle with other depressive music obsessives at the John Peel stage. She is thinking about it again.

Did not tell her about Sad Ed's mojo. She needs to realize how much she loves being with him first. Shock of revelation now could actually kill her.

. . . .

Wednesday 25

Hurrah. Scarlet has agreed to go to Glastonbury with Sad Ed. There are several caveats though:

1. They do not purchase civilian tickets but use Suzy and Bob's VIP ones. That way they can poo in comfort, and in proximity to superior celebrity bottoms.
2. Sad Ed sleeps in separate tent pod, does not consume any bean-based produce, and does not attempt to infiltrate Leonard Cohen's trailer and suggest campfire singalong.
3. I whip up ill feeling in common room and initiate riot in time for Scarlet's triumphant return. Possibly involving injury to Trevor that requires Scarlet's nursing skills.

We have agreed to all of them. Although Sad Ed is hoping Scarlet will not be lovingly tending Trevor's wounded wings, as will be too overwhelmed with love for Sad Ed after weekend. Asked how he was going to persuade Scarlet to seize the day and hop pods. He said he is hoping time spent together will be like epiphany and she will realize she cannot spend another minute apart from him. Did not say anything as did not want to

dishearten him so asked how he is going to persuade Mrs Thomas to let him go in first place, as she is still convinced he is going to get engaged every time he leaves house. He says he is going to tell her he is staying at mine. Which, he says, is better than prison in Mrs Thomas's eyes. It is true. Mum's regime makes HMP Pentonville look lax.

. . . .

Thursday 26

Hurrah. The potentially happy couple have left for Somerset. Bob is dropping them at railway station in sick-smelling Volvo. He and Suzy are not going this year due to potential for eel-helmet man pills to compromise adoption chances. Plus he says he is backed up at maternity clinic due to refusal of Saffron Walden to embrace new drop-in anti-sex condom clinic. He says he cannot understand why. Did not mention persistent presence of Marjory and digital camera outside door.

Signs on Sad Ed and Scarlet front not too promising as yet. Mostly due to Sad Ed's outfit of choice, i.e. enormous David Bowie T-shirt, combats, and waterproof hat. Which I know for fact is not at all mojo arousing for Scarlet. She is much more moved by bat capes and tight vegetarian leather trousers. In fact ideal man is Noel from *Mighty Boosh*, whereas Sad Ed more like fat Nabu or the gorilla. Plus they have already had three arguments over Sad Ed's food supplies, i.e. a twenty-four pack of Nik Naks, which Scarlet says is too bulky and will cause tent-pollution issues. But it is early days. And am confident that heady atmosphere of late nights, starry skies, and groundbreaking music, or if that fails, excess of hot cider, will break down tent pod divide between Sad Ed and Scarlet, and they will be united in pro-mojo love.

11 p.m.
Have just got text from Scarlet. It says TENT FALLEN DOWN. AND SAD ED FORGOTTEN SLEEPING BAG. IS MORON.

Think this is actually good news though. In their attempts to find shelter, they will be forced to share each other's body warmth and will be utterly aroused. Hurrah.

. . . .

Friday 27

Have tried and failed to whip up anarchy in common room. Everyone is too demob-happy to argue about pot noodle residue in the leaky microwave. Plus half the BTECers are on field trip to Ridgeon's Building Supplies to identify tools. Will try again on Monday when new Lower Sixth invade for induction. That is bound to get backs up. Besides, do not want to peak too early.

3 p.m.
Have had phone call from Sad Ed. Asked how things were going tent-wise. He said not brilliantly and he

spent most of last night huddled under shelter of giant Nik Nak bag. So on plus side, he has been proven right in insisting on bringing crisps. Asked where Scarlet spent night. He said he is not sure but she came back this morning to 'freshen up' and said she might see him at Kings of Leon later. I said she has probably just gone to Green Fields to be at one with Mother Earth. Sad Ed said he not so sure and possibly being at one with dirty looking VIP musician who was lurking outside tent while Scarlet changed her knickers. Asked where he was during pant change. He said inside tent. I said that was excellent news, mojo-wise. But he says it just proves she thinks of him as emasculated, despite his massive mojo, and to her he will always be one of the girls. He is too depressed to watch bands now and is going to sit inside the tent, or failing that, the Nik Nak bag, and read Sartre. He is hopeless.

5 p.m.
Have had phone call from Mrs Sad Ed worried that Sad Ed has left his trusty bedtime companion Frobisher the toy rabbit at home. Said he cannot come to phone as was helping Mum prepare nutritious Welsh cakes (i.e. pro-Aled) and that I have lent him Smithers the monkey to make up for missing Frobisher. Am brilliant liar. Which is why struggle with honesty thing. Is wasting talent.

Saturday 28

11 a.m.

No news from Glastonbury as yet. Which am taking as good sign, i.e. that Scarlet has noticed that Sad Ed has functioning man penis and is overcome with feelings and they are at this very minute sharing smelly sleeping/Nik Nak bag of love.

Wish they were here though. Am utterly bored. James and Mad Harry are practising camping in the garden. Though thankfully, are concentrating on tent construction skills, not pooing ones. Maybe Sad Ed should have had session. They have put tent up five times now and have got it down to three minutes forty-three seconds, with only a partial collapse of front awning. Will go into town for wander. Possibly in vicinity of Waitrose. Just in case Jack is doing the shopping again.

3 p.m.

Did not bump into Jack at Waitrose. He is obviously too busy plotting his great escape to Hull. Or Cambridge. Did, however, bump into Reuben Tull, literally, who was busy trying to herd all trolleys in absence of Sad Ed. Trolleys seemed to be also plotting escape as several broke loose and ploughed into back of Mr Wilmott's Vauxhall. He said they are trickier than cows. Offered to help (and thus prove my ability as potential employee) but he said it is against Health and Safety regulations to allow amateurs behind the wheels. Plus my aura might 'bring them down'. Pointed out that *a*) trolleys not alive or affected by auras, *b*) since when has he been blessed with second sight, and *c*) even if he is, he needs glasses as am completely happy. He said, 'Whatever you're telling yourself, Riley. But I see it differently. You need to follow your dream, Rach. Stop holding yourself back.' Said, 'Whatever,' and went to buy doughnut instead. He is obviously doing way too many illicit things if he thinks that trolleys are alive. Or that I am unhappy.

5 p.m.
Oh. Have had awful thought. Maybe all drugs have opened up new levels of perception and Reuben can see things beyond wit of human understanding. Because am, in fact, unhappy. Am racked with potential loss of Jack. And at my failure to seize day with him. Reuben is right (except about trolleys being alive; that is just mentalism) I must follow my dream. I must tell Jack how I feel. Yes, am inspired. Will do it tomorrow. Once have planned speech. And wardobe.

8 p.m.
And watched *Casualty*.

11 p.m.
Have called Ed to tell him about trolley-related revelation. He said Reuben is always seeing things. Some come true, e.g. Les Dennis will make a comeback; and some do

not, e.g. monkeys will rise up and conquer world with superior opposable thumbs and prehensile tails. But that he hopes mine is fulfilled. Asked if he had been fulfilled yet. He said not unless you count eating all twenty-four packets of Nik Naks and sleeping through Neil Diamond. Scarlet is still MIA. Though on plus side eel-helmet man arrested last night, so wherever she is, she is not in herbal-pill-induced coma.

. . . .

Sunday 29

1 p.m.

Is D-Day Jack-wise. Have spent hour doing 'barely there' make-up, as recommended by Grandpa Riley from this month's *New Woman*. Though is utterly tricky and would be lot quicker to do 'definitely there' claggy mascara and lipgloss. But Grandpa says men go for natural look and my hard work now will pay dividends later. He is utterly pro Jack thing. It is because he had unrequited love for relative of best friend for years and regrets never acting on impulse. Asked who it was. He said it was Bert Holmes's gran. He is weird. Anyway, am taking plunge now. Just hope he is in. And that Bob and Suzy are not. Do not want their gigantic mojos overshadowing me and Jack.

Feel sick. Is because in just few hours could be in arms of true love. Or possibly blackberry pie that ate for lunch.

263

5 p.m.

Am not in arms of anyone. Am hopeless seizing day chicken. This is what said (ish):

JACK: What are you doing here? Scarlet's at Glasters.

ME: Er. I know. I just . . . er . . . wondered if you'd heard from her. If she'd . . . um . . . said anything about . . . er. . . her and . . . er . . . Sad Ed.

JACK: No. Why? What's going on?

ME: Um. Nothing.

JACK: Riley, you are crap liar. You are totally red in face. Oh no. That is just blusher.

ME: Is not blusher as am wearing imperceptible make-up. Is actual blush. Sad Ed has found mojo. Mojo is in love with Scarlet.

JACK: Shit.

ME: Yes.

JACK: Shit.

ME: Yes.

JACK: ——

ME: Do not say 'shit' or we stuck on endless loop.

JACK: OK.

ME: Why shit? Do you think he's wrong for her?

JACK: Er. No. Not necessarily. And, anyway, does it matter?

ME: So you don't think it matters if someone is wrong for you?

JACK: No. Not if you love them.

ME: Really?

JACK: No . . . Are we still talking about Sad Ed here. Or
        is this about someone else, Rach?

ME: No. Er. Still Sad Ed.

JACK: You really need to do something about your
        blushing.

ME: Am not blushing. Is blusher. Was misadvised
        make-up-wise . . .

JACK: So, Riley, any more Frankensteins on the
        horizon? Exams are over. You can experiment
        again.

ME: Frankenstein was creator, not monster. As well
        you should know. And, like, bog off. I've given
        that up. That's not what I really want.

JACK: So what do you really want, Rach?

ME: . . .

And I could have said it then. It was begging to be said.
Like it was hovering in the air above us in neon letters
shouting, 'YOU, JACK, I WANT YOU!' But I didn't say it.
Because what if I don't have second sight like Reuben?
What if I'm just seeing living trolleys all the time and not
any truth? Or what if the truth hurts?

So I just said 'I can't tell you.' Which I know is a cop
out. But at least was honest. And he just said, 'Right.'
And then I said, 'Got to go.' And he said, 'You know
where I am.' And I said, 'Do I?' Because thought he was
speaking metaphorically. But turns out not as he said,

'Er . . . am here, Riley.' Said 'Oh.' And left. Actually. Not metaphorically.

Got home to find Mum celebrating golfing victory. She beat Dad by record twelve shots. So at least one Riley female is fulfilling her dreams.

. . . .

Monday 30
9 a.m.

Yet another day of living utter lie, i.e. that am in love with Jack Stone but am too chicken to admit it. Being honest is not at all as easy as it sounds. It is utterly fraught with rejection potential. At least he is not in school this week so can sit mournfully on saggy sofa without arousing suspicion. Will claim am just traumatized by death of CD player (irreparable after someone tried to 'play' a strawberry Pop Tart).

4 p.m.

Oh God. Have just remembered was supposed to initiate riot at school. But the thing is, even with new intake trying to stake claim on Um Bongo cushion, the common room is place of relative peace. Fat Kylie is doing good business giving minigoths purple highlights and lack of CD player means there is no argument over Take That versus T-Rex. Actually think Scarlet could be root cause of all discord. It does not matter though. She will not care. She will be happy with her higher prize, i.e. true love

266

with Sad Ed. Though have heard nothing for two days now. But think is good sign. They were probably too busy consummating relationship under canopy of canvas. Or stars, if tent has fallen down again.

6 p.m.
They were not consummating relationship under anything. In fact were not even under same canopy at all. Sad Ed says he has not seen Scarlet since Saturday morning, when she made brief appearance to commandeer her smelly sleeping bag. Asked how Sad Ed had managed to keep warm. He said he had sheltered under cocoon of Nik Nak wrappers and polystyrene noodle dishes. Said he was pathetic and had utterly missed once-in-lifetime chance to reveal true feelings. He said, 'What, so you told Jack, then?' Said no. Was not right moment. Sad Ed said am more pathetic as at least Jack in same room. Asked where Scarlet was now. Sad Ed says he does not know. She is probably on a tour bus somewhere having sex with an Arctic Monkey. He is even more depressed than ever.

8 p.m.
Scarlet is not on a tour bus having sex with an Arctic Monkey. She is at home in vile mood. It turns out that she spent entire weekend trying to find Sad Ed but that tent had weirdly disappeared so she assumed he had gone home. (Asked Sad Ed about this and he said is true, he

was sick of tent pegs falling out every time drunken liggers and C-listers tripped over them, so he just tied the tent on to a Winnebago instead. Asked whose. He said some ginger girl with weird accent. Said Kate Nash? He said possibly. Asked Scarlet about Arctic Monkey man. She said it turns out he is not an Arctic Monkey at all. He is not even in band. He is charlatan, i.e. substandard roadie (and not even for Verve but for Neil Diamond) who tried to lure her into sexually compromising position in portaloo with pair of maracas. She said she ended up sleeping on floor of caravan in Lost Vagueness with transsexual called Kitty Sometimes and her only comforting thought was that I was busy at home paving the way for her head girl glory. I said 'Yes.' Do not want to pee on her already soggy bonfire by telling her that Middle East has lasting and secure peace and that Fat Kylie might turn out to be Madeleine Albright after all.

Tuesday 1

Common room is back to full-scale war. And is all
Scarlet's fault. She has been refusing to talk to Sad Ed all
day and instead has been hurling macadamias at him
across nylon carpet. Mark Lambert got caught in crossfire
and then full-scale nut riot ensued. On plus side ceasefire
is forgotten so Scarlet is none the wiser about my failure
to initiate conflict. Plus Sad Ed says the angrier she is, the
more he loves her. So he is in unrequited love heaven.
Nut fights are not the same without Jack though. His precision with yoghurt-coated cranberries is unsurpassed.

At least James has been despatched on his camping
trip so house will be place of quiet contemplation etc. for
four days. Mum has issued him with list of no less than
twenty-four instructions including:

1. Do not drink from anything other than tamperproof bottles of Evian.
2. Do not eat wild fungi, suspicious berries, or pork
that has not been heated to 77°C for at least ten
minutes.
3. Do not attempt to become forest dwelling hermit or
Hobbit of any variety.

James is not best pleased. He says there are times when
real men have to rip up the rule book and use their wits
and whatever is lying about to survive. Mum says if he
even thinks of trying to rip up the rule book or build huts
using bits of twig and bin liners she will be up the B172

in the Fiesta faster than he can say Bear Grylls. She has instructed him to phone home every evening and has lent him Dad's mobile for this purpose. James says Scott of the Antarctic did not have a mobile phone so it is not a proper man-challenge. Mum says Scott died and if he doesn't ring she will be up the B172 in the Fiesta etc., etc. I pointed out that Mum was taking a risk and that James could use the phone to call premium rate quiz lines, far-flung relatives, or sex workers. Mum said James is not like me, and knows the value of money. This is true. He makes Scrooge look generous. Plus relatives limited to Cornwall, which, contrary to popular belief, is in same country.

· ·

Wednesday 2

4 p.m.

Went round Sad Ed's after school. We are both still in unrequited love misery. I said it was more depressing than missing mojo misery. But Sad Ed said nothing is worse than unresponsive pants. In fact he seems quite revived. He says it is because unrequited love is like air or water to a true poet and he is utterly inspired, music-wise. He has already written a song. It is called 'Ballad of the Scarlet Woman' and involves not a lot of rhyming and way too many adjectives. Plus tune is totally lifted from Nick Cave. But said was excellent as did not want to ruin his rare moment of happiness. Maybe he is right though and unrequited love good for literary types. Look at Britney. Her best work was when she was pining over Justin. Sad Ed's ballad just rubbish because he is compromised talent-wise. Will write poem immediately, inspired by Jack situation.

6 p.m.
Is harder than thought. Have got possible title, i.e. 'Stone in Love With You', which is totally appropriate. Even if is stolen from Stylistics. But trouble is every time I try to think of Jack for inspiration just get too depressed at potential loss to write. Plus disturbed by phone call from James to report back from Camp Moron. Asked him how things were going, whittling-wise. He said whittling is for amateurs and so far they have risked their lives crossing a ravine on nothing but nylon rope and adrenalin. Asked how deep was ravine. He said several feet. Said hardly life threatening. He said *au contraire*, Maggot fell off and got bitten by a rattlesnake and might be dead within hours. Said rattlesnakes do not live in Epping Forest. He said might have been slow-worm. Said slow-worms do not bite. He said might have actually just licked him then. Or looked at him funny. But was still terrifying and manly. Then Mum commandeered phone to check he is eating properly. He said he has had apple a day, as dictated by Rule 5, and had a poo, inside latrine tent (Rule 17). Mum said what about Mad Harry's Wagon Wheels. James said he had resisted temptation. He is lying. There is no way

anyone can resist the clever mallow-biscuit combination. Even though guaranteed to feel sick immediately afterwards. Then he said he had to go as they were about to build a giant campfire and sing songs around it. Mum said to wear protective clothing and stay outside a one-metre radius of flames. James said they are not actually going to set fire to campfire as is environmentally unfriendly plus against Health and Safety. Mum put phone down satisfied. Think she is warming to Nige's accident-aware attitude.

8 p.m.
Still struggling with Jack poem. Have got opening line. Which is most important, as any novelist or tragic poet will tell you. Is:
> *I'm stone in love with you*

Which is admittedly just repeat of title. But reinforces message, I think.

10 p.m.
Have given up on Jack poem. Clearly am so in love have been rendered speechless.

10.15 p.m.
Or am just rubbish poet.

10.30 p.m.
No, that is not it. Still have prize (macramé owl) won in Year Two for poem about Terry Wogan featuring brilliant

line where managed to rhyme toupe with hooray). Am excellent poet. Just that brain too compromised by confusing feelings.

. . . .

Thursday 3

9 a.m.
Sad Ed has begged me to test Scarlet waters, i.e. see if he stands chance with her. Have agreed. Though think answer at moment will be no as she has not uttered more than 'knob off' to him all week.

3 p.m.
Asked Scarlet if she was thinking of forgiving Sad Ed at any point. She said she has more important things on her mind than the idiocy of the bingo-winged one, i.e. her maiden speech as head girl. Said still got week to go before announcement. Plus Sad Ed has worked hard to eliminate the sag on upper arms. She said is hard to tell under cavernous T-shirt.

So this has good and bad elements, i.e. she is not at all annoyed about his tent-moving antics any more. But physically, he is possibly repulsive. Will only tell him first bit. And lend him Mum's fitball for extra arm exercise.

6 p.m.
James has phoned in his final camp report. Today Archie Knox (son of hairy librarian and philosophy teacher, also

hairy) got bitten by a beaver, or possibly a guinea pig, and he and Mumtaz swam across shark-infested pond to win bet. Said *a*) what did he win, *b*) Mum forbade any 'wild swimming' in Rule 22, and *c*) did not think he and Mumtaz were friends any more. He said, *a*) £1.30 and a packet of fruit pastilles, *b*) she specifically stated 'rivers or lakes', and *c*) he is hoping they will be more than that after tonight's farewell disco. God, even James is luckier in love than me. And he wears an anorak and can sing the books of the Bible off by heart. There is no justice in world.

. . . .

Friday 4

Sad Ed has a black eye. Asked if he had riled Scarlet again and got brained with a rogue brazil, but he says it is fitball injury. He was trying to do press-ups, and ball burst and he hit head on coffee table. He said I should send ball back as is possibly faulty. Have checked small print. It has weight limit. Think Sad Ed's hefty girth may have voided guarantee.

Also James is back from camp. But something is afoot. He is not at all jubilant at having fulfilled man challenge. Mum tried to despatch him into immediate bath, as smell quite overpowering, but he said he cannot even muster the energy to wash and anyway what is the point. Mum said, 'To avoid chafing, and fungal infection, as well you know.'

But James said, 'Not of soap. Of life.' He has shut himself in bedroom with dog and can clearly hear sound of Elvish being spoken (by James, dog still unable to communicate in any form).

6 p.m.
James has refused to come down for his chicken goujons. He says what is point of food. Mum was about to go into growth/energy answer but I said he is probably just tired from all healthy fresh air and will take him nutritious bed-based supper, e.g. Marmite on toast. Mum has agreed. But says he had better be up and fully washed for Shreddies in the morning as she is not having any malingering under her roof. It was bad enough when Grandpa Riley was here. I said would pass on message. And will do. Once have gleaned information from him about cause of malingering using my brilliant sympathetic 'I totally feel your pain' interview technique, as practised by Phil Schofield. I predict it is Mumtaz-related.

8 p.m.
James has confessed all. Would make excellent tabloid journalist. (Although he did not fall for 'feel your pain' line and had to offer him Graham Norton's autograph (as faked by Mark Lambert) instead.) As predicted it was Mumtaz-related. But is on gigantic Jeremy Kyle scale of rejection, i.e. not only did Mumtaz turn down his advances, but she has spurned him for another, i.e. Mad

277

Harry. James said it was utter tragedy. Especially when he had to watch them slow dance to 'In the Gloaming' in front of the latrine tent (he was peeping through flap at time, trying to fulfil Mum's strict poo instructions). I said it is hard when love is over before it even began. James says it is not just love. It is career. Said what career. He said Beastly Boys. He said he cannot possibly be expected to go on world tours with his love rival.

He is right. It is tragic. In an eleven-year-old deluded pop star kind of way, i.e not at all. Whereas me and Jack is on *Tess of D'Urbervilles* scale.

Saturday 5

The pop world has been shattered by devastating news. Beastly Boys have definitely split up. Plus James also has black eye. But is not fitball-related. He went round Mad Harry's this morning to give him one last chance, and said he had to choose between Mumtaz and stardom. Harry chose Mumtaz. James says he is throwing away his dreams for a cheap kiss. Harry said Mumtaz is his dream, and she is not cheap, she does not even eat own brand baked beans. And then he hit James with a stormtrooper. James said black eye is a badge of his commitment to higher art and he wears it with pride. Mum said it is a sign of being common and has sent him to his room with a tube of concealer.

On plus side, bumped into interesting person in town,

i.e former meat mincer, future rock star, and ex-boyfriend Justin Statham. Was in Waitrose car park with Reuben and Sad Ed when saw his unmistakable blond hair wafting in sunlight. Was like halo of an angel. Possibly. Anyway, he came over and said the Braintree lot (i.e. rock foundation, art foundation, and other made-up courses) are having a farewell party up at the acropolis next Friday and we are totally invited. Said will be at prom but might come over after. He said, 'Nice one, Ray.' Which he has never called me before, despite me spending several months trying to instigate it! Then he ambled off like Archangel Gabriel in Nirvana T-shirt towards the tinned fish aisle.

But not everyone so happy at encounter. Reuben said, 'I don't like his vibes, man.' I said, 'You think trolleys are sentient beings, so what would you know.' Sad Ed said, 'Don't even think about it, Rach.' I said I am not. My interest in Justin is utterly non-mojo-related and attendance at party would be purely platonic nostalgia sort of thing. And it would. I am so over Justin. My heart is Jack's.

9 p.m.
Although Jack possibly doesn't want it. And Justin does owe me a snog.

. . . .

Sunday 6
No, am definitely not going to snog Justin. Jack called today to check I am going to prom. Though was not

actually asking me to be date to prom. Which think he should have made clearer at start, i.e. I said, 'I would love to go.' He said, 'Er . . . I'm in the band so I'm going to be sound checking. I can't pick you up or anything. Sorry. I was just wondering if you were going already.' Said I had considered it (was backtracking and playing hard to get, which is hard to do at same time). He said, 'Good. I've got something I want to show you.'

Hurrah. It is my portrait.

7 p.m.
At least think it is. Could feasibly be mojo.

7.30 p.m.
No, Jack is not like that. Is either portrait, or he has finally conquered the Jon Bonham twenty-minute drum solo thing.

7.45 p.m.
Though is shame about mojo.

. . . .

Monday 7
9 a.m.
There has been another body blow to James. He has lost his appeal for a place at St Gregory's Girls. The letter arrived this morning. James says is final nail in coffin of his hopeless life and begged Mum to let him stay off school as he cannot bear to see Harry basking in

happiness when he is so unbasky. Mum told him to belt up and take the dog for a wee. Said she was being oddly calm in face of rejection. She says school is making mistake, as his SATs results will show. Then they will come crawling back to her begging to send James to their hallowed halls. Said hope this is case. Although halls at St Gregory's Girls not that hallowed. They let Thin Kylie in for a month until she refused to wear regulation pants, sexually provoked the caretaker, and threatened Sister Ignatia with a gel pen.

5 p.m.
Like lightning, or rather, unlike lightning, tragedy has struck Riley household twice in one day. Although is actually Cleggs that has hit so technically is only once. But repercussions have made way to 24 Summerdale Road, so think it counts. Anyway, point is, the Belleview/Pasty Manor Bruce amnesty is over. Granny has finally thrown Grandpa out for his persistent racist/sexist/idiotic tendencies. Dad said he was amazed it had taken this long, but Mum commandeered phone and demanded to know what was straw that broke camel's back. Apparently it is Trelawney's Army, aka Grandpa, Denzil, and Pig Gibbons. They have been arrested for trying to overturn seat of power, i.e. Julia Goldsworthy MP (Lib Dem, Falmouth and Camborne). Mum asked if they have been charged but Granny said no because their weapons were water pistol and cake spatula. Police have

suggested psychiatric care instead. Mum said that is good suggestion and he should remain at home during assessment. But Granny says she cannot harbour a criminal any longer and he is staying at Denzil's. Mum said, 'Until he comes to his senses?' Dad said he wouldn't hold his breath on that one. But apparently that is not it anyway. Granny said her mind is made up and she is determined to stick to her guns (or spatulas), even if it means being a single mum struggling on benefits. Mum pointed out that her children were middle-aged and financially independent. But Granny said Auntie Joyless borrowed a fiver off her last week for a box of fish fingers and a loaf of Nimble and anyway it is symbolic. Mum said she is not worried. Granny will get bored, or will need someone to prise the lid off the Fray Bentos, and Grandpa will be back on the broken Parker Knoll by the end of the week.

Tuesday 8

Grandpa Clegg has rung. He is not full of remorse, as predicted by Mum. Instead, was to moan about conditions at Denzil's. He is sleeping on a chair in the kitchen, and ate jar of beetroot for dinner last night. Mum told him to swallow pride (instead of pickles) and say sorry to Granny and then he can move back. But Grandpa says the only way he is moving back to Pasty Manor is if Granny moves out. That will never happen. Granny is like Hammerite. Immovable.

Wednesday 9

There has been movement in St Slaughter situation. It is Grandpa. He says he cannot be expected to cope with conditions at Denzil's any more (the floor is so sticky he actually got stranded last night and had to be heaved to safety by Pig). Instead he is back on the broken Parker Knoll with the *Daily Mail* and a cup of Ovaltine. BUT it is not with permission of Granny, is in breach of her demands and she is going mental with rage. Grandpa says he is man of Pasty Manor and, if Granny does not like it, then she can leave. But Granny says she is steadfast in her determination to remain at Herbert House and has God and Hilary on her side. James suggested that offspring should decide who can stay, like in custody battle. And in absence of resident minors, it should be Bruce. Mum said there is no way she is leaving fate of her parents to that moron. He has gone missing five times since his testicles were removed plus he drinks Harpic. She says instead, Granny and Grandpa are going to have to find a way to live with each other's foibles. Like she and Dad have. Dad said that was unfair as he has never brandished a kitchen implement at an MP, or Hammerited his face. But Mum raised the ugly spectre of the morris dancing hoo-ha so Dad went off to strim the lawn before his ego could be battered any further.

Thank God it is head girl announcement tomorrow to take mind off idiotic family. Also because Scarlet is becoming unbearable in her zeal to follow in Jack's footsteps and lead the masses. Or the common room at least. So far this week she has initiated a hockey field sheep-poo pick, a common room carpet shampoo (carpet now frightening royal blue colour, causing eye damage threat to stoners, who need to wear sunglasses at all times) and a wipe down of leaky microwave. Plus she has tried to woo Mrs Leech's vote by giving her some Nigella recipe Florentines. This could backfire though. Not because Mrs Leech is not open to bribery (she is) but she has simpler biscuit tastes, i.e. Malted Milks and Jammie Dodgers. She thinks Florentines are too bitty. On plus side, campaign has brought Sad Ed and Scarlet closer. He has undergone an utter transformation and is her willing slave in all matters. It is amazing. Normally he barely heaves his mass off Um Bongo cushion unless it is to use toilet facility (and even then he has been known to withhold wee for up to an hour to avoid effort). But now his mojo is revived he cannot jump to her assistance fast enough. And as bonus is losing weight! Arms of T-shirts are no longer threat to circulation.

Thursday 10
A political travesty has occurred. Scarlet has not been appointed head girl. Unbelievably, it is Thin Kylie! Mr Wilmott said he has decided to go for Northern Ireland style power sharing, i.e. one BTECer and one A leveller.

Kylie must be Martin McGuinness, i.e. possibly evil, definitely controversial, but weirdly respected amongst her peers (i.e the Criminals and Retards). BUT, in another shock move, Ian Paisley is Sad Ed (i.e. grumpy and fat). Mr Wilmott says he has shown a new side recently, i.e. involving himself in all recent common room changes. Yes, plus he is always giving Mrs Leech his gypsy creams. Scarlet is outraged. She says he only got the job thanks to her efforts. But that she has been passed over for the less controversial candidate, and it is like Tony and Gordon at Granita all over again. But, in cunning diplomatic manoeuvre, I said in fact was excellent, as Sad Ed is clueless and will rely on her for all guidance. So she can still do what she wants, and take glory when things are good and blame it on stooge when goes badly. She will be puppetmaster, pulling strings, and he will be mere marionette. She is now excited by idea and is going to use him to introduce her controversial compulsory vegetarian footwear next term.

Sad Ed was not too happy about it either as he does not embrace responsibility of any kind. But said, *a*) he gets to spend more time with Scarlet, and *b*) there are biscuit privileges, i.e. he gets key to Mrs Leech's store cupboard, home of the Jaffa Cake. Hurrah. Am like Alastair Campbell, greasing the wheels of power, or whatever it was that he did.

Walked home with Martin McGuinness, aka Thin Kylie, in spirit of cross-party co-operation. Asked what her first act as head girl would be. She said she is going to do Mark Lambert in the language lab tomorrow night. Said that was more information than was looking for.

. . . .

Friday 11

5 p.m.

Hurrah. Is prom in less than two hours. And official anointment of Thin Kylie and Sad Ed as lords of the saggy sofa, i.e. head boy and girl. Plus is Jack Stone Five farewell gig. And official unveiling of portrait of me, Rachel Riley, muse and general artistic type person. Am wearing best woman dress. Was going to wear Jack's Led Zeppelin T-shirt and cat-hair-covered socks, so that am instantly recognizable as subject of painting, but dog has chewed several sections of T-shirt so it just reads 'Le Z', which think will overexcite BTECers. Think aura of muse will shine through anyway.

Also, have made momentous decision. Am going to tell Jack tonight that am actually, in fact, in love with him. Prom is utterly a seizing day sort of moment. Just need to find courage this time. Will maybe have little drink of Mum's cooking sherry. James says is not proper alcohol drink for men. Is for ladies. Like Listerine Softmint. Plus has been open for month so probably lost most of potency.

6 p.m.
Sherry definitely lost potency. Have drunk half of bottle and do not feel any different.

Oooh. Is door. Will be Sad Ed and Scarlet in limousine, i.e. sick-smelling Volvo. Hurrah. Tonight am just run-of-mill Essex sixth former, with a poor record on snogging. But tomorrow will wake up as famous muse, in arms of renegade artist, drum genius, and lover, Jack.

· ·

Saturday 12
9 a.m.
Feel sick. And am not sure where am. Will shut eyes and try again in hour.

10 a.m.
Oh God still do not know where am. Perhaps am in bedroom of Jack. Except walls not black. Are magnolia. Will shut eyes again and try to remember.

10.30 a.m.
Is definitely not Jack's room. Oh God. Maybe is Justin's room.

10.45 a.m.
Oh. Is my room. Was just upside down. James has just come in with patented hangover cure breakfast of Marmitey eggs on toast. Said in fact do not have hangover. As

287

was not drunk. James said if was not drunk, then why did wake him up at two in morning singing 'Back for Good'. Do not remember that. But think maybe was little bit drunk. Asked where Mum was. James said she is at driving range, practising her chip shot, but that I can expect full punishment on her return later.

11.30 a.m.
Oh God. Have remembered stuff. Is not good. Is not at all as planned. Is coming back in flashes, e.g:
- Tripping over Dean Denley during coronation and impaling head on Thin Kylie's tiara;
- Reuben Tull giving me 'something for headache';
- me going to look at Jack portrait and it not being beautiful Pre-Raphaelite thing but hideous wonky woman;
- me telling Reuben Tull he prescient genius and was going to seize day and follow dream;
- me staggering to acropolis and seizing day by flinging self on Justin;
- me and Justin going back to his house and taking some, possibly all, clothes off;
- Justin saying, hang on minute, Riley, am having whitey, think need to be sick;
- me coming home and finishing off Jack poem.

Oooh. Maybe have written work of genius in state of trauma. Where is poem? Oh, is here under pants. Says:

Ten Things I Hate About You. Oooh. Is like in film. Am Julia
Stiles repressed but weirdly attractive type.
1. You are shite at drums even dwarf thinks so;
2. Justin has much better nipples;
3. You are complete knob;
4. Can't think of any more but is enough anyway.

Oh. Maybe not like in film. Is not very good really at all.
Am not weirdly attractive. Just weird.
  Oh God. Is all mess.
1. Jack does not love me but sees me as ugly witch
   woman and only good for painting in freak show
   kind of way;
2. Have only narrowly avoided having sex with Mr
   Small Nipples because he so repulsed by naked self
   that he actually sick;
3. I have subconscious nipple issues;
4. Am completely pants at poetry of any kind.

Only plus side is that at least did not humiliate self and
tell Jack I love him.

12 noon
Oh God. Have just remembered something else. Need to
check phone.

12.15 p.m.
Oh, is bad. Think may have told Jack love him after all.

According to phone, drunk dialled him at 10 p.m., i.e. on way to acropolis. Do not remember talking to him though. Maybe he not there so hung up.

12.30 p.m.
No. Do remember shouting into phone. Must have left message. Is not good at all. Oh. Is doorbell. Is probably Sad Ed. Thank God. Need friendly face in time of trauma.

12.35 p.m.
Oh God. Is not Sad Ed. Is Jack! James has conveyed message that he is on John Lewis sofa and is demanding talks. Have told James to tell him am dead. Or at least have leprosy.

12.40 p.m.
James says Jack says it is important and he needs to see me. Plus has large parcel. Asked what shape parcel. He said rectangular, inch thick. Possibly jigsaw of historic building, or large board game like Pictionary or Buckeroo. Have said to bring parcel up. But leave Jack downstairs if at all possible.

12.45 p.m.
Parcel is not jigsaw of Buckingham Palace. Or Buckeroo. It is portrait. Of me. But is not same one as last night, i.e. this one is not wonky. Is pretty. Beautiful even. Think

290

may need to talk to Jack after all. Oh, can hear steps again. Is James. Will send him down to tell Jack to come back tomorrow when do not look like witch. Or smell of Justin.

3 p.m.

Was not James. Was Jack. And he is still here. And think am possibly going to burst with day seizing and honesty issues. But need to write this down now as is historic. And want to remember for the rest of life!

So Jack came in. He said, 'You look peaky, Riley.' Said, 'Yes, have possibly leprosy.' He said, 'No, you do not.' Said, 'No do not. Is true,' (i.e being honest). He said, 'What do you think then?' I said, 'Of what? Third world debt? The Barnett formula?' i.e. was witty even in face of supreme humiliation. He said, 'No, Rach. The picture.' I said is very nice. Is just shame he did not think to put that one in exhibition last night. He said, 'Are you still drunk?' Said, 'No do not think so.' He said, 'Is same one.' Said, 'Where is giant nose and eyes like Miss Beadle (bulgy, like Joey in *Friends* or rabbit with myxomatosis).' Jack said is possible sight was affected by mushrooms. Said did not have mushrooms for tea. Had ham omelette. He said not Waitrose ones, Reuben Tull ones that I ingested at gig. Said thought was aspirin. In herbally liquid form. Jack said was not. Was mild hallucinogen. Said, 'Shit.' He said, 'Yes.' Said am not getting in that endless cycle again. He said, 'Good.' Said, 'So am not hideous ugly freak then.'

He said, 'No. Can't believe you would think that's how I saw you.' Said was how saw self sometimes. He said am blind. Or mad. Said very possibly. Then was pause for long time like in films where you can hear clock ticking etc. but could not hear clock, only James singing 'Bleeding Love'. Then Jack said, 'So was it true what you said on phone last night.' I said, 'Maybe.' He said, 'Well either it was or wasn't.' I said, 'I understand semantics of possibility. Just that do not remember what actually said.' He said, 'Was something like, "You are total bastard, Jack Stone, and cannot believe thought liked you in pants-based way. Hope penis falls off. Oh shit, who put drain there?"' Said, 'Yes is true. Look still have bruise.' Jack said, 'Not bloody drain, Rach. The liking bit.'

And could have said no was all drunken/mushroom-based lie. Except that did not want to. Wanted to tell truth. So said, 'Yes, thought—no, think—am in like with you. So is all true. Oh. Except bit about penis falling off. That not nice. And you being bastard. You are not bastard.' He said, 'Really?' Said, 'No. You are like the coolest person I've ever met and you don't even have to try.' He said, 'I try really hard actually.' Then I said, 'So does sun shine out of ass?' And he said, 'Yes sun definitely shines out of ass.' And then was about to do more brilliant and relevant *Juno* quoting but could not. Because mouth was too busy. Being kissed!

And was utterly best mojo-moving kiss of life. Even had twinkly sounds and head spinning. Although that

292

could be after-effects of mushrooms. Anyway, it doesn't matter. Because I love Jack. And think he loves me. And is all because we have seized day and been utterly honest.

Well, mostly. Have not told him about almost doing it with Justin. But only because there is no point. Is so over. Jack is only one I care about.

Plus he will never find out. Is secret that will take to grave.

Or possibly reveal in biopic, with Summer out of *The OC* playing me.

No. As knowing my luck would probably end up with bloaty one out of *EastEnders* anyway. Will keep secret. Jack will never know he was second in snogging queue again. And now am going to do more. Snogging I mean. Before Mum gets back and grounds me for ever.

Is funny how things turn out. Maybe luck is about to change after all. And from now on will have utterly brilliant life. Just like in books.

Is about time, after all.

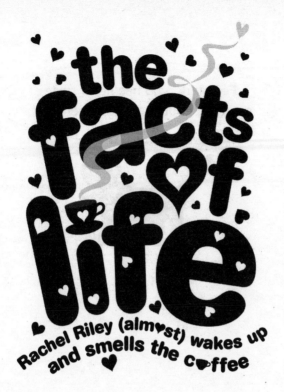

the facts of life

Rachel Riley (almost) wakes up and smells the coffee

CORNISH
FLAG

Sunday 13

4 p.m.

OMG. Am actually weak at knees. In fact think may need to lie down for a bit. Is unprecedented. Is utter revelation. Am happy! Not just 'thank God it is chocolate sponge instead of povvy yoghurt for pudding' happy, but when Baby does the lift at the end of *Dirty Dancing* happy. Or when James got a laminator for his birthday happy. Oh. Am actually going to have to lie down as think may swoon, Jane Austen-like, in my delirium.

4.30 p.m.

OK. Am temporarily unswooned and can confirm that am in love with Jack Stone. Oh, even writing his name makes me feel breathless and dizzy. Although that could be dog, who has eaten Glade Plug-In and is emitting over-powering scent of hyacinth every three minutes. Or possibly low blood sugar as have used up all joules of energy snogging. Will stop for bit again.

4.50 p.m.

Have had replenishing Marmite on toast. But only one slice. As am in love, cannot eat properly, it is well-documented fact. But is enough to be able to write coherently, if only for brief moment. Am likely to hit wall of pain any minute, i.e. start pining and panicking as have not seen him for more than an hour.

Cannot believe I feel like this. Have been utter fool.

True love has been staring me in face for years but was blinded by shiny but hollow bauble, i.e. Justin Statham and his halo of blond hair, small nipples, and ability to play 'Stairway to Heaven' on guitar. These trappings are meaningless to me now. Jack is my true destiny. He is my Paulie and I am his Juno. Except not pregnant and with better dress sense. We are inseparable. Or at least we would be if he hadn't had to go home for Sunday lunch (at 4 p.m. in Stone household due to various issues involving tantric yoga classes, biorhythms, and scheduling on T4). But I will see him again tomorrow after school. Point is, we are soul mates, i.e. we like all the same things, for example The Doors and Waitrose hummus. Plus I can tell him anything. Like the time I ate sheep poo because I thought it was a Malteser. Or when I got my hand stuck down a drain trying to reach a Sylvanian something.

Except fact that am actually in love with him. Am going to build up to that. As *a*) do not want to appear like overkeen stalker type; *b*) am waiting for him to say it first, and *c*) declaration needs romantic setting, e.g. sunset, or beach, or balcony in unspoilt peasant village, i.e. not John-Lewis-decorated bedroom contaminated with odour of hyacinth-scented dog and within earshot of eleven year old singing 'Nessun Dorma'. Which is obviously why Jack has not told me yet either.

Also have not told him what actually happened on the night of prom, obviously. He did ask me where I went

300

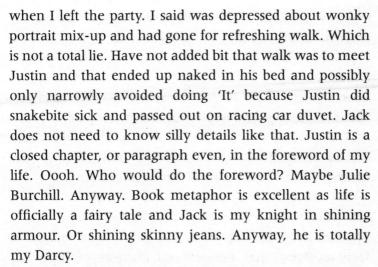

when I left the party. I said was depressed about wonky portrait mix-up and had gone for refreshing walk. Which is not a total lie. Have not added bit that walk was to meet Justin and that ended up naked in his bed and possibly only narrowly avoided doing 'It' because Justin did snakebite sick and passed out on racing car duvet. Jack does not need to know silly details like that. Justin is a closed chapter, or paragraph even, in the foreword of my life. Oooh. Who would do the foreword? Maybe Julie Burchill. Anyway. Book metaphor is excellent as life is officially a fairy tale and Jack is my knight in shining armour. Or shining skinny jeans. Anyway, he is totally my Darcy.

This is it. This is my happy ever after. I just know it.

Ooh, doorbell. Maybe that is him. He cannot bear to be apart from me and has sacrificed his nut roast in order to gaze once more on my features.

5.30 p.m.
Was not Jack. Was Sad Ed, who has already eaten (two helpings) and is engulfed in gloom, as usual. It is because his mojo has decided to fall in love with our best friend and Jack's sister Scarlet, who is oblivious to Sad Ed's (admittedly not many) charms and is still pining after bat boy Trevor. I said surely my happiness could lift the veil of tears that is strapped permanently to his head but he said, *au contraire*, it is nauseating, and if I want to help I can tell Scarlet asap about me and Jack, and then she

might be inspired to reassess her friends, i.e. Sad Ed, for potential boyfriend material. I said would think about it.

6 p.m.
Have thought about it. Am not going to tell Scarlet yet. She is just too judgemental. And sometimes plain mental.

Mum is also in a bad mood. Do not know why. She should be delighted about me and Jack. He is clean, brainy and has never worn a Kappa tracksuit.

6.30 p.m.
Apparently Mum's misery is not in any way related to Jack, as James has pointed out, as part of his well-practised 'the world does not revolve around you' lecture. It turns out that was in such bubble of bliss that have made grave error in judgement and forgotten that today is Mum's birthday. That is why I only got one roast potato at lunchtime and the soggy Yorkshire pudding.

7 p.m.
Have solved birthday dilemma and given Mum Jack's portrait of me as present. And pointed out that this was yet further evidence of Jack being such excellent boyfriend as he has painted picture that can adorn her walls and remind her of me for ever. Mum said 'hmm'. And Dad said, 'Why would a picture of Princess Margaret remind her of you?' There is no pleasing some people. It is because they have forgotten what it is like to be

302

consumed with passion. Or possibly never knew in first place. Cannot imagine habitual vest-wearers Janet and Colin in heated clinch. Or rather do not want to imagine it. Ick.

Nothing can dampen my good mood though. Jack's portrait has saved me from domestic abuse. It is like magic talisman. Will text him to tell him that.

7.30 p.m.
And to tell him that had four fishfingers and peas for tea.

11 p.m.
James has just been in to demand an end to texting. He has counted no less than sixty-three beeps in five hours and has calculated that so far today my love has cost £7.56 plus several pence in battery recharging electricity. He is right. I do not need to text Jack. We are so in tune I will send my thought-waves out of window and he will telepathically know what I am saying.

11.45 p.m.
Just got text from Jack checking am still alive as had not replied to previous text. Think thoughts ensnared on Clive and Marjory's leylandii. Have texted back. But is last one of night.

12.05 a.m.
Is new day. So can text again. Have sent him message to say cannot sleep.

1.30 a.m.
No reply. Maybe he is dead. Maybe should ring and check. Yes will do that.

1.45 a.m.
He not dead. He asleep. Or rather was. Will do same. So can meet in our dreams. Plus James has confiscated phone.

. . . .

Monday 14
8 a.m.
Am still in utter bubble of bliss. Love, as effete Tory Bryan Ferry says, is the drug. Mum did ask if 'crack marijuana' was in fact the drug due to my uncharacteristic perpetual smile and fact that did not get minty with dog when it coughed on my Shreddies. She is still in bad mood about temporarily overlooked birthday yesterday. I said inconsequential matters such as dog spit and birthdays are of no interest to me since I now operate on a higher plain. Which made her suspicious again. So pointed out higher plain was love, and that I do not need artificial stimulants as Jack is more than enough. But mention of stimulation and Jack in one sentence made her eyes perceptibly bulge and lips go thin so left house before either she or James could launch into anti-teenage pregnancy sex lecture. James is very much anti-sex. And love. It is because he is still reeling from the devastating union (in pathetic

eleven-year-old sense) of Mad Harry and Mumtaz. Though am not sure if he is more distressed at Mumtaz's choice, or at the demise of Beastly Boys and untimely end of his boy band dream. He says only the dog understands him. Which is possibly true.

4 p.m.
The saggy sofa is just not the same without Jack. I cannot believe his buttocks have graced Yazoo-stained cushion for the last time (except for annual last day silly string/release the sheep ritual). I miss him. I miss the sweet sound of his voice shouting at Fat Kylie to stop microwaving Wagon Wheels. I miss the thud, click of his boots with the drawing pin in the toe chasing rogue Retards and Criminals along B Corridor. John Major High is an empty shell without him. Yet just a few weeks ago I barely noticed him among the crowd of pasty faces and Arctic Monkey hairdos. Oh, it is utterly poetic.

Plus his head boy replacement, i.e. Sad Ed, is clearly not up to the job. He is too busy being consumed with lust over his self-appointed Chief of Staff/Director of Communications aka Scarlet to enforce any kind of control. Scarlet, *au contraire*, is consumed only by power. She has already been to see ineffectual headmaster Mr Wilmott three times to demand *a*) a ban on Dolphin-unfriendly tuna in the canteen, *b*) a ban on pupil-unfriendly Mrs Brain in the canteen, and *c*) an overhaul of the fruit and nut dispensing machine as there is a

packet of dried figs in there that is potential chemical weapon. He says they will not be able to implement any changes until September, and possibly never in the case of Mrs Brain. Scarlet is unperturbed and says it will give her time to draw up a manifesto for lasting change. Asked what I got to do in the new regime. She says I can be Peter Mandelson. Normally would be utterly peeved at weird-voiced and potentially evil role but luckily am too busy being in love. Am going round to Jack's house now. Ostensibly to visit Scarlet in her war room (aka the den), but mostly to gaze at Jack.

9 p.m.
Have done several hours of gazing, four minutes, thirty-three seconds of snogging when Scarlet went to the toilet, and some minor under table footsie while she comforted Suzy over birth of Jolie-Pitt twins (Suzy boiling with jealousy at vast and multicultural family when her own ovaries are withering on vine). Jack said maybe we should reveal our new relationship to cheer her up but I said this was further proof why we cannot, as our young and potentially fruitful union might push Suzy even further over the edge. Plus think having secret love is utterly literary. Is like *Romeo and Juliet*. Our families are from opposite sides of the tracks, well, Debden Road anyway, and might fight to keep us apart. Jack pointed out that my mum already knows what is going on and has not forbidden anything except closing of the bedroom door at

any time so that she can see into every crevice to make sure we are not doing 'It'. But I said she is only not declaring war yet because she is gloating in her superior position of knowing something before Suzy. Jack rolled eyes, but luckily at that point Scarlet came in to demand my immediate repatriation to presidential headquarters to take tea orders.

In contrast, Mumtaz and Mad Harry's love is very much not secret. Apparently they were all over each other on the St Regina's junior log (official territory of Years Five and Six) in first break. James says it is disgusting and he is minded to inform Mr Mumtaz who is not a fan of snogging, or Mad Harry. The only reason he is holding his tongue is because he gets his SATs results tomorrow and is confidently expecting them to be so high that he will be instantly admitted to Eton, and thus avoid having to go to substandard John Major High, which not only has a broken locust tank and unhygienic toilet facilities, but is where the Mumtaz and Mad Harry love nest will be ensconced come September. He is heading for certain disappointment.

· ·

Tuesday 15

As predicted, James's SATs results have not magically opened the doors of Eton, Rugby, or Hogwart's. In fact, according to official statistics, he is utterly not as boffiny as everyone thought. Mum says it is the influence of

deadly Keanu O'Grady who is ruining not only his own life, with his endless consumption of Peperami and Capri-Sun, but the lives of those around him. James says it is not Keanu, it is that no exam can do justice to his unique intellect, and is begging to be sent to private school. Dad says we cannot afford it in these austerity times and we are all going to have to make sacrifices in the harsh months ahead. I asked what his were. He says he has been using the same golf balls now for several months.

I suggested we could move to Hull, i.e. potential new home of Jack and utterly cheap, according to Phil and Kirstie. But Mum says she would rather move to the Whiteshot Estate than north of Watford, i.e. not at all. James says there is nothing else for it then, and is demanding to be home-schooled. He has clearly had some kind of emotional breakdown. I can think of nothing worse than being trapped in the dining room with Mum for seven hours a day while she bangs on about osmosis.

- -

Wednesday 16
10 p.m.
The home schooling dream is over. Mum says if the credit crunch continues, then come September she will not be available for tuition as she will be looking for a job. It is because she is worried we will be forced to shop at Lidl or give up Cillit Bang for own-brand substandard cleaner.

James warned her that we will become latchkey children, and get obese on microwave meals and that the house will go downhill and we will be festering in discarded Pot Noodle cartons and Mars bar wrappers within weeks. Which sounded excellently tragic. But Mum has put paid to any dreams of Dickensian squalor. She says she will only work part-time and we will continue to consume a balanced diet including liver once a week and oily fish on Tuesdays.

Also Granny Clegg has rung. Apparently Grandpa Clegg is up in arms about the curfew in Redruth, i.e. all menacing local youths have to be inside their houses by nine p.m. He says it is anti-Cornish and wants it imposed on anyone who eats olives, wears coloured wellies, or drives a 4X4, regardless of age. Granny says he is showing no signs of giving up his allegiance to the Cornish Liberation Army and that she does not know how much longer she can take it. This morning he claimed his blood ran black like the Cornish flag, and said if he ever needs a tranfusion, it has to be from someone born within the county boundaries. Granny is now sleeping in the spare room with Bruce. Said did that not compromise 'relations'? She said they hadn't had 'relations' since Boris Becker won Wimbledon in 1985 (no idea) so there is no change there. Plus Bruce does not sing mining songs and his breath is less deadly.

It is utterly sad. Jack and I will never end up like that, i.e. locked in political conflict. Or wearing elasticated

trousers. We will be at one for eternity. Even though he is at band practice, I feel utterly connected to him. In fact, can feel him telling me to call.

10.15 p.m.
Think maybe he was just telling me NOT to call him. So just marginal error. He had left mobile at home and Scarlet answered and demanded to know why was ringing him 'out of hours'. Said *a*) needed political advice relating to inbred Cornish relatives, and *b*) did not know Jack had official office hours. She said *a*) to tell Granny Clegg to embrace life and possibly join match.com to find a like-minded pensioner who does not think the Health Secretary is someone who types up prescriptions; and *b*) after ten is reserved for head girl (i.e. smelly Oona) business, band business, or girlfriend business, and I am none of the above. Said will bear that in mind in future. There is no way am telling Granny Clegg about match.com though. She has had a hip replacement. Plus am still holding out hope for a Clegg reunion. She may have forsaken her racist and generally moronic tendencies for newfound left-wing feminism, but she still thinks *Doc Martin* is real so all is not lost.

. . . .

Thursday 17
There has been another relationship breakdown. Wonky-jawed Welsh Lib Dem Lembit Opik has been dumped by

the Cheeky Girl. It was obviously not true love. He should have stuck to his own kind, i.e. the wide-mouthed weather woman, also from Wales and also habitual shopper in Marks & Spencer's 'sensible' department, instead of being seduced by hot pants and exotic Transylvanian accent. James says it is utterly like his own situation, i.e. Mumtaz has been swayed by Mad Harry's bottom and has ignored James's superior intellect and interest in chess. Although he is visibly less despondent today. It is because Keanu has taken James's side and has banished Mad Harry from the gang. I said it was an empty gesture as in a week neither of them will be in the gang anyway as they are leaving St Regina's and Keanu will have to recruit a whole new set of idiotic minions. James says, *au contraire*, it is replete with symbolism, as it means he will enjoy the protection of the O'Gradys at John Major High. Said O'Gradys are not the mafia, they are just over-large family of helmet-headed mentalists. And that includes the girls. James said exactly.

Friday 18

Scarlet is getting more suspicious of me and Jack. It is because had to offer apologies for non-attendance at saggy sofa summit this lunchtime (to discuss potential ban on kettle on environmental grounds, i.e. it is giving off odd fumes since I tried to heat milk up in it for Ready Brek) because was meeting Jack for romantic walk down

Battleditch Lane (aka snoggers paradise aka dogshit alley). Obviously did not say was going for romantic walk, said was going to help head boy round up escaped lower school snoggees. Luckily Sad Ed came to rescue by saying he had a few things he needed to run by her in private. Do not think he meant strategy though. He is still hoping she will suddenly develop interest in his pants area. Thank God she is out tomorrow (on PA duty for Suzy, attending lubricant convention in Ipswich ('Sliding into the Future')). Which means Jack and I can spend entire day enjoying secret love. It is utter serendipity (new favourite word) that we do not have Saturday jobs any more. We do not need money—we can live on love alone. Think Mr Goldstein (hunchback, Fiat Multipla, proprietor of lentil-smelling wholefood outlet Nuts In May) must have known this when he sacked me.

. . . .

Saturday 19

10 a.m.

Hurrah. A day of love beckons. Am glad to be alive. Unlike Sad Ed, who has already texted to say he has only been herding trolleys for half an hour and is already suicidal and if he does not unite with Scarlet soon he will have to revive untimely death plans. Asked him how fellow herder Reuben Tull was, i.e. was he not cheered up by his seemingly endless ponderings on whether God is a

dog-headed lizard with lasers for eyes? But apparently
Reuben has other withdrawal symptoms (crop failure,
and not the wheat kind) and is 'on a total downer, man'.
As is Scarlet. Though is not drug- or Sad Ed-related. It is
because she is stuck in traffic on the A14 and Suzy is
insisting on playing her hypnotic anti-smoking CD, which
is not at all conducive to driving. Or giving up smoking,
as Suzy has been listening to it for three years and still has
a packet of Silk Cut permanently stuck down her bra.
Told her to call Sad Ed, as will be busy for rest of day. She
said 'doing what?' Said charity work. Is not complete lie.
Is utterly kind to Jack to snog him. And anyway, lie is for
good cause. Is essential she does not find out. Or secret
love will just be normal run-of-mill love. Which is not at
all literary or tragic. Will be OK. Convention does not fin-
ish until five and traffic clearly awful, so she will not be
back until six at earliest. If leave by half five she will be
utterly in dark still.

5.45 p.m.
It is all over. Scarlet very much not in dark any more but
bathed in 100 watt polar ice-cap melting light, i.e. she
knows about me and Jack. She burst in on us in den and
said, 'Oh God, it is true. Ugh, ugh, make them stop, Suzy,
make them stop.' Which was pointless as *a*) Suzy in
favour of all sex and *b*) were not actually engaged in any
nakedity, were in seventies loveswing watching *Scrubs*,
but was clearly in non-just-good-friends way as one of his

hands was twirling curl of hair and other was hovering dangerously close to left breast. Said I had thought she wouldn't be back and had not intended for her to find out like this and it is fault of unusually favourable traffic conditions rather than my fault per se. But Scarlet said in fact is Sad Ed's fault as he confessed on phone what sordidness was going on in her absence and is why she made Suzy ignore speed limit and traffic impediments in order to stage utter bust. Jack said it is better that it is all out in the open and that Scarlet should be happy for us. But Scarlet not in agreement. She demanded that all non-Stones (i.e. me) depart forthwith so she can lie down in darkened room and meditate in bid to calm mind. Jack said not to worry, and that he will talk her round and all will be fine by tomorrow. I said he had better as do not want to be forced to choose between best friend and lover. Although then realized that, actually, would be good as is utterly Shakespearean. But Jack said, 'I know what you are thinking and you are wrong, it would not be good, or literary, or tragic. Just annoying.' Oh, I love him even more. He is in tune with all my innermost thoughts and feelings.

Unlike Sad Ed who is utter traitor and in tune with nothing, as his misguided mojo only serves to testify. Rang him on way home to demand to know why he had spilt proverbial beans. He said he had hoped it would win him points for being loyal and also that she would collapse into his arms in either *a*) face of our horrifying

forbidden love, or *b*) realization that he is her Jack, only not her brother, and with slightly 'more developed' (aka fat) upper arms. He is utterly disappointed though. Not only did he miss the crucial revelation moment, but he is on overtime untangling a nest of trolleys that Reuben jammed behind the pay and display machine. Which, frankly, is divine justice.

- -

Sunday 20
9 a.m.
Am racked with torture. Every second I do not hear from Scarlet is another potential nail in the coffin of our sixteen-year alliance. Is excellent. Am totally living in episode of *Skins*.

11 a.m.
Still no news from Stone household. James says whatever happens, I am my own person, and do not need the approval of my friends. I said I was glad to see he has forgiven Mad Harry and is moving on in his life. He said on the contrary, Mad Harry is a treacherous villain and he is hoping to wreak revenge by going solo and securing five-album deal thus showing Mad Harry what he is missing by breaking up Beastly Boys. He wandered off singing 'The Promise'. Which was ironic as it did not show any. Plus the glory is never the same after the band has split. Look at Duncan out of Blue.

2 p.m.
Scarlet has texted. She is coming round now for a peace summit. Have texted Jack to come over too but he says is better if we sort this out together and not to worry, Scarlet is calm and has no discernible weapons on her. He is right. I will be brave and face my fate alone.

2.10 p.m.
Have texted Sad Ed for back-up. Calmness is worrying and Scarlet has been known to cause injury with only a strawberry bootlace.

4 p.m.
Hurrah. Am injury free, and still officially best friends with Scarlet. (Sad Ed permanently downgraded to second best friend due to betrayal, and also presence of penis.) Scarlet said it was an extremely difficult decision for her, as it compromises all her beliefs, i.e. snogging only weirdy bat people or oddballs you pick up at Glastonbury, but that, on reflection, it is not friendship-ending stuff, and is probably only a phase as Jack is going to college in a few weeks. So as long as I do not mention Jack's genitals then she will accept it. As have not actually seen Jack's genitals yet, cannot discuss them, so agreed. She is wrong about it being only a phase though. He is my ONE. Am sure of it.

Sad Ed is not happy though. It is because Scarlet said she hoped no one else was harbouring weird and unnatural lust secrets as she could not cope with any more

horrifying revelations. He pretended to be lost in musical reverie, but as was Snow Patrol on radio at time, was not utterly convincing as he is renowned for thinking they are mawkish sellouts.

Monday 21

And as one fledgling relationship begins to soar, another is mired in the bird poo of life (could not think of other bird-related metaphors except dead seagulls or swivelly owl heads). It is the Cleggs. There has been more Cornish Liberation Army related hoo-ha in St Slaughter. Grandpa, Pig, and Denzil are now under curfew along with unsavoury youths. It is for picketing the sundried tomatoes and pesto shelf (aka the tourist section) in Spar. Maureen said she had no option but to call the police after Pig started telling customers he had injected the olives with contaminatory urine. They are now forbidden to walk the streets of St Slaughter, Redruth or surrounding conurbations at any time after nine p.m., and are instead holed up in Pasty Manor (aka Belleview, aka Chez Clegg) drinking Pig's potato wine, eating pickled eggs, and singing sea shanties. Granny says sound and smell is overpowering and she can bear it no longer. She is demanding that Mum comes to retrieve her immediately or she may well be under curfew for murder. Mum suggested she could stay with Aunty Joyless, or with Hilary (former boyfriend of Scarlet, future first-ever black Prime Minister, home

help to Cleggs), who is partially responsible for all the hoo-ha, having politically educated Granny above and beyond her place in life. But Granny says Aunty Joyless has a house full of zealots on exchange from a church in Bodmin and the Nuamahs are having their spare room painted (something called Dead Salmon, despite Granny suggesting a nice roll of lupin-printed Sanderson). Mum has given in and is going on Saturday. But not to collect Granny, to broker peace as a matter of emergency, as she does not want a Clegg here getting under her feet, even a newly politicized one. Dad is in agreement. He says it is bad enough having to endure that level of idiocy once a year, let alone 24-7. Although I think he secretly would welcome the addition of Viennetta to the Riley household. The credit crunch has hit puddings hard and we are on fruit or plain yoghurt only.

· ·

Tuesday 22
5 p.m.
James has drawn up a list of pros and cons of housing a Clegg at 24 Summerdale Road as follows:

GRANNY CLEGG

FOR	AGAINST
Enlightened opinions on minorities.	Will bring Bruce, thus initiating almighty battle
No longer thinks hummus	of the moronic dogs,

318

is 'spit of the devil'.

with inevitable ensuing mess and shouting.

GRANDPA CLEGG

FOR	AGAINST
Will not bring Bruce.	Does not like: black people, gay people, tall people, ginger people, or anyone born east of Tamar. Is still not talking to Grandpa Riley (although Grandpa says this is a positive thing).

It is in case Mum's peace-brokering fails. I would offer Jack's services, as he is excellent negotiator (saggy sofa accord is still holding, admittedly by a thread since Mark Lambert showered sofa aka Jerusalem with a can of Vimto) but Saturday is beginning of our utterly romantic first summer holiday together, and do not want to spend it in contraceptive atmosphere of Pasty Manor, i.e. confined space with Grandpa Clegg (anti-romance) or Mum (anti-most things). They are both guaranteed to dampen desire.

6 p.m.
Not that am planning to do 'It' yet. Not until love has been officially declared by both parties, and not just in

sexual lubricant manner, but in true, non-pants-based
Jane Austen-type way.

* *

Wednesday 23

It is utterly frustrating to be finally immersed in fairytale-
style love but unable to share details of passion with best
friend. I have tried but every time I mention Jack's lips
(soft and taste of peppermint)/eyes (smoulder-
ing)/shoulders (broad and smooth with scar on right one
where Scarlet stabbed him with a Bill Clinton figurine)
Scarlet covers ears and says, 'La la la, I can't hear you.'
Even Sad Ed has shut up shop. He says it is more than his
frustrated mojo can bear at the moment. Have even
broached the Um Bongo cushion to speak to Thin Kylie in
my desperation (she is renowned for being interested in
all things love-based (or sex-based anyway)) but she just
said, 'I can't believe you, like, dumped Davey for that
knob-brain. Are you, like, blind, or mental?'

* *

Thursday 24

Tomorrow is the last day of school. It is utterly poignant
moment as is officially Jack's last day at John Major High,
i.e. end of an era. Scarlet says it is not the end, it is the
beginning, i.e. of her and Sad Ed's new and improved
regime. Reminded her that she is locked in power-sharing
government with Thin Kylie, but she says Kylie will lose

320

interest by October and be back in the West Bank microwaving cola cubes and fiddling with Mark Lambert's sherbet lemons, leaving her free to impose absolute rule. She is sounding more like Hitler every day. But have not told her that as do not want to alienate her further. She said she has had to ban Jack from talking about me at breakfast as she is struggling to keep her muesli down. Which sounds bad, but in fact is excellent as it means we are being gagged like political prisoners, trapped by the love that dare not speak its name.

6 p.m.
James says the love that dare not speak its name is 'boy-on-boy love' which ours is most certainly not. Said how did he know. He said Grandpa Riley told him. Asked how did Grandpa know, as was worried he might turn out to be closet Oscar Wilde or Graham Norton, thus throwing Baby Jesus's life into even more Jeremy Kyle-style turmoil than it already is. But James said Grandpa read it in *Take A Break*.

. . . .

Friday 25
Last day of school.
8 a.m.
Am too sad to even chew Shreddies. Have been forced to consume porridge, which takes no effort, but is now sitting in stomach like leaden ball, adding to my misery. In

contrast James has had two slices of toast and an under-ripe pear and is dancing to Leona Lewis on Radio 2 with dog. I said historic nature of occasion, i.e. last day of primary school, will hit him later like giant rounders bat, and he will collapse in heap of sorrow. He said not likely as Mumtaz is going to Pakistan for six weeks and it will be the ultimate test of devotion for Mad Harry, who has attention span of gnat and will be begging James to reform Beastly Boys within a week, and then James can spurn him to give him a taste of his own medicine. I said that was a bit harsh. He said 'harsh is as harsh does'. Which does not make sense and suspect he has been talking to Granny Clegg on phone, who is renowned for inventing crap proverbs.

4 p.m.
Sadness has been dispelled. Not by joyous atmosphere of silly string and stray sheep (exceeding all expectations this year by getting trapped on top of Mrs Leech's biscuit cupboard), but by Jack's tongue. Have made up for wasted years by snogging all over school including: common room, library, and against nut dispensing machine. Would have gone for Mr Wilmott's office but Fat Kylie in there with Davey MacDonald (Mr Whippy on Donkey Dawson's (weird shaped head, allegedly large thing) stag do in Clacton). We have left our indelible mark on every inch. Metaphorically-speaking. Now every time walk down C Corridor will be struck by memory of his hands

pinning me against sky blue walls while sheep milled around us like slightly smelly clouds. Notice that some-one, possibly Mark Lambert, has left actual indelible mark, i.e. stubby pen picture of genitals. Lou (caretaker, former Criminal and Retard, once ate school rabbit) was at it with a damp sponge when we left. He needs to have lesson with Mum. He will never get it off without at least a mild abrasive. It would be easier to turn it into a sort of erupting, though hairy, rocket.

Upper Sixth and substandard Year Elevens are not only ones leaving though. There is to be another departure from hallowed, albeit sheep-poo-strewn, halls. It is Mr Vaughan (head of Drama, lover of Sophie Microwave Muffins, proud owner of supersize nipples). He has got a new job in Bath. Scarlet said he will regret it as it is full of upper-middle-class Boden-wearing blonde airheads. Saw Sophie by nut dispensing machine while Jack having essential wee break from snogging. To show did not bear grudge over whole Justin/Jack thing, and that empathize with lover moving many miles away, said, 'It'll be OK, you'll see.' She said whatever, she will be glad to be out of this smalltown hellhole and get to uni. Asked where she was going. She said Bath.

. . . .

Saturday 26
Hurrah, it is the first day of the holidays, and the long, hot summer stretches ahead of me. Except without hot bit as

is raining, as usual. But is still excellent as Mum is going to Cornwall this morning, plus she is taking mini menace James. He says his absence will only fuel Mad Harry's desire to rekindle their friendship. Mum was not at all happy about leaving me behind as she says Dad cannot be trusted to make sure I am 'controlling my urges'. Ick. But James has told Mum not to worry, he has given Dad a lesson in surveillance. Am unperturbed. Dad is renowned for being utterly lax when it comes to Mum's many and varied rules and regulations. Is lucky she is not leaving next-door neighbour Marjory PI in charge, with her ear for gossip and arsenal of digital spyware. Hurrah, will commence contraventions by inviting Jack, Scarlet, and Sad Ed round later to play loud music and take drugs.

10.30 a.m.
Or at least drink alcohol.

10.35 a.m.
Or possibly Ribena.

10 p.m.
Do not need Dad to meddle with urges as Scarlet is contraceptive enough already. Was only giving Jack minor snog (partial tongue, but no hands) when Scarlet started screaming 'My eyes, my eyes!' And squirted us with apple juice (near sell-by so possibly fermenting and cidery). Sad Ed just sighed and ate another Pringle. He is still waiting

for her to realize what is standing right in front of her, i.e. not largish son of Aled Jones obsessives with flabby upper arms and a stained Smiths T-shirt, but towering god of love. He will be waiting a long time. To make matters worse, the dog has eaten the volume knob on the CD player and it is stuck on 'barely audible'. Which is not at all edgy or law-breaking.

Sunday 27

10 a.m.

It is utterly poetic. Am being forced by Mum to stay away from Jack. She is Mrs Capulet, i.e. blind to my needs and desires. Mum said it is not poetic, and she is not Mrs Capulet, it is just that Dad cannot be trusted to cook Sunday lunch without burning or exploding it, so she has arranged for us to go to Grandpa Riley's. I said she was risking my love life, if not actual life, with this rash decision but she says she has given Treena a copy of Delia's complete cookery course and strict instructions not to let Dad or Baby Jesus or dog suck frozen sausages pretending they are Cuban cigars. Asked her how Operation Clegg was going. She said not entirely according to plan. Granny is still refusing to leave the spare room, Grandpa is refusing to leave the broken Parker Knoll and Bruce is refusing to leave the cereal cupboard. Said this must be very disappointing as is almighty blip in her record of imposing military rule, but she says she is hoping to

achieve small victory by corralling Grandpa into bath in minute. He has been on 'dirty protest' for a week. Then could clearly hear sound of someone singing 'Blow the Man Down' and James shrieking 'No more, Pig, no more,' and Mum hung up.

5 p.m.
Was wrong about lunch. Was excellent as Treena forgot rule about leaving dog unattended in room with unsecured meat and it ate two packets of mince including the polystyrene trays so Dad took everyone to pub instead for prawn cocktails and scampi (banned on myriads of grounds including hygiene, fat content, and so-called thousand island dressing). I bet James is regretting his choice of parent now. He is probably trying to digest several pounds of health-giving vegetables in the company of dirty-protest Grandpa Clegg, plus a man who smells like pig (Pig) and one who looks like one (Denzil).

At least Grandpa Riley is relatively fresh-smelling. And utterly understands me. Had forgotten he is very much au fait with matters of the heart. It is all the glossy magazines he is reading. And *Hollyoaks*. He said if feel it in my toes when Jack kisses me then is love for sure. Said feel it everywhere. He said then options are pill, condom, or femidom, but he wouldn't go for that as is like wearing plastic bag in chuff, according to seventy-six per cent of readers who have tried it. Said was not at that stage yet. Grandpa said I was in thirty-eight per cent minority and had better not wait too long, as Jack is hot-blooded male and eyes, and hands, might start to wander—look what happened to Britney.

He is wrong. Jack would never leave me. Even if took vow of chastity. Though will not do that as am not anti-sex. Just worried will be rubbish at it. Like hockey, all over again. Think might be time to tell him I love him though. Because is true. Utterly utterly do.

* *

Monday 28

Mum and her demonic assistant James are jubilant. Not only are Grandpa Clegg's many orifices clean and lemon-scented (James says he used washing-up brush and bottle of Fairy Liquid and kept eyes averted at all times to pre-serve dignity, and contents of stomach), but Pig and Denzil have left the building, i.e. Pasty Manor. Asked if they had gone voluntarily. James said no, they had fallen prey to one of his expert 'hustles'. Apparently he used phone box outside Spar to call Chez Clegg pretending to be Trelawney, symbolic patron of Cornish Liberation Army, demanding Pig's and Denzil's presence at anti-Jamie Oliver march from the 24-hour garage (shuts at 8, on Mum's to-do list of complaint letters) to Watergate Bay. Said that Trelawney was dead and had been since 1721. James said clearly they are unaware of that fact.

James is right, it is excellent victory. Now they just need to persuade Grandpa Clegg to perform romantic

gesture in bid to win back heart of true love. Like paint over Hammerite Cornish flag on cladding. Or cut toenails.

12.15 a.m.
Or climb silently up *Dawson's-Creek*-style ladder for illicit midnight snog! Which is what Jack did fifteen minutes ago. Was excellent, although did have panic when heard knocking at window, as was having dream about Dracula at time. Although think it could just have been Trevor Pledger in full winged costume. Anyway, Dad is none the wiser. Hurrah, our love is utterly like mid-90s TV series, i.e. tragi-comedy, with clever postmodern script and big hair. May suggest *Dawson's Creek* idea to James. Although the Cleggs' record of injury through misadventure is quite high.

· ·

Tuesday 29
Dad has warned me that he will confiscate *Dawson's Creek* ladder if I continue to abuse its presence. As it is, he is fighting a losing battle with Mum, who claims leaving it in the side return is tantamount to an open invitation to burgling O'Gradys everywhere. Will have to tell Jack to be more careful. Clearly his drawing-pin boot tapped too loudly on the rungs. Though is odd as usually Dad sleeps through anything, including Mum changing the bed linen.

Also James has rung with grave news. Pig and Denzil

are back in Pasty Manor. Asked if they had realized the very dead nature of Trelawney and got wise to James's substandard hustle. James said, *au contraire*, he is Lord of the Hustle (which sounds hideous), but that they got hungry waiting at not-at-all 24-hour garage and decided to have armchair, or broken Parker Knoll, protest instead. Mum and Granny Clegg are now both in spare room having lie down.

11 p.m.
Oh my God. There has been another bedroom intruder. But horrifyingly, was not Jack this time, was Justin Statham—former boyfriend, future rock god, and possessor of small nipples! Worse, he has informed me that he bitterly regrets post-prom snakebite sick incident, as being mostly naked in bed with me was in fact opposite of vomit-inducing. I said he should have thought of that before he dumped me for Sophie Microwave Muffins Jacobs, especially given she had dumped him for Mr Supersize Nipples Vaughan. He said, 'I made a mistake.' I said, 'Yeah, well, me too, i.e. going out with you in first place. But I'm with Jack now, and we are in like. Possibly in love. We are soulmates and can tell each other anything. Unlike me and you, who had more secrets than episode of *Miss Marple*.' He said, 'Have you told him about mostly naked prom night?'

And then had complete panic and said 'yes'. Which I know is utter lie. But do not want Justin to think there is

chink of possibility we might still have chance. He just nodded blond Kurt Cobain hair and said, 'OK, Rach. I cede the battle. But not the war.' Which is very poetic for someone who only got D in English lit GCSE. And also somewhat ominous.

This is typical. Have waited years for a boy (i.e. not Sad Ed, who is boy, but only in loose sense) to ascend sacred *Dawson's Creek* ladder in bid to snog me, and now has happened twice in two days. At least Dad does not seem to have noticed this time. He is too busy enjoying Mum-free home and has been in living room since 6 p.m. with two cans of John Smith's Extra Smooth, a box set of *The Sopranos*, and a bag of Doritos. Is like when Berlin Wall came down and deprived communists went mad for Western excess.

· ·

Wednesday 30
11 a.m.
There has been weird and worrying incident chez Riley. Was enjoying Mum-free breakfast at Shreddies table (aka Crunchy Nut Cornflakes, Nutella, and doughnut table) and trying not to think about *Dawson's Creek* ladder hoo-ha, when Dad said, 'I hope you are not thinking about engaging in hanky panky with Justin Statham. Jack is bad enough but I do not like the cut of Justin's jib.'

Is terrifying. Dad has developed an all-seeing eye in Mum's absence. Is contagious, like measles. He does not

330

need to worry anyway, as am not fan of Justin's jib either (ick). Plus Mum is back in seven hours so there will be no hanky panky of any kind. Like Justin, she has ceded the battle and is bringing Granny Clegg back to 24 Summerdale Road. But she also of opinion war is not lost. She says is only temporary arrangement as she is hoping our noughties 'wayward living' will be too much for Granny, who will realize that she is best suited to Grandpa Clegg and the environs of St Slaughter, which are both still stuck somewhere in the 1970s. Mum is confident Granny will be packing the Spar bags in days. She clearly has a skewed concept of wayward living though. The last time anyone did anything wayward here was when Dad tried a can of Red Bull. He paid for it later though when he lost a four-ball because his chip shot was caffeine-compromised.

Have emptied Nutella and Crunchy Nut Cornflakes in preparation for return of austerity rule (i.e. fed contents to dog). They are high on banned list for double whammy of contravention, i.e. sugary evil masquerading as nutritious by involvement of protein-based nuts.

8 p.m.
Granny Clegg is here and is installed in the spare room with Bruce, who has been chained to radiator until he can learn to follow simple instructions like 'sit' and 'stay' and 'don't eat the stairs, you moron'.

Plus Mum wants to know why father of Bruce, i.e.

331

dog, is having apparent sugar rush (it has been running round garden in circle for ten minutes). Said it is just excitement at return of supreme leader, a feeling also shared by her loving and obedient daughter. James snorted and said my 'hustle' was inferior, as give away signs were fiddling with ear, refusing to look at subject, and use of word obedient. But luckily Mum too busy questioning Dad about suspicious orange powdery residue on remote control to notice.

9 p.m.
Bruce unchained from radiator, having also engaged in dirty protest. Though hope Grandpa Clegg did not poo on carpet as part of his.

Thursday 31
Hurrah, tomorrow is my birthday and is set to be historic occasion. Not only will turn 17, which means will be fully-fledged provisional driver—but will also mark highly anticipated joint declaration of love. Hopefully.

Have decided am going to do it tomorrow night during party. Which will not be usual childish affair, involving rogue O'Gradys, Bacardi breezer or shaving the dog, but will be intimate dinner soirée involving fine wine, haute cuisine, and me, Jack, Scarlet, and Sad Ed. Had hoped not to have to invite latter two, but Sad Ed says romantic candlelight will be aphrodisiac overload and Scarlet is bound to lunge at him over the lobster thermidor. Said he was making quite a lot of assumptions, not least presence of candles, which, as well he knows, are banned from Riley household on grounds of fire and melty wax mess risk. As are lobsters, on grounds of them being *a*) overpriced and *b*) eating poo and therefore at high risk of harbouring life- or bottom-threatening disease, and *c*) having tappy legs and feelers (me not Mum on that one). Plus Scarlet will not eat them as she is strictly vegetarian. Caved in anyway. Cannot forsake friends just because am in love. Will kick them out after pudding and do declaration then.

Amazingly Mum has agreed to arrangement, including request for her to vacate property for evening. Think it is because she is already struggling with perpetual presence of Clegg. She has issued several caveats though:

1. She will do cooking (Delia's wild mushroom stroganoff) and we can warm up in low oven later.
2. Granny Clegg will remain in the house. But will be installed in own bedroom with audio CDs of Mary Wesley and individual Fray Bentos pie.
3. Bruce and dog will remain in house. But in downstairs and upstairs toilets respectively, with doors to remain closed at all times.
4. There will be no alcohol, bar one can each of Dad's Shandy Bass (pseudo-alcohol and less potent than Benylin).
5. There will be no swinging, or 'sexual play' (Mum's horrendous words, not mine).

Will still be excellent night though. Do not need alcohol.
Will be drunk on utterly heady mix of stimulating conversation, sparkling wit, and potent love of Jack. He has
already given me my present. Do not know what it is, as
is in envelope, with strict instructions not to open until
tomorrow. But is probably poem he has written inspired
by our love.

10 p.m.
Although can feel something jangling, in unpoetic way.
But will not open. Am grown-up. Not seven year old who
prises open flap of paper to check that all gifts are up to
standard (James), or rips them open on Christmas Eve,
thus instigating the Riley 'no presents under tree until
Shreddies have been consumed' rule (me).

10.30 p.m.
But is not wrong to hold envelope. Am not actually opening it. Just using telepathic oneness with Jack to deter-
mine contents.

10.35 p.m.
Or maybe just feel outline of jangly thing.

10.36 p.m.
Is key. Oh my God. Is symbolic key to heart. Is poetic after
all. This is it. It is his boy-way of saying he loves me! Have
texted Jack to say also have gift for him (i.e. love) and will

be unveiling tomorrow night, privacy pending. He said, 'Can't wait to see them.' Texted back to say, 'Is not breasts. Is more metaphysical. Breasts later.' Grandpa is right. Even under exterior of progressive political and musical genius lurks oversexed *Nuts*-reader. But do not care. He is The One. And anyway, does not read *Nuts*. He is more *Guitar Monthly* man.

august

BABY MONITOR

THE HIGHWAY CODE

Friday 1
9 a.m.

Have opened Jack's envelope. Was not key to heart. Was actual key—i.e. to non-sick-smelling car of the people, i.e. Jack's Beetle. Envelope also contained note, which was not love poem, but declaration that he is giving me driving lessons for my birthday, starting this afternoon. BUT, if he goes to Cambridge University, he is giving me custody of car as he is going to use traditional bicycle power instead as is economical (plus is very *Brideshead Revisited*)! Is excellent thoughtful gift. Plus tension over gearstick is renowned for inducing atmosphere of love. Look at Mike Wandering Hands Majors (bouffy hair, driving instructor, rumoured to be father of five children by former pupils in Saffron Walden environs). Dad is jubilant that am not going to be driving one of his fleet of Ford Fiestas. Not only is he saving £25 a week, Mum will not get to ogle Mike's vice-like grip on the faux leather steering wheel from the dining room window.

Have also had somewhat less thoughtful presents from family i.e.:

- Copy of *Highway Code* (Mum and Dad—credit crunch clearly affecting presents as well as puddings);
- Feu Orange car deodorizer (James—affected not so much by credit crunch but by fact that he is addicted to odd smell);
- Bar of Dairy Milk (Granny Clegg—also not affected by crunch, just habitually povvy);

- Driving gloves (dog and Bruce—not crunchy but unwearable as make me look like mentalist);
- Stack of glossy magazines (used and in some cases stuck together with suspicious substance—Grandpa Riley, Treena, and Baby Jesus);
- Kernow car sticker (Grandpa, Pig, and Denzil).

Do not care, as am about to take flight in Jack's winged chariot of love. Hurrah! Am not at all worried about doing as told, as am used to following strict instructions (17 years of experience), plus how hard can driving be?

6 p.m.
Driving is impossible task. Every time look in mirror, swerve into kerb. Plus gear stick hand apparently has invisible thread connecting to accelerator foot, which is apparently not at all good for health of *a*) car, *b*) approaching pedestrians, and *c*) Jack. No wonder Sad Ed is still struggling, with his oversized fingers and flat feet. Jack says next time we will concentrate on the basics, e.g. turning engine on. Asked when next time might be, but he deferred question with kiss. So even though chariot not winged, is still one of love. Cannot wait until tonight and historic declarations. The wild mushroom stroganoff is warming in oven, the four cans of Shandy Bass are chilling in fridge and the best tablecloth is out of quarantine, but with a severe warning that any spillages are to be tackled immediately with a damp sponge and appropriate

340

Stain Devil. As predicted candles have been banned, but Mum has agreed to using Dad's emergency camping light to give appropriate mood lighting. Thank God they have gone out and have taken James with them. They are round at Malcolm from IT's and Mrs Malcolm's. Mum is hoping James will bond with Alastair (10, squint, entire *Lord of Rings* Panini sticker set collection), elevating him out of the circle of devilment that is Mad Harry and Keanu for good. Granny Clegg also safely out of way in spare room with steak and kidney pie and audio version of *The Camomile Lawn* (as read by Joanna Lumley), and dogs shut in toilets with Radio 4. Being watched while weeing is small price to pay for avoiding colossal idiocy that hovers over dogs at all times. Now all I have to do is wait for my guests in utterly glamorous hostessy manner, i.e. sipping wine (aka lemon barley) and playing classical music (aka Glasvegas), which is utter modern classic, according to Jack.

6.30 p.m.
Have had minor setback. Had to go to toilet (oversipping lemon barley) and was not quick enough with lock. Bruce made bid for freedom and threw itself at upstairs bathroom door having established that mortal enemy, i.e. dog, was inside (trying to dig tunnel through lino). Which sent dog into frenzy of door butting and then strange silence. Further investigation revealed dog to be concussed, possibly through mistaken butting of sink so had

341

to give it reviving shower. Am now slightly moist all over, and emanating odour of wet dog, which is not at all love inducing. Have sprayed self liberally with Mum's Tweed. Plus have shut dog in James's bedroom where any damage will be a blessing. Bruce is in with Granny Clegg, listening to Joanna Lumley and eating congealed kidneys. On plus side at least will be able to wee in private from now on. Bruce worryingly interested in wee and potential for drinking thereof.

7.30 p.m.

Oooh. Doorbell. This is it. In just a few hours, relationship with Jack will have shifted up a gear (without hitting kerb), plus Sad Ed and Scarlet will possibly be entwined in mojo-satisfying love. Hurrah!

10 p.m.

Oh God. Horrifying thing has happened. Have not had night of love at all. Instead think may have been dumped. Am too shocked to write now. Will go to bed in hope that either *a*) am wrong or *b*) overnight, body will block traumatizing memory from brain and will be in state of ignorant bliss.

. . . .

Saturday 2

8 a.m.

Body not blocked traumatizing memory at all. And think

342

am not wrong. Think am definitely dumped. According to annoyingly disobliging brain, events occurred as follows:

Friday 7.30 p.m.
Guests arrive and hostess takes coats etc. upstairs in professional manner. Scarlet demands that hostess also take self upstairs and wash as odour of dog/Tweed is overpowering and could cause hives.

7.45 p.m.
Hostess returns refreshed and slightly less odorous and announces dinner is served. Menu as follows:
Canapes: Twiglets and Frazzles (as purchased by Dad, in contravention of several rules of state, as birthday 'treat');
Mains: Delia's mushroom stroganoff (as made by Mum);
Pudding: Apple 'snow', as made by James or cheese (Cathedral City) and biscuits (cream crackers not Jacob's, but Waitrose, so not totally povvy);
After dinner mints: Matchmakers (as brought by Sad Ed for light snack).
Party consumes canapés and mains but rejects pudding and mints on various grounds (meltiness of snow, non-organic nature of Cheddar, Nestlé's buyout of Rowntree Macintosh).

8.15 p.m.
Party finishes allocated Shandy Bass. Scarlet opens bag to reveal two bottles of Merlot donated by Suzy for occasion

(she is cutting down to five bottles a week in case she has to have medical for adoption interview). Jack opens Merlot. Hostess tackles ensuing stain according to instructions.

8.30 p.m.
Party opens second bottle of Merlot. Hostess refuses second glass, citing fact that Mum is recent purchaser of portable breath test gadget, and is likely to use it without provocation on her return, in less than three hours.

8.45 p.m.
Sad Ed decides Nestlé not so evil after all and consumes entire box of Matchmakers.

9.30 p.m.
Discussion on guitarist out of Franz Ferdinand (scary or just unfortunate positioning of instrument) cut short by ominous crashing sound upstairs. Hostess goes to investigate inevitable Granny Clegg/Bruce/dog misdemeanour.

9.31 p.m.
Hostess discovers cause of crash is, unbelievably, not any of usual suspects but in fact Justin Statham falling through open bedroom window having slipped on last rung of *Dawson's Creek* ladder due to ill-advised wearing of flip-flops in rain.

9.33 p.m.
Justin declares he is not giving up in fight for Rachel and cannot believe Jack's kisses as potent as own. Hostess says Jack's kisses indeed more potent. Justin demands kiss-off experiment. Hostess says Ick. Justin says he is not leaving without test results. Hostess gives in for betterment of science and snogs Justin. Earth does not move. Hostess informs Justin this is case and demands departure forthwith. Justin says 'Then if am not potent love god then why did you get naked in bed on prom night and at one point touch small nipple, before did sick everywhere . . . '

All of which would have been fine had this schedule not been going on simultaneously in dining room:

9.31 p.m.
James Riley and Colin Riley arrive home having had *a*) argument with Alastair over the latent heat capacity of toluene and *b*) argument with Mum over whether or not two helpings of rhubarb crumble constitute a breach of dietary regulations. Both demand to know whereabouts of hostess. Party informs rogue Rileys that hostess upstairs with dogs and Clegg sorting out 'incident'.

9.32 p.m.
Instead of going upstairs, James Riley reaches behind love talisman portrait of hostess and pulls out baby monitor (which had been informed was in attic in pieces after Mad

Harry tried to get dog to eat it in bid to project his voice from bowels of animal, but has apparently been revived and now has pride of place in James's anti-Marjory arsenal of surveillance equipment).

9.33 p.m.
Baby monitor switched on and party witnesses entire chemical kiss experiment.

9.37 p.m.
Party, plus rogue Rileys, burst into hostess's bedroom. Scarlet manhandles Justin to floor. James is caught in crossfire by flailing flip-flop and is removed by Colin Riley for first aid.

9.38 p.m.
Jack says, 'Yes, Rachel, why did you get naked in bed with him and touch small nipple, when had just rung me and declared that were in like.'

Hostess says, 'Because was high on fake herbal aspirin aka psychedelic mushroom stuff and thought you had done wonky portrait because thought I was wonky minger.'

Justin says, 'Thanks a lot.'

Jack says, 'Ditto.'

Hostess says, 'Sorry. Was huge mistake. Is not fault. Is fault of Reuben Tull. And possibly Justin as he is one who said would be good revenge to do "It".'

Jack says, 'You were going to do "It" with Justin?'

Hostess says, 'Yes. I mean, no. I don't know. Point is I didn't.'

Justin says, 'But only because I had whitey.'

Sad Ed says, 'Yeah, man.'

Scarlet hits Sad Ed with sticky copy of *New Woman*.

Jack says, 'Great, so every time we have a row or you have too much to drink, or take mushroom-based drugs by mistake, you're going to go running back to Mr Small Nipples.'

Hostess, who is having flashbacks to Mum and her lecture, says, 'No,' in very quiet voice in practised manner.

Jack says, 'You said you could tell me everything but you didn't tell me this.'

Justin says, 'You're such a liar, Riley. You said you'd told him.'

Hostess looks at floor willing it to swallow up. Floor does not oblige.

Jack says, 'You know what, I can't do this.' And descends dramatically down *Dawson's Creek* ladder.

Justin says, 'Me too.' And descends less dramatically due to limp, bare feet, and getting Foo Fighters T-shirt snagged on boiler overflow pipe.

Scarlet declares need to lie down in darkened room. Sad Ed offers his own bedroom. They exeunt, stage right. Leaving villainess alone, clutching flip-flop, and fighting back snotty tears.

(Saturday 8.30 a.m.)
Oh God. Have fallen for classic baby monitor scam. Life is
not fairy tale. It is cheap ITV drama. Why, oh why did I
not drink too much Merlot? Punishment from Mum
would be welcome as would have bonus of either *a*) being
too drunk to conduct conversation with Justin in first
place, possibly even to get up stairs, or *b*) at least mind
would be blank at moment.

Unless, maybe is all bad dream. Or at least exaggera-
tion in own mind. Am prone to overactive imagination.
Will text Scarlet to check.

8.45 a.m.
Have sent text: AM I DESTITUTE ONCE MORE?

8.47 a.m.
Scarlet has texted back: YES.

Oh how can one small word be so utterly life
destroying?

8.48 a.m.
What if actually is life destroying? Must text Scarlet again.
HAS JACK KILLED SELF?

8.49 a.m.
NO HE IN ROOM DRUMMING TO DEEP PURPLE. AND
STOP TEXTING. AM NOT TALKING TO YOU. YOU ARE
SMALL NIPPLE FANCYING LOVE CHEAT.

It is worse than I thought. Well not worse than death. But almost. As know for a fact that Deep Purple is emergency-only music. Plus now have potentially lost best friend as well. Am going to sob into pillow for a bit.

9 a.m.
James has been in to inform me my presence is required at the Shreddies table to explain several suspicious matters. Said was too depressed to consume food as am love reject. (Love, and lack of, is entirely compromising nutritious needs. Will get scurvy if carry on at this rate.) James said *a*) Mum's lips are very thin and *b*) at least he fought for his love instead of falling at first hurdle. Said *a*) how thin and *b*) he did not fight for love, he got clouted by Mad Harry for referring to Mumtaz as cheap. James said *a*) thinner than the time Dad let the dog drink two glasses of Marks & Spencer cognac, *b*) whatever, and *c*) I can either i) wallow ii) fight for Jack, or iii) follow James's lead and rise triumphantly, stronger and more manly from experience.

He is right. (Not about rising more manly from experience. He is utterly not manly. He is weedy weirdo.) But about fighting for Jack. Is totally unliterary to allow rubbish baby monitor incident to ruin love. That is sort of thing that happens in *Coronation Street* (I imagine, as have never seen due to double ban for being *a*) Northern and *b*) common). Whereas my life is utterly high-class BBC in-house period production and only thing that can

349

separate me and Jack is dose of consumption. Will go round Jack's immediately for fight and ensuing snog-filled reunion.

Once have eaten slice of toast. Cannot fight for man on empty stomach.

11 a.m.

Have had two rounds of toast and Marmite, a bowl of Cheerios and an apple (for vitamins) and am going to get my man. In metaphorical and hopefully physical sense. Have texted him to meet me on common ground, i.e. the common.

4 p.m.

Have not got man. In any sense. Was catalogue of disaster.

1. Jack thought I meant bench next to car park (aka Barry Island) not bench next to slide of death, so spent an hour watching Whitney O'Grady hurl herself into oblivion whilst Jack was on other side of common getting mintier by minute.

2. Once had established confusion (and vacated to Jack's bench as O'Gradys quite distracting), then spent another twenty minutes sitting in gloomy silence.

3. Then wished was still in gloomy silence as words that finally came out of Jack's mouth were not at all complimentary, i.e. 'You're just not who I thought you were. No, scratch that. You're exactly

who I thought you were. I just hoped I was wrong. You've humiliated me, Rach. Again.' Said, 'Have humiliated self.' Jack in agreement this time. But then hit me with silver bullet, i.e. said, 'I think maybe we are just not meant to be.' Which felt like had pierced heart. As we are totally meant to be. Like Darcy and Elizabeth Bennet. Or the two fat ones out of Gavin and Stacey. Realized then that had to do love declaration immediately, before was completely too late. So followed James's Ninja advice, which was to close eyes and pull on reserve inner strength. But when opened them, Jack was gone, and had said 'I love you' to local madman Barry the Blade who was looking in the bin for kebab bits.

This is utterly the worst day of my life. I have lost my boyfriend and my best friend and have been given relationship advice by a man who has not changed pants in two years and is rumoured to have stabbed first wife to death.

On plus side, things cannot possibly get any worse.

11 p.m.
Dog has fused electricity by eating fridge cable. Am now in dark, with screams of small children (i.e. James) haunting me in my misery. Is utter metaphor for life.

* *

Sunday 3

10 a.m.

Ugh. Am still engulfed in giant thundercloud of gloom. (Though is not actual gloom as fuse mended and all appliances fully functioning.) Have texted Scarlet to see if she has reconsidered her communication shutdown and wants to come over and comfort me in hour of need/ watch T4, but she says she is operating a period of official radio silence and cannot cross my threshold as would be betraying Jack. Plus she has to go to Waitrose to get some raspberry balsamic vinegar. At least Sad Ed is not so choosy. He says he is also depressed as Scarlet utterly did not take advantage of him in his darkened bedroom and several times demanded that he stop staring at her as was like horror movie when friend turns out to be mentalist zombie and eats you. So at least we can be united in our status as pariahs.

3 p.m.

Am in bedroom with Sad Ed listening to morose music and watching him eat peanut M&Ms. Love is afflicting him in opposite manner, i.e. he has gone into confectionery overdrive and consumed ten Crème Eggs, four Snickers, and half a pound of Galaxy in last twenty-four hours. He in agreement that Stones are unworthy of our affections and we should stop getting hopes up that they are key to our happy endings in life.

3.15 p.m.

Can hear something outside. Is familiar. What is it?

3.16 p.m.

OMG. Is unmistakable sound of rumble of non-sick-smelling car of people on pea gravel. Jack has realized we are meant to be. Hurrah. Any second now he will ascend perilous heights of *Dawson's Creek* ladder and fling me against John Lewis painted pine wardrobe in fit of passion.

3.18 p.m.

Or possibly use more traditional method. Doorbell has just gone. He is obviously trying not to upset Mum and general anti-ladder feeling. He is so considerate! Will await thud, click on stairs instead.

3.20 p.m.

Oh. Jack has gone. And did not fling me against anything. Did not even come upstairs at all. Instead James, i.e. portent of doom, has delivered note. It says, 'Have taken key.' Said is metaphorical. Is to heart. He has sealed it up and I cannot penetrate it any longer. Is devastating. James said is not metaphorical or devastating. Is key to non-sick-smelling car of people. Sad Ed said is devastating as he was hoping to use Beetle for untimely death once passed test. James pointed out he was more likely to die of old age. Which even Sad Ed agreed was true. Though

353

has made him more depressed than ever. And me. I could have been passenger and we could have driven over edge of Grand Canyon (or at least ditch behind Homebase) like Thelma and Louise. Instead have no car, no boyfriend and no hope of suicide. Will end up as withered old woman staring out of bus window talking to self and wondering where life and love has gone. Am Miss Havisham. Or Granny Clegg.

Am going to retreat into hermit-like hovel for rest of summer. Sad Ed and I have agreed is only way to minimize torment. We are going to stage bed protest. Against unfairness of life and vehicular access. Starting tomorrow.

. . . .

Monday 4

9 a.m.
Is Day One of bed protest. Have got supplies, i.e. bottled water (to be sipped slowly to minimize loo requirements), Kendal Mint Cake (for joules of energy, and fresh breath) and stack of Grandpa-soiled magazines.

11 a.m.
Mum not happy about bed protest. She says is bad enough having Granny Clegg malingering under the covers until gone nine but I am young and fit and should be out enjoying healthy walk in countryside, or at least lurking around bus stops. Said was not fit. Was sick,

354

i.e. heart is broken. Mum said, 'Oh for heaven's sake, not again.' And went off to delimescale the bathroom sink. Thank God. Now can go back to tormented sleep in peace.

11.15 a.m.
Or not. Granny Clegg has been in to offer remedy to cheer me up. Said what is remedy. She said Bruce—i.e. his happy face can make even the terminally ill feel vital. Looked at Bruce. Bruce wearing same hairy glare as usual. Plus was chewing pair of Dad's pants. Said am beyond any cure. She said would leave Bruce anyway.

11.30 a.m.
Have had yet more interruptions. This time was James with reviving cup of tea and invigorating talk. Which is better, but only marginally. He said he has 'been to that dark place and feels my pain'. But that I need to take a leaf out of his book and get over it. Said was not taking leaves out of James's book as book has also involved mysterious dancing in leotards and furry pants in recent past. And to please leave and take Bruce with him as his smell and perpetual burrowing in carpet are not all conducive to peaceful protest.

Have barricaded door (locks banned due to potential for *a*) underage sex and *b*) underage chemical experiments). Am alone now. Nothing can interrupt my hermit-like existence.

11.40 a.m.
Need loo. Should not have drunk tea. Was secret weapon planted by Mum to get me to cave in. But will not. Have weed in Pringles tube in times of emergency. Am practically Bear Grylls. Will just wee in cup. Is bound to fit as is only what went in one way.

11.45 a.m.
Have had slight wee spillage. Tea expanded inexplicably inside body to fill cup and had to divert into pencil holder. Wish had kept Bruce after all. He very interested in wee and would probably drink if let him. Have mopped up with odd sock. Will limit fluid intake and concentrate on reading instead to lift me above trivial bodily needs and on to more cerebral plain where words are my only sustenance.

2 p.m.
Have read *Vogue, Elle,* and *Take a Break* and am thirsty, hungry, and weirdly twitchy. Think must be getting cabin fever. Oooh. Am like James Cracknell and that one with the gigantic teeth off *Animal Park*. Except am not rowing around world naked. But is almost the same. Will just text Sad Ed to see if he also jittery. That is not official contact with outside world as Ed also on hermit protest.

2.05 p.m.
Sad Ed says *au contraire*, he is perfectly happy in his saggy

bed of hermitude. This is because it is utterly normal for him to stay under covers for days at a time (his record is seventy-six hours, during a *Buffy* marathon), whereas I am like fragile flower, and crave light in order to blossom. Curtains are my barricades (literal and metaphorical) trapping me in my torment until someone rescues me from my plight. Oooh. Is like Rapunzel. And Jack is my prince. Maybe if send him telepathic message he will rescue me from tower of imprisonment.

2.07 p.m.
Though will not let him climb up hair. Is wiry and quite long, but still patchy after claggy raisin/hoover haircut incident.

2.10 p.m.
OMG. The *Dawson's Creek* ladder is moving. Can hear it scraping along wall. Is knock at window. Hurrah! It is Jack, i.e. handsome prince, come to take me into his manly arms.

2.15 p.m.
Was not Jack. Was Mum. Who is utterly not handsome prince but wicked stepmother type. Said her SAS protest-breaking tactics did not wash with me and try as she might she will not get me out of the bedroom. She said, *au contraire*, she was conducting a thorough assessment of our security arrangements and was removing ladder as it

contravened several regulations, as she had informed Dad on no less than eight occasions. It is utterly unfair. Not only is my bedroom now non-TV style one with door as only egress (excellent word, gleaned from *Oxford English Dictionary*, along with tine (prongy fork bit), uvula (dangly bit in mouth, not genital as had thought) and merkin (pubic wig—ick)). But now Jack cannot rescue me even if he wanted to. Am stuck in prison of my own making.

4 p.m.
Oh God. Need poo. Should not have eaten fruit. Is Mum's fault for hammering home vitamin consumption message on daily basis. But is crisis as do not think even Bear Grylls would poo in pencil holder. Why oh why did I not think of chamber pot à la Grandpa Clegg. (Is not out of necessity, they have had indoor toilet for four years. He just likes convenience, and feel.) There is nothing else for it. Am going to have to use bathroom. But will be fine. Will do stealth poo. Like Ninja.

4.15 p.m.
OMG. Poo not as stealthy as thought. The picket lines have been crossed and my bed has been stripped of sprig-patterned duvet cover and pillowcases, plus the curtains have been pulled back and room thoroughly aired. It is an outrage. Nobody respects my beliefs. Or toilet requirements. Have demanded Mum's presence immediately, using non-hermit method i.e. shouting.

4.20 p.m.

Mum has ignored request but sent her minion of choice i.e. James. He says I made a fatal error in thinking I could mess with laundry day. Said thought laundry day moved to Wednesday, due to mid-week uniform emergencies relating to St Regina's 'cookery' lessons (chocolate crispy cakes and cheese on toast). James said is now extended to bi-weekly event for limited time only, in order to cope with excess Clegg-wear and dog-related spillages. Ugh. Is so unfair. Even laundry conspires against me. Plus is lovely sunny day. Is typical. Sun decided to show face when heart is immersed in darkness. Brightness is hurting eyes. Maybe bed protest has damaged retina. Am like wolf child emerging from cave. Will have to wear sunglasses for ever more.

Though now am up might as well have lunch and watch bit of TV. Will have sofa protest instead. Is comfier, although Granny Clegg has assumed full control of remote which means endless *Heartbeat*.

5 p.m.

Have taken sunglasses off. Cannot see sepia-tinted 1960s rural England properly.

9 p.m.

Am back in bed. Though is not protest as much as TV has been commandeered by Dad to watch *Top Gear*. Am being philosophical though (am excellent philosopher, as fast

approaching AS level result will testify) i.e. tomorrow is another day.

9.10 p.m.
James says that is not philosophy, that is stating obvious. And anyway, tomorrow never comes. Said it did yesterday.

．．．．．．．．．．．．．．．．．．．．．．．．．．．．．．

Tuesday 5
9 a.m.
Tomorrow is here. Ha. And am still gloomy. But am out of bed, which is progress. Although is partially due to fact that dog is in it. It has seemingly followed my example and is on anti-Bruce protest. Bruce is not on protest. It is busy looking triumphant on the sofa while James serenades it with a medley of Take That hits. He is an utter traitor. James says he is not, but that Bruce may in fact be genetically superior to dog, due to its mother's pedigree DNA. Reminded him its mother is Fiddy Britcher, who exists on diet of Kraft cheese slices and chicken tikka sandwiches, which is far from intellectual. He said I will change my mind when Bruce sniffs out truffles or buried treasure. I said I would not hold breath.

2 p.m.
Oooh. Have forgotten to inform Sad Ed that bed protest is over and he can get up and pull back the curtains on his

life—actual and metaphorical. Will text him immediately. Then he can come over and resume normal moping instead.

2.10 p.m.
Sad Ed has texted back. He says he is quite happy where he is as Mrs Thomas has given him a bell to ring for assistance (one dong for sausage sandwiches, two for Jaffa cakes). It is so unfair. He is lucky to have a mother who understands his plight. Even if she is in the Aled Jones fan club. Will just spend day in normal summer holiday mode instead, i.e. watching TV and sighing a bit.

4 p.m.
Have stopped sighing. James said it was disturbing his police dog training with Bruce. They are hunting for dead bodies, i.e. Granny Clegg, using only the power of smell. I said it was unrealistic as any dog could find Granny Clegg, given her ingrained odour of beef pie, but James says it is the timing that is crucial and Bruce has got it down to forty-eight seconds. Said he should test it against dog in case dog is superior after all. He has agreed in name of science.

5 p.m.
Dog took thirty-seven minutes twenty-two seconds. It is back in bedroom in disgrace. Mum has ended police dog training for day. She says shock of seeing Granny Clegg

slumped on stairs with tongue lolling out gave her near heart attack. Plus the dog managed to pull the dining room curtains down during its hunt.

8 p.m.

Am not sure which is worse—Granny Clegg as murdered corpse or as live version. Now she has taken to doling out love advice. She says she remembers when she had her heart broken by her true love. She said she wept for weeks every time she saw a milk float. Said *a*) thought Grandpa Clegg was true love and *b*) milkman is cliché. She said, *a*) no, first love was boy from Praze-an-Beeble called Curly Collins who *b*) was not milkman, but did party trick of drinking pint of gold top in four seconds. Said so Grandpa Clegg was rebound man. She said no, he mender of heart. Said what with. She said a steady job with the gas board. Then she looked a bit wistful and sighed heavily. Which is a good sign. Her heart is not dead to the power of Norman Clegg yet. Shudder.

. . . .

Wednesday 6

1 p.m.

Am going out. Cannot lock myself away for ever. Even Sleeping Beauty got up eventually. Am just going for fresh air. Possibly in direction of Jack's house. But is act of defiance, i.e. only to show him that am alive and that he

cannot break me. Although possibly if he sees am alive he may fling himself at my mercy and beg for a second chance.

1.05 p.m.
Or try to break me.

4 p.m.
Am back from walk of defiance. Which less defiant than hoped, i.e. Jack did not see me being alive and vigorous despite me walking past house twenty-seven times. Scarlet however did see me and sent me text saying she had called police to report stalker menace.

Bumped into Thin Kylie on way home. She was sitting on wall with Fiddy smoking a Benson and Hedges and chewing Nicorette. Said why was she not in kidney-shaped pool enjoying brief display of sun. She said there are two dead pigeons in it and Cherie and Terry are arguing over who fishes them out. Told her about love plight. She said that's what happens if you go out with nerds who think with brain instead of knob. Asked her how her fiancé, i.e. Mark Lambert, (definitely does not think with brain) was. She said the Lamborghini is in better nick than ever. Was about to point out that Mark Lambert did not own Lamborghini—he owned Toyota held together with No More Nails and parcel tape, and minibike (semi-crushed). But luckily at that point Fiddy started choking, possibly on Nicorette, so escaped without confirmation of

fear that Lamborghini in fact Lambert penis, i.e. centre of his thought processes.

- -

Thursday 7

There has been contact from enemy headquarters, i.e. Grandpa Clegg has rung from Pasty Manor. Thought it might be to announce end of mentalism but was further confirmation, i.e. to ask Mum to ask Granny how does the cooker work as he has had some pig in there for four hours and it is still raw. Mum was worried he had turned into cannibal in desperation and was consuming fellow anti-curfew protestor but Grandpa said it is not Pig, it is one of Pig's pigs. Then he asked where does toilet roll come from as they have run out and are using *Daily Mail* which is not at all absorbent plus his bottom has gone a bit inky. Mum lost temper and told Granny Clegg she should go where she is needed, i.e. her own home, i.e. not 24 Summerdale Road, where everyone is fully aware of location of oven switch and provenance of Andrex. But Granny says she is not going anywhere until Grandpa renounces his allegiance to the Liberation Army, evicts Pig and Denzil, and trims toenails, which are actually clacking on floor now. Plus the Olympics starts tomorrow and our telly is much bigger. Reminded her that she was anti-China, due to their treatment of Tibet etc. etc. but she said that's as maybe, but they do know how to put on a good show.

- -

Friday 8

Granny was right. The Olympic opening ceremony was fantastic. How do they get the thronged thousands to move in time like that? Saffron Walden Amateur Operatic Society struggle with a chorus of ten and one of them always falls off the stage. Is wonder of world.

Scarlet has texted to say is not wonder of world, is utter display of fascism, and all participants are probably facing certain death if they so much as blink off beat.

Which is weird, as had not texted her. Think oneness not with Jack at all but possibly with Scarlet. Which is not good as do not want her reading innermost thoughts. Especially when am thinking about snogging her brother. Oh. Have to stop thinking it. Have to empty mind.

8.45 p.m.

Mind successfully emptied of thought. Was not through meditation. Was through display of idiocy in front room, i.e. weeping and mental barking at telly. Not at prowess of Olympians, but at apparently devastating news that moronic TV Alsatian Wellard is dead. Pointed out to Mum that was mistake allowing Granny Clegg to break house rule Number 4 and watch *EastEnders* but Granny says is part of her education about real life beyond the river Tamar. On plus side, dog and Bruce seem to be united in their grief, which is good news as far as furniture destruction goes.

Also Sad Ed is still in bed. It is new record. Asked how he was managing toilet wise but he says he has en suite so in fact he can poo within eyesight of bed. Said did not need to think about that. Especially if Scarlet listening in. She will never love him if she has seen him poo. Telepathically or otherwise.

. . . .

Saturday 9

Sad Ed is still in bed. Went to observe him on trolley herding duty at Waitrose at lunchtime but Reuben Tull (giant afro, purveyor of medicinal mushrooms, apprentice herder) said he had called in sick. Said what with. He said 'weirdness'. Said I was sicker, i.e. had no man, no job, and no meaning in life any more. He asked if had tried God. Said thought he believed supreme being was in fact laser-eyed dog thing. He said 'affirmative'. So said no, had not pinned hopes of happiness on battery-powered Lassie. Hounds in our house are bad enough. The fighting is over, but now they are both 'helping' James with his investigations, i.e. they are trying to dig for murdered corpses in the compost heap.

. . . .

Sunday 10

Today has reached new lows in Riley household shouting levels and things being banned. Everyone has been sent to their rooms, one dog is in the garage and one is

having a 'holiday' at another location, i.e. the Whiteshot Estate, until all foreigners (i.e. Granny and Bruce) are returned to their places of origin. Have pointed out that it was Mum's fault for inviting Riley senior household (i.e. Grandpa, Treena, and Baby Jesus) over for lunch when house already contaminated with presence of Clegg. But Mum said it is not her fault, it is Treena's fault for telling Granny Clegg she needed a makeover, James's fault for giving Granny Clegg a makeover, Granny Clegg's fault for showing Bruce makeover, Bruce's fault for biting Grandpa Riley in panic, Grandpa Riley's fault for bleeding all over Dad, Dad's fault for bringing up time Grandpa Riley got him to feed his fingers to a Muscovy duck 'for a laugh' at lunch, and the dog's fault for bringing up its lunch. Said on plus side I am scot-free for once. She said, *au contraire*, it is also my fault that Baby Jesus ate a miniature Crabtree and Evelyn avocado-flavour soap, as I was in charge of taking him to loo, which is further proof that is good thing am single, as risk of pregnancy and child rearing, which am clearly not cut out for, reduced by several percentage points. Voluntarily went to room at that point before Mum could do more shouting/use of words like subnormal or fallopian tubes.

At least one person is out of their room. It is Sad Ed. Asked if was because he had overcome his broken heart or found alternative target for Scarlet-loving mojo, but he said no it is that his portable TV blew up. Said that must

have been frightening. He said it was as he missed the end of *Grey's Anatomy* and now he will never know if Dr McDreamy shaves his beard off or not.

8 p.m.
He does. James googled it.

. . . .

Monday 11

Mum is mental with anti-social behaviour/criminal madman potential. Marjory has rung to warn her that someone is lurking outside the house. Reminded Mum of fatal error in judgement when she thought Al Qaeda were about to blow her up and it turned out to be Weirdy Edie ogling Dad but she is adamant that the perpetrator is male this time. He is currently hiding in a rhododendron. James is also in overdrive. He says it is his first real job as a PI, it is just a shame that he is down to one tracker dog, i.e. Bruce, now that dog has taken up residence at 19 Harvey Road for foreseeable future. It is not a shame. Bruce can only detect Granny Clegg and neither of them are stealthlike. James is undeterred though and is determined to beat Marjory in identification of criminal lurker. Is bound to be an O'Grady. Or Barry the Blade. Oh God, what if he has fallen for me after my accidental bin love declaration and has earmarked me to become Mrs Blade, so that he can marry me and then murder me in a crazed knife attack?

368

3 p.m.

Lurker is gone but James said is not Barry the Blade as Marjory has already phoned in with a field report and says he is outside Goddards eating a pork pie. Said I thought he and Marjory were PI rivals. He said he has duped her into acting as his mentor, but it will be him who revels in the glory as the young upstart. Said he could have solved mystery by just going downstairs and confronting lurker. But James says where is the challenge in that?

. . . .

Tuesday 12

11 a.m.

Am racked by shocking news. It is that Peaches Geldof (who is totally me, except that she has tattoos, lives in London, and Dad is ageing muso type with cool hair and Crombie versus Colin Riley who is ageing accountant with short back and sides and cagoule from Millets) has got married. This is yet further reminder of what I have lost. I could have had Las Vegas wedding with own young upstart musician and spent rest of teenage years lounging in Brooklyn loft reading Bret Easton Ellis. Instead am in spare room watching bush with binoculars while James takes break from detecting for wee break and brain-stimulating snack (i.e. Omega-rich Flora on seedy granary).

11.05 a.m.

Oooh. What if lurker is Jack? What if he has been inspired

369

by Peaches Geldof true love too and has come to beg me to become Mrs Stone? Am going down immediately.

11.10 a.m.
Lurker was not Jack. Was Mad Harry! (So slightly mad, and criminal.) He is lingering around house in the hope that James will beg him to reform Beastly Boys. Said what about Mumtaz? He said, 'While the cat's away.' Said Mumtaz not cat, she girl. Mad Harry said whatever, he is bored rigid and she isn't back from Islamabad for five weeks. At which point James appeared from observation point number two (i.e. upstairs bathroom) and said he should have thought of that before he chose sex over musical supremacy. Mad Harry said Mumtaz's kisses cannot compare to the sheer joy of performing 'You Raise Me Up' alongside James. James said talk to the hand, and that he can lurk all he wants but Beastly Boys are dead, and their dream died with it. But Mad Harry said he still believes in Boy Power and went back to his lurking post. He is clinging to hope, like wreck of the *Hesperus*, clutching on for dear life. But James has already swum ashore and is reading magazine by the pool. It is utterly sad. Although on plus side will not have to witness any more renditions of 'Bleeding Love' in matching shiny T-shirts.

· ·

Wednesday 13
Mad Harry is still in the bush. He went home for tea and

sleep but was back at eight this morning with a carton of juice and a Harry Potter. This is what comes from being an only child. If your girlfriend and best friend desert you then you walk alone in the world, with just literature for company. At least I have sibling to take mind off trauma in hour of need.

3 p.m.
Sibling busy sifting tomato bed for bones. Think would be better off as only child. Or in bush with Mad Harry.

Anyway. Have more pressing and potentially tragic matters to concern self with, i.e. tomorrow is A level results day. Am not concerned for my performance (is AS levels so not even real exams) but is Jack. He cannot leave environs of Saffron Walden until have persuaded him that we are each other's destiny after all. Which may take more time than hoped. So either he has to get all As so he can go to boffiny Cambridge, i.e. only thirteen miles along A11. Or he has to fail completely so that not even Hull will take him. Am pinning hopes on him having had minor seizure in exam hall. Or Edexcel getting his papers mixed up with Fat Kylie's hairdressing multiple choice. Is feasible. Curse second-rate universities for setting low entry criteria.

. . . .

Thursday 14
8.30 a.m.
Feel sick. Cannot even eat Granny's Ready Brek (usually

371

banned for being too smooth). Is D-Day, i.e. will fate put 155 miles and the murky Humber between me and Jack, or will she deal him a hand of Fs and keep him trapped in non-fish-smelling Saffron Walden for another year? I hope so.

Mum is already pacing around the Shreddies table in anticipation (at my results, not Jack's). I do not know why she is so het up. As James has pointed out, I get a second go next year anyway. And, even if I do get an A in philosophy, there is no way she will let me take it for A2 in case it compromises my 'real' subject, i.e. English (drama and politics verge on BTEC bricklaying in her eyes).

9 a.m.
This is it. Am going to school. Have to face Jack. And my future. And also remember to get own results before Mum implodes.

2 p.m.
OMG. Fate has dealt me giant hand of Aces. Or a Royal Flush. Or whichever is good hand (poker banned in house under rules pertaining to gambling, fluorescent lighting, and green sun visors), i.e. Jack got As in everything. But isn't going to Cambridge, or Hull. Not yet anyway. He is deferring for a year. Did not find this out from Jack. He got results online as is still too angry to see me apparently, according to Sad Ed, who got it off Scarlet.

372

But do not care as means he will be within my clutches, aka reach of loving arms for another year. Hurrah!

Also Sad Ed and I got Bs in everything. Which would have been almost as excellent, had Scarlet not got three As, so is now eyeing me with superior brain anti-nipple love cheat stance instead of just anti-nipple one. (And Sad Ed with 'Cannot believe you are head boy and I am mere head of communications, is like Blair and Campbell all over again' stance.) Am rising above it. Now have another entire year to win back heart of true love. Will not give up. Will be persistent, like superglue. Or Mad Harry. He has moved on from lurking in the bush and is now on public display, i.e. is sitting on wall singing 'Back for Good'. Mum says if James doesn't hurry up and sort their relationship out she is going to hose Mad Harry down and will not spare the weedkiller attachment.

. . . .

Friday 15
Mad Harry is no longer lurking outside. He is inside, in James's bedroom, and I can distinctly hear the sound of scale practice. James is pathetic. He has no willpower. He claims he is just using Mad Harry and will dump him come September like the turncoat he is. He will not. Mad Harry is his destiny.

On the plus side, it proves persistence pays off, which bodes well for me and Jack. And me and Scarlet. Am going to commence campaign to win them back immediately.

Or possibly on Monday. As need to formulate plan. Plus Mum is out, Granny Clegg is asleep with Bruce on chest, and I have control of remote.

. . . .

Saturday 16

There has been a shock manoeuvre from Camp Pasty. Grandpa Clegg has rung and has surrendered and begged Granny Clegg to return to her rightful place! He says he cannot cope alone any more. Asked where Pig and Denzil were. He says they have gone to Pig's for a bath as conditions at Pasty Manor have deteriorated beyond comprehension. There is no hot water (Grandpa cannot work the thermostat), no food bar frozen Yorkshire puddings, no toilet roll (they have run out of *Daily Mail* and are on *Parker's Used Car Guide*, which has very small pages), and the sink has fallen off the wall. Grandpa says it is like 1950s all over again. Although personally thought it was like that before the whole coup thing.

Anyway, Granny is having none of it. She has told Mum she wants to have her pension book transferred to Summerdale Road as she is thinking of moving in permanently. Mum went pale and told her not to be too hasty. But Granny says she can see herself eking out her days on our sofa, with her loving family around her. Mum is now in emergency panic mode. She says she is not prepared to look after a Clegg on anything other

374

than a temporary basis. James pointed out the advantages of a multi-generational household, i.e. free TV licence, dog number one stays at Whiteshot Estate. But Mum said dog is picnic compared to Bruce. This is true. After Granny made her announcement I actually saw Bruce smile ominously. Think he evil, like Cujo.

. . . .

Sunday 17

Multigenerational household tension is palpable. Granny is issuing a litany of demands, now that the spare room is to become her permanent abode, including:

1. New curtains. She says oatmeal (Mum's preferred hue, of everything—clothes, walls, linen, food) is too depressing and she wants a bold rose design.
2. Some nice Axminster carpet to replace current (oatmeal) shade.
3. And a portable TV in bedroom (worse than heroin in Mum's book, which as have pointed out before, is actual book).

Mum's lips have disappeared, i.e. is advisable to give her at least ten-metre berth. In fact, Dad has gone to play golf and James has volunteered to caddy for half his usual rate. Think will follow their example and exeunt to Scarlet's. Will be chance to rekindle our best friend status, and to initiate my year-long win-back-Jack campaign.

5 p.m.

Am also in emergency mode. There has been more shock-ing permanent residence news—this time from house of Stone. It started off well, i.e. actually persuaded Scarlet to let me in. She said are you here to apologize to me, or to moon around over Jack in hope he will change his mind and stick tongue in orifice again? Said to apologize to you, obviously. Do not even like Jack any more. Have accepted our relationship has run course. And orifices now her-metically sealed. But then she said, 'Good. And anyway, he too busy to be mooned over, even if wanted to, which he does not.' Said why he too busy. Scarlet said he is packing. Said for what? Assuming it was for brief post-A level celebratory holiday, e.g. yurting in Brecon Beacons. But it was not. He is going to build schools for impover-ished and uneducated children. And is not even in Wales. Is in Guatemala! Bob is driving him to the airport in the sick-smelling Volvo tomorrow morning! Said it is awful. Sight of me so unbearable he is having to flee to war-torn third world country, where he will live on refried beans and possibly get that thing where a hooky fish swims up your penis and you die (Sad Ed saw it on *Grey's Anatomy*). Scarlet said I was overreacting and not all beans refried (why do they do that?), plus he knows better than to sway penis in contaminated water. And anyway, at least I had her back again as probationary best friend. Asked her what had changed her mind. She said she had thought about it and, on balance, even though utterly broke Jack's

heart, she preferred it when best friend not hovering near brother's genitals as is too ickky to contemplate. Said hmm. But was too busy thinking about Jack's genitals. And broken heart, obviously. Oh it is utterly romantic. He is selfless charity worker, as well as musical prodigy and political genius. I love him even more! Maybe he will become non-religious missionary, i.e. spreading the word of Keynesian economics. Oooh. Or I can go out there and work alongside him in a giant hat and khaki hot pants. Will be like Indiana Jones film. But without Nazis and giant rolling ball thing. Hurrah! Am actually happy again.

. . . .

Monday 18

9 a.m.
Or maybe he will meet love of his life over a cholera-infested latrine pit and they will both catch leprosy and die in each other's arms. OMG. It is AWFUL. I have to stop him.

9.15 a.m.
Have had genius idea. Am going to do airport dash. Is utterly romantic and always works in films, e.g. *Love Actually* (although is eight-year-old boy, but all the same, is very tear-jerking). Am going to Scarlet's immediately. Or at least, in an hour. Want to ensure Jack actually departed before set off otherwise is not dash, is just drive in silence in same sicky Volvo, which is not at all

romantic or life-changing. Will text Sad Ed to come too. Is possible romantic airport atmosphere will aid in his plight, i.e. Scarlet will hurl self on him at boarding gate. Or more likely cake section of Costa Coffee.

10 a.m.
This is it. Am going to change the course of history! Or stop Jack getting a fish up his penis, anyway.

5 p.m.
Have failed. Jack has gone. And can hear the fish swimming towards his pant area as we speak. Events as follows:

10.05 a.m.
Arrive at Scarlet's.

10.09 a.m.
Sad Ed arrives at Scarlet's, despite having less distance to travel and having left five minutes before me.

10.10 a.m.
Sad Ed given pint of water and emergency pain au chocolat to revive sugar levels. Scarlet refuses to do mouth to mouth citing potential risk of 'cooties'.

10.11 a.m.
Rachel Riley points out 'cooties' not real but made up American thing like malt shops and bobby pins.

10.12 a.m.
Sad Ed says no cooties real. He has had them twice.

10.13 a.m.
Scarlet refuses to countenance airport dash on several grounds, i.e. *a*) she does not want to encourage me going near brother's bits, as is as bad as fish, *b*) it is utter cliché, *c*) she is boycotting Stansted due to kerosene melting polar bears etc., as well I know, and *d*) none of us can drive, except Suzy, who is still over limit from drowning sorrows at departure of first-born into wide world.

10.14 a.m.
Suzy declares that *a*) Jack's genitals are free territory, *b*) was not a cliché in *Love Actually*, was utterly tear-jerking, *c*) we are preventing Jack from flying so is pro-polar bear, and *d*) Sad Ed can drive and she will invigilate.

10.16 a.m.
Party gets into non-sick-smelling car of people.

10.26 a.m.
Sad Ed finds first gear. Non-sick-smelling car of people departs chez Stone block paving on eight-mile journey towards destiny.

11.26 a.m.
Car of people arrives at destiny, i.e. short-stay car park,

with only thirty-four minutes to go until Jack departs for certain fish-related death.

11.36 a.m.
Party dashes through airport in excellent cinematic display.

11.37 a.m.
Sad Ed crashes into herd of trolleys (oh, the irony), ruining cinematic effect, and costing several seconds.

11.38 a.m.
Party arrives at departure gates. Heroine (i.e. me) searches desperately for hero among crowd lining up for boarding.

11.39 a.m.
Hero appears behind heroine with copy of *Melody Maker* and Double Decker (not the same without raisins) and says, 'What the hell are you doing here, Rach?' Heroine says, 'Why you not in queue. Have you changed mind?' Hero says, 'No, flight delayed for hour. That is queue for Formentera. Look, there is Thin Kylie.' Heroine observes Thin Kylie with tongue in Mark Lambert's mouth and hand down back of trousers.

11.40 a.m.
Heroine says, 'Have come to change your destiny. Need to

tell you something. Um. Thing is. Um. Am in love with you.' Hero looks away and shakes head and says 'Rach' in way that does not indicate he in agreement. Heroine says, 'But have done romantic airport dash and everything.' Hero says, 'Life is just one big drama for you, Rach. You think you're Elizabeth Bennet or Bridget bloody Jones. But I don't want Bridget Jones. Or anyone from Richard Curtis style rom-com. I want you. The real you.' Said, 'But this is the real me.' Hero says, 'That's what I'm worried about, Rach.' Said, 'But will try harder. Honest. Will never snog Justin again. Even though last one was not actual kiss, was scientific, i.e. to prove you are better at it. So am like Marie Curie, if you think about it.' But Jack not in agreement with this. He said, 'There you go again. Jesus, Rach. You shouldn't want to be anyone else. You should want to be yourself. Life isn't a bloody film, or a book.' Said, 'But you are knight in shining whatever.' Hero says, 'No, am really not knight in shining whatever. And you don't need rescuing anyway, except possibly from self.' Heroine tries blackmail tactic, i.e. 'But I thought you cared about me. Was obviously utter lie.' Hero sighs and says, 'Look, I do care. That's why I'm telling you this. You need to give up on the fairytale stuff. You need to grow up, Rach. Otherwise we don't stand a chance.' Heroine says, 'Mmmmggghh', as is doing snotty crying. Hero kisses heroine on forehead (carefully avoiding snot-smeared areas), and departs in direction of destiny, i.e. Gate 12.

And now hero is several thousand miles away in war-torn and exotic Guatemala. And heroine is back in war-tornish but not at all exotic Summerdale Road, lying on bed, staring at poster of Ophelia drowning. Oh God. Am Ophelia. Going mad with grief. Am literally drowning in own tears.

. . . .

Tuesday 19

Have had revelation. Am not Ophelia. Am Rachel Riley. And do not care. Sad Ed and Scarlet have been round to comfort me in hour of need/point out that Jack is right, i.e. we should be proud to be ourselves, even if we are only seventeen, white, and from Saffron Walden, and is much more exciting to be black or drug dealer or lesbian. Anyway, point is, we do not need knights in shining armour. We are strong, intelligent women (and penis-compromised man) and can rescue ourselves from dragons, and selves. Sad Ed not entirely happy with that point. He has been planning for weeks to engineer situation whereby he has to rescue Scarlet from terrifying wild animal so that she is indebted to him for ever and will be forced to love him. But Scarlet told him he had better not be showing any signs of anti-feminism or she will be petitioning Mr Wilmott for a rethink of head boy appointment on sex discrimination grounds and their happy team will be split irrevocably. Sad Ed made pledge.

Scarlet is right. Basing life on books is utterly childish. Have taken down Ophelia poster and boxed up all false-hope-inducing romance-based books, e.g. *Pride and Prejudice*, *Emma*, and *Sugar Rush*.

From now on, am just me. Am going to grow up. And accept that, in this life, there are no happy endings. There is just tomorrow.

. . . .

Wednesday 20

Unless your surname is Clegg. There has been news on the grand reunion/happy ending front. Granny Clegg has sustained a severe head injury, i.e. she tripped over Bruce and knocked herself out on a curtain cleat. Which is excellent as, despite the bloodstain on oatmeal carpet, which makes house look like set on *Crimewatch/EastEnders*, Granny Clegg is experiencing partial amnesia! When she came round she demanded to know where she was, and why house smelt weird (i.e. of hyacinth-flavour Glade plug-in instead of Fray Bentos and feet). Plus she has refused reviving cup of ginger and lemon tea as it was 'for lesbians' and has demanded the Spar bags and a return to Pasty Manor immediately! James said Mum was under moral obligation to tell her of her political awakening and her decision to move to Summerdale Road following the Pig and Denzil hoo-ha. But Mum says what she doesn't know won't hurt her. She is repatriating her first thing tomorrow. Hopefully the sight

of malnourished and soiled Grandpa Clegg will not effect total recall.

In fact, might go with her. Am utterly bored. Life is empty without romance-based books, TV, or films. Under current rules can only watch fact-based things, i.e. news (as long as do not imagine am Kirsty Wark) and documentaries (as long as do not imagine I am sex trafficked Russian being abused by criminal overlord). Even *Lovejoy* is banned as have been known to imagine was Tinker, under extreme circumstances.

. . . .

Thursday 21

Have changed mind. Utterly brilliant fact-based thing has happened, i.e. there is a wild beast on loose. It is an ocelot called Brian who has escaped from Linton Zoo and was last seen heading along B1052 towards Saffron Walden. Local news is mental with excitement. Granny Clegg says is old hat and ocelot is nothing compared to Beast of Bodmin, which she has seen several times including once when it did poo outside Hester's. (She has not, it was overweight cat from launderette.) Mum is jubilant as is proof Granny still mentally incapacitated/back to normal self. The Spar bags are packed and they are departing as soon as Bruce has had a wee.

James and Mad Harry are also mad with excitement. They have built up an arsenal of equipment to locate and capture beast. Though Mum has already confiscated the

Hoover. She says it is still recovering from its stint in 'Ghost Hustlers' when it was used to suck up ectoplasm (dog vomit/soup/Badedas bubble bath). They are going round to Grandpa Riley's in a minute to fetch the dog. They claim its anti-cat instinct will prove essential in successful ocelot capture. They will be lucky if they can persuade dog to leave 19 Harvey Road. I know for a fact it is enjoying low-protein high-crisp diet.

3 p.m.
Ocelot fever has also hit Loompits Way. Sad Ed wants to join the hunt so he can rescue Scarlet from its rapacious claws. Reminded him of ban on rescuing knights of any sort, but he says she will change her mind when its jagged teeth are sinking into her milky white thigh. He is mental.

7 p.m.
Have walked round town twice and there is no sign of ocelot anywhere. Am back home in safety of living room, watching alternative wild beast chew its own tail, i.e. dog. James and Mad Harry managed to get it away from Grandpa Riley but it did not in any way aid ocelot hunt as has put on several pounds in crisp weight, so it has been sacked and they are going to rely on their wit and cunning alone. They have no hope. Plus, according to news, ocelot is miracle cat, i.e. has been spotted in several places at once, e.g. savaging mole on fourteenth hole of golf course, stalking small children in Bridge End Gardens,

and looking at screenwash in Halford's. If ocelot has any sense it is heading for bright lights of city, e.g. Cambridge, where at least there is a McDonald's to scavenge.

. . . .

Friday 22
10 a.m.

Grandpa Riley has rung with an ocelot sighting. He claims it is at this very minute next-door in the O'Gradys' living room, he has seen it through the grimy nets. (Theirs, not his. His were confiscated by Mum for being common.) He thinks it has chosen them for their superior size and meat-based diet and has rounded them up. Asked him if he had rung police yet. He said no, as Mum had issued him with new rule that he was only allowed to ring police after checking with her first that emergency was actual emergency. (He is on blacklist for false alarms, e.g. 'cannot find can opener', 'someone has stolen BBC1' (aerial fallen out), and 'Jesus is stuck up a tree' (though this was actual emergency not Messiah-based fantasy as assumed by PC Doone).) James said he had done the right thing, and that it was best not to involve the police at all, and that he and Mad Harry are going instead. Is good job Mum is in Cornwall as she would be issuing several more bans.

11 a.m.

Have texted Sad Ed to tell him to lure Scarlet in direction of Whiteshot Estate for savaging.

386

2 p.m.
James and Mad Harry are back. So is Sad Ed. Was not man-eating ocelot in O'Grady living room. Was stuffed lion called Maurice. Stacey and one of the Liams stole it from the museum in a ransom bid. Is utterly disappointing. Had hoped someone would be minorly maimed. James and Mad Harry say *au contraire* is triumph as they have solved mysterious plot and are hoping to secure grand reward for endeavour. Plus they say it is the inaugural case for their new detective/safari agency Beastly Investigations. Said did not think there was going to be much call for wild-beast-related crime solving in Saffron Walden. James said, 'That's what you think.' He is moron. Sad Ed is depressed though. He has been pinning his hopes on seizing Scarlet from jaws of woman-eating wildcat. Instead she ended up fending off Fat Kylie who threatened to hit him with Mr Whippy's ice cream scoop for 'being twathead'.

5 p.m.
Ocelot has been caught. Was not on golf course. Or in Halford's. Was on common looking in bins with Barry the Blade.

. . . .

Saturday 23
Mum is back from Cornwall. She says Pasty Manor is restored to its former glory, i.e. both Cleggs are happily

inside it, arguing over who gets the broken Parker Knoll. Apparently scene was of utter devastation, i.e. toilet blocked with several Anne Leslie columns, suggested costs for 1985 Mini Metro, and a flyer for Bobby Helmet. Plus somehow Pig and Denzil had managed to get diesel oil, or possibly treacle, all over the spare beds. Pointed out that Mum lives for challenges like that. She said yes, it was a three-cloth job. Asked if she had had words with Pig and Denzil about staying away but she said apparently is unnecessary as newly unprogressive Granny is talking about joining them in the fight for independence. She even refused to let Grandpa change house name back to Belleview as gesture of surrender. Said was romantic. She said is not, is shameful. But at least is 300 miles away, as is Bruce, who apparently was utterly overjoyed at return. Although it took several washings before he recognized Grandpa Clegg. Mum said he looked like a tree protestor what with his matted dreadlocks, withered limbs, and haunted look of the perpetually undernourished.

Sunday 24
9 a.m.
Not only am I loveless, and trapped in small town without even romantic comedy to fill me with hope for the future, but also have no hope of getting out as Jack has ridden into sunset (on board DC10, as opposed to astride white charger. And not so much sunset as mid-afternoon

gloom, but you get the point) with key to non-sick smelling car of people. Is nothing else for it. Am going to have to beg Dad to pay for lessons.

10 a.m.
Dad says he absolutely cannot afford to pay for driving lessons in the face of economic gloom and that is waste of money anyway as he is perfectly capable of teaching me to drive. Mum says *au contraire* he is perfectly incapable, as his previous speeding fine/obsession with Jeremy Clarkson/inability to stick to the ten-to-two position proves, and that she will teach me, as she is known for her rigid abiding to all speed limits, as well as ferocious mirror, signal, maneouevring. Have got first lesson in four hours. Is like woke up in minor bad dream, but now has turned into full-scale nightmare with demonic homunculus thrown in for good measure.

3 p.m.
Dad is booking me in with Mike Majors next week. It is because Mum says she cannot be expected to teach someone who turns a simple request to turn right into a philosophical discussion. I said I cannot be expected to learn from someone who insists that I wear her brogues (not on-trend Alexa Chung ones, hideous Clarks' ones) as Converse might slip on accelerator and cause fatal accident. Especially when did not get above five miles an hour as Mum kept saying, 'Careful, careful, watch that

pedestrian', when *a*) pedestrian was several hundred yards away, and *b*) was an O'Grady so prime target for mowing down. Dad said he cannot be expected to listen to this nonsense any more, it is enough to make him turn to drink. At which point Mum turned her minty attention to him so could escape to bedroom to read fact-based books.

. . . .

Monday 25
Bank Holiday
Am so full of facts am turning into nerd. Is dangerous stance. May well end up repelling all members of opposite sex for good. Look at James. In fact do not look at James. He and Mad Harry are currently dressed as James Bond (black polo-necks, dark glasses, and swimming trunks (in case of water-based emergencies)) and are practising spy tactics, i.e. rolling across lawn whilst shooting dog with water pistol. Dog does not mind. Plus it is still too fat from the crisp diet to move if it did.

. . . .

Tuesday 26
Am beyond bored. Scarlet is away on economy drive ironic caravan holiday in Bognor Regis and Sad Ed is on unironic Aled Jones tour of Bangor. James says I can join Beastly Investigations if I want. Asked if he had any commissions. He said no but they are going to stake out Mr

Hosepipe (aka Mr Lambert, father of Mark, former stripper, current fireman) later as it is possible he is running white slave trade from back of fire station. He is not. He is running a crap lookylikey agency, e.g. PC Doone as Freddie Mercury (PC Doone looks nothing like Freddie Mercury. Looks like Bobby Davro with false moustache) and Mark Lambert as David Beckham (with cunning aid of sunglasses and cucumber down pants).

Will go for walk instead. Though will utterly not pretend am Elizabeth Bennet on wistful stroll around grounds of Pemberley. Or Cathy staggering to Wuthering Heights. Will be romance-free, fact-based walk. Will identify wild plants. Or note locations of dog poo.

4 p.m.
OMG. Have bumped into man on walk. Literally. Was not even looking for one, and was utterly not pretending to be Tess of d'Urbervilles lowly-birth type but actually related to rich but evil aristo, when there he was, standing in front of me, rubbing bruise on nose, looking completely like Johnny Borrell, but with less tight trousers, and a packet of custard creams in hand instead of vodka bottle. Said sorry, was not looking where was going, was thinking about important fact-based matter. Like, er, mortgage crisis. He said, 'No worries. Sometimes I go into another world when I get going on politics.' Then he walked off past Marjory's humming theme from Channel 4 news.

Is fate.

5 p.m.

No is not fate. Is pure coincidence. Am not going to fall at first romantic comedy hurdle.

7 p.m.

But he is older man, i.e. at least 22, judging by out-of-date Strokes tour T-shirt. And Jack told me I had to grow up, and what better way than by going out with older man?

. . . .

Wednesday 27

Have walked round block five times but older man not in evidence. James says I can hire Beastly Investigations to track him down for one pound fifty. Said one pound twenty-three and half a packet of Polos? He has agreed. He and Mad Harry are behind the wall with the binoculars and aquatic disguises as we speak. Pointed out lack of water hazards in Summerdale Road environs but James said his namesake, Mr Bond, would never have lived to die another day if he had ignored water peril. And anyway Thin Kylie has a kidney-shaped pool and Marjory has an ornamental pond, both of which are utterly hazardous (and lower middle class) as verified by Mum.

4 p.m.

There has been a positive sighting of T-shirt man. To be

fair did not require binoculars or aquatic-wear, or even detective agency. He just walked past house and nodded and said hi. Which would have been good if had not been in full view of me in front garden trying to get dog to hurry up and poo by singing the 'poo song' to it (i.e. Kenny Rogers and Dolly Parton 'Islands in the Stream', which for some reason has laxative effect on dog). Plus Mum was hovering in background with rubber gloves, smelly Bob spade and poobag, ready to dispense with poo as soon as it made appearance. James is jubilant none the less. He says his services were essential as they now have him on camera and can trace him back to his lair. So he is fully deserving of his £1.23 and mint-based confectionery. Mum not so happy. She said hopes I am not having romantic urges towards strangers, especially ones who are old enough to be my father. Said *a*) am anti-romance and only interested in facts, which is why *b*) I know he is not at all old enough to be father as no one of Dad's age would know who Strokes are let alone have body to wear a figure-hugging T-shirt bearing their 2004 tour dates. And *c*) he does not live in lair as is not cartoon baddie or Osama Bin Laden. But then decided to exit to house as Mum was armed and dangerous, i.e. pointing poo-laden smelly Bob spade at me.

. . . .

Thursday 28

James and Mad Harry have garnered further inside

information on T-shirt man. According to their investigations, he is possibly in league with Mr Patel of Mr Patel's
fame, as he spent fifty-eight minutes in the shop this
morning. So either they are running a black market ticket
tout ring, or he has a porn/Pot Noodle/sticky lino fetish.
Also he is not a vegetarian as he came out eating a
Ginster's pasty (contravening Mum's many rules pertaining to Ginster's use of mince rather than cubed steak, and
purchasing convenience food from corner shops where it
is kept in unhygienic conditions and rarely warmed to
required temperatures).

4 p.m.
Mum says he is none of the above. Except for foolhardy
regarding pasty consumption. According to Marjory, who
got it off Mrs Dyer (unconvincing dye job, fat feet, smells
of Yardley), he is lodging at Chestnuts B&B (1950s semi,
manky conker tree in garden, proprietors Les and Ying
Brewster of sex bar and Siam Smile restaurant fame) until
he finds a flat, which is why he was talking to Mr Patel as
Mr Patel is property magnate (not magnet, have made
that mistake before) and owns half of Saffron Walden.
Also, he is 23, which, while not technically being old
enough to be my father, is still utterly out of bounds. Also
she has banned James from any more detecting/wearing
of swimming trunks anywhere other than municipal
pools/beach-based areas. She says *a*) he clearly has no
talent in this area, and *b*) he starts secondary school in

394

four days' time and if doesn't want to get dragged down by the hordes of gum-chewing knife-toting O'Gradys then he had better start getting his head in the game. Said *a*) no one totes knives at school, it is banned, although gum is encouraged due to plaque fighting properties, but it has to be dispensed into bin, not stuck to desk or Mr Wilmott, and *b*) did not know she had seen *High School Musical*. She said *a*) I have had just about enough of your fact spouting, I think it was better when you read Enid Blyton all day and thought you were Darrell because you both had curly hair, and *b*) Operatics are doing it as winter show. Said *a*) is true, am quite like Darrell, and *b*) in that case hoped she and Dad are not auditioning after the *Grease* fiasco. She said no, but Clive and Marjory are hoping to be cast as Ryan and Sharpay. Said would not hold breath. She said nor would she as is bound to go to sadistic dentist Mrs Wong and Russell Rayner (closet homosexual, golf professional, once in an Erasure video).

* *

Friday 29

James is in room with Mad Harry planning for school. They are sharpening their pencils, tying their ties and checking their trousers are regulation length. They are so going to get heads flushed down toilets on Monday. Will pretend do not know them. Cannot be associated with such levels of weirdness. Instead have done detecting on

own, i.e. wandered past B&B on pretext of poo trip. But to no avail. T-shirt man is very much not in evidence. Which is possibly good thing as dog bit Chestnuts sign off the gate and swallowed it before could prise it out of hairy jaws.

9 p.m.
Mum has banned me from taking dog on any more poo trips. She says it is exhausted. Plus it will lose the ability to control its bowels and start needing to poo every two hours. Like Dad. Did not ask. She is right though. I am wasting my time. It was not fate bumping into T-shirt man. Was just idiotic Riley-esque accident. I do not believe in romance or happy endings. I just believe in facts. And the fact is, he knows where I live, and hasn't been back. Although the sight of Mum with poo-spade could be deterring him. Not even Dad could find that pleasant. Thank God Scarlet is back tomorrow. She will reinforce my fact-based mission.

· ·

Saturday 30

Scarlet is back. But is out of bounds. I rang to ask if she wanted to come round once Sad Ed has finished trolley herding but she says we cannot see her until her transformation is complete. Apparently she has had a revelation in Bognor Regis and will unveil all on Monday at school. Sad Ed says it had better not be Wicca again as he is

still sad after melting his wand, aka light sabre, in ritual sacrifice.

. . . .

Sunday 31

James is going mental with grown-upness, i.e. in anticipation of his first day at secondary school. He is already wearing his uniform (with full sleeve painting apron on top to alleviate potential porridge spillages). He is going to be severely disappointed. All he will do in first week is draw locusts, burn peanuts, and get chewed by the school sheep. A timetable that will continue for weeks, if not years. Real learning does not begin until Year Ten, as any fool know.

september

NAPPY

Monday 1

First day of school.

Hurrah. It is finally here. After several arduous years, am at pinnacle of career at John Major High, i.e. am Upper Sixth. Which gives me instant rights to barge to front in chips and beans queue, access top shelf in library (Usborne Pop-Up Guide to Body) and wee in superior A Corridor toilets. *Au contraire*, James is at bottom of food chain, i.e. Year Seven, doomed to tinned sweetcorn (ick), *Sweet Valley High*, and the no-seat loo. Have given him essential survival tips, i.e. do not look a Criminal and Retard in the eye, do not offer to find a valuable they claim to have dropped down toilet in exchange for reward, do not join maths club, chess club, science club, or farm club (double whammy of mentalism as not only is geeky but you smell of goat poo all day). Plus have warned him it can take weeks to make friends and, if he gets scared, then Mrs Leech (school secretary, too much face powder, biscuit habit) has a ready supply of bourbons and orange squash. Have also warned him that under no circumstances is he to lurk around common room or in any way reveal that I am related to him.

Mum has taken at least twenty photographs of him looking like Little Lord Fauntleroy. Asked why I was not allowed in picture to mark historic day, but she said my miniskirt and dog-chewed Led Zeppelin T-shirt did not reflect theme of academic prowess. Plus my hair takes up too much room.

5 p.m.

School was excellent. Me and Sad Ed are utterly imbued with Upper Sixth authority, i.e. Year Sevens stare in awe when we pass in corridors. Although that could be down to dog-chewed T-shirt which now reads 'Le Z'. Plus Sad Ed was wearing skinny jeans, which are not at all flattering to his 'unique build', as have pointed out on several occasions, but apparently his combats are in wash following incident on Aled Jones tour so he is limited wardrobe-wise. James has failed to abide by any of my rules though. Already he and Mad Harry are nestled in the cocoon of geekery that is the mathletes lunch table. Apparently they impressed the 'boss' (aka Ali Hassan) with their ability to sing the periodic table and correctly identify the valency of boron. As did Mumtaz. Though James says she is only there by default because she is related to Ali so it is totally like the mafia, or Nicolas Cage. Said mathletes not in any way like the mafia and anyway I thought he was going to dump Mad Harry come September once Mumtaz was back on the scene. James says Mad Harry says Mumtaz has been offish with him since her return and that six weeks in Pakistan may have restricted her, love-wise, so James is just biding his time to see which way the wind, or Mumtaz, blows.

There is other, non-nerd-related canteen hoo-ha. It is Scarlet. In shock fashion/lifestyle move, she has turned back into a goth, i.e. black fishnets, pasty complexion,

perpetual smell of patchouli. She says she had an epiphany in Bognor, which was not ironic at all, just wet and crap, so she spent entire week in bunk reading seminal vampire-based novel *Twilight*, plus several sequels, and has seen the light, or rather dark, again. I said this was potential breaking of pact as reading gothic romance utterly not OK under terms and conditions, but she said, *au contraire*, she has learned all sorts of important facts about vampires, Native American culture, and pick-up trucks, so it was educational, rather than emotional stimulation. She has lent me book to see for myself. But can tell she is lying. I can see suspicious glow on cheeks even under chalky sedimentary layer.

Anyway, rebirth has upset Goth Corners Mark I and II no end, as, according to official John Major rules, her age, seniority and ownership of vegetarian leather coat give her right to be declared Head Goth and sit on the Throne of Darkness (plastic chair with bats drawn on in chubby marker). But that position is currently occupied by Tamsin Bacon, former Wiccan novice, and current girlfriend of Trevor Pledger (former Head Goth, ex-boyfriend of Scarlet, currently on gap year in shuttlecock factory). Scarlet says this is a mere detail. She is going to get Sad Ed to impose head boy authority and take possession of the throne. Sad Ed is bound to do it. I caught him gazing at her ankles (only bit visible due to return of voluminous goth skirt) in English with utter boy lust.

8 p.m.
May just read bit of *Twilight* for research purposes. All facts are equal in eyes of education.

1 a.m.
Oh my God. Scarlet is right. Is totally seminal. Am in love with moody vampire Edward Cullen, and possibly with werewolf enemy. Plus am utterly heroine Bella Swan, i.e. cool, bookish, with father who can't cook. Although he not chief of police, and Saffron Walden not really at all like Forks, i.e. Forks is big wet forest with swirly grey clouds and Saffron Walden is leafy commuter town with Starbucks. God it is so unfair. Why can't we move to somewhere with vampire potential. Like Forks. Or possibly Leeds, which is wet, at least.

1.30 a.m.
Although obviously and most importantly have gleaned lots of good vampire facts, e.g. reason can't go out in sunlight is because they go all glowy and twinkly. See— would never have known important vampire-detecting fact if had not read romance. So is not breaking rules. Plus, is horror, so cannot have happy ending.

. . . .

Tuesday 2
Ramadan begins
There has been a goth-related fight in canteen. Sad Ed imposed authority, and weight advantage, by sitting in

Throne of Darkness, to reserve it for Scarlet. But four minigoths managed to topple him forwards into Mrs Brain's healthy soup of day (baked bean and sausage) and move chair to Goth Corner Mark II, instantly designating it as Goth Corner Mark I. So now there are two rival goth camps. And although Scarlet is leader of one, it is the substandard Mark II version. She says she is going to use plan B. Which is get Sad Ed to build a new and bigger throne, thereby outdoing the Throne of Darkness, and transferring authority back to her table. I said a) Sad Ed is not known for his carpentry, or indeed any, skills, and b) wouldn't it be easier just to settle dispute in traditional John Major High fashion, i.e. fight on sheep field. But Scarlet says a) he offered, and b) fighting is going to be banned under Sad Ed's new head boy rules, and they are going to introduce a system of heated debate instead. Plus c) (which came from nowhere, but is further proof that she is invading me telepathically) neither of us is anybody other than ourselves, but if push came to shove, she is Bella, not me. I said but Bella has car, and I am at least taking driving lessons, unlike Scarlet who refuses on various grounds (anti polar-bear, potential for road deaths, leather steering wheels). Plus her dad can cook vegetarian toad in the hole. Scarlet said it is not about cars or cookery skills, it is about essence de goth, which she has, and I do not. I said I can buy patchouli tomorrow if that is all that matters but Scarlet just said 'point proven' and ate another sesame snap.

Also, Mumtaz was noticeably absent from the math-lete table. Asked James if this was indicative of post-separation decline of her relationship with Mad Harry. James said potentially. Although mainly is because is Ramadan and she does not want to be around all those granary sandwiches. But that this is causing love-divide issues as Mad Harry is very food-orientated, and not so respecting of her religious beliefs as James, who has been known to observe Ramadan in past, albeit only for few hours, and ending in fainting on netball court. Said hoped James not thinking of embracing Islam again in bid to vie for affections. He said the only affections he is interested in are Mad Harry's. But not in a man-love way.

8 p.m.
Although thinking about it, James and Mad Harry do enjoy dressing up in leotards and fake fur. Plus they like Will Young. And *Hannah Montana*. Maybe they are gay. That would be excellent as not only would I be instantly cool, but Mum would go mental. Will tell him to come out of closet immediately.

8.30 p.m.
James still in closet. Though he claims there is no closet. He says he is 100 per cent heterosexual. Said not even just 90 per cent? He said possibly 99 per cent, if you count his admiration for the physique of young Kirk Douglas. Which he does not. And to stop bothering him as he is

406

'fagging' for 'the boss' tomorrow. Said aha, he is Ali's maths bitch, which is totally gay. He said it is not, he is just calculator monitor. So is just nerdy, not gay. How utterly disappointing.

. . . .

Wednesday 3

8 a.m.

Hurrah. It is drama today. And we have new teacher now that Mr Vaughan is ensconced in Bath, with his supersize nipples and Sophie Microwave Muffins. It is sad, because Mr Vaughan had excellent, forward-thinking approach to teaching, e.g. not minding if anyone was late for lessons. Or even showed up for lessons. Although he was potential pervert-in-school. Plus new teacher will possibly be RSC actor taking philanthropic sabbatical to pass on cavernous experience to the next generation of stars. Oooh. Maybe it is Dr Who!

9 a.m.

New teacher rumours have reached epic proportions. According to James, odds are 10–1 on Dr Who, 5–2 on Simon Cowell, and evens on Mrs Best from Burger King Sports Academy, who is vaguely related to someone on *The Bill*, and who Mr Wilmott has had his eye on for years, ever since her groundbreaking production of *Joseph* with actual locust plague. James is now fully entrenched in the mathletes illegal gambling ring. He and Mad Harry are

debt collectors, due to them being former gang members. I said I did not think a few months as henchmen to Keanu O'Grady was necessarily satisfactory qualification but James says it is the closest to menace any of the mathletes have ever been—they are like superheroes. How sad.

4 p.m.
Oh. My. God. New drama teacher is not Dr Who. Or even Mrs Best. It is Older T-Shirt Man from B&B! Who is not actually called T-Shirt Man but is officially Mr Pringle! On downside, he is not RSC actor, or even related to someone on *Bill*, but on plus side he looked utterly gorgeous sitting astride back to front chair in faded black T-shirt and position that says 'I am completely in charge, but in leftfield, maverick kind of way.' Now I know how Sophie Microwave Muffins must have felt when confronted with Mr Vaughan and his smoking habit and big nipples. Am utterly smitten. He is my handsome prince. Hurrah! Will have happy ending after all.

4.30 p.m.
Have had rethink. Am not smitten. Am not looking for romantic fairytale happy endings etc., etc. Am only interested in facts.

4.45 p.m.
And, obviously, he is teacher, which is out of bounds and illegal. In Mum's eyes, if not in actual eyes of law.

5 p.m.

Scarlet has texted to say is illegal in actual eyes of law. How does she do that? Anyway, am determined to enjoy only cerebral relationship with him. He can be my mentor, like Alan Sugar. We will not snog, but will have grown-up fact-based relationship.

. . . .

Thursday 4

Have demanded that Sad Ed use his head boy privileges to get school secretary Mrs Leech to divulge any facts (see, am sticking to rules) she may have on Mr Pringle's provenance, and preference, woman-wise. It will be cinch. She is anyone's for a cup of tea and a gypsy cream.

12 noon

Fact: Mr Pringle has degree in drama and media studies from University of Stoke on Trent.

Fact: He is NOT on sex offenders' register.

Fact: His first name is Patrick. But he prefers Paddy.

Hurrah. So now know he is pro-working class, i.e. chose Stoke (not too thick to get into Manchester, which is what Mrs Leech claimed), irony-embracing (Paddy, despite not being Irish), and officially NOT a pervert.

Said that was not many facts, really, but Sad Ed said apparently he over-sugared the cup of tea and his iced rings were stale. Plus Mr Wilmott came in to demand to know where his swivelly orthopaedic seat was. Mrs Leech

said is utter mystery, maybe the Criminals and Retards have borrowed it for corridor racing again. They have not. It is installed in Goth Corner, complete with velvet cushion, superglue bat attachments and Scarlet enthroned in it. She is like that supreme Dalek, Davros—half evil dictator, half chair. There is no contest with Melody Bean. Her chair has no wheels or orthopaedic back support and in fact only pretension to gothness is felt tip cartoon. She has been forced to concede defeat, thus avoiding splitting the Goths further (already suffering due to a difference of opinion on admitting EMOS and the Tim Burton freaks).

. . . .

Friday 5

There is fact-based hoo-ha at 24 Summerdale Road, which is threatening love-based hoo-ha (Mum and Dad's, not mine or James's. Or dog's. As he is still genital-free). It is Mum's new job hunt. She has been scouring the *Walden Chronicle* for suitable (part-time) appointments and has ringed two potentials:

- Trainee traffic warden (uniform and notebook included)
- Vice-Chancellor of Essex University.

Dad said, 'Fact, Janet: you are not qualified to be a Vice-Chancellor. Plus we can manage quite well enough on my salary, with a few minor cutbacks.'

Mum said, 'Facts, Colin: I can spot a traffic violation

when I see one. There are NO qualifications to be a Vice-Chancellor. Plus no one uses paperclips any more, so your job future is looking increasingly dubious.'

Dad said, 'Fact, Janet: Wainwright and Beacham is the county's top-ranking treasury tag supplier, so my future is assured.'

Mum said, 'Fact—' but at that point me, James, and dog left before we got caught in fact crossfire. James is right though, she would be excellent traffic warden. Although we would have to run away due to potential for O'Grady menace. I am still taking flak for her dog-poo-wars.

. . . .

Saturday 6

9 a.m.

Hurrah. It is my first driving lesson today. Or at least first lesson involving properly qualified instructor, i.e. Mike Wandering Hands. Although hope he will not be doing any hand wandering with me. As, despite being older man, he is utterly ick-making. Given his taste in women, i.e. Mum, it is unlikely anyway. Hopefully will be triumph. As will not be distracted by either desire to snog him (Jack) or eject him from front seat (Mum). Plus must have inherited some of Mum's driving skills.

11 a.m.

Have inherited none of Mum's skills. Or charm, according to Mr Wandering Hands. He said is a miracle I was even

'born of her womb'. I said I had thought same thing. And in fact hoped it on number of occasions. But sadly all signs point to her being biologically related. He seized opportunity to discuss my shortcomings with owner of womb, who agreed with him, having watched proceedings from window using Beastly Investigations binoculars. He said it might be advisable for me to have intensive lessons. Mum said she would run it past Dad. Mike said he didn't think Mum was kind of woman to need permission (ick). Mum said she does not need permission, just satisfaction of proving why she is right to apply to be traffic warden in order to fund lessons. Then luckily Mike had to go to teach Ying Brewster (wife of Les, former sex worker, landlady of Mr Pringle) who has been having lessons for four years and has failed a record thirteen times. Though Mum says it is deliberate, and she is only doing it to be close to Mike, now that Les has had a vasectomy. But Mike has no interest in her as she is walking cliché (low tops, high boots, perpetual smell of Poison).

1 p.m.
Mum and Dad are not speaking. It is because Mum told Dad that Mike was supportive of her traffic warden dream. Dad said it is only because he wants to ogle her in a uniform and black tights. Mum said Mike was no admirer of uniform, purely of authority, and that anyway she will be opting for sensible trousers and lace-ups.

Cannot stand arguing. Is like love-kindling *Grease*

episode never happened. Although in fact do wish that had never happened. Anyway, am going to go and mope with Sad Ed on the trolleys for a bit. Now I feel his driving lesson pain. So far he has cost Mr and Mrs Thomas over £300 and he still cannot do a three-point turn without mounting the kerb or stalling or pranging several other vehicles. Or all three.

6 p.m.
Sad Ed says it is possible that it is the rest of the world who is wrong and that we are the only ones with natural driving ability. Though fact that at that very moment he crashed a herd of trolleys into car park exit barrier does not bear this out. Reuben Tull said maybe we needed to see beyond the steering wheel and white lines and chill about the whole driving thing. Said if that was an offer of drugs then the answer was no. Asked if he could drive. He said he doesn't need to, he soars above the people trapped in their tin boxes and travels in his mind. Case proven.

On plus side, am going for Sunday lunch at house of Stone, i.e. Scarlet's. Sad Ed is coming too. Scarlet says it is a power lunch, i.e. to discuss campaigning matters. Whatever. Suzy is vastly better cook than Mum, lets you drink wine at the table and her house is imbued with essence of Jack, so can osmotically ingest his aura. Plus glean essential info off Suzy as to his state of mind, and penis (fish-free, hopefully).

413

Sunday 7

Atmosphere at Shreddies table is decidedly frosty. Is the Mike Majors thing rearing its ugly head, or ugly wandering hands, again. Plus Grandpa Riley is coming to lunch with Treena and Baby Jesus. Which means Mum will be in preemptive strike mode all morning concerning spills and fighting. Thank God am going to Scarlet's.

Am utterly going to show off fact-based stance, so Suzy and Bob can report back that am grown-up and not happy-ending, fairytale obsessed child person. They do not need to know about Bella/vampire thing. Although finished second book in series last night and it is clear that Scarlet is mistaken as to who is who. Is obvious. Jack is Edward Cullen (mysterious and broody), I am Bella (brainy and misunderstood), and Sad Ed (or potentially dog) is werewolf boy (hairy but loyal). Scarlet is one of vampiric sisters, i.e. irritating and superior.

5 p.m.

Why oh why are my parents not sexperts and abortionists? Or at very least open to culinary experimentation? Not only was lunch at Scarlet's fascinating feast of canapés (Suzy nesting like mad pre-potential adoption by cooking entire Nigella party food book), but conversation at table was dynamic row encompassing the Gaza Strip (actual one, not carpet in common room), Jerusalem (saggy sofa in common room, not actual one) and which Miliband has better potential Prime Ministerial hair

(answer neither, although at least Ed's can go in more than one direction). Chez Riley, it is nutritionally balanced casserole or shepherd's pie rotated on fortnightly basis, with occasional roast thrown in to baffle everybody, plus conversation is limited to what the dog/James/Dad has/hasn't done.

On down side, Jack is having excellent time in Guatemala. Had secretly hoped he might be yearning to come back to my loving and very adult arms. But Suzy says he is embracing back-to-basics lifestyle and shedding all his Western trappings. Plus his penis is fine. Said maybe we should Skype him immediately so that he feels homesick for parmesan straws and aubergine dip but Suzy says there are no computers or mobile phones in Chichicastenango. She only heard by letter and he said that might be last as a goat ate the postbox last week.

Apparently lunch Chez Riley also vaguely successful, i.e. only one major spillage (Treena's elderflower cordial, though that could have been deliberate), two breakages (the freezer handle and Dad's nine iron, both Jesus), and one dog-related incident (it chipped tooth on nine iron). Plus, sexual/financial tension somewhat relieved by stunning announcement that Mum has got a job. It is looking after Baby Jesus. Apparently Grandpa can no longer cope with the trials of childcare (i.e. he cannot run fast enough to prevent Jesus escaping to Mr Patel's 2 or the O'Gradys' house, which he has taken a fancy to, it is all the junk

415

food and endless *QVC*—in both cases). Plus he says Jesus's conversation is doing nothing for his potential Alzheimer's as is limited to endless questions about Macca Pacca and where the Wattingers are (he does not have Alzheimer's, he has a Guinness habit). He is desperate to go back to Twilight Years Day Centre. He says it will be new lease of life. Which is possibly true, though from experience conversation tends to revolve around what happened to Lord Lucan and who is going to die next, so not entirely brain stimulating. Plus I have seen the communal TV tuned into *Night Garden* on more than one occasion. Anyway, he begged Mum to take Jesus in to save his sanity, and (in cunning, well-played move) to impose her excellent record of raising intelligent, socially-adjusted children. Mum has accepted. She is going to have Jesus on Mondays and Tuesdays, and over-time by prior arrangement. There has been some discrepancy over payment, as Grandpa thought reward of passing on cavernous knowledge of phonics should be enough, but he has agreed to hand over his magazine money instead. Mum is going to be minted—he spends at least £50 a week. Dad says she is going to regret her decision and wish she had waited for an office-based position, with perks, e.g. a pension scheme and Nespresso machine. As it is she is going to be up to her elbows in J-cloths and Cillit Bang. James pointed out that will be perk enough.

Monday 8

There was more hoo-ha at the mathlete table this lunchtime. It is Mumtaz. She has dumped Mad Harry. I said was inevitable, culturally, as she has probably been promised to a cousin in Pakistan. But James said it is not that, she has fallen for Damon Parker, who has memorized the dates of every ascension to the throne since Ethelred the Unready, and is in Year Eight. So she too is prey to the significant charms of the older man.

7 p.m.

Not that am going to fall for older man. Just am aware that there are attractions, e.g. experience of world, ability to purchase alcohol legally, no urges to let sheep out in 'hilarious' prank.

. . . .

Tuesday 9

Had tour of new John Major High childcare facility today, i.e. The Camilla Parker Bowles Memorial Crèche (Camilla not actually dead, but Mr Wilmott has thing about her and is hoping naming in her honour will secure visit). It is being staffed by Mark Lambert and both Kylies, who have transferred from bricklaying and hair and beauty respectively. Asked if they were following burning ambitions to become Supernanny. But apparently it is not that. It is because it is warmer, and there is a television and endless supply of rusks. Plus the Kylies are hoping to keep

up their training by using the 'inmates' (Fat Kylie's word, not mine) as live models. They will have trouble keeping them still enough judging by the cupboard full of Capri-Sun.

. . . .

Wednesday 10

8 a.m.
Have slight sick feeling. Maybe ate dodgy sausage last night. I know for a fact the dog had licked one of them before it made it into the oven. Or possibly is because have drama later. With Paddy.

8.15 a.m.
I mean Mr Pringle. Obviously. And it is not that. I have no feelings for him other than age-appropriate ones.

8.30 a.m.
Still feel odd though.

5 p.m.
Oh my God. Sick feeling was hands of fate swirling around in stomach. I think Mr Pringle could be my ONE. It turns out he is utterly anti-fairytale too and has similar fact-based stance to my own. Although his involves cutting edge documentary drama and *Das Capital*, not *Richard Hammond's Blast Lab* and the *Usborne Pocket Guide to Birds*. But none the less, it is utter meeting of minds. He says

Hollywood endings are the opium of the masses and dupe us all into subordination, instead of fighting for social justice. And that only hard-hitting factual drama has the power to change the course of political history. Am going to educate self immediately so can prove I am utterly his Juliet.

5.15 p.m.
Not that he is Romeo, nor I Juliet, as that is not hard-hitting or factual. Although they both die, which is not very Hollywood. But maybe they should have just staged a hunger strike or got up a petition instead and solved the family feud that way.

5.20 p.m.
And also he is not ONE as Jack is ONE, which will prove by being grown-up and fact based and utterly anti-love.

. . . .

Thursday 11

Granny Clegg has rung in a panic. It is the Hadron Collider, i.e. giant machine to recreate the Big Bang. She is terrified that it is Armageddon and that we are going to be blown into a black hole and devoured by 'strangelets'. James gave her lecture on difference between science fact and science fiction (e.g. gravity and fire: real; ET and Mr Spock: made-up) but Granny Clegg says Auntie Joyless (God-bothering sister of Mum,

mother to badly dressed cousins Boaz Jehosaphat and Mary Hepzibah) says Collider is 'vessel of the devil and all his cloven-hoofed minions'. (She is just minty as it contradicts theory that earth not created by Big Bang but by God.) She is now getting Grandpa, Pig, and Denzil (now taken up semi-permanent residence at the Fray Bentos table) to build a nuclear bunker in the outside toilet and will be stocking it with tinned beans and anti-alien/Beelzebub weapons (aka Pig's pigeon pistol) immediately.

. . . .

Friday 12

There has been another victim of the impending economic meltdown. KXL airline has collapsed, trapping thousands of people on Costa Del Sol, including Cherie Britcher. Mum says it is natural selection and she will only start to worry if BA, with its roster of culturally superior destinations, starts to suffer.

. . . .

Saturday 13

Hurrah, have another driving lesson today and am anticipating leap in improvement. Have eaten brain- and manual-dexterity-stimulating breakfast of scrambled eggs. In contrast Dad very much not calm. He is determined that Mum will not be in when Mr Wandering Hands arrives and is making up spurious plans to lure

her away from Summerdale Road. He will have a hard time. She has already got the binoculars out. Though she insists they are to observe my parallel parking at close quarters, rather than Mike's manly gear arm. (She said manly, though not in earshot of Dad.)

If she has sense she will get out of house though as house is currently full of Mad Harry who is very much not mad but is moping in Sad Ed-like manner. It is Mumtaz. He says life is meaningless without her in it, solving logarithms and snogging during *University Challenge* (they are both stimulated by the boffiny presence of Jeremy Paxman). James is undeterred. He says a day of Beastly Investigations will have him restored to normal mentalism in no time. They are going to attempt to track down Archie Knox's (son of hairy librarian Mr Knox, also hirsute) lost guinea pig Cecilia, once Mum has repatriated the binoculars. Which is better than original plan, which was to dredge shopping-trolley-clogged Slade for alligators. It is hard to believe they are at secondary school.

4 p.m.
Driving lesson marginally improved on last week, i.e. did not mistake clutch for brake pedal, and remembered to manoeuvre after have checked mirror, not other way round. Although Mr Wandering Hands raised spectre of intense lessons again. Said not sure that Mum's new job would stretch to that. He said, 'Ah, so Janet is following

my, I mean her, traffic warden dream.' Said no, she is going to babysit Jesus.

Got him to drop me in Waitrose car park, which he seemed disappointed about. (Not least because Reuben came perilously close to the Fiesta with a record forty-seven conjoined trolleys (maximum allowed is twenty but he and Sad Ed are having competition to herd the most in one go).) But, anyway, was not to avoid love triangle issues, was because had important purchase, i.e. birthday card for Jack. He is 19 on Monday. Have chosen factual and political theme, i.e. picture of Saffron Walden Town Hall, and signed off 'yours truly', which is utterly grown up and anti-romance. Had to get his address off Mr Goldstein (former employer of me and Jack, hunchback, owner of lentil-smelling healthfood emporium Nuts In May). Which was totally like Mutya going back to ask favour from other superior Sugababes, considering he heartlessly sacked me (albeit for potential defecting to Waitrose toiletries aisle). But needs must, as there is no way Scarlet will hand it over.

Got home to find blood on floor in kitchen and Mad Harry writhing in agony at hands of Mum. Was not murder though, as first suspected. It was a Beastly Investigations wild-animal-related injury. He tripped over dog and cut forehead open on cheese grater. Mum was administering TCP in usual aggressive manner.

· ·

Sunday 14

Went round Sad Ed's today, following shepherd's pie (no surprises there, but bizarre inclusion of sweetcorn instead of habitual peas caused raised eyebrows all round, including dog). He is stepping up his campaign to win Scarlet's heart and mind and mojo, i.e. he is thinking of going Goth. I said he has advantage of pale complexion (he fears the sun, preferring to lie in bed watching *Angel* box sets) but that his build is not at all vampiric. Unless vampires also gorge on Toffee Crisps. He says he is minded to go on diet. Not of blood (unless in form of black pudding, which do not think is slimming), but cutting down to two packets of Nik Naks a day, and replacing Mars Milk with milk milk. I said was good idea. Though am not at all sure it will do trick with Scarlet. Edward Cullen can move with superhuman speed, whereas Sad Ed can barely manage a slow jog (he gets nipple rub and stomach chafing). Plus only twinkling he has done was when Mark Lambert entwined him in the school fairy lights in Year Seven and plugged him into the mains. He has never recovered.

. . . .

Monday 15

Today is historic occasion in bipartite (good facty word) manner:

1. It is nineteenth birthday of Jack Stone—former love of life. And still future love of life, once have done requested growing up. Will be sending him facty

thoughts across the Atlantic. And hope that Scarlet does not intercept them with her spooky and militant sixth sense. Which have realized is further indication that she is not Bella but a Cullen, as they are ones with ability to read minds. And oddball dress sense.

2. Is Mum's first day as official carer for Baby Jesus Harvey Nichols Riley. She has already drawn up a pre-emptive strike list, involving Jesus and dog. Mostly concerning not allowing them in the same place at same time, and restricting all access to remote controls, as they have both been known to interfere with television by stealing/ingesting the indigestible.

4 p.m.
Oooh. Forgot another historic fact.

3. Is last ever *Grange Hill*. John Major High is awash with sadness. I wish I could join in but *a*) am unmoved by fictitious fayre, and *b*) have never seen *Grange Hill* due to Mum's ferocious parental controls.

Anyway, has been triumph on one count. Not Jack. Have heard nothing back, telepathically or otherwise. It is Jesus. Mum has declared her regime a success, i.e. there have been no major breakages and only a minor spillage (liquid soap, so self-cleaning). Jesus is not so jubilant at the arrangement. He is used to at least six hours of Cartoon Network, four Fruit Shoots, and several packets

424

of Wotsits a day. In stark contrast he got half an hour of David Attenborough, a glass of milk, and a wholemeal oatcake. He is currently looking glassy eyed in a corner clutching James's naked Will Young doll. James says it is like *Trainspotting* when that heroin addict went cold turkey. He says it is calm before the storm and Mum will have to lock him in the spare room tomorrow with a bucket. Mum demanded to know when James had seen *Trainspotting* (banned for glamorizing drugs, shaven heads, and Scotland) but luckily the dog fell down the stairs before he could reveal source (i.e. Scarlet, which means official shouting goes to me).

Tuesday 16

Mum is taking James's advice and taking Jesus out of house for afternoon. She says if he is going to get violent and messy then she does not want him within range of her oatmeal furnishings. She is taking him to soft play at the Lord Butler Leisure Centre. She says according to website it encourages physical and mental skills and will be safe and happy environment. It will not be. I have seen what can happen in an unsupervised ball pool. Scarlet is still traumatized by the sight of spherical plastic to this day.

4 p.m.

I was right. Mum has added Soft Play to her list of banned items on grounds of hygiene (three plasters and a

dead earwig in the ball pool), injury risk (woefully inadequate thickness of crash mat) and O'Grady count (Whitney and Mrs O'Grady both hurling themselves menacingly down the inflatable slide, which in Mrs O'Grady's case is potential manslaughter). She is having a lie down and Jesus is watching television. It is not Cartoon Network, is History Channel, but I can tell he is claiming a minor victory. He has same semi-smug look as dog when it has been begging for a KitKat and gets a custard cream.

More importantly, is drama tomorrow. Think may have wardrobe revamp in order to reflect new grown-up Upper Sixth status.

4.30 p.m.
Not that the two are related. Is just that need outfit that says 'am serious fact-based individual' rather than ironic Brownies T-shirt, gold lamé miniskirt (actually boob tube), and purple Converse, a look that only says 'am underage, colour blind, and possibly slightly retarded'.

. . . .

Wednesday 17
8 a.m.
Am wearing black. Black is utterly grown-up and facty. Plus will win me points with Scarlet as is goth-friendly wear. Hurrah.

8.15 a.m.
But not points with Mum, who says I had better not be thinking of getting any of my nether regions pierced or tattooed. Have pointed out that am not actual goth, and that black is uniform of all serious minded academic types. She said she does not recall Moira Stewart (favourite helmet-haired multicultural newsreader) wearing lace gloves and a cloche hat. Do not know why she is so minty. It is a non-Jesus day today so she can focus on her leisure activities, i.e. hoovering the mattresses and scouring mildew out of grouting with a toothbrush.

4 p.m.
Scarlet also not impressed with pseudo-goth wear. She says I cannot pull the look off with my voluminous hair and freckles. At least did not look as bad as Sad Ed. He was wearing eyeliner and face had definite powdery white glow. He denies use of make-up but saw packet of Waitrose self-raising flour in locker at first break. Anyway, it does not matter what Scarlet thinks. Mr Pringle aka Patrick aka Paddy was definitely in approval. He says black is the blank canvas on which we can paint our characters and is uniform of his old drama group Clause 4, who did something called gorilla theatre. It sounds excellent and groundbreaking. Is probably about mimicking our base instincts and returning to nature. May try it for next week's practical lesson.

Thursday 18
8 a.m.

Mum is in vile mood. It is because she has got Jesus again today. It is not so Grandpa can go to Twilight Years Day Centre. It is so he can have hair cut. Mum pointed out the prior arrangement clause in the contract (which is actual contract, drawn up by James and countersigned by Mum and Grandpa) but Grandpa said he had given her two hours' notice. She is only in a mood because it will compromise her plans to realphabetize the CDs (following some confusion over whether the Nolans should be filed under N for Nolans (Mum), T for The (Dad), or C for crap (me and James)). Jesus is not at all alphabet-friendly. Or CD-friendly. He has tendency to file them in random manner, i.e. by inserting them into small cracks.

5 p.m.

As predicted Mum's day not entire triumph. It is her own fault. She should never have let Jesus be in charge of dusting the cases. At least only Kenny G and Crystal Gayle are missing. And, personally, would have said this was a blessing.

Friday 19

Granny Clegg rang again to tell us that the world is not going to end after all. It is not her hip of doom (previous allegedly fortune telling hip, now replaced with metal

428

one) or any other portentous body parts telling her this.
It is GMTV. Apparently the Hadron Collider has developed
an electrical fault and so there will be no Big Bangs and
we will not be eaten by strangelets any time soon. Granny
thinks they probably got it from Dixons in Truro. She says
she got her hairdryer from there and it has a mind of its
own. It does not. It has Bruce-related damage. Mum is
jubilant at latest idiotic missive from Cornwall, i.e. there is
still no sign of Granny Clegg's memory reactivating. Mum
does not believe in elevating anyone beyond their station
in life, even if that station is Hammerited terrace called
Pasty Manor replete with a man called Pig.

Saturday 20

Ugh. Have got driving lesson this morning. Is odd how
have been awaiting this seminal moment for years, yet
now has arrived, wish was 16 again and limited to walking or sick-smelling Volvo. Is utter disappointment. Like
being tall enough to go on Waltzers at fair and then you
realize is just electric roundabout being spun by halfwit.

5 p.m.

As predicted driving lesson entirely not good, i.e. am still
having spatial awareness issues, i.e. think car twice width
that actually is and have tendency to shut eyes and panic
when approaching any other vehicles. Pointed out that at
least do not think car thinner than is, which would be

429

whole lot messier. Mum says I am bringing shame to the Riley name. I said what about Dad. But Mum says at least he knows an inch is an inch. James told her not to worry as in less than six years he will singlehandedly restore the House of Riley to its splendour when he passes within a week of starting lessons. This is possibly true. Though he also thinks cars will be defunct by 2014 and that we'll all be wearing jetpacks and silver suits and eating fishfingers in pill form. Am going round Scarlet's to escape mentalism. She is not even learning to drive so at least will feel vaguely superior.

10 p.m.
Am not feeling superior at all. Is because Scarlet pointed out that she can already drive, including handbrake turns (illegal) and hill starts (impossible), as Bob taught her when she was ten. She just chooses not to on environmental and economic grounds. Also dinner was not usual hotbed of Nigella-based canapés and stimulating conversation (also frequently Nigella-based). Was beans on toast and row about Suzy's erotic art collection (aka filthy porn pictures). It is because Suzy and Bob got a letter from Mr Lemon at the council (formerly of housing and school admissions, now in charge of adoption and refuse collection) this morning. Their adoption interview aka interrogation is on Monday and Suzy is worried their normalizing measures may not have gone far enough. They are right. Do not think removing Kama Sutra and a

Gordon Brown mask even scratches the surface. Plus Scarlet is hardly a model of wholesomeness. She was wearing bust-revealing corset and reading *Your Vagina, Your Call* at the table. If only Jack was still here, with his intelligent aura and chest-covering outfits of choice. Mr Lemon would be begging them to take a horde of waifs and strays off his hands.

Sunday 21
Mum says Suzy is mad wanting another baby at her age. Pointed out that Suzy is in fact a full year younger than Mum and so may have more youthful invigoration, plus she is more lenient when it comes to stains, junk food, and Channel 5. Mum went visibly thin-lipped. She is showing classic symptoms of post-weekend deflation, in anticipation of day of hard grind tomorrow, instilling discipline and food groups other than crisps into Baby Jesus.

Monday 22
Mum is more determined than ever to sway Suzy away from having another child. It is because she spent the afternoon at 'Mummy and Me' aka tedious toddler group at Bernard Evans Youth Centre. James pointed out that, by rights, she was there illegally, as she is not officially Jesus's mum, but Mum says that was problem. Brenda Marsh (also runs Fat Busters, four foot nine, fifteen stone)

congratulated her on getting her figure back after birth. Mum says it is ultimate humiliation to be considered the parent of a boy dressed as a Power Ranger.

James suggested she should set up her own rival toddler group called 'Carer and Me' (i.e non-sexist, and non-ageist). James is idiot. Mum got sudden faraway look in eye, i.e. is now mental with anticipation at becoming Gina Fordesque baby guru, imposing strict routines and stain-free bibs. At happy-go-lucky and very stained end of spectrum Scarlet has texted to say Bob and Suzy's checks went fine, although there was slight mishap when Mr Lemon asked about the sex swing. Apparently Suzy said it was state of art baby bouncer. They are now confidently expecting the arrival of a Chinese or Malawian orphan (their stated preference) within a matter of weeks.

. . . .

Tuesday 23
4 p.m.
Have remembered have to do practical for Mr Pringle tomorrow. Will watch some monkey-based David Attenborough to get gorilla tips. Baby Jesus will not mind. He has taken to wildlife regime very well. There is more sex and violence than Nickelodeon.

6 p.m.
Will make excellent gorilla. Am totally immersed in

character. Plus know loads of gorilla facts, like they are utterly vegetarian, and they live in nests (who knew!— am amazed they do not fall through). Baby Jesus also demonstrating gorilla tendencies. Though Mum not so amused at him trying to nest on windowsill. Asked what he was still doing here anyway, as Grandpa usually picks him up before *Home and Away*. Mum says Grandpa and Treena have gone for a quick drink after work. James asked if it was by prior arrangement. Mum said yes, but only by five minutes. James shook his head and said it is tip of slippery iceberg. Mum said it is not, Jesus is going home after *Look East* and will not be back until next Monday.

. . . .

Wednesday 24

8 a.m.

Jesus is already at the Shreddies table. Grandpa dropped him off at half seven, with no prior arrangement other than shouting up at Mum's bedroom window. James raised practised eyebrow at Mum but Mum too busy trying to keep Jesus and dog away from the bran flakes. They are both banned following excess poo issues. Also, have texted Sad Ed to make sure he is in character for drama. Am already in gorilla mindset, i.e. admiring leaves on hydrangeas as potential nesting material. Although James says gorillas do not nest in hydrangeas, due to weight versus twig width ratio, as I would know, were

I to join him and Mad Harry as part of Beastly Investigations. Declined again. They are only offering me substandard position, i.e. binocular monitor, which is not at all befitting my superior Upper Sixth stature.

8.30 a.m.
Sad Ed has texted back. It says, 'Vy, yes, pretty maiden.' Have texted back to ask who the hell he is supposed to be.

8.35 a.m.
Sad Ed has texted back. It says, 'Is Dracula, duh.' He is idiot. As if anyone, i.e. Scarlet, is going to believe that. Whereas gorilla theatre is not only convincing, but is utterly left-wing. Though am not entirely sure how.

4 p.m.
Oh. Apparently gorilla theatre is not about gorillas at all. Or any animals. It is actually 'guerrilla' theatre, i.e. edgy underground maverick style drama, as opposed to monkey impressions. Mr Pringle said it was easy mistake to make and not to feel bad. I said was not mistake, was deliberate undermining of expectation. He said, oh, well in that case, I get *dix points*. Although think it may have been sarcastic. On plus side, my arm waving and hooting was nothing compared to Sad Ed's Dracula impression. Reuben Tull actually fell off a chair laughing (though that might also be the 'refreshment' he had partaken of at lunchtime).

434

Also, Jesus is still here. He is staying the night. James says it is like Granny Clegg all over again, and he will be a permanent resident by Christmas. Mum says it is not like Granny Clegg, as Grandpa is definitely repatriating him tomorrow after breakfast. Plus Jesus does not say 'hooge'.

. . . .

Thursday 25
8 a.m.
There has been a handover of power at Shreddies table this morning. Dad has been left in charge of administering nutritious breakfast and vitamins while Mum has lie down in darkened bedroom. It is because she was up fourteen times in night to attend to Jesus's many and varied demands including seven pickings up of 'Baby' (naked Will Young), two cups of water, one poo, one wee, one check for Wattingers under the bed and one removing him from top of chest of drawers. James said she should be thankful that we were never like that. But Dad said *au contraire* I had nightmares about falling off my unicorn and James used to appear ghoulishly at the end of the bed and demand to know how gravity worked. James said at least his showed burgeoning intelligence, whereas mine was early signs of living in fantasy world. Reminded him of time he claimed he was a hobbit. He said 'there's nothing fantasy about middle world'. He is moron. Anyway, on plus side Dad let us eat

435

marmalade out of the jar. Jesus was doing it anyway so was only fair.

4 p.m.
Jesus is still here. Grandpa and Treena have got food poisoning and have begged Mum to keep Jesus. James says they have not got food poisoning, as is impossible to get food poisoning from Frazzles, which they were apparently consuming in vast quantities in the Queen Lizzie last night. Asked how he knew. He says off Mumtaz, who got it off Damon Parker, who got it off his cousin 'Nosey'. Apparently Ali Hassan has agreed to secondary business activity (alongside illegal gambling ring) i.e. spy network. Their slogan is 'a geek in every corner'. Shudder. Anyway, Jesus's unholy presence is useful distraction tool as need to ask Mum's permission to join utterly excellent new non-geek-based school club. It is Film Club and is being run by Mr Pringle. He is going to show seminal documentary drama on Friday nights and then we will discuss films, like on *Culture Show* with Mark Kermode, but with smaller foreheads and less of look of giant toad. First one is *La Haine*, which is about disaffected inner-city French youths. Which I totally identify with. Except the French bit. And the city bit. But am disaffected. I think.

5 p.m.
Mum has agreed. Or rather, she said 'whatever'. Which is the same. But is also unprecedented as 'whatever' is on

436

banned list. But think fact that Jesus had just inserted
raisin into wall socket possibly pushed her to limit.

. . . .

Friday 26
8 a.m.
Dad is wearing stubble and haunted look of crimewatch
photofit. It is because Mum has found solution to having
to get up for Jesus's demands. It is to let him sleep in bed
with her and Dad. James said is outrage as it goes against
all her anti-new-age-hippy ideals, and pointed out that
we were not even allowed to get in bed for morning cud-
dles. Mum said it was not anti-hippy, it was to avoid bac-
terial cross-contamination. Dad also in agreement with
James. He says he has been kicked, poked, and weed on
in night and now has to go and spend eight hours chained
to desk auditing the drawing pin department. Mum said
he could always stay at home and childmind his brother,
i.e. Jesus. Dad took box of Shreddies and spoon and shut
himself in Passat before she could enforce idea. Jesus is
utterly jubilant though. He is like devil child slowly turning host family against each other, before he eats us all
alive. Possibly. Not that will be here to witness it as have
seminal film club date tonight with Mr Pringle.

8.15 a.m.
And is not date. Is club. So there will be other people
there.

8.30 a.m.
Although will be in dark, and French theme is utterly romantic, and possibly no one else will sign up so we will be alone in charged atmosphere of fact-based love. Oooh.

10 p.m.
Was not at all charged atmosphere. For a start was not even in dark, was in overlit 'audio-visual suite' aka the library, with strict instructions not to turn lights off as Mr Wilmott does not want teen pregnancy quota up as we are already lagging behind Burger King Sports Academy since Debs Donaldson in Year Nine had twins. Plus Scarlet, Sad Ed, Reuben Tull, Dean 'the dwarf' Denley (part-time meat mincer and full-time midget), Stan Barrett (once saw Paul Weller in John Lewis) and half of the music table (admission criteria: owning a guitar or an Arctic Monkeys CD) were also in attendance. Did not even get to sit next to Mr Pringle. Instead was wedged in between Sad Ed and Scarlet who argued over my head, or rather through my hair, about whether or not *Gone in 60 Seconds* is classic of modern cinema. (Answer not, unless you also include *Fast and Furious* and *Chronicles of Riddick* in canon. Which Scarlet does not.) Hair had definite powdery residue afterwards due to Sad Ed still sporting his self-raising corpse look. It is not winning him any points with Scarlet. Although the minigoths are definitely showing him more respect, i.e. they have stopped tripping him outside the fruit and nut-dispensing machine. Melody Bean

is still not talking to him though since their wedding fell through. She was also at film club, flicking carob-coated peanuts at his head. Have found several in hair. Have eaten them. Waste not want not, as Mum says. Or at least she would say if was not imbued with minty Jesus-based rage. He is upstairs in bed. Grandpa and Treena are now not answering their phone. Dad says he is going to leave Jesus on doorstep of 19 Harvey Road tomorrow morning like foundling child. Although Mum has forbidden this in case the baby-mad O'Gradys kidnap him and raise him as their own. She says wolves would do a better job.

Saturday 27

Dad has issued a Jesus-related ultimatum. He says if 'the child' is not repatriated by *You've Been Framed* then he is going to move in with Grandpa Riley instead. Mum looked tempted for a minute, as Dad's sweat glands are high maintenance in the laundry department, but then Jesus reasserted his idiocy by trying to iron the dog. It is agreed. James (as second most authoritative Riley) has been sent round to Harvey Road to inform Grandpa. And also take dog out of house before it chews any more chair legs. It is showing signs of increased mentalism, also Jesus-related. Am not surprised. So far it has been dressed up as a Harboo (wrapped in coloured sheets), 'hidden' in airing cupboard (for four hours, necessitating decontamination of all towels), and had novelty troll-topped pencil

inserted in nostril, troll-end first. Am actually glad have got driving lesson. Three point turns and emergency stops are almost zen-like compared to trying to manoeuvre around living room.

5 p.m.
Dad is jubilant. Not only is Jesus out of the house, but Mum has given up her job as childminder. His manly position as main breadwinner is restored, along with peace. Apparently Grandpa actually cried when Jesus was handed over. He begged Mum to reconsider and said he was only just getting his life back, which was limited anyway as possibly he has fatal bowel obstruction. Mum said he does not have fatal bowel obstruction, he needs to eat more fibre and fewer Bird's Eye Steak Grills, and anyway, he should have thought of that before he got his care worker pregnant at the age of 73 (Grandpa not Treena, she was 28).

. . . .

Sunday 28
Dad is less jubilant. Jesus is not back. But Mum and James have shut themselves in the dining room and are having a career assessment, i.e. James has got his highlighters and Post-Its out and they are listing pros and cons of various job opportunities. I said Dad should be happy that Mum is so keen to share his money-earning burden, but he says he is worried she will revive the ill-fated 2004

housework roster and make him share in that burden, which as we all know, will only end in tears and shouting when he uses the wrong sponge or hoovers when he should be sweeping or lightly rubbing with a damp cloth. (Also why I am not allowed to partake in housework. Only James passes strict entry requirements.)

3 p.m.
Mum and James have narrowed down her ideal career to three:
- accountant (i.e. what she is qualified for in first place)
- police officer
- head of emergency post-murder cleaning company.

Said there was not much call for latter in Saffron Walden, but James says they are including Harlow in catchment.

. . . .

Monday 29
9 a.m.
Something suspicious is going on. Am sure have just seen Jesus Riley disappear around end of D Corridor in (hefty) arms of Fat Kylie. Possibly am hallucinating. Is flashback to Reuben Tull mushroom madness.

1 p.m.
Oh my God. Was not hallucination. Have had Riley summit meeting (i.e. me and James) outside lower school

toilets, (i.e. neutral territory as Scarlet is refusing to allow James and Mad Harry within a metre of Goth corner on grounds of their involvement in Ghost Hustlers). Anyway, according to James, who got it off Mumtaz, who got it off Damon, who got it off Nosey, who got it off Mrs Leech for a Tunnock's Teacake, Jesus is now fully enrolled in the Camilla Parker Bowles Memorial Crèche. Fat Kylie is bringing him in every day with Whitney, her brown baby sister. This is huge mistake. Not only is Jesus consorting with O'Gradys on official basis, but he is being educated by a host of former Criminals and Retards including Mark Lambert (owner of the 'Lamborghini'), plus Thin Kylie. It is like prison, where all the criminal masterminds pass on their illegal skills. He will be carjacking within a fortnight. Will tell Mum she needs to reconsider her resignation.

4 p.m.
Mum says Jesus can be taught by Reggie Kray himself there is no way she is having him back in the house. She has only just unclogged the sink with a crochet hook (residue included half packet of Shreddies, four dried apricots, and a Lego head). She will change her mind when he is on the front page of the *Walden Chronicle*, bringing shame on the Riley name. Although is possible that she will be doing that herself if her job hunt continues. She has filled in application to join fast-track police officer course. She will not get on. She is no good at

442

taking orders from hard-boiled, hard-drinking, chain-smoking Scots (Rebus) or hard-boiled, hard-drinking, chain-smoking Northerners (Gene Hunt).

. . . .

Tuesday 30

Jewish New Year

It has already started. Mr Wilmott cornered me outside language lab to inform me that my 'brother' Jesus and his 'accomplice' Whitney O'Grady had managed to flood the Camilla Parker Bowles Memorial Crèche. Said *a*) he was not my brother, in fact, had no idea who he was talking about, and *b*) why had no one removed plugs as is elementary rule when looking after delinquents or toddlers (plugs on Mum's banned list during Jesus residence). Mr Wilmott said *a*) how odd, he looks just like me, and *b*) the plugs had been removed but Jesus and Whitney made cunning use of Jammie Dodgers and toilet paper then turned all taps on full to enjoy the lake effect. Said then can only blame operator error, i.e. Criminals and Retards, or Mrs Leech for choosing notoriously claggy jam-based biscuits as official snack. Mr Wilmott will have forgotten by tomorrow anyway as one of BTECers is bound to have tried to blow up, maim, or melt something. Plus he is still consumed by the mystery of his disappearing swivelly orthopaedic chair. Clearly the bat disguise works as Scarlet actually wheeled past him down A Corridor yesterday and he utterly failed to identify her bottom half.

443

School filled with gloom as well as water. It is Sad Ed and impending eighteenth birthday, i.e. tomorrow. He had planned to be dead musical genius with grieving groupies by now. Whereas he is very much alive, single, and singularly untalented music-wise. Plus is covered in layer of flour. He says is utterly depressing to be entering middle age with nothing to show for creative endeavours. Said *au contraire* he is in position of utter power and public acclaim, i.e. is head boy. But he says all that gets him is a daily shouting from Scarlet because he is not following her media strategy. Plus his head girl (i.e. Thin Kylie) looks like Paris Hilton as dental nurse. (Crèche uniform is, inexplicably, white coats. Which makes it look like cross between science lab and lunatic asylum. So quite appropriate really.) Have got Sad Ed Vampire Weekend album for birthday. He wanted limited edition 'Hatful of Hollow' on vinyl. But Woolworth's only does chart CDs so it was that or Pussycat Dolls.

October

Wednesday 1

Hurrah, it is utter landmark day, i.e. is Sad Ed's eighteenth birthday. Which means we now have stooge to purchase alcohol, cigarettes, fireworks, and porn. Although in reality have been able to buy alcohol off Mr Patel for several years by cunning use of hat and sunglasses disguise. Plus none of us smoke or require sparklers or *Big Ones International*. But is excellent grown-up occasion none the less. Sad Ed is not having party today. He says he is going to be too busy wallowing in failed untimely death gloom. We are going to defer until Saturday instead, and stake our claim on table in Duke of Wellington pub (squelchy carpet, well-stocked snack shelf including Cheese Moments, absolutely not favoured by beardy and potentially grassing teachers (aka Cowpat Cheesmond and Mrs Buttfield (aka Buttface)) who prefer folk night and pickled eggs at King's Arms).

5 p.m.

Has been successful older man-based day all round, i.e. *a*) Sad Ed very much liking his birthday presents. Although CD outdone somewhat by packet of condoms from Scarlet. Sad Ed says it is a token of her true affections for him. It is not. It is a freebie from Suzy's sex show. Also *b*) drama was excellent fact-based lesson on using theatre to resolve conflict. Mr Pringle made us choose sides in Middle East and argue our way to compromise. Sad Ed was Yasser Arafat and Reuben Tull was Ehud Olmert. I got

447

to be Saddam Hussein, who had cameo appearance as sort of evil *deus ex machina*. There was a fraught bit where Ehud Olmert tried to resolve crisis by having a game of musical statues, but in end, debate won the day and they joined forces and decided to populate Sweden instead.

On theme of older men/birthdays/anti-war politics, I have heard nothing back from Jack thanking me for fact-based birthday card. Maybe a goat has consumed letter, or postman, as well as postbox. On plus-side, think no news is good news, penis-fish-wise.

. . . .

Thursday 2

There has been another Jesus-related incident in the Camilla Parker Bowles Memorial Crèche, i.e. a prison break. Lesbian PE teachers Miss Beadle (overweight, bulgy eyes like Joey in *Friends* and rabbits with myxamatosis) and Miss Vicar (stick thin, no breasts, facial hair) found Whitney burying him in the long jump pit, aka cat toilet. Is lucky they saw him before Whitney finished project. There is no way he would have survived Fionnula Flack (Year Eight, alleged 'gland' problem, actual cheese consumption problem) and her hop, skip, and jump.

I fear Jesus is being sacrificed for the sins of others though. I blame Whitney. She is the one who stole the spade from Cowpat Cheesmond's potting shed. Or Fat Kylie for failing to look up from article on Kerry Katona's

new haircut in time. That is what happens when you put power in the hands of the populace. They just buy *Heat* magazine and claim they were on a tea break.

. . . .

Friday 3
1 p.m.

Am having fact versus fiction financial quandary. It is following revelation that JK Rowling now earns £5 a second, thanks to utterly fairytale (though non-happy-ending) Harry Potter. On one hand, is against all writerly principles, i.e. point of being writer is that is hideous impoverished existence whereby you are forced to live in bohemian squat and consume Marmite soup and cat biscuits. But on other hand, would quite like to be millionaire. Scarlet says am pathetic money-lusting capitalist who is swayed from political cause by chink chink of gold sovereigns and ker-ching of metaphorical till. I said that's as may be but I could have earned £25 pounds in the time it took her to say that and then spent it on leprous midgets or harpoon-threatened whales. Plus it is now up to £60 pounds. No £65 . . . £70 . . . £75 . . . At which point Scarlet hit me with a Grizzly Bar as she said it was like watching *Bargain Hunt*, including the absurd hairdo. Thank God is film club tonight, which will restore my faith in fact, and banish the Harry Potter money madness whence it came (i.e. BBC Breakfast News). Film is *Control*, i.e. about moany dead Manchester musician. Sad

Ed is mental with untimely death musical genius anticipation. Am mental with Mr Pringle anticipation. Am
wearing Joy Division T-shirt (borrowed off Sad Ed so
actually more of capacious dress) and will be nodding and
saying 'God, yes' at intervals to indicate agreement at
theme of wasted youth and Northern deprivation. Am
hoping Mr Pringle will be imbued with Northerny passion, or at least blinded by glare of fluorescent library
lighting, and fling me older manfully against stack of Enid
Blytons.

1.10 p.m.
Except that would be illegal.

1.15 p.m.
But all best things are illegal.

1.20 p.m.
But not murder, obviously. Or drugs. Actually most illegal
things are not good at all. Maybe that is why they are
illegal.

9 p.m.
Luckily Mr Pringle was not imbued with Northerny passion or blinded by fluorescent glare. In fact was too busy
arguing with Sad Ed about New Order and brilliance/
crapness thereof to even notice me 'God, yes'ing artfully
in utterly grown-up manner. Scarlet did notice however

450

and said, 'This is not *When Harry Met Sally* and if that is the kind of performance you give then you need to see Suzy.' Have no idea what she is talking about. Have seen film but Mum always fast forwards through a bit of it as she says there is a hideous murder which could psychologically damage both James and me. Plus the dog does not like Meg Ryan so by that point a lot of fast forwarding gets done to alleviate the leg/furniture chewing and frenzied barking at her inexplicably immovable hairdo.

- -

Saturday 4

Have had driving lesson. Is utter torture. Would give up except that will need ability to drive in order to have life-changing road trip across America/transport first aid supplies to refugee camps/get job delivering pizza. Told Mum do not know what she ever saw in Mr Wandering Hands though. He has no patience when it comes to forgetting which switch is windscreen wipers and which is to turn left. Mum looked wistfully through Windolene-smeared door and said he can change from first to second as if he is cutting through melted butter, plus his hair smells of pine furniture polish. But then face of Dad loomed idiotically through glass and Mum returned to planet Janet and pointed out that these were objective observations and that in fact she did not see anything in him and their relationship was merely one of mentor and protégée. I hope she is not getting all heated about Mike again. It is

Dad's fault for letting himself go. He has been wearing the same trousers since 2002 (obviously not every day, he is not Barry Blade, just unprogressive fashion-wise). Plus he has no regard for his physical health, as Mum has pointed out to him on several occasions. He claims he weighs exactly what he did at age of 30. Mum said, 'That's as may be, but it has all redistributed itself to your stomach.' It is totally sad. I will never let self go in middle-age and take up golf or start drinking Horlicks. Will be utterly edgy Kate Moss-type (but with bigger hair, and body) until am ancient fifty year old when will turn into Vivienne Westwood. Except will wear knickers. But not waist-hugging M & S ones am currently limited to due to mysterious disappearance of black minimalist pair (potentially gone way of dog, or Mad Harry) and tiny Topshop pair (confiscated by Mum for contravention of lace/buttock coverage rules). It is so unfair. Scarlet actually has pants from Agent Provocateur. Although at least am not Sad Ed who I have seen in Power Ranger Y-fronts. Maybe now he is eighteen he will break free from confines of Mr and Mrs Thomas and their Aled Jones ambitions and assert his authority when it comes to underwear. It is inaugural Sad Ed/Scarlet/Rachel pub drinking outing tonight. Hurrah. By last orders will be hardened Duke regular with seat at bar and whisky habit.

11.45 p.m.
Or not. Was allowed in pub, but was not permitted to

purchase or in any way consume alcohol. Landlord 'Shorty' McNulty (former police dog trainer, half left ear missing, seven feet tall) is apparently stricter than Mum when it comes to serving underage drinkers. At least Mum lets me sip shandy on special occasions. Shorty limited me to a pint of soda and lime and a packet of Twiglets. Kev Banner's dog gets preferential treatment. It is allowed beer in a bowl and has its own stool at the bar. On the plus side we have staked a claim on a table in saloon, i.e. the wobbly one next to loos. It has advantage of clear jukebox access, but pervading odour of wee and Toilet Duck. Scarlet says it is swings and roundabouts and anyway we will be upgraded as soon as Wizard Weeks (beard, long hair, once came fifth in all-Essex Dungeons and Dragons marathon) goes into rehab again and we will have all-essential squishy seats and a view of the roundabout.

Was excellent grown-up evening though, i.e. had raging argument about minimum wage with Wizard Weeks (for) and Shorty and Kev Banner (and dog) (against). Plus now know all words to 'Here I Go Again' by Whitesnake, which was on jukebox thirteen consecutive times (is Kev's dog's 'theme tune' apparently), much to Scarlet's anger as she paid 50p for 'Oxford Comma' and it never got played. Shorty refused a refund on grounds it will get airing tomorrow around five and she is welcome to come back in for a listen then. She declined, but we are going in extra early next week to line up a better

playlist. Sad Ed also happy with coming-of-age pub evening due to free birthday crisps on the house. Shorty is like drug dealer—getting him hooked on Cheese Moments then charging him 70p a packet next week. He is still compromised on pant front though. Waistband of Rhino Ranger Y-fronts definitely visible above low slung combat trousers (not in hip way, in more 'can't get them over Cheese Moment and beer-filled stomach' way).

· ·

Sunday 5
10 a.m.
Called Sad Ed to check on his first legal hangover. He is racked with remorse. It is not due to shameful drink consumption leading to shameful behaviour. It is shameful snack consumption leading to not-at-all-vampiric stomach. He says he is thinking of taking up bulimia (he has already failed spectacularly at anorexia). Reminded him of sick phobia and suggested he could exercise off snacks by walking round here and watching documentary on coal miners' strike. He said he would but he has just opened a packet of Buttons and *Hollyoaks* is on.

How I pity him and his lust for third-rate fictional soap operas. Or third-rate fictional soap opera actresses. Instead will spend entire day consuming fact-based *Sunday Telegraph* from cover to cover, i.e. not just fashion supplement or cartoons, which is usual limit.

11.15 a.m.

May just go out for walk instead. And possibly purchase fact-based *Grazia* or at least borrow it from Grandpa Riley. *Sunday Telegraph* is sorely mistaken if it thinks Andrew Lloyd Webber or Archbishop of Canterbury of interest to general populace.

1 p.m.

Have abandoned walk without purchase or borrowing of celebrity gossip magazines of any kind. Is not due to sudden appreciation of frog-like impresario Mr Lloyd Webber. Is due to sudden appearance of utterly non-frog-like, and in fact annoyingly handsome princeish, Justin Statham outside Mr Patel's. He said, 'So, Rach, you and Jack back together then?' Said, 'Uh, yeah.' (As did not want to encourage him trying to win war, even though had lost battle etc. Despite his hair looking totally halo-ey and definite visibility of six-pack through ripped Velvet Underground T-shirt.) He said, 'No you're not.' Said, 'Yes I am.' He said, 'No you're not.' Said, 'Yes I am.' He said, 'No. You're. Not.' Said, 'Is not bloody pantomime season, and how would you know if I'm not anyway?' He said Scarlet told Rosamund (works in Nuts In May, ailment-ridden, nits) who told Dean Denley (midget, meat mincer, works opposite Nuts In May) who told Stan Barrett (once saw Paul Weller in John Lewis) who told Barney Smith-Watson (white, dreadlocks, fake Jamaican accent) who is also on rock foundation at Braintree. Said, 'OK. Am not.

But does not mean am on market as am in fact totally anti-romance as am busy being grown-up and above all things pant-based.' He said, 'What's in my pants is pretty grown-up, Rach.' Said, 'No thank you, as have already proven we are chemically incompatible. Plus ICK.' And left before could change mind, or ogle pants area.

Only now have pants areas on brain and am being forced to read about Andrew Lloyd Webber as contraceptive measure. Is good tool as he is utterly repellent, pants and all areas wise.

. . . .

Monday 6

Had special Upper Sixth assembly with fact-based, grown-up theme, i.e. the fact is that deadline for Oxbridge applications is in less than two weeks and it is time to grow up and think hard about future if do not want to eke out days on minimum wage stacking bean cans or sweeping up hair clippings. Mr Wilmott is minty because Emily Reeve (owner of Lola Lambert, knee-length socks (not in Japanese way), cracked nipples) has decided to train as Jo Jingles instructor which only leaves Ali Hassan and he is hell-bent on St Andrews. Scarlet says she is minded to apply so that she can subvert the idle rich from within. I said as long as it was that, and not rekindling of interest in Hilary Aneurin Bevan Nuamah, formerly ensconced at Pasty Manor helping inbred Cleggs clean toilet and restock freezer with Viennetta, now ensconced

456

in Fray-Bentos free Magdalene College, studying to become first-ever black Prime Minister. She said *au contraire*, she prefers Oxford as it has produced more politicians by volume, and anyway Hilary is too muscly to stir her vampire-obsessed mojo. She is going for pale and weedy, i.e. malnourished with possible scurvy/rickets, i.e. not Sad Ed, who, while he has potential scurvy due to replacement of oranges in diet with orange-flavoured TicTacs, is far from malnourished. (He has given up on bulimia already. He says it is too hard fitting fat fingers in mouth.) Sad Ed is not applying to Oxford or Cambridge. He says there is no point wasting money on a top-notch education as he will be dead by the time he's twenty-seven. He claims it is mystical age by which time all musical geniuses have written their best work and either die (Jimi Hendrix, Janis Joplin, Jim Morrison) or turn into tedious do-gooders (Bono, Chris Martin). He is going to try for Braintree Art Foundation instead. Am also not applying. Is not because want to die. It is because *a*) they do not do media studies at Cambridge and *b*) even if they did, there is no way I would get in as am not working class ethnic minority who has had to tramp twenty miles to school in freezing snow in order to educate self above lowly birth. Am not even from North. Why, oh why couldn't Mum and Dad be Newcastle Brown-swilling Geordies. Or at very least live in Harrogate. It is so unfair. Being middle class and Southern is utter curse.

Tuesday 7

Mum says there is no way I am doing media studies as it is a totally made up subject like BSc Golf Course Design and BA Surfing. Dad made fatal error of declaring that he wished he had done golf course design instead of accountancy as then he could be drawing water hazards and hanging out with Tiger Woods instead of spending eight hours a day trying to find out why Malcolm from IT needs twenty-five packets of Post-Its a week. He got despatched immediately from the Shreddies table without a second slice of toast and marmalade as punishment. But it is hollow victory as Dad just went round to Clive's where there is no limit on toast slices, and Nutella. James is fully backing Mum in her made-up subjects proscribed list (also banned: Stage Combat, Homeopathy, and Women's Studies). He says media studies will only qualify me to wear nobbish glasses and take cocaine. At which point he also got despatched, missing out on his second Marmite-on-granary. The dog is jubilant though. It was allowed the confiscated goods as a prize for not eating the wall.

But am now in complete degree subject choice quandary. Cannot do English literature any more as is utterly fiction-based. Nor can I do any of Mum's approved subjects, i.e. medicine, accountancy, or engineering, due to non-boffiny choice of A levels. Plus would rather die than do engineering. It is bad enough having to sit near the mathletes at lunch without voluntarily joining their

betank-topped ranks. Maybe will not do degree at all, but will go to university of life instead. Is utter grow-up-fast experience. Will travel war-torn countries and document horrors with naive yet insightful authentic voice of youth. Hurrah!

5 p.m.
Mum says I am not going to the university of life. I am going to an actual university, with halls of residence, on-site canteen, and at least four stars according to the *Times* rankings. And not in London.

. . . .

Wednesday 8
Told Scarlet and Sad Ed about thwarted university of life dream. Unbelievably Scarlet is on Mum's side. She says it is my duty as an underprivileged state-educated female to claim my rightful place amongst the elite ranks. She said I should be aiming for Durham, Manchester, or the LSE. Pointed out LSE is in London, i.e. banned, due to overinflated rent costs/potential to become crack whore. Scarlet said I can commute from Saffron Walden and live with Suzy, which is almost like being in student housing, due to abundance of incense sticks, marijuana, and cheap sex. Said that would all be over once the new baby arrives. But apparently there is still no news on that front and Suzy is back on the Merlot and funny fags. Sad Ed is more on my side. He says university

459

is only a back-up plan if his garage band fails to get signed. Said what band? And what garage? He only has a shed. He said is not real one, is virtual Garageband garage band. He is experimenting with a new sound and is confident of being the next Kate Nash. At which point had to vacate Goth Corner as thought of Sad Ed in vintage dress singing about sick on trainers too much to bear.

Anyway, have more pressing matter than the rest of my life. It is Mr Pringle. He has announced that instead of churning out mass-oppressing musicals like *Miss Saigon* or *Cats* (though surely this is cat-oppressing not mass-oppressing) at the end of term, we are going to write our own political documusical. We have to come up with a key historic event for a brainstorm next week. Sad Ed is mental with anticipation. Though pointed out that I do not think the death of Kurt Cobain is necessarily what Mr Pringle is after. Scarlet said since when do you know what Mr Pringle is after? Luckily at that point two Year Sevens started flicking tapioca at each other and she had to go and assert Sad Ed's authority for him. (Sad Ed has tried to do it on his own but he is too slow, and not at all scary. Mostly shoutees just roll eyes at him.) Though do not know why she is getting minty. She is utterly pro older men. Especially political ones. She had a crush on Neil Kinnock for years. Sad Ed said I am wrong and the death of Kurt has changed the course of music history and history history. Plus I could be Courtney Love. Was

swayed for instant as am totally like Courtney Love, i.e. prone to fashion mishaps. But then remembered *a*) am own person and *b*) there is no way would get part anyway as Daisy Devlin has fake tattoos, bigger breasts, and once overdosed on Junior Disprin. Will rack brain, or *Children's Illustrated History of the World*, later for genius idea instead.

8 p.m.
Hurrah. Have narrowed down docudrama suggestion to following (with aid of James, and his trusty companion Google):

- veteran BBC journalist John Simpson invading Afghanistan dressed as woman (has excellent transvestite theme potential)
- Anthrax terrorism scare (thus finding useful role for school sheep, who are renowned for carrying disease)
- infighting in Labour Press Office over giving Gordon Gok Wan style makeover (everyone loves a transformation scene).

Am total documentary fact-based genius. Though possibly not entirely grown-up. As list-making delayed by fight over who got the swivelly chair, plus James insisted on weighing our peanut and raisin mix snack to ensure there was fair division of spoils.

Thursday 9
Yom Kippur

Mum has been dealt a double credit-crunch-related blow.

1. She is still jobless. The police have turned down her application for fast-track detective status. The Inspector Morse dream is over before it has even begun. James says she should fight them on grounds of sexism. But apparently it is not that she is a woman. Just that her demands on flexible working (i.e. she will only work 9–3 in term-time) were too rigid.

2. A For Sale sign has gone up next door. Mum is mental with potential ASBO neighbour panic. She has gone round to Clive and Marjory's to demand a full explanation, and potential withdrawal of sign and moving ambitions.

4.30 p.m.

Mum is back having secured a partial victory. On down side, Marjory has refused Mum's demands to not move. She says Clive's job (have no idea what job is, but possibly something to do with pet food) is in balance, and they are downsizing before they get repossessed, in utter forward-thinking move (which Mum cannot argue with as she is all for forward thinking, and economizing). Sign is also still up. Marjory says it is not a blot on the landscape, or a threat to security, or a distraction to drivers causing potential crashing into low level wall and pea gravel,

which James had listed as bargaining tools. BUT, in ill-thought-out concession, she has agreed to involve Mum in choice of new occupiers. This is fatal. Mum's list of banned neighbours is vast, e.g: anyone from North, anyone with potential to hang Austrian blinds, and anyone vaguely related to an O'Grady. Marjory will be stuck there for ever. James is in agreement. Though he says it will not be because Mum and Marjory are turning the hordes away, it is that at £395,000, the house is vastly overpriced, considering the avocado bathroom suite, the ill-advised carpet in the kitchen, and the lack of all-important stormporch, and that in fact they will be lucky to get any viewings at all in the current climate.

· ·

Friday 10

Is my turn to be dealt a double blow. Is not credit crunch related. Is Jesus- and Criminal and Retard- and mathlete-related, i.e.

1. Grandpa fell asleep during *Diagnosis Murder*, and forgot to pick Jesus up from the Camilla Parker Bowles Memorial Crèche this afternoon. Fat Kylie tried to ring Mum but Mum does not converse with O'Gradys and put the phone down on principle. So Mr Wilmott nominated me to take Jesus home. Said James was more responsible (official declaration by Mum) but Mr Wilmott said he was well aware of that but James's many talents were needed

elsewhere, i.e. in a crucial chess-off against Burger King Sports Academy. Fat Kylie gave me Jesus's weekly school crèche report to take home. It said 'Weed in Wendy house and hit other child on head with hammer.' I blame Mark Lambert. He is the one who lent Jesus his toolbox.

2. Film Club has been cancelled tonight, i.e. there will be no Pringle-gazing. It is due to a domino effect of catastrophic events, i.e. an unnamed Retard (widely believed to be Kyle O'Grady) tried to overturn authority by gassing Mr Potter (Physics, underarm issues, beard with bits of food in it), i.e. leaving all Bunsen burners on, which meant that A Corridor had to be temporarily sealed off to avoid potential explosion, which meant that One Fenton's double geography lesson had to decamp to Mr Knox's audio-visual suite, but during journey Mad Harry bet Evan Fletcher that he couldn't drink a can of Nutriment in four seconds. He could, thus winning 45p. But bet null and voided after Nutriment made reappearance on audio-visual suite carpet five minutes later, which meant that library had to be sealed off until tomorrow to avoid vomit-smell moaning.

4.30 p.m.
I mean discussion of brain-stimulating cinematic experience. Not Pringle-gazing. Obviously. Though as didn't happen, doesn't matter. No one will know.

4.45 p.m.

Just got text from Scarlet. It says 'No Pringle gazing 4 U'. How does she do it? It is the throne of Davros. It is imbuing her with weird Dalek-like powers. And laziness. She actually used it to navigate beans queue at lunchtime. She will be commuting on it next.

. . . .

Saturday 11

Hurrah. Have achieved older man cancelling karma, i.e. Mr Wandering Hands cannot do driving lesson today. According to Mrs Wandering Hands (who knew??), he has sustained a repetitive strain gear-knob-related injury. Dad says it is more likely a Mrs Wandering Hands wandering hands-related injury. Then Mum got all het up and said it was like talking ill of Jesus (churchy one, not uncle. She is all for talking ill of that one), and at least Mike took an interest in his physical health. But James pointed out that *a*) Mum is an atheist therefore Jesus is no more than a fictional construct; *b*) gear knob RSI is utterly made up, according to Google; and *c*) Mr Wandering Hands has previous. At which point Mum stormed upstairs with the Beastly binoculars to keep an eye on viewings next door. She is probably just minty about finding out there is a Mrs Wandering Hands. It has ruined her hopes of being driven off into sunset in an X-reg Fiesta. She is still trying to reduce Dad's calorie intake. He is only allowed one almond slice at teatime and no sugar on his Shreddies.

He says it is worse than wartime rationing. James pointed out that rationing ended in 1953, i.e. a full eleven years before Dad was born. But Dad said he meant the Falklands, when Grandma Riley got stingy with the corned beef in case Argentina stopped exporting cattle.

5 p.m.
James is jubilant with his real estate assessment, i.e. there have been no viewings at Clive and Marjory's. There was a near panic when Les Brewster and Ying showed up, but through cunning deduction (i.e. James being sent over to borrow cup of flour (wholemeal, i.e. utterly plausible, although Mum running out of anything not at all plausible)) it turns out they were buying a second-hand abdominizer (Marjory also selling off random household goods in financial crisis averting move). But Mum not so jubilant as is annoyed at bargain-missing potential as abdominizer could have been answer to Dad's stomach issues.

Thank God have got welcoming refuge of Duke to escape to. Is utter grown-up activity, i.e. sink sorrows in pint (of diet Coke) and relate family-based woes to world weary but sympathetic regulars.

11 p.m.
Or place bets on how many bottles of Pale Ale Kev's dog can drink before it falls off stool (answer five).

466

Sunday 12

Have remembered have appointment with destiny tomorrow, aka careers counsellor 'Bonkers' Batty (long hair, adult onset acne, obsession with obscure German heavy-metal bands). James says is like psychometric testing, i.e. they will delve into the murky depths of my personality to see if I am geared to working with people or should stick to hermit-like shelf-stacking menial labour. It sounds excellent, like diary room in *Big Brother*. Oooh. Maybe will find out am utterly meant to be tragic poetess like Sylvia Plath.

8 p.m.
Or fact-based Christiane Amanpour newshound type.

Monday 13

Careers meeting not at all like psychometric delving into personality nor in *Big Brother* diary room style mentalist suite. Was crap multiple choice questionnaire in library (now free of vomit smell—must find out recipe to pass on to Bob for sick-smelling Volvo), i.e. surrounded by Year Sevens trying to look up 'knob' in OED.

Plus, according to results, am not tragic poetess or newshound. In fact am ideally suited to being 'data processor', which have no idea what is, but sounds crap. Said test was utterly wrong. Bonkers Batty said Carol Ann Duffy and Christiane Amanpour not on listed options and

test is never wrong, is infallible judgement of character. Made him take test. It told him to be a careers adviser or premier league footballer. He said see, is accurate, except that test does not know about his rheumatoid arthritis. Said, whatever, there is no way am being a data processor, as despite having no idea what it is, it is obviously pants. Bonkers said maybe I should consider having a gap year until have made up mind about future. I said I would, except gap years are banned in our house due to risk of: *a*) catching dysentery, *b*) being sucked into cult by yogic guru/Operation Raleigh leader, and *c*) getting overused to amassing wealth from temp jobs and refusing to return to studies. And fish up penises (not on Mum's list, but will suggest it as amendment).

Scarlet got 'civil servant'. She is citing it as further evidence of her government potential on her Cambridge application. Said did not think the dons would be persuaded by the equivalent of a *Cosmo* sex quiz (question example: Do you prefer working with *a*) your hands, *b*) your brain *c*) children). But she says *au contraire* it is world-respected accurate test, and I would do well to consider its conclusions on my own potential.

Sad Ed is on my side. He got 'fisherman' (is because he said he likes gloom and solitude, and is not scared of dying). But he also found out twenty-four words for penis (Mad Harry, James, and the OED), so he says it is not entirely a wasted afternoon.

Tuesday 14

Grandpa Clegg has rung. There is devastating news from Pasty Manor. It is not that Granny has remembered she is progressive non-racist type, it is that Bruce has had a fight with Pig over a leftover chipolata and the neighbours are complaining about the barking (both Bruce and Pig, who claims he can 'talk to the animals'). Apparently Granny says one of them is going to have to move out. I said *a*) did not know Pig was permanent resident, *b*) if he is, who is looking after the pigs, and *c*) since when had Pig taken precedence over Bruce in Granny's affections. Grandpa said *a*) semi-permanent, i.e. he sleeps on broken Parker Knoll when *CSI* is on as he can't get reception on the farm, *b*) Mrs Pig (who knew!), and *c*) since Bruce took a dislike to Eamonn Holmes. Put the phone down. There is no way anyone can solve such an idiotic conundrum.

6 p.m.

Unless it is weird boffin boy James Riley. He has drawn up infallible mathematic equation that proves it is Pig who has to move out. He is ringing Grandpa with the joyous news as we speak.

6.15 p.m.

Equation redundant as condundrum already solved. Bruce is apparently taken with Dr Doolittle barking, or possibly hairy face and essence de pig, and is treating him as new leader of house. Granny says she does not mind as

Pig is in her thrall anyway so she is still in actual charge of them, and Grandpa does not mind because he is in charge of Granny, due to mere dint of owning a penis, so he is actual top dog. Is sorry state of affairs when top dog is a man who has Hammerited own face and thinks Cold War was fought with ice throwers.

. . . .

Wednesday 15

Mr Wilmott is jubilant. He has a record fourteen applications for Oxbridge including Scarlet, Alan Wong (son of sadistic dentist Mrs Wong, Mars Bar habit, rumoured to be in triads), and at least four Criminals and Retards. He says it shows how times are changing and positive attitudes to comprehensive pupils are encouraging high-flying academic ambitions. It is not that. It is because everyone who applies gets next Wednesday morning off to watch *Chariots of Fire* to introduce them to world of boffiny elite. Am unmoved by academic ambitions though. What is high-flying about moving thirteen miles up road. Or to Oxford, which is basically Cambridge, but with Inspector Morse location tours. Am thinking instead will form guerrilla (not gorilla) theatre troupe and travel bombed-out cities performing life-changing fact-based political drama. Have submitted all my ideas to Mr Pringle. Think he was utterly impressed by breadth of my fact-based (i.e. Wikipedia-based) knowledge. Though he did point out that John Simpson one was potentially

470

libellous (had changed character slightly to make him evil Western warlord). It is still better idea than Sad Ed or Reuben Tull though. Sad Ed is still clinging to his Kurt Cobain dream (despite being a foot too short and four stone too heavy to in any way play him convincingly). And Reuben Tull wanted to recreate Woodstock including hiring the Rolling Stones and making the audience take mind-altering drugs. He is moron. Anyway, Mr Pringle is announcing the result next Wednesday and we start rehearsing straight away. Hurrah.

. . . .

Thursday 16

There is further proof that going out with older man is way forward. It is Madonna who is divorcing pseudo-cockney toy boy Guy Ritchie. According to Grandpa Riley (who got news from *Heat* Online—number three most popular website at Twilight Years Day Centre, after Times Obituaries and Viagra shop) she needs to focus her sights on someone at least ten years older, who will appreciate her dedication to leotards, instead of realizing she is rad-dled old has-been. Is true. Look at him and Treena. There is forty-something-year age gap and they still do it twice a week and extra on Saturdays if Treena has been watching *X Factor*. (It is not Simon Cowell. It is midget impresario Louis Walsh. Treena says he makes her 'go funny down there'. Said Ick.) Will refocus sights on Mr Pringle tomor-row night in film club. We are watching *The Doors* starring

471

Batman as Jim Morrison and Meg Ryan as a groupie with
bad wig. Sad Ed is mental with anticipation. He says he is
thinking of resubmitting a stage version for our play.
Pointed out that *a*) Jim Morrison spent most of his life
wandering around semi-naked and did he really want to
expose his manboobs to the Year Nine Criminals and
Retards, and *b*) on the subject of fighting the flab, what
has happened to his vampiric ambitions as have seen him
eat four Twix fingers and a packet of Monster Munch
Flamin' Hot in less than an hour. Sad Ed said it is comfort
eating. Scarlet's demands as Chief of Staff are getting
absurd. She wants him to demand funding for lesbian and
gay caucus minibus to ferry anyone afeared of discrimination around in comfort and safety. (She is mental. There
is no way she will secure backing from head girl Thin
Kylie, who is anti-all things lezzer, let alone Mr Wilmott.)
Plus, according to minigoth Harriet Pucklechurch, who
got it off Melody Bean, former head goth and lover of
Scarlet Trevor Pledger is on verge of breaking up with
Tamsin Bacon. Melody says they had a row outside the
Co-Op about badminton being anti-goth due to white
clothing requirement and she has given him his rat back
(Hedges, inferior in every way to Benson, according to
Scarlet). Sad Ed says it will be all over for him the minute
she gets a whiff of Trevor's patchouli-ingrained vegetarian
leather coat. I said to be fair, it had never really begun. Sad
Ed sighed and unwrapped a Chomp bar.

Friday 17

Sad Ed is right about Scarlet. Mr Pringle had to shush her four times during *The Doors* due to her comparing Trevor favourably to Batman in terms of hair, nipples, and the way he leans on stuff. I told him is because Trevor is older man and it is the way of nature for me and her to pursue grown-ups. Sad Ed said he was utter older man. I said twenty days does not count, especially when backed up by evidence of childness, i.e. fact that he broke another spring on saggy sofa at lunch when he attempted to use as trampoline to reach the legendary flump that has been stuck on ceiling since 2002. Sad Ed said was not childishness, was rite of passage John Major tradition, i.e. totally grown-up older man. Then Scarlet overheard and demanded to know what was discussion about older men? I said is nothing. Just that older man is utterly way forward for fact-based grown-up style relationship etc. Scarlet said is true, plus they have cars and are better at finding G spot. At which point Mr Pringle demanded to know what was conversation about so we said trade unions and went back to concentrating on film, and eating Sad Ed's Revels (stealth chocolates, i.e. you think you have delicious Malteser but turns out to be ickky orange thing).

. . . .

Saturday 18

2 p.m.

Something fishy is going on next door. There is a man in

a pinstripe suit with scary hair and a clipboard peering through Marjory's letterbox. Mum has got the Beastly binoculars out and is keeping an eye in case he is a burglar or a Mormon. The dog is also keeping an eye. (Although not with binoculars. It cannot control the focus bit. It is just staring menacingly out of the window.) It is its aversion to spookily helmet-like hairdos (Natasha Kaplinsky, Moira Stewart, Mrs Noakes. Even Granny Clegg has to be careful when she has a wash and set.) Dad says we are all overreacting and it is probably just a Cable TV salesman. James said they are more persuasive than the Mormons so the vigil was doubly necessary. Dad rolled eyes and and went back to putting golf balls into Nescafé jar. He should be happy. At least Mum is focusing her binoculars, and attentions, on potential criminals/religious fanatics, rather than Mr Wandering Hands. He was visibly disappointed at the lack of spying he got when he dropped me off.

2.15 p.m.
All signs point to helmet hair man being burglar. He has been joined on doorstep by Mrs O'Grady and several smaller O'Gradys. Mum is thinking of calling the police. Have pointed out that if they are planning burglary then they are not being very surreptitious, i.e. *a*) they are at front of house in full view of passers-by and the Beastly binoculars, *b*) since when do burglars wear pinstripe suits, and *c*) they have brought Whitney, who will surely only

be a hindrance in any crime situation. James says, *au contraire*, *a*) it is a cunning deceptive tactic to throw us off the scent and as we speak one of the Liams is probably shinning up a drainpipe and jimmying open Marjory's bathroom window, *b*) it might be a banker forced to turn to crime in the current economic climate, and *c*) Whitney is ideally suited to crime, they can funnel her into crevices and down chimneys and then she can undo doors from inside. Said he is mental. Plus Marjory has just opened the front door and let them all in, so either she is expecting them, or she is an accomplice in the crime, which is unlikely given her militant pro-*NYPD Blue* tendencies. James said possibly she is committing massive insurance fraud to avoid having to downsize and sell house.

2.45 p.m.
Marjory has just been over. Is not insurance fraud. Is bigger crime, i.e. potentially selling the house to the O'Gradys! Mum is mental with ASBO panic. She said it is bad enough having the Britchers opposite with their kidney-shaped pool (banned) and Union Jack flag (banned) but now it is as if *The Sopranos* are moving in as well. Pointed out that Mum had never seen *The Sopranos*, due to her own vigorous controls, and that if she had, she would know that comparing Mrs O'Grady to Carmela Soprano is like claiming Granny Clegg is Helen Mirren. Or so I had been told, as had obviously never seen it due to it being banned (did not mention *Sopranos* marathon

475

with Jack last year). Mum eyed me with suspicion but was too busy panicking with O'Grady menace to dole out punishment. Marjory says it is unlikely they will be able to afford it anyway, given their no jobs and penchant for gas-guzzling 4x4s. But James said they probably had a million stashed away in the microwave in used notes. He has been watching too much *Lovejoy*. Besides, there is no way they would keep it in microwave, it is only source of hot food.

. . . .

Sunday 19

Shreddies table was utter war zone this morning. Mum is still seething over anticipated O'Grady invasion, which is having detrimental effect on rest of house in terms of shoutiness. Dog got two for walking into door and licking genitals at mealtime, Dad got one for saying word 'genitals' at mealtime, and I got a stern talking to for cross-contamination of Marmite and marmalade. Only James remains shout-free. It is because he is in agreement with Mum. He says it is the beginning of the end for his 'manor'. Said *a*) he had said that about Thin Kylie and *b*) he is not Guy Ritchie, so please stop talking like a twit. He said *a*) Britchers are breeze compared to seasoned menaces the O'Gradys and *b*) the mathletes are adopting a 'street talk' stance in attempt to overhaul their public image and boost ranks. They are also going to be adopting a new look, which he will be unveiling tomorrow.

Said *a*) he was, officially, friends with foremost O'Grady menace Keanu, first toughest in the juniors, so he should be welcoming them to his 'manor' and *b*) please don't let it be waistcoats or cravats or will have to utterly disown him. He said, *a*) he may admire Keanu's skills as gang member, but he does not want a Daihatsu with a 'Honk if You're Horny' sticker miring Summerdale Road in chavdom and *b*) it is not cravats, it is much more ambitious and manly.

* *

Monday 20
7.30 a.m.
Oh my God. James has revealed new look. Is not manly. Is moronic, i.e. is trousers halfway down bottom, revealing underpants (Marks & Spencer), tie undone, and back to front baseball cap (Mole Hall Wildlife Park) on abundantly gelled hair. He was right on one count though, i.e. is utterly ambitious. He is mental if he thinks he is going to get that past Mum.

7.35 a.m.
As predicted, James has been sent to his room to *a*) change and *b*) reflect on his use of the word 'ho' when referring to Mum, or indeed any woman. James said it's not his fault if the 'old lady is wigging about the 'hood'. Told him to quit while he was ahead, i.e. he may have lost the baseball cap and gel but he can pull his trousers down

477

as soon as he gets to school. Although, would not recommend it as it is tantamount to open invitation to get wedgied by a Criminal and Retard. He said, 'Props, blud.' He is idiot.

5 p.m.
Mum is in buoyant mood. It is the O'Gradys. They are not moving into Clive and Marjory's. Apparently the avocado suite is too 'minging'. Marjory is not so jubilant. It is having her interior design shunned by someone who wears velour. Personally I am with the O'Gradys. Green toilets are just wrong.

Also Mum has demanded to know why James is walking 'like he did the time he had a poo incident on the M5'. James says he sustained minor bruising from a rogue hacky sack in PE. He did not. He got three wedgies, and an 'up and over' (pants stretched to reach head—speciality of Criminals and Retards) in first break. Mad Harry got off worse. He had to see Mrs Leech for some Savlon and a glass of medicinal lemon barley. He is having difficulty sitting down at all.

· ·

Tuesday 21
8 a.m.
James's trousers are firmly back where they belong, i.e. covering his buttocks, with no visible wedgie targets. He says he is limiting his streetwise style to language only,

and then promptly got sent back upstairs for calling the dog a 'beeyatch', which is not only rude, but inaccurate. He also called Dad a 'dawg', which may be rude, but is at least genitally-correct. Dad took it as compliment anyway. They are both idiots. There is no way a man in a vest and Hush Puppies and reading the *Telegraph* is in any way 'dawg'-like. Mum is preparing herself for a summit meeting at Marjory's to discuss the housing crisis, i.e. the potential sale of Number 22 to unsavoury characters. She says she cannot be expected to live the next God knows how many months in perpetual fear that she is going to wake up to find Barry the Blade waving at her over the fence. Said that was unlikely given that Barry the Blade lives in an Austin Allegro, so his next step up the ladder is likely to be a Montego estate, not a four-bed detached with decking and a breakfast bar.

5 p.m.
Mum is utterly not jubilant. She says Marjory is unwilling to embrace change and move with the times. Said this was odd, as Mum is usually pro not moving with times, e.g. when Jif changed its name to Cif, when they turned Milky Ways white inside, and when Blue Peter stopped making Advent crowns in favour of hosting cheerleading displays. Mum said, *au contraire*, she is thoroughly modern, and cited acceptance of dark chocolate as potential health food, purchase of non-tapered trousers, and embracing of John Humphrys as Magnus Magnusson

replacement on *Mastermind* as proof. Did not retaliate, though have plenty of ammunition, as wanted to know what hoo-ha was about. It is that Mum had come up with genius scheme to avoid potential moving horror, i.e. renting out Marjory's spare rooms (two, as despite having four bedrooms, she and Clive have separate beds due to 'snoring issues', i.e. Clive's according to Marjory and Marjory's according to Clive). But Marjory says taking in a lodger is like inviting reclusive pervert into the house and they will be rifling your undies and eating all your HobNobs before the rent cheque has cleared. Marjory watches too much ITV. But, it is I who am (are/is?) genius, as pointed out that Mum could use own idea to avoid impending credit crunch crisis at Number 24, and save herself finding job (she has been rejected by Barclays, Saffron Walden Building Society, and, controversially, which cannot even begin to go into, Wainwright and Beacham in last few days). Mum says she is going to mull it over with Dad, i.e. tell him that she is doing it, and then ignore his objections. Is brilliant. Having a lodger is excellent for broadening minds and horizons, e.g. Humbert Humbert in *Lolita*, who is very much older man.

5.15 p.m.
And fictional.

5.20 p.m.
And potential pant-sniffing pervert. But still, it is good

idea. Oooh. Could lure Mr Pringle away from Chestnuts B&B. We have much more hygienic toilet facilities (i.e. Mum does not have bikini-line trimmer, let alone leave it on edge of sink). Although am not sure he could cope with the proscribed items list. Would be excellent to be in same house though. Then he could see how am utterly fact-based and grown-up. Think he may well be falling for my charms already. Bumped into him at fruit and nut dispensing machine at last break (or rather, had followed him down two corridors, using Sad Ed as visibility protection) and he said I would like the play announcement tomorrow. So he must have gone for my Gordon Brown makeover idea. Hurrah!

. . . .

Wednesday 22

4 p.m.

Play is not Gok Wan Prime Ministerial makeover. Or John Simpson thing. But is better. It is *Secret Diary of Anne Frank—the Musical!* Which was no one's idea, but Mr Pringle said trying to re-enact the taking of Kabul in the lower school canteen would have proved problematic. Whereas this is smaller in actual scale, but bigger in metaphorical scale, i.e. is not just about Jews in hiding in a few rooms in Amsterdam, but about persecuted minorities everywhere, i.e. like me on my bed protest! I am totally Anne Frank! Caris Kelp (eats glue) says in fact she is Anne Frank, as she has been to Holland. But I

481

have hair like Barbra streisand, i.e. unmanageable. Plus, more importantly, I am diary-keeping, fact-based, sexual-awakening teenage prodigy type. Hurrah! As long as Sad Ed does not get cast as Peter. I am a good actress but faking sexual interest in him would be impossible. Anyway, is unlikely as his five a day (Mars bars, not fruit) diet is conducive to looking neither like a vampire, nor a ghettoized Jewish boy subsisting on cabbage soup and hope. Mr Pringle says at this stage no one is anyone, and we just need to read the book and get into the mindset of being effectively imprisoned. But I definitely saw him look meaningfully at me at that point.

4.15 p.m.
Unless he has lazy eye like Dr Braithwaite (huge hands, bottle of whisky in drawer) and was actually looking meaningfully at Reuben Tull in bid to stop him air drumming to theme from *Big Barn Farm*. Anyway, does not matter as am going to subsume self into book at half term so that Anne Frank's very aura transwhatevers into me then he will have no choice but to cast me.

. . . .

Thursday 23
There has been another Jesus-related incident at school. He, and all other inmates of the Camilla Parker Bowles Memorial Crèche, have been banned from the school farm. According to Sad Ed, who got it off Mrs Leech,

Cowpat Cheesmond says the sheep have not been so terrified since the Criminals and Retards (yes, he did use that phrase, though is rich, considering his own swarthy and slightly backwoods tendencies) were allowed to try sheep shearing. It is Fat Kylie's fault. She was supposed to be supervising them, i.e. keeping them behind the fence at all times and ensuring sheep were only fed health-giving pellets. She said it is not her fault she is 'allergic to sheep shite', or that Whitney had concealed a packet of Hubba Bubba in her pull-up pants.

10 p.m.
Oh my God. I AM Anne Frank. Not only is she philosophical and poetic. But her mother is irritating stickler for rules! Oh, cannot wait for ending. Hope it is tension-fuelled *Sound of Music*-style night flit to Edelweiss studded green hills of neutral territory like Austria or Belgium. Or Isle of Man.

. . . .

Friday 24
Last day of school

Scarlet says I am not Anne Frank, I am Rachel Riley. Not least because *a*) I am NOT Jewish. I just have crap hair, *b*) I have never been persecuted, and *c*) consistently painting oneself as fictional construct is not at all helpful mental-health- or Jack-wise. Said *a*) hair is not crap and she is utter anti-Semite for saying so, *b*) I live under

restrictive regime that makes Taliban look lenient, c i) Anne Frank is not a fictional fairytale construct but is actual dead real person, so conforms to all rules, not that there are any, and why does she care because she doesn't want me to go out with Jack anyway, and c ii) that's rich coming from someone who claims to be the lover of a fictional 106-year-old vampire (i.e. older man but with lithe body of youth, so best of all worlds, according to Scarlet). Then she whizzed menacingly round the table at me on the Davros chair so did not say anything else as she was armed with pot of Petit Filous, which is not only stain-making, but substandard apricot flavour. She is obviously not taking news that Bob and Suzy have passed all their tests to become adoptive parents as well as thought. It is utter miracle though. I bet they did not disclose the time they accidentally left Scarlet aged three in the John Lewis car park for four hours while they tested mattresses. Or the time Jack ingested an entire packet of Suzy's contraceptive pills and grew temporary breasts. Although there is downside to joy. They are not allowed to adopt a black baby. Mr Lemon is insisting that it is not culturally beneficial to either party. Suzy says it is utterly racist, and that they will happily adopt customs and native dress if necessary. Mr Lemon said that was utterly racist and then they got into a tit for tat 'who is more PC' fight, won marginally by Suzy for knowing Martin Luther King's 'I have a Dream' speech by heart. Anyway, they are not getting a black, or brown, or Chinese baby. They

are getting a much more whitish one, if and when one shows up.

11 p.m.
Have finished *Anne Frank*. And am somewhat disappointed by downbeat gritty non-fairytale ending. But that is reality for you—no snogging in flower-filled meadows, no making snow angels, and no comedy airport dashes. Maybe will persuade Mr Pringle to do alternative finale, involving Anne single-handedly overpowering Nazis and escaping with Peter to America where they become world famous literary commentators and also invent fat-free mayonnaise.

Saturday 25

A blow has been struck to general grown-upness. It is Mum (as usual). She has decided that going to pub regularly is potentially life-destroying and that I will end up with shaky arms, thousand yard stare, and compromised complexion of alcoholic if I do not tackle my addiction. Have pointed out that so far only addiction is Sad Ed's to Cheese Moments, which, though junk food, do contain calcium, so are not at all as lethal or chav-based as Wotsits. Mum says *a*) The only permissable pub-based snack is protein-rich cashew nuts (unsalted, unroasted), and *b*) she is no longer funding my sordid lifestyle through pocket money. Said *a*) What about Twiglets

485

(Marmitey so with folic acid) and *b*) yet you are content to fund James's penchant for Warhammer crap? She said *a*) Absolutely not, as Marmite level minimal and out-weighed by preservative content, and *b*) that is entirely different, as Warhammer is mind-expanding and encourages concentration and is thus good for his chess. Was about to argue that in fact just creates unemployable nerds with no social skills and bad facial hair but then the dog managed to turn the Magimix on and whizzed eggs all over the ceiling, thus ending conversation.

It is utterly unfair. Going to the pub is mind-expanding (and stomach-expanding in Sad Ed's case). For instance, where else would I have learnt the ingredients of a Mudslide (anything, according to Shorty, including cherry-ade and Malibu, as the Baileys overpowers everything else), or the words to 'Crystal Chandelier'? Will just have to economize, e.g. no more Frazzles and tap water instead of lime and soda. Will still be excellent night.

11.30 p.m.
Have had utterly pants night, i.e. have been downgraded to leaning on toilet door or hovering on sticky carpet. It is gangly landlord Shorty. He says we cannot have custody of the sought-after wobbly table if all we are going to consume is a pint of cider, a Britvic, and some tap water. It is Sad Ed's fault for deciding to revive his vampiric diet. Otherwise we could have guaranteed at least £7.70 on Cheese Moments. Scarlet pointed out that he was being

anti-poverty, i.e. classist. But he said he was not being classist, he was being an economist. And Scarlet couldn't argue with that as it is uber-political. We are going to think of money-raising schemes instead so that we can oust Reuben Tull (drug dealer, so flush) and his enormous-haired cohorts from their new-found table of glory. I did suggest joining forces but Sad Ed takes up too much seat room and there is no way I am sitting on Reuben's lap. Scarlet says Shorty will get bored with them soon because they clog up the jukebox with Pink Floyd, which is not at all conducive to selling Bacardi Breezer, and it is statistically proven that Phil Collins encourages far greater alcohol consumption. Is possibly true. As would personally only suffer Phil Collins if was heinously drunk.

. . . .

Sunday 26
British Summer Time ends

Mum is going mental with Russell Brand prank phonecall hoo-ha. She is very much anti-Russell Brand already, on grounds of height of hair, tightness of trousers, and indiscriminate nature of penis. But now he has apparently gone too far by insulting her favourite comedy racist Spanish waiter actor. She is writing to the BBC to demand an immediate ban on Russell and Jonathan Ross, who is also very much proscribed due to outlandish suits, large-breasted wife, and speech impediments. Mum does

not believe anyone with a speech impediment should be in position of public broadcasting, including a stutter, lisp, or Birmingham accent.

Have retired to bedroom to escape idiotic discussion and immerse self in *Diary of Anne Frank*. Oh how our lives intermingle. She reads great literature, I read great literature (or at least I did until became fact-based). She hates dentists, I hate dentists. It is like she is reincarnated in me.

3 p.m.
Ooh. Maybe she is reincarnated in me! Which would mean I AM Anne Frank, not Rachel Riley after all!

3.15 p.m.
James says she is not reincarnated in me. If anyone is reincarnated in me it is a plague-ridden haggle-toothed gypsy. Asked who was reincarnated in him. He said Nelson. Said Nelson Mandela not dead. He said Lord not Mandela, which is further evidence of why no one uber-intelligent is camping out in my body. He is wrong. Even if Anne Frank not in me, am still utterly at one with her plight.

4 p.m.
James has persuaded Mum to add Noel Fielding to her BBC ban demand letter, citing scary eyes, overlarge teeth, and revealingness of catsuits. Have told them that they are not to trouble me with such trivia any more, as am

persecuted Jew with deeper concerns than the petty-minded flippant whines of the overprivileged. Honestly. They do not know they are born.

5 p.m.
Oooh. Have had genius character-building fact-based idea. Am going to annexe self off from rest of world, and subsist on meagre rations, my diary, and an occasional news update from my helpers, i.e. James and dog. Although dog potentially not great source of news. But will be comfort in my incarceration.

5.15 p.m.
Unless it has criminal wind. I do not know why Mum persists in giving it health-giving vegetables. They are not at all good for health of anyone else within twenty-metre radius. Anyway. Is definite. Am going into hiding. Have instructed Mum that am only to be allowed war-based food from now on, which is to be brought to my room, in secret, by a sympathizer, i.e. James. Although he is not utterly sympathetic, i.e. he said am mental, but he is best I can do as dog cannot carry tray (James has tested this in past, it ended in Rice Krispy spillage and a level two shouting). Mum says I will not last past *Watchdog* tomorrow night. She is wrong. I am iron-willed in my determination to evade my Nazi persecutors. Plus *Watchdog* isn't on because of the snooker.

Monday 27

Half term

10 a.m.

Hurrah. It is Day One of Anne Frank annexation. Have consumed two bowls of Shreddies and stood in garden for ten minutes to boost Vitamin D levels in preparation. And am now back in room with diary and jug of tap water. Is utterly war-like. Except for possibly Chris Moyles's breakfast show (even Anne Frank had radio).

10.15 a.m.

And *Heatworld*. Was present from Grandpa Riley to sustain me in hour of need. Though have finished already. There is only so long you can look at Calum Best without gagging.

1 p.m.

Mum is wrong. There is no way am going to cave. Besides, is easier than bed protest as am allowed to use bathroom. Although will not flush toilet for authenticity. James is taking role very seriously. He has brought cottage cheese on jacket potato for lunch, which is not cabbage soup, but is still war-like in blandness. Plus he has reviving news of the outside world, i.e. Mum has made new clothes for naked Will Young out of old Action Man outfit, although now he looks like Prince William; Beefy (postman, dyslexic, notorious gossip) says Mr Patel got red gas bill (so obviously porn, junk food, and nicotine

490

patch empire not as lucrative as thought) plus Mad Harry has worms.

He is sending Mouchi, i.e. the dog, up later for some pet therapy. Plus he is going to test my ability to move about the house undetected by the Nazi enemy (i.e. Mum).

3.30 p.m.
Have sent Mouchi back whence it came. Watching it trying to eat piece of gum entangled in paw fur is not at all therapeutic. Am going to attempt surreptitious foray to kitchen in minute to secure rich tea biscuit (utterly povvy and warlike).

3.40 p.m.
Have failed foray test. James sprang out on me from under table and issued yellow card (actual yellow card, embossed with swastika). He says I will have to forego snack as punishment, and await austerity dinner instead.

5 p.m.
Am starving. Thank God is tea in half an hour. Maybe will be celebratory war-like casserole.

6 p.m.
Was not celebratory casserole. Was authentic dried bean soup. Mum is trying to flush me out with meanness. It will not work. She underestimates my Jewish resolve.

8 p.m.

Am going to sleep. James has issued authentic lights out warning. And cannot listen to any more Radio One as it is making nerves jangly. Being Anne Frank not as much fun as thought. Am starving and bored. Plus do not even have love interest to moon over. Sad Ed did offer but there is no way I am being incarcerated with his depression, or bowels, for any length of time.

. . . .

Tuesday 28

10 a.m.

A new day dawns in the ghetto, and, despite my peril and persecution, am revived in my optimism for life. Plus got Edam sandwich for breakfast, on grounds that it is Dutch. Have made resolution to stop complaining and utilize time wisely, i.e. do homework.

11 a.m.

Cannot do homework in ghetto as am plagued by sound of *a*) stomach that is used to at least a bowl of Shreddies, a piece of granary toast and Marmite, and several rich teas by this time, and *b*) James and Mad Harry who are combining Beastly Boys and Beastly Investigations by singing 'The Lion Sleeps Tonight' on the landing, complete with dog howling the chorus bit. I bet Anne Frank didn't have to put up with this sort of hoo-ha.

1 p.m.
Have eaten lunch. Four crackers (dry) and an apple with a brown bit. Ate brown bit despite maggot potential. Think need protein as can feel muscles depleting.

3 p.m.
Have failed yet again in foray test. Was trying to liberate cheese (Edam, so legal) from fridge while Hitler, i.e. Mum, safely replenishing slug traps in garden but Mussolini, aka Mad Harry, had installed himself inside boiler cupboard and burst out, causing me to hit head on fridge door and sustain medium to severe bruising. Plus cheese confiscated.

8 p.m.
Another day closes. Feel like have been locked up for months. Maybe it will get easier. Deprivation will become second nature and I will be unable to rehabilitate into outside world, like lifers when they are released from Broadmoor. Hurrah.

. . . .

Wednesday 29
9 a.m.
Uggh. Deprivation is not any easier. Cannot be expected to survive on Edam and crackers. Only thing keeping me going now is prospect of visit from James. He is my Miep, bringing hope, joy, and digestive biscuits.

493

11 a.m.

Was not digestive. Was oatcake. Which is not biscuit at all but sliver of savoury concrete. Plus news from outside world is not at all hope-imbuing, i.e. Mum is bulk-soaking dried beans, Granny Clegg has rung to say Pig has got hand stuck in jar trying to retrieve liquorice allsort, and the dog has attacked Mad Harry which is utterly like when lions turn on their tamers. It is not, it is like when crocodiles eat annoying morons who jump into their zoo enclosures. Mad Harry is always pestering the dog.

James has brought me more fact-based reading though, as have exhausted the *Children's Illustrated Encyclopaedia* and the Penguin *Guide to Punctuation* (there is nothing I do not know about semi-colons now). It is Mum's hypochondriac's bible aka Dr Le Fanu's *Book of Family Health*.

7 p.m.

Am dangerously ill. Have looked in mirror and have definite look of concentration camp. Have checked symptoms and have narrowed it down to:

- Hepatitis B
- Yellow fever
- Bird flu (sparrows on windowsill looking bit sickly and may have sent germs through glass by osmosis)

Death is imminent. So am recording poignant, yet mysterious, last words for immortality.

7.15 p.m.
Cannot think of anything mysterious. Plus need a poo.

7.16 p.m.
But what if die on loo. Cannot have 'need a poo' as last words. Oooh. Will borrow meaningful phrase instead.

7.20 p.m.
Aha. Have got it. 'The World Is Not Enough'. Is utterly mysterious and deep. Cannot remember where comes from though.

7.30 p.m.
Did not die mid-poo. Which is lucky as have remembered it is name of James Bond film and not even good one as has Pierce Brosnan in who is neither retro cool (Sean Connery) nor postmodern macho (Daniel Craig). Is just Mr Wandering Hands with better hair and weird accent.

Am retiring to deathbed now, with following, final words: *No one understands me.*

. . . .

Thursday 30

10 a.m.
Am not dead. But wish was. Was not Edam for breakfast. Was authentic soused herrings. Feel sick now. That will teach Mum for trying to break me with pickled fish as

cannot flush sick away, thus breaking all sorts of cross-contamination rules.

3 p.m.
There has been reviving news from the free world. It is Mum. According to James she is mental with anticipation as her lodger advert is in the *Walden Chronicle*. Have begged him to bring me contraband newspaper to see joyous news for myself.

4 p.m.
Have read joyous news. And am less joyous. Advert says:

> **WANTED**
>
> Non-smoking, non-drinking, drug-free professional tenant to join our clean and comfortable household. Must uphold high levels of tidiness and hygiene and be dog-friendly. £70 a week, bills included. References, CRB check, and credit rating required.

She will not get any replies. Plus it is unfair as Mum is not at all friendly to the dog herself—I have heard her shout at it three times today for something to do with the washing machine temperature knob.

4.05 p.m.
Miep, i.e. James, says, *au contraire*, there have been two calls already and I am under strict instructions that this Anne Frank nonsense is to end by tea tomorrow as Mum does not want any potential tenants thinking she has a mentally deficient child on the premises as they could demand a rent reduction. Apparently James and Mum are showing them round on Sunday, when they will undergo a thirty-minute interview and written test. Is utter farce. No one will pass test as it is bound to include trick questions about Jif, and James's notorious general knowledge round. I am unmoved. Anyone moving to 24 Summerdale Road will have to take me as I am—i.e. fact-based, politically committed and utterly grown-up.

4.10 p.m.
And also demented looking. It is the lack of sunlight. I tried sticking my head out of the bathroom window to soak up essential rays but Beastly Investigations, i.e. Miep and Mad Harry, were busy in the side return and issued a red card and three-match ban. They are morons.

. . . .

Friday 31
Hallowe'en
10 a.m.
Breakfast has been reduced to oatcakes and margarine. Miep says enemy forces have commandeered the ghetto

food supplies. They have not. It is Mum employing CIA tactics to get me to give myself up to the occupying forces. But I am strong. My Jewish resolve will not falter.

2 p.m.
The toilet roll is missing. Have had to use several pages of Dr Le Fanu instead (concussion, conjunctivitis, and constipation, *quelle* irony). I do not mind. I am hardened to adverse conditions like this.

5 p.m.
Sad Ed has been round. Miep let him up on grounds he was Jewish sympathizer (he likes Matzo balls) and had essential news from free world. It is that Scarlet is having Hallowe'en party tonight. Said was not interested in non-Kosher goth-based celebrations as am hardened fact-based individual, but to hand over any contraband confectionery concealed about person immediately. Sad Ed said he would, but Mum had conducted a full body search on entry and confiscated two Picnics, a packet of Minstrels, and four Freddos. Have sent him away.

7 p.m.
Although do slightly wish was at Scarlet's party. Not only would be gleaning essential facts such as how many glasses of rum and blackcurrant can one drink without doing purple sick on Habitat rug, but there would be endless Waitrose mini snacks. Have begged Miep for

498

sustenance but he says he can no longer risk his life for mine. Said he was not risking life, just a shouting and potential limiting of biscuit privileges, but Miep says that is more than my life is worth. It is utterly like Anne. But will not give up. Am here to the bitter end, and the pounding of Nazi boots on the stairs. Or at least the shuffle slap of Mum's Marks & Spencer's slipper mules.

november

Saturday 1
9 a.m.
Oh. Am on sofa. And head hurts. And have no idea how
got here. Maybe Nazis arrived in annexe after all and
knocked me out with Dyson handle. Though do not
remember shuffle slap sound. Will ask Miep.

9.15 a.m.
Miep says *a*) he is not called Miep he is called James, or
Jimmy Boy (it is idiotic 'street' mathlete nickname) and
b) there were no Nazi boots, or shuffling slippers, but that
I attempted a foray to steal the Nazis' supply of Shreddies
and dog got excited and jumped on me and in weakened
state I fell backwards and knocked self out on cereal cupboard door handle. Asked if had been rushed to hospital.
James said no. Mum made Dad put me on the sofa while
they watched *ER*. I said what is point of consuming
endless medical-based drama when they do not take hint
from plotlines and call swarthy paramedics to give me
mouth to mouth. James said they tried to check symptoms but the concussion page of Dr Le Fanu was mysteriously missing.

So ghetto dream is over. Like tragic Anne Frank, my
number was up from the very start. But on plus side,
James and Mad Harry have given me two Chupa Chups
and a Boost bar from trick or treating. They went as
Wolverine and the Bionic Woman. Plus my driving lesson
is cancelled on grounds that I am bad enough at operating

heavy machinery at best of times let alone after sustaining head injury. Hurrah. Will luxuriate on sofa all day and appreciate the freedoms of post-war society, which hitherto have taken for granted.

10.30 a.m.
Mum has confiscated Chupa Chups, banned me from sofa, and issued instructions that I am to have shower, shampoo, and vigorous nit comb as according to Marjory, two O'Gradys were scratching vigorously outside Mr Patel's earlier. *Plus ça change.*

* *

Sunday 2

11 a.m.
It is D-Day for Mum's recession-busting, crisis-averting, spare room-clogging lodger plan. James has typed and printed their checklist of infallible questions, designed to root out perverts, evangelical Christians, and murderers, and Mum has set up an interview/torture area, complete with blinding anglepoise lamp and unnerving, or at least annoying, presence of dog to sniff out drugs, and chav-based snacks. Pointed out that they are trying to find kind, helpful, and hygienic tenant, not interrogate Al Qaeda suspect but Mum says you can never be too careful. Dad is not at all happy about the idea. He is worried his place as head of the household may be usurped by young dynamic intellectual who shares Mum's obsessions

504

with Jeremy Paxman, mung beans, and Cillit Bang.
James has pointed out that *a*) he is not, and has never
been, head of household, and *b*) it will mean the Cleggs
can never again infest the spare room with their Spar
bags, racist tendencies, and odour of Fray Bentos. Dad is
marginally happier now. And has agreed to assume air of
authoritative, yet benign presence, by reading boffiny
Sunday Times (main section, not sport), and listening to
Classic FM (not Radio 5).

Asked what my role was in grand plan. James says I
am to go to Sad Ed's and stay there until at least 5 o'clock
lest I put either interviewee off with my bad hair,
appalling taste in music, or habit of engaging guests in
crap philosophical discussions. He is wrong on all counts.
But have agreed none the less. Do not want to witness
mentalism that is Mum and James's bad cop idiot cop
routine. Plus need to find out if Sad Ed snogged Scarlet at
the Hallowe'en party. It is possible, given the strength of
Suzy's uber-alcoholic punch.

5 p.m.
Sad Ed did not snog Scarlet. Apparently percentage proof
of punch did not compensate for *a*) non-vampiric nature
of bulgy tummy and bingo wings and *b*) presence of former head goth and current shuttlecock checker Trevor
Pledger—twenty-eight inch waistband, upper arm fat
quotient minimal. Demanded to know if Scarlet had
locked fangs with bat boy, but Sad Ed said only plus point

was that while punch not strong enough to force Scarlet to fling self into his (flabby) arms, was strong enough to make her throw up on Tuscan tiled floor and pass out in hovery love swing. Said am surprised Bob and Suzy allowed such debauchery, given their newfound responsibility as soon-to-be adoptive parents. Sad Ed said they are getting the revelry in while they can. It is a shame I missed it. Although it wouldn't have been the same without Jack. I wonder if they have Hallowe'en in Chichicastenango. Probably not. Although goats are quite devilish.

Got home to unsurprising news that 24 Summerdale Road is still tenantless. Mr Garamond disqualified on grounds of wonky eyes and shifty legs and Mr Tennick on grounds of actually being Mr Whippy! Is utter relief. Thought of Fat Kylie testing his 99 in spare room potentially horrifying.

They will never find a lodger at this rate. Even Paxo would fail to make the grade. As would Dad. He is in trouble for losing the sink plunger. Plus he is still battling weight issues and Mum has never quite grown to love the mole on his right ankle. Thank God is school tomorrow so can escape fat and money-based tension that pervades every Cif-scented corner.

5.30 p.m.
Oooh. And see Mr Pringle. Will tell him of my excellent half-term annexization experiment. Then he will not

506

only immediately cast me as Anne, but also want to move into fact-based 24 Summerdale Road! He will totally pass test as his eyes are straight, his stomach is flat, and he has no discernible blemishes. Am genius!

. . . .

Monday 3
3 p.m.
Am not genius. Mr Pringle said annexe experiment good, but he is operating a cunning Auschwitz-style casting system whereby we pull number out of hat to seal our fate. Said that was open to all sorts of horror, e.g. Nigel Moore (impetigo, not potato blight) as Mrs Frank or Sad Ed as the cat. Mr Pringle said the point is not to create beautiful art, it is to get the cold hard facts across. He will struggle if Reuben Tull gets a lead role. He thinks learning lines is too much pandering to 'The Man'. Whoever he is. But on plus side, he says he is totally interested in position as lodger as Chestnuts is not only overpriced, but Ying's breakfast is sliced Nimble and Nutella. Said it was health-giving granary all the way at 24 Summerdale. Have given him phone number and hints to pass James's hygiene and spillage test, e.g. count to fifteen elephants while soaping hands and red wine does NOT come out with salt, that is only adding insult to injury. Hurrah. May well be under same roof as Mr Pringle within days. Our age gap chemistry will pervade the air like a brace of Glade plug-ins.

Also school is mental with Barack Obama madness.

Scarlet says it is less than two days until America has its first ever black President. Said she shouldn't count her chickens as that other man (old, bit wrinkly, no idea of name) looks quite kindly, like benign grandpa, plus Sarah Palin has excellent glasses and a pregnant daughter, which is complete liberal vote-winner. Scarlet told Sad Ed to remove me from her vicinity before she did something she may well regret later. Said *a*) since when is Sad Ed acting as bodyguard and *b*) she never regretted any act of violence, not even when Tracey Hughes had to go to hospital in Year Seven with a pair of compasses stuck in her left thigh. Sad Ed shrugged and carried me to saggy sofa using one arm. He is quite manly really. Although he did have to stop for emergency deep breathing halfway down the Gaza Strip.

The mathletes table is also over-run with black president anticipation. I heard Ali Hassan call James 'bro' twice during Mrs Brain's fruit-based pudding (Spotted Dick). They have taken forty-eight bets on Barack winning, twenty-three bets on no one winning, and one bet on Sarah Palin actually being Ross Perot in a wig.

· ·

Tuesday 4

9 a.m.

Scarlet is still not speaking to me on account of my potential racist tendencies and general air of political idiocy. Have pointed out that am not racist, am realist, and am

not political idiot, just that I do not have advantage of parents who spent 1980s stuffing envelopes in militant wing of Bethnal Green and Bow Labour party, as well she knows. Scarlet said well I had better shape up fast if I want to attend her all-night CNN election vigil in the den. Have bought an Obama badge for £1 off the mathletes' fly trader market stall (behind the bins aka Rat Corner). They are making them out of a copy of the *Observer* colour supplement and James's laminating machine.

4 p.m.

Scarlet has relented and agreed I can come to CNN vigil, if only because it will educate me in the workings of the American Electoral College. I wish we had an electoral college here, I would go and stun Scarlet with my prowess at naming marginal seats and swings to gain. Mum is not at all happy as it is a school night but have pointed out that is utterly part of history, e.g. where was she when Kennedy was shot, or when Tony Blair swept to power in landslide? Mum said *a*) inside Granny Clegg (ick) and *b*) in the bathroom cleaning up James's sick after he swallowed the Monopoly iron (ick ick, especially as know for fact we are still using said iron).

8 p.m.

Chez Stone is infused with Obama/potential adoptive baby madness. The kitchen is crawling with Saffron Walden Labour Party members (all seven of them)

blogging via their BlackBerries and furiously checking Twitter. Suzy says she is utterly calling her new arrival Barack, even if it is white (which it will be) and a girl (quite possibly). Scarlet says this is without doubt the most seminal night of her life, beating even the time she saw Germaine Greer in Tesco and the time Trevor touched her right breast (under T-shirt but over bra). She is right, is utterly seminal. Although to be fair not much is happening at moment, and *Friends* is on E4 and would quite like to switch over.

8.05 p.m.
Scarlet says there is no way we are switching over and this just further illustrates why I am no more than a pretender, i.e. am Duffy to her Dusty Springfield.

8.10 p.m.
We are watching *Friends*. Is one where Joey wears all of Chandler's clothes. Genius.

11 p.m.
There is still nothing actually happening in America. Although Kay Burley is barking mentally with excitement at pictures of people at polling stations and milling aimlessly round a park in big hats. She will be hospitalized by the time somewhere actually declares. Thank God we don't have Sky. The dog could not cope with her hair or starey eyes.

12 midnight

Politics is time consuming and essentially dull. Wish the history part would hurry up. May just rest eyes a little bit. Will be fine for five minutes. They are still showing pictures of Arnold Schwarzenegger grinning manically at a polling station.

- -

Wednesday 5

Guy Fawkes Night

8 a.m.

Oh. It is all over. Apparently Obama did win. Asked Scarlet what historic thing I was doing when this was declared. She said I was drooling slightly, but was not as bad as Sad Ed who was snoring and had hand inside pants. Will not mention that in future years. Will say I was opening bottle of vintage Krug in celebration. Or possibly carton of Ribena. At least am going to school in same slightly sweaty clothes as yesterday, which is badge of utter honour as indicates political commitment.

8.05 a.m.

Or night of debauchery with Mr Whippy's Rocket in Fat Kylie's case.

12 noon

Oooh. Mr Pringle is also in same clothes as yesterday! So

he is utterly politically committed. Asked if he had stayed up at Chestnuts to watch but he said he went to his friend Henry's up in London, as Ying was watching *Bid-Up* to get a Diamonique necklace set for £3.99. Apparently Henry works for BBC. Did not mention myriads of TV rules in our house. Or antipathy towards anyone who works in media. Cannot wait until drama though. It is well known fact that post-election atmosphere is hotbed for extra curricular snogging.

12.05 p.m.
Not that am hoping he snogs me, as is illegal.

12.10 p.m.
Or that am keeping mental note of Mr Pringle's wardrobe.

12.15 p.m.
Except that he does look good in chest hair revealing V-neck T-shirt.

4 p.m.
Drama was not hotbed of victory snogging. But was excellent none the less, i.e. I AM ANNE FRANK! Hurrah. Reuben Tull is moany Mrs Frank, Sad Ed is dodgy dentist Mr Dussel and Caris Kelp is Peter. Which adds interesting lesbian frisson to annexe.

On downside Mr Pringle not amenable to idea of incorporating Barack Obama as voice of Jesus on grounds

that *a*) play is JEWISH and *b*) there is no one in the group who is remotely black and the favoured John Major High method of portraying anyone of colour (i.e. boot polish) is not acceptable. Mr Pringle also not amenable to rewriting of ending to include uplifting escape scenario. He said that is the sort of schmaltz that has ruined the New Hollywood. He is utterly right of course. Although I do excellent terrified fleeing face (as practised in magnifying bathroom mirror).

Sad Ed is also mental with Anne Frank-based joy. It is not at not being minty Mrs Frank. It is because he and Reuben are writing the songs. He says it is the break he needs and could potentially lead to a concept album and slot on the Peel stage at Glastonbury. He is wrong. It will lead to embarassment and flying Criminal and Retard-related Skittles if his rendition of 'Eleanor Rigby' in the Year Seven All-Faith-Embracing Beatles medley concert is anything to go by.

. . . .

Thursday 6

There has been a bitter blow to my fact-based grown-up older man stance. It is that film club has been suspended. It is because hairy librarian Mr Knox lent the DVD player to the Camilla Parker Bowles Memorial Crèche so they could watch *Underground Ernie*, and someone (probably Jesus but also possibly Mark Lambert) inserted two party rings and a chocolate finger into the

slot. I offered to host the club in our living room but Mr Pringle says we can better use the time to work on the musical. He is right. Plus there is no way Mum would let us watch *Sid and Nancy*. Or let Reuben Tull over the threshold. He looks like a mentalist and smells like a badger.

4 p.m.

Not that have smelt a badger. But they look a bit ripe.

4.05 p.m.

James says that according to Beastly Investigations research, badgers are not foul-smelling creatures, but are in fact quite hygienic, like gerbils. Reuben Tull is more of a stoat.

. . . .

Friday 7

Oh my God. Mr Pringle has called to ask if lodger vacancy is still vacant! James has informed him that there is indeed an opening for a tenant at 24 Summerdale Road, and has invited him for interrogation on Sunday! Hurrah. So it is swings and roundabouts as far as fact-based film sessions are concerned as will be on John Lewis sofa discussing jump cuts, fade outs, and the seminal influence of the *Blair Witch Project* wonky camera technique within days.

. . . .

Saturday 8

11 a.m.

Ugh. Have driving lesson. Was hoping that Mr Wandering Hands would get domestically abused again by Mrs Wandering Hands, preferably fatally compromising his accelerator foot or gear-knob hand. But he is foot and knob-intact and due to guide me round the hell that is the Hockley one-way system any minute. Mum is also slightly disappointed. I think she was hoping he might be in need of temporary accommodation. He is her dream tenant: clean nails, bouffy hair, embracer of laws of all kinds. Dad would have gone mental though. He is still fully convinced that Mr Wandering Hands wants to embrace more than Mum's rules. Shudder.

2 p.m.

Why, oh why can I not learn to drive around nice quiet village, e.g. Catmere End (three houses and a bus shelter). Negotiating Bishop's Stortford on a Saturday is utterly worse than Oxford Circus, i.e. clogged with traffic impediments, 4X4s, and nine year olds high on Haribo. Pointed out to Mr Wandering Hands that I should not be penalized points-wise in my test for knocking over one if not several of these dangers to driving. He did not reply as was too busy using his emergency instructor brake to avoid a Jeep Cherokee. Maybe should give up lessons and use money instead for more enlightening activity, e.g. going to Duke tonight for political discussion and/or close

harmony rendition of 'The Gambler' with Kev's dog on percussion. Will suggest it. Is just redeployment of funds. Not actual extra money.

2.15 p.m.
Mum says there is no way I am redeploying £20 a week from the fluff-free pockets of Mr Wandering Hands to the filth-filled coffers of Shorty McNulty. I pointed out she could consider an increase in pocket money (still languishing around the £3 mark) given that she will be flush tomorrow with a rent cheque and hefty breakages/soiled goods deposit (contract includes forfeits for damages to soft furnishings, hard furnishings, and mung bean cultivator). But Mum said there is no guarantee Mr Pringle will pass muster, and even if he does, the money is earmarked for a mini Dustbuster and a new rotary washing line. (Old one broken due to repeated hanging off and whizzing round by Mad Harry and James. And me. And Dad.)

6 p.m.
Yet another evening of *Casualty* beckons. Poverty is utterly hampering my horizon-widening, philosophical pub ambitions. May well write to Gordon Brown to complain about mad-eyebrowed Chancellor Alistair Darling. His poor money management could compromise an entire generation, condemning us to hospital soaps and *A Touch of Frost* when we could be more usefully

516

keeping economy afloat by purchasing beverages and snacks.

8.15 p.m.
Oooh. Have found £2.30 down the back of the sofa. James claims it is his and that he got it off Mad Harry for successfully predicting that he couldn't eat more than two cream crackers in two minutes. (Is weird phenomenon. Have tried. Is utterly impossible.) Dad says *au contraire* it is his, because the right hand cushion is his *Lovejoy* viewing area and he has notoriously leaky pockets. Luckily Mum is round Marjory's looking at seed catalogues so am going down Duke to splurge it all on Cheese Moments and lime and soda before she can lay claim to it, under Rule 91 of household management law.

12 midnight
Hurrah. Have had excellent night in pub, despite still being relegated to the swirly carpet until we can prove our increase in Britvic and peanut consumption is long-term rather than a rogue blip. Scarlet is in agreement that Mr Pringle moving into house will be excellent, education-wise. She says my parents are restricting me with their *Telegraph* editorial outlook, and Mr Pringle will inject refreshing new views. Sad Ed asked if he could move into Scarlet's as he is utterly compromised by having to reside with two members of the Aled Jones fan

club and she can inject him with whatever she likes. She said no.

. . . .

Sunday 9
Remembrance Sunday
1 p.m.
It is less than an hour until Mr Pringle's interrogation commences. James is armed with his clipboard and Mum is armed with fleaspray (this is not for Mr Pringle, it is for the dog, who is scratching uncontrollably). Have begged them to look favourably on his position as pillar of community (i.e. teacher) and impeccable academic record but James says drama is not pillar-style subject and Stoke got no stars in *Times* guide last year so unless he has an MA from either Harvard or Yale, then he will have to ace his hygiene test to get through.

1.59 p.m.
Oh my God. Doorbell has gone. He is here, and is punctual, which is five points before he has even got over threshold. Hurrah!

3 p.m.
Oh my God. Mr Pringle is moving in. He got an unprecedented seventy-nine points out of a hundred, which is, according to the *Which* rules of consumer testing, a guarantee of customer satisfaction, and worthy of a coveted

Best Buy award. Hurrah! He is giving Ying and Les notice tonight and will be bringing his allotted two bags and a bicycle (with lights) round next Sunday.

Thin Kylie was sitting on the wall with Fiddy when I went to take dog out for a poo. (Mum claims he has been holding it in in bid to gain access to Bran Flakes, which I said shows remarkable intelligence, but Mum says shows new levels of idiocy. But it is not withholding, it is probably just stuck behind a sock or a stapler.) She demanded to know what business Mr Pringle had been conducting at 24 Summerdale Road. Actually what she said was, 'Oh my God. Are you, like, knobbing Pringle? He is a minger. Lambo saw his thing in the staff toilet and it is, like, totally ginger down there. And he wears Hi-Tecs. Knob.' I said *a*) No, he is our new tenant, *b*) what was Mark Lambert doing in staff toilet, and *c*) what is wrong with Hi-Tecs (which were, as far as I knew, de rigeur in world of chav). She said, *a*) 'Oh my God, he is totally, like, going to get in your knickers, Riley. Minging,' *b*) 'He had drunk, like, five cans of Fanta and it was leaking out. But he won £3.40 off Fat Kylie so he don't care about the stain,' and *c*) 'Oh. My. God. I, like, can't believe you just said that.' And at that point she flounced off dragging Fiddy out from under dog, who is still determined to mate her despite several feet in height difference and no testicles. It is hard to believe she is head girl. She is so not a role model for enlightened leadership. Last week she banned hummus sandwiches from common room on the grounds

it 'like stinks, innit'. Anyway, she is wrong. Mr Pringle does not want to get into my knickers.

5 p.m.
Does he? Oh. My. God. Maybe he does fancy me after all. It is totally possible. I am bohemianish, fact-based, and my hair is marginally less mental at the moment due to unseasonally clement weather conditions. Oooh, the Shreddies table will be boiling with sexual chemistry.

5.15 p.m.
Except that Mum is bound to add a million caveats to her already fourteen page banned list to include any lusting over the Marmite jar. It is so unfair.

5.30 p.m.
And also wrong. Have remembered that he is teacher and is out of bounds, no matter how potent our love for each other.

5.45 p.m.
Also am not sure he has potent love for me.

5.50 p.m.
And utterly do not have potent love for him. Love is fictional happy ending construct, and not in any sense fact based. Yes. Will think on him as benign uncleish presence.

6 p.m.
Or at least will try.

. . . .

Monday 10

12 noon
Think may have been wrong about Mr Pringle. Have just seen him in B Corridor (having discussion with Miss Beadle about who has to monitor the lower school playground on a Friday, i.e. notorious demob-happy day). Said hello and his gaze definitely lingered on my legs! Oh my God. It is totally potent love!

12.10 p.m.
Was not potent love. Was Dairylea cheese triangle that had somehow adhered itself to back of thigh. Possibly during emergency visit to Camilla Parker Bowles Memorial Crèche to separate Jesus and someone called Samson Judd who were locked in a no-win situation over a sticklebrick.

. . . .

Tuesday 11

Another milestone looms along our arduous passage to utter grown-upness, i.e. tomorrow is Scarlet Marjory Mowlam Stone's eighteenth birthday. James says from now on it is all utterly downhill and she needs to start doing stomach crunches and using Oil of Olay to combat

521

the seven signs of ageing, e.g. fine lines, dark patches, and wearing criminal sandals. Have no money to purchase present, as spent it all in Duke on Saturday. So have written her meaningful fact-based poem instead.

The Lady in Scarlet (i.e. utter genius play on Granny Clegg's favourite crap ballad 'The Lady in Red' by monobrowed midget Chris De Burgh.)

> *You cloak yourself in black.*
> *The uniform of the Goth.*
> *Of the semi-EMO.*
> *Of every angst-ridden teen.*
> *But it shines through.*
> *Your true colour.*
> *You are Scarlet!*
> *Red like fire.*
> *Like menstrual blood.*
> *Like the corpses of slaughtered lambs.*
> *Scarlet.*
> *Bright and shining.*
> *Like the top off full fat milk.*
> *Like an old phone box before they replaced them with*
>   *plexiglass and aluminium.*
> *Scarlet. Scarlet. Scarlet.*

Scarlet will be moved to point of tears. It is utterly better than bottle of gin, which is what Sad Ed is getting her.

Wednesday 12

Scarlet says *au contraire* she would have quite liked another bottle of gin in order to drown her monumental sorrows. It is not fear of wrinkles. It is devastating news that Bob and Suzy have utterly forgotten her birthday! She says they are consumed with thoughts of their potential adoptive child and this is just a precursor of life to come where she will be forgotten, the abandoned middle child. And will possibly turn to crime or drugs or marginal political causes. Apparently even Edna, the non-Filipina Labour-friendly Rothman's-smoking cleaner remembered (she got her a box of Toffifee). Scarlet says she is thinking of adopting her as a new mother. Said that is the trouble with progressive parents. All the tantric sex and drugs have messed with their priorities. Whereas mine might wear vests and have not had sex since 1996 (James) but our birthdays are noted and highlighted in a WH Smith diary and checked on a weekly basis. Thin Kylie said *au contraire* (actually she didn't, as is too French, she said 'Yeah, well, whatever'), we are all wrong and pointed out that in fact it is brilliant as now Scarlet can totally blackmail them. Apparently Cherie forgot her birthday one year and she got £150 and a PS2 in compensation. Maybe she is more political than I thought after all.

Also Scarlet says it is semi-skimmed milk that has red top, and as a vegetarian she takes offence at the corpses line. Luckily had to go to drama rehearsal before she could deconstruct poem any further. Now I know how

poet laureate Andrew Motion must feel, having the words he has poured his soul into being pulled to pieces by cack-handed A-level students.

Rehearsals went well though. Mr Pringle said my Anne showed acute understanding of the torment of metaphorical entrapment, i.e. in the body of a teenager, with the mind of a young woman. It is so utterly true. I am mature beyond my years mentally, yet my breasts have only just grown to 34B.

. . . .

Thursday 13

Thin Kylie is not political genius. Her solution to today's common room row over whether Mark Lambert had spilt Pepsi Max on Ali Hassan's iPod and was it deliberate, and possibly even justified, was to make them battle it out on sheep field with shaken up bottles of a carbonated beverage of their choice. She was right about the blackmail though. Apparently Suzy remembered last night, when Jack's email arrived from Chichicastenango (they have finally got reliable electricity and a twenty-year-old Dell). She was racked with remorse and has given her £100, two bottles of vodka, and a giant Toblerone. Scarlet is utterly jubilant. Said she should not allow them to buy her affections, and what about her new mother Edna? Scarlet said she has changed her mind about Edna. She may have left-wing credentials (husband was a miner), but she buys non-organic vegetables and has a fur hat.

524

Plus she thinks Penelope Keith is the greatest living actress. Asked if Jack's email mentioned me. It did not.

. . . .

Friday 14

Went round Sad Ed's after school. He is utterly depressed about the Scarlet/mojo situation. He says his attempts at a *Twilight* look have not curried favour, and, to top it all, he is not even an older man any more. Said that skinny jeans was possibly a step too far in the vampiric fashion stakes for someone of his unique build, but that he will always be an older man, even if it is only by a crucial few weeks. He is marginally revived and is pinning his hopes on tomorrow night's celebration in the Duke. Scarlet has vowed to spend at least £75 of her birthday money on beverages and snacks. She says it is an utterly economic strategy to fiscally stimulate a valuable local business. It is also utterly economic strategy to win us back custody of the wobbly table. There is no way Reuben Tull can top that on a trolley-herder's wages.

. . . .

Saturday 15

5 p.m.
Is shaping up to be excellent two days.

1. This morning Mr Wandering Hands said my three-point turn was down to five points, which is vast improvement on 13-point turn previously.

525

2. Tonight is Scarlet's utterly grown-up eighteenth party when she will finally realize that Sad Ed is her utter destiny, despite his non-batlike build and penchant for buffalo wings (i.e. chicken wings, not actual wings of buffalo, which was confusing for quite a few years).

3. Tomorrow Mr Pringle moves into the spare room, with his library of fact-based DVDs, wardrobe of fading nineties tour T-shirts and potential potent love for me.

Hurrah. Is recipe for weekend of utter success on grown-up front. I predict that by this time tomorrow, Scarlet and I will both be in the arms of older men, or at least in close proximity to them on the John Lewis sofa watching *Antiques Roadshow*.

. . . .

Sunday 16

6 p.m.

Am in close proximity to older man. In fact, am almost in (flabby) arms of older man. But is utterly wrong one, i.e. is not fact-based media studies expert Mr Pringle. He is currently in dining room, going through a checklist of do's and don'ts with Mum (heavy on the don'ts) whereas I am in bed, with Sad Ed, glass of water and emergency sick bucket.

It is all Scarlet's fault for fiscally stimulating Shorty

McNulty. If I ever see another Cheese Moment will possibly die of anaphylactic shock. In fact feel sick again just writing words. Yes, definitely sick coming.

6.10 p.m.
Have rinsed out bucket with bleach and anti-bacterial spray concoction, according to Mum's instructions (typed, laminated (to protect against projectile emissions) and inserted under door). Oh. Sick is endless. Sad Ed also sick (five times, beating my three and a half (no sick last time, just weird green stuff)). It is not Cheese Moments though for him. It is beer. He drank eight pints in bid to prove his older man credentials but effect slightly lost when he did the Macarena with Kev Banner and the dog. Had to get Dad to fetch us at half nine in Passat (with Sad Ed hanging head out of window like giant St Bernard, to avoid sick-smelling Volvo repeat). Dad wanted to deposit him at Loompits Way but Sad Ed begged him to carry his addled body upstairs as Mrs Thomas is under impression that Saturday nights are spent drinking Ovaltine and singing campfire songs and he did not want to shatter her illusions. Mum was not at all happy with arrangement but James pointed out that it gives her excellent trump card leverage against future misdemeanours of mine. Credit crunch is turning everyone into Machiavellian wheeler-dealers. Or morons. Mum agreed but only if he slept in my room as did not want Mr Pringle's contaminated with sick, or sweaty Morrisey T-shirts.

527

Jack was right. This is typical Riley mess. Am not at all grown-up. Grown-ups do not eat twenty-four packets of Cheese Moments. And four pickled onions. And past sell-by pork scratchings that have been open for fortnight and are meant for dog. Cannot face Mr Pringle. Will stay in room, alone with shame, for ever.

6.30 p.m.
Except am not alone with shame, am wedged in junior bed with giant bulk of Sad Ed hogging sprig-patterned duvet. Will eject him. He is not at all conducive to penitent thoughts.

6.45 p.m.
Am alone. Will think pure Joan of Arc-style factual thoughts.

8.40 p.m.
There is funny noise under bed. Maybe my shame has taken on human form, like ghost of Christmas past, and is hiding like homunculus under bed to torment me.

8.45 p.m.
Was not homunculus of shame. Was dog eating one of Mum's shuffly slippers. Am giving up on today. Tomorrow will be better. Will be grown-up by then. Or at least vomit-free.

. . . .

Monday 17
7.30 a.m.
Am revived. Have purged myself of childishness, with Cheese Moments sick. Am ready to take my place next to Mr Pringle at Shreddies table as utter grown-up. And if his potent love pervades air like steam off coffee, will rebut it with my penitent facty breakfast of granary toast with no butter.

8 a.m.
Did not take seat next to Mr Pringle (Mum has allotted him official place between her and James, i.e. where he is least likely to get mooned over by me or harangued by Dad over antipathy towards *Top Gear*), and did not notice potent love wafting around table as James too busy testing him on 'house rules', i.e.

- No shoes beyond doormat, but stack carefully, away from jaws of dog;
- No food to be consumed whilst walking around house;
- No biscuits to be consumed except at allocated snack time. Ad infinitum.

But on plus side, at least have not shamed self further.

8.15 a.m.
James has just returned my *Railway Children* DVD in full view of Mr Pringle. Said, 'Um, thank you. It is excellent

chance to observe the full workings of Britain's pre-nationalized rail system.' James said, 'And you always cry in "Daddy, my Daddy" bit.' Thank God am going to school. Common Room is utterly more grown-up atmosphere than 24 Summerdale Road. Plus can get gossip from Scarlet about what happened in Duke after Passat rescue on Saturday.

4 p.m.

Oh my God. Scarlet did snog an older man in the Duke! It is Kev Banner (26, works in BJ Video, owner of alcoholic dog). She said it is utter rite of passage and she feels no shame. She should. He shops in Next. On plus side, we have regained control of wobbly toilet table. Reuben Tull is in the car park due to suspicious herbal smell.

Also Common Room not entirely grown-up due to incident involving Thin Kylie, Mark Lambert, and jar of peanut butter. Part of West Bank (aka microwave corner) has been cordoned off and will remain a no-go zone for several days.

. . . .

Tuesday 18

Mum has drawn up strict bathroom timetable. Said she need not worry about me walking in on Mr Pringle having shower as I am utter woman of world and have seen it all before. Mum said *a*) what exactly have I seen before and *b*) it is not me she is protecting it is Mr Pringle who

walked in on James having poo this morning, which is distressing enough but he was also trying to clean dog's teeth at same time. Said was talking metaphorically. Which is true. As Jack kept pants on, and was too drunk to remember what Justin's looked like. Which limits penis-memory to Grandpa's, James's, and Sad Ed's. Which is not at all worldly. Or pleasant.

Sad Ed is in agreement about his penis, i.e. that it is not at all worldly. Although he says it is due to underuse, rather than size or shape. He says he is thinking of joining me in my pursuit and redirecting his affections for Scarlet to an older woman as it is very rock-starrish to have Mrs Robinson-style experience. Plus then Scarlet will get all minty and jealous and beg him to bestow his penis on her.

Think he is overegging it somewhat as do not think Scarlet will be begging for his penis anywhere near her, whether it has been near an older woman or not, but agreed it is good idea to experiment, as cannot cope much longer with his mojo-related depression. Asked if he has set his sights on a lucky lady yet. He said no, but he is going to check out the market over the next few days.

. . . .

Wednesday 19
5 p.m.
Grandpa Riley has rung in panic. It is Jesus. Apparently he is lying on faux leather sofa in silent shock. Asked if it

was this morning's incident in Camilla Parker Bowles Memorial Crèche (he headbutted Samson for putting Whitney's Bratz doll in the soiled nappy receptacle). Grandpa said no, and what is wrong with that, it shows chivalry. It is news that hobbit-like political pundit John Sergeant has quit *Strictly Come Dancing*. Jesus has been glued to screen for weeks and is very much taken with him, particularly in his tight tango outfit. I do not know why, he looks and dances like Granny Clegg, but there is no accounting for taste. Grandpa says he does not know how to comfort Jesus, who has spurned all his usual tricks, including Wagon Wheels, Wotsits, and the Patrick Swayze DVD. Said there is nothing to do but wait. Jesus is grieving a significant loss, and time will heal his wounds, i.e. utterly grown-up answer, as Mr Pringle in room at time trying to rescue shoe from dog. Think it impressed him, especially when I threw in brilliant fact that John Sergeant was also actually a sergeant in Welsh Guard.

5.15 p.m.
John Sergeant not sergeant. James Googled it. Curse Scarlet and her propensity for evil. And my gullibility.

. . . .

Thursday 20
Went to see Jesus in Camilla Parker Bowles Memorial Crèche at lunchtime. He is still in mourning, i.e. is lying

on cushion in Wendy House while Whitney strokes him with a filthy Iggle Piggle. Fat Kylie said he even refused his snack-time Cheese String so things are really bad. Grandpa is writing to BBC to complain about the debacle. He is demanding reinstatement of John Sergeant, who he says is a role model for pensioners and the facially-afflicted everywhere, and a replacement of Arlene Phillips with Amanda Holden, who cries at anything. He will be waiting a long time.

. . . .

Friday 21
Mr Pringle said an old man rang and went on about pigs for five minutes then hung up. Said did he sound a bit retarded and have a tendency to say 'arrr' a lot. He said yes. Said it was a wrong number. It was not. It was Grandpa Clegg. Cannot let Mr Pringle know I am related to inbred racist, homophobic, and Hammerited man. He will never bestow love, potent or otherwise, on me.

6 p.m.
Not that I want his potent love, as am utterly Paxman-like—i.e. only interested in facts.

. . . .

Saturday 22
It is typical. Have utterly turned corner (real and metaphorical) in my grown-up pursuit of wheel-based

freedom (i.e. am finally allowed to negotiate Hockerill lights and notorious Sparrow's Hill), and driving lesson is cancelled so that Mr Wandering Hands can take Mrs Wandering Hands on a relationship-rekindling trip to Madeira. Mum is not at all happy. She says it is not the relationship-kindling. It is the lack of commitment to his pupils. She says she is minded to become driving instructor herself and offer her services as substitute teacher. Have begged her not to. It is bad enough she wears waterproof trousers in public without barking at half the teenage population of Saffron Walden about their emergency stops. Was hoping to spend time discussing Anne Frank's sexual awakening with Mr Pringle but he has gone to visit his friend Henry for the weekend. (They are going on an 'end the occupation' march. Not sure what occupation they mean. Could be Iraq. Or Afghanistan. Or possibly Isle of Wight, which I know for fact he thinks should be independent principality.) So am going to Waitrose car park instead to see if Sad Ed has found a potential Mrs Robinson for his unworldly penis.

5 p.m.
Sad Ed has narrowed the field down to three possible penis contenders, i.e. Suzy, Miss Mustard (lab assistant, not Cluedo piece) and Janine off Waitrose meat counter. Said that while Suzy was clearly the front runner, given her pro-sex stance and heaving bosom, she is also *a*) Scarlet's mum and *b*) Scarlet's mum and therefore utterly

out of bounds. Have also ruled out Miss Mustard on grounds of greasiness of hair and fact that she is engaged to Mr Waiting (economics, bad ties, distracting mole). Reuben Tull suggested Mrs Stimpson, who is wee-smelling white-flare-wearing lady tramp. But Sad Ed said he didn't want to tread on Barry the Blade's toes. Literally or otherwise. Or go near the source of the wee smell. So it is down to Janine off meat. Made surreptitious browse of ham and gala pie on way home in order to 'check out the goods'. She is at least 30, has a tattoo of Daffy Duck on her bicep and wields a meat cleaver with conviction. Sad Ed will be putty in her swarthy hands.

. . . .

Sunday 23

2 p.m.
Am utterly bored. Scarlet is giving Sad Ed assertiveness training, and James is round at Mad Harry's having a Beastly Investigations crisis summit. If only Paddy (i.e. Mr Pringle) was here. Have started calling him Paddy in head, now that our relationship has moved to a new more informal level. May actually try calling him it out loud at some point. Is utterly modern. And is less weird to think about snogging someone called Paddy than someone called Mr Pringle.

2.10 p.m.
Not that am thinking about snogging him.

2.15 p.m.

Although I bet he is excellent at snogging. Radical political types always are, according to Scarlet. Which would partially explain John Prescott. But not entirely.

3 p.m.

Mum not in agreement about 'modernizing' my relationship with lodger. Asked her when Paddy was getting back from Henry's. She said it is Mr Pringle to you and if I hear you call him that again you will be delimescaling the draining board for a week. She is just minty because Dad managed to beat her on golf driving range. Dad says it is his superior man strength, and eagle-eyes. Mum says it is not that, it is that she has tennis elbow from excess Cillit Banging. Am going round to Grandpa's to escape fraught atmosphere. And to comfort Jesus in his hour of need. Maybe he is political prodigy, i.e. he can sense John Sergeant's superior intellect.

6 p.m.

Jesus is not political prodigy. He is over his John Sergeant-based grief and has instead latched on to a new and improved celebrity. Was hoping it might be continuing with the current affairs theme, i.e. Trevor McDonald, but it is someone called Mister Maker who has unfeasibly large forehead and does stuff with PVA glue and buttons. Paddy still not back from Henry's, which has only added to tension as Mum had made meat loaf for

tea and his portion will be wasted. She has offered it to Dad, who has declined. As has dog. Do not blame them. There is nothing normal about meat masquerading as bread.

. . . .

Monday 24

8 a.m.
Mum is going mental with potential murder excitement. It is Paddy, who is completely absent from Shreddies table, and has not been in bed for at least seventy-two hours, according to James, who was sent to do forensic check. Mum is blaming Henry, who she thinks is crack-addicted anarchist. She thinks everyone who lives in London or works in telly is on drugs or about to blow something up. So Henry is utter evil overlord in her eyes. She is thinking of calling police. Or Marjory, who watches *Waking the Dead* and several *CSIs*, so is expert in all murderous matters.

9 a.m.
Paddy is not dead. He is in staff room with black coffee and funny red mark on neck. Sad Ed says it is lovebite. But he is wrong. It is probably a truncheon wound from a radical march. Anyway, have rung Mum before her and Marjory start serial killer scare. She sounded disappointed. It is Paddy I feel sorry for. She is bound to wreak revenge.

537

5 p.m.

Was right about Mum. She has removed Paddy's TV remote privileges for a week. She says she will not be treated like a hotel. Paddy pointed out that she was in fact a hotel of sorts. But then Mum made her lips go super thin and he said he had some marking to do and disappeared into dining room.

. . . .

Tuesday 25

8 a.m.

Hurrah! Shreddies table is hotbed of political debate. Is like *Newsnight* live version with Mum as self-important Paxo and Paddy as ubiquitous Shami Chakrabarti. It is at news that first ID cards for foreigners were introduced today. Heated discussion ensued, i.e. 'It will end in insidious function creep' (Paddy) versus, 'It is small price to pay to stop Osama Bin Laden being able to wander around Waitrose willy-nilly and inject chemical weapons into tins of cling peaches' (versus 'Oh for heaven's sake, I'm going round to Clive's to listen to Terry Wogan' (Dad)). Scarlet was right. Having lodger is excellent for political enlightenment of Riley household. Although Paddy did not win argument. Mum will not be moved in her quest for more curtailment on personal freedom. She thinks everyone should have ID cards, and is fully in favour of function creep and invasion of privacy. It is why she likes this house so much with its panopticon-like

538

central hallway, i.e. she can stand in single vantage point and monitor all occupants with one sweep of her all-seeing eye. She says it is why Clive and Marjory's is not selling as it has a dogleg corridor that can hide a multitude of murderers or miscreants. It is not. It is the overpricedness. And the gnomes.

6 p.m.
The ID card row is still rumbling on. Mum only gave Paddy two fishfingers for tea and he got the potato with the brown bit on. Said it was excellent and house had not been this intellectual since Grandpa Clegg and Dad had the week-long argument about Tony Blair (to be fair, was not about policy, was about teeth, but was feisty all the same). James said that's as may be, but the smart money (i.e. him, Damon Parker, and five Year Nines) is on Paddy moving out before Christmas. He is betting obsessed. It is the mathletes and their illegal gambling ring. Anyway he is wrong. There is no way Paddy will move out before Christmas. He has to give a month's notice and it is the 25th of November already.

. . . .

Wednesday 26
5 p.m.
Oh my God. Sad Ed has got a date with Janine off meat! He says two days lurking by the brisket after school has utterly paid off. Asked if he was going to take her out for

romantic dinner and walk by river (or shopping-trolley clogged Slade). He said no, duh, he is bringing her to Duke, so that Scarlet can observe his manly pulling power, then hopefully it will be straight back to hers for lessons in love. Ick.

It is like miracle though. He is imbued with optimism. Or at least is not dragging feet listening to German new wave on iPod all day and thinking of new ways to achieve untimely death, i.e. he has also written two songs for *Anne Frank the Musical*, i.e. 'Beanfeast' and 'Dreams of a Drilling' (thwarted dental theme). Paddy says they are excellent. Although he has banned him from including version of 'I Kissed a Girl' for Anne and Peter's pseudo lesbian kiss. Pointed out that we will not actually be kissing anyway, as that is too naturalistic and fairytale. Plus do not want to get superglued to Caris Kelp's mouth mid performance. Instead we will be hugging and exchanging metaphorical red paper roses as symbols of our love and leftwingishness. Think am definitely going to apply to do Drama and Politics at university. It is ultimate theatre of debate combination of creativity and evil-minded genius.

5.15 p.m.
I mean philanthropical drive to create better world.

. . . .

Thursday 27
Scarlet says Drama is not ultimate left-wing university

dream. Is self-obsessed wannabes with more ego than brain or talent. She says economics is the only real subject and we should be more concerned with the effect of the US subprime market than whether or not spirit fingers are the same as jazz hands. (Answer: not. Spirit fingers involves definite additional wiggle.) Said would be plenty of time for learning about that when I go to electoral college in America for my Masters degree and anyway Paddy said we are utterly Brechtian and world-changing. Scarlet said *a*) oh my God, you are so-o-o-o retarded, *b*) I think not, and *c*) since when do you call him Paddy? Said *a*) obviously not or wouldn't be going to electoral college in first place, *b*) whatever, and *c*) sorry, thought had just said it in head, did not know it had come out of mouth. Scarlet said Hmm. And wheeled herself off mysteriously in the Davros throne in direction of Mrs Brain's healthy jelly surprise (segment of tinned mandarin at bottom of pot).

. . . .

Friday 28

Oh my God. Have lost height. James did my official measurement before school and have gone down by a centimetre and is crucial centimetre as am now only four centimetres off being medical midget, according to James. Dad says it is because dog ate old John Lewis tape measure (semi-retracted—God knows how it got it down) and now we have substandard B&Q one. But Mum is not in

agreement. She says it is down to my louche teenage lifestyle and lurking in darkened bedrooms, which is renowned for depleting your Vitamin D. And possibly your height. She is putting me on extra protein for the next month and prescribing at least half an hour healthy outdoor activity a day. Have agreed to walk around sheep field at lunchtime. Do not want to deplete any more. It is utterly depressing. Am not growing up at all. Am actually shrinking.

. . . .

Saturday 29

1 p.m.

It is D-Day for Sad Ed and his unworldly penis. Tonight he will be snogging Janine off meat in the utterly grown-up surroundings of the Duke saloon bar, before having Mrs Robinson experience in her flat above BJ video. Had thought of inviting Paddy to come too, as potential inspiration, but he has gone to Henry's again. Although he has agreed to return by 8 p.m. on Sunday, and will have left-over tea of cold cuts and pickles. Have measured self again. Am still centimetre under height. But have styled hair in Amy Winehouse beehive do which has added five inches so am now relative giant.

5 p.m.

Have unstyled beehive. It would not fit in Mr Wandering Hands's Fiesta. Pointed out he should have more

capacious car for extra tall people and policy was possibly heightist, and racist as Somalians are renowned for being ultra lofty. He said he was not heightist, or racist, but that my hairdo was a danger to driving in case of partial collapse, thus obscuring my vision and potentially killing several pedestrians. He is so like Mum it is frightening. Anyway, am undeterred. Have put on ironic hat instead (is bowler from James's brief fling with tap dancing). Look like Kelsi from *High School Musical*, i.e. small, but with utter geek-turned-beauty potential. Will report back tomorrow on Sad Ed's coming-of-age older-woman worldly-penis moment. And Scarlet's raging jealousy. And will utterly not be eating any Cheese Moments. Will restrict self to ready salted crisps and one packet of peanuts for height-attaining protein content.

5.15 p.m.
James says I do not look like Kelsi, as she is ultimate in boffiny undiscovered-talent-and-beauty womanhood, whereas I am a hirsute midget in a hat.

. . . .

Sunday 30
St Andrew's Day
Coming-of-age older-woman worldly-penis night has been disaster on several fronts.

1. Sad Ed did not get to snog Janine off meat or have Mrs Robinson experience at flat above BJ video.

She ended up in ladies with Kev Banner. And noises from wobbly table vantage point indicate they were not discussing pork belly. It is the dog I feel sorry for. It sat on its stool alone all night with no one to talk to except Wizard Weeks.

2. Scarlet not at all jealous, but now even mintier with Sad Ed for bringing rogue element into pub and ruining her older man snog potential. I pointed out that she does not even fancy Kev Banner unless she has had six vodka and blackcurrants but then she threatened to get Shorty McNulty to banish me to the car park with Reuben Tull so I shut up. It is true though. She only wants Kev because she can't have Trevor. He is back with Tamsin Bacon according to James who got it off Melody Bean who got it off the other Tamsin. Apparently they were all over each other by the Gayhomes mop display at lunchtime.

3. I ate five packets of Cheese Moments. Could not stop myself. Every time went to bar they were calling out to me in all their savoury deliciousness. They are utterly like heroin. I am pathetic addict.

Oooh. Maybe Cheese Moments have depleted height! Will get James to Google for potential side effects.

3 p.m.
James said it is not Cheese Moments that are making me a midget. It is my Clegg blood. I am destined to be

underheight. And of limited intelligence. Plus will have a moustache by the time I am thirty. Said that Mum did not have any of these symptoms but James said she is genetic throwback from the one generation when a Clegg mated with superior middle-class stock.

december

£20

PAPER
ROSE

TICKET

Monday 1

Am utterly depressed. It is not my height. Although am still nine millimetres down, according to the tape measure of doom (millimetre possibly gained from late night ham slice snack). It is the credit crisis, which has not only crunched me, but has chewed me up and spat me out, i.e. I have no job and no savings and not many shopping days until Christmas. James says it is always the low-skilled and mentally subnormal who fall victim first and I should just be grateful that Gordon Brown is pumping money into counselling services for the fiscally challenged. He is a moron. But he is a rich moron. He is making a fortune from the mathletes gambling ring. It is because he and Mad Harry persuaded Reuben Tull to take out a two-way accumulator on Mrs Buttfield's weight loss programme (she has gained at least a stone so far). Have begged him to lend me some of his amassed fortune but he says I have a history of debt, and it is people like me who brought the economy to its knees in the first place.

Tuesday 2

Scarlet has refused to lend me money as well. Pointed out that it is ultra left-wing to redistribute wealth to the impoverished proletariat, i.e. me. But she says that is outdated old labour attitude and new labour is all about doing business with business. Then she went into a lecture about negative inflation at which point

549

brain switched off as have no idea what any of it means.

. . . .

Wednesday 3

Thank God for Anne Frank and her Nazi persecutors to cheer me up and take my mind off my hideous misfortune and curtailed life. Paddy says we need to knuckle down though as only have two weeks left until the show and Sad Ed still has a finale to write ('Kinky Boots' and 'These Boots Were Made for Stalking' have both been rejected). Plus Reuben Tull is not at all convincing as Mrs Frank. Unless she was secretly smoking skunk in the toilet. We are having an extra rehearsal day on Sunday to 'nail it'. Hurrah. Maybe he will give me lift on his bicycle. Will be utterly romantic, but environmentally-friendly and economical. Is ultimate in credit crunch love.

7 p.m.

Will not be getting lift on left-wing bicycle of love. It is not because Paddy is against idea (though to be fair, have not actually asked him). Or Mum. Though she would be, on grounds of peril, common-ness, and fact that no bike helmet stays on on huge hairdo. It is dog, who has chewed through the front tyre and now has head entangled in spokes. Mum is leaving it there for an hour to teach it a lesson. She is wasting her time. You

550

cannot teach an old dog new tricks. Or anything for that matter.

Thursday 4

Mum is in a fiscal crisis panic. It is James's grave news (gleaned from Radio 4) that interest rates could dip below zero, meaning in theory she would be paying Barclays to look after her millions. He has offered to investigate off-shore potential, but her non-throwback Clegg genes have reared their (criminally) ugly heads and revived the shoe-box under bed might be better idea. James said she is wrong as dog is renowned for consuming cardboard of all persuasions (he is still mourning the loss of cereal packet robot from four years ago). Mum said she did not mean an actual shoebox, but a metaphorical one, possibly in the shape of an iron safe with two combination locks and a potential anti-theft attack device. James says he will see what he can do. He was right after all. Mathletes is like the mafia. There is seemingly nothing he can't procure.

Friday 5

Mum is writing to the BBC again. This time it is financial guru Robert Peston who is the object of her ire. She says his constant talking down of the economy, plus ferretish features and faulty turntable drawl, are potentially responsible for shoebox dilemma, if not entire credit

crunch, and that they need to bring back baby-faced business reporter Declan, who may have been Irish, but at least he had benign look of shoe salesman. Paddy pointed out that Robert Peston in fact has stutter which he controls with his unique declamatory style, but Mum says that it is even more reason to get him off our screens. She is still reeling from the Gareth Gates debacle.

Mum is sounding more like Granny Clegg every day. Maybe it is true, and we do all turn into our mothers. Oh God. Is bad enough have got her knees. Let alone inheriting her hygiene obsession and ferocious parental controls.

8 p.m.
Crisis averted. Granny Clegg has just rung to ask if veal comes from rabbits.

· ·

Saturday 6
8 a.m.
Have woken imbued with new-found economic optimism. It is thanks to dream involving Robert Peston, Barack Obama, and Fern Britton (who was irrelevant, but did save Saffron Walden from tidal wave with power of magic microphone). Anyway, point is Obama did not let his colour stand in way of success. He rose against prejudice to ultimate triumph. So am utterly going to take leaf out of his book and not let my background (shortness and bad hair, rather than blackness) hold me back. Instead am

going to write list of transferable skills and tread mean streets of Saffron Walden hawking myself to traders until someone gives me a job.

10 a.m.
Have written list of skills:
1. Have maths GCSE, i.e. can add up using calculator.
2. Thanks to months of experience on Nuts In May till of doom, am unafraid of perilous or baffling mechanical equipment (though have slightly mis-shapen right index finger).
3. Am adaptable to new and complicated shelf stacking systems thanks to Mum's patented alphabetized, height-co-ordinated and in use-by-date order method.

James says I should add that have experience caring for the elderly and infirm, i.e. Granny Clegg last year, and see if I can get work at the Twilight Years Day Centre. Said no. It is not that am ageist. It is that would have to work with Treena and go on pub crawls that involve her cousin Donna who is 'double mental'. Anyway, am aiming higher, for job that involves monetary responsibility, or at least avoids the smell of bleach and endless Jeremy Kyle. Oooh. Have had excellent idea. Will offer skills to Mr Wandering Hands. I could run office and be in charge of booking out the fleet of Ford Fiestas! Is all phone-based so hair and shortness not in any way impediment. Am genius.

1 p.m.

Am not genius. Mr Wandering Hands says he does not have office, he has Mrs Wandering Hands and a week-to-view A4 WHSmith diary and no I cannot wash the Fiestas for £5 a time because he has it on good authority that my cleaning skills leave a lot to be desired. Curse Mum and her honesty is the best policy policy. Will have to tread mean streets after all. Am like Oliver Twist. Or Dick Whittington. Or someone who had to walk a long way in cold, rain, and endless dog poo.

5 p.m.

Have beaten credit crunch and ferret-faced Robert Peston and have got job! On downside, it is in Woolworth's, which requires *a*) crap overall wearing and *b*) willpower to stay away from pick-and-mix lest I put on two stone in violet creams by New Year, but is job none the less and means will be able to purchase presents, and go down Duke on regular basis (to reinvest in local economy). I start December 19 (said cannot do before then due to theatrical commitments). Anyway Mr Luton (trousers an inch too short, hair in ears, dandruff) could obviously see my excellent potential as he said that was fine, as long as I could do Christmas Eve, because that's when it gets totally mental.

Mum says my joy is ill-founded as according to her sources (James and Mad Harry) Woolworth's is in dire financial straits and could be about to 'go to the fence'.

Said *a*) it is 'go to the wall' and *b*) she is wrong, the atmosphere there is positively festive (tinsel hats all round) and she will be eating her poorly chosen words when I am furnishing her with lavish seasonal gifts. She is such a doom-monger. As is Sad Ed. He refused to even ask Mrs Noakes (bad perm, calls trousers 'slacks', notorious gossip) to put me back on the waiting list for trolley-herding. He says he and Reuben are barely clinging to their jobs as it is in this climate, and they do not need fresh-faced competition. Pointed out that if he and Reuben did more herding and less crashing then they would not be on final warnings. But at that point there was distinctive crunch of metal on metal and Sad Ed had to go and untangle Reuben and a Ford Ka. Anyway do not care. Am no longer one of Brown's job-less millions.

7 p.m.

Paddy has pointed out that was never one of jobless millions in first place as, being under eighteen, I am not included within official statistics. He said he and Henry are fighting to get people like me the right to be counted. Which just proves that in his eyes my age is no barrier to being grown-up. Oh God. I think I love him.

8 p.m.

Scarlet has rung to demand to know why I am not seated

at the wobbly toilet table in the Duke. Said I was feeling a bit below par and needed to conserve joules for tomorrow's all-day Anne Frankathon. She said but Sad Ed is not conserving joules, he is at very minute at bar securing Cheese Moments. Did not tell her he is only following the demands of his unworldly penis, i.e. trailing Scarlet wherever she goes. Nor that I am following mine. (Not penis obviously. Do not have one, unworldly or otherwise, despite recurring nightmare at age of eight. More my heart. Or head. Or possibly pants.) Anyway, am staying in so can watch telly with Paddy. Atmosphere of fact-based love marred only by fact that he is on other side of room whereas I am wedged in on sofa between dog and James who are both taking advantage of Mum and Dad being at Mr Wainwright and Mrs Wainwright Mark II's for wine and nibbles by eating crackers with no crumb-catching plates.

10 p.m.
Think it is definite and Paddy is potently in love with me, i.e. there was discernible atmosphere of tension during *Midsomer Murders*. Will assess situation further tomorrow. Am going to call him Paddy to face. Is time we were on first name terms. It will be last barrier to be broken down before he flings me against wardrobe department (i.e. broken wardrobe) and snogs me in left-wing fact-based grown-up manner. Hurrah!

Sunday 7

Paddy has not flung me against wardrobe in fact-based or any other manner. He has been too busy trying to rescue *Anne Frank the Musical* from current state of disaster. It is utterly Caris Kelp's fault for making herself sick on Pritt Stick in the Beanfeast number. And possibly mine for slipping on sick and elbowing Mouchi in eye. Paddy said he has no idea how we are going to be ready for Thursday. I said, 'Don't worry, Paddy. We'll pull something out of the hat. That's showbusiness!' He said, *a*) we had better do, *b*) it is not showbusiness, it is docudrama, which is utterly different, and *c*) please don't call him Paddy, it is Mr Pringle.

It is a bitter blow. But I understand. It is school rules, and we cannot let our love compromise his job in the face of Mr Wilmott's oppressive (though ineffectual) authority. We must bide our time before revealing our relationship to an un-understanding world.

10 p.m.
And actually have relationship.

. . . .

Monday 8

Scarlet summoned me to Davros throne at lunchtime. Thought it might be to discuss her plans to persuade Sad Ed to persuade Mr Wilmott to have a goths-only toilet but it was not, it was to discuss my 'erratic behaviour'. She

says as my first best friend she demands to know why I would turn down an opportunity to consume savoury snacks and sing 'Crystal Chandelier' to spend an evening watching John Nettles, who do not even like, with my brother, who is an irritating mathlete, the dog, who is just irritating, and Mr Pringle, who I must surely be sick of the sight of, given that I am in rehearsal with him every day. Said I do not know what she was talking about and oh my God, is that Robert Pattinson in the apple pie queue? It was not, it was Sad Ed with a voluminous hairdo and too much eyebrow pencil (he is relentless in his bid to win Scarlet's bat-based love). But it gave me time to hide behind the mathletes. Cannot let her know about Mr Pringle. Our love is a secret. Forbidden, like Eve's apple. Or Ribena in the vicinity of oatmeal wool carpet.

5 p.m.
And not actually real at the moment.

. . . .

Tuesday 9

The crapness of *Anne Frank the Musical* does not seem to have reached the public arena, i.e. the rest of John Major High, yet. Tickets have officially sold out and the math-letes are touting them on the black market (i.e. nicotine patch corner, i.e. behind the bike sheds) for double face value. Oh my God. Is like when Prince played the O2.

5 p.m.
James says it is not like when Prince played the O2. It is like when Bobby Helmet plays the Miners' Arms in Goonbell, i.e. the public love a good car crash.

. . . .

Wednesday 10
9.30 p.m.
James is right. *Anne Frank* is utter car crash. In fact is three-lorry pile-up with oil spillage, minor injuries, and sheep all over the carriageways (Criminals and Retards, again). It is Mr Pringle I feel sorry for. This is his life's ambition—using popular drama to change politics. And what he has got is a load of teenagers in black T-shirts and tights singing about beans and falling off edge of stage (Mrs Frank aka Reuben Tull, due to 'compromised sense of perspective'). Oh his grief is unbearable. I long to comfort him in his hour of need. To stroke his hair. And whisper gentle nothings. And then gasp as he kisses me gently, yet masterfully, in the staff toilets . . .

10 p.m.
Oh. Had funny turn there. Am revived now. Thanks to Mum who burst into bedroom to demand if had eaten last Fruesli bar. Said no, was dog on fibre mission.

Must not fail Paddy though. Will channel grief and anguish into critic-silencing performance of lifetime. This time tomorrow I will be etched on everyone's memory as

the definitive Anne Frank. Vulnerable, yet assured. And beautiful, despite Barbra hair.

∙ ∙

Thursday 11
10 p.m.
Or as Rachel Riley, the girl who got a paper rose stuck in left nostril during Secret Lover routine (is Caris Kelp and her Uhu residue).

On plus side, there was catalogue of other misdemeanours i.e.:

- Mrs Frank aka Reuben Tull fell asleep in soup.
- Mr Dussel aka Sad Ed accidentally drilled hole in Mouchi's cardboard cat ears with Black and Decker (couldn't get actual dental drill due to unfeasibly high price demanded by potential triad Alan Wong).
- Nazis missed cue due to argument about Wayne Rooney in green room and Mrs Frank (with soupy face) had to go and remind them to come and arrest us all, which kind of ruined the surprise effect.

Is not good. Actually saw Mr Pringle bang his head on trophy cabinet in despair several times. But it is first night. And first nights always go wrong. He is hardened theatre professional and used to such setbacks. I predict he will be back in upbeat mode giving us director's notes first thing tomorrow.

∙ ∙

Friday 12

10 a.m.

Mr Pringle is not in school. Which is odd as he left house at usual time, i.e. 8.17 a.m., according to James's infallible timings, following a health-giving, if silent breakfast of Alpen (original, not luxury, variety). Although he was not wearing his usual school outfit or even suitable coat. Oh God. Maybe he is like Captain Oates, i.e. has gone out into the snow and ice (or at least drizzle) to seal his fate. Is all my fault. And possibly Reuben Tull's. And definitely Caris Kelp's for eating glue in first place. Her thirst for adhesives has sent grown man to his death.

1 p.m.

Scarlet is still mental with suspicion. She demanded to know why my eyes filled with tears over my cheese and chutney bap at lunch. I said it was the astringent pickle. Cannot tell her I am grieving for my lost dead forbidden love.

4 p.m.

Have informed Mum of my Oates theory. James says Mr Pringle would have to be naked for at least two weeks to sustain hypothermia and ensuing death, given the clement temperature today. He is wrong. At this very moment Mr Pringle is probably lying blue-lipped in a waterlogged ditch. Or behind the meat bins at Goddards. But we will not fail him. The show must go on.

4.15 p.m.
Unless Lou (school caretaker, former Criminal and Retard, once ate school rabbit) has forgotten to replace the safety curtain, which accidentally got wrapped around Sad Ed and fell down during attempts to extricate rose, in which case it can't due to fire regulations.

5 p.m.
Mr Pringle is not in a ditch. He is at the dining table consuming pre-show salmon fishcakes, and his lips are not blue but are pink and smiley. Though tight, i.e. he is not revealing where he has been. It is probably hell, metaphorically speaking (unless he actually did get as far as meat bins). But think he has had some kind of Saul on Road to Damascus revelation and is renewed in his commitment to fact-based theatre as he is definitely coming to supervise show. Hurrah!

5.15 p.m.
Though it would have been utterly brilliant if he had been dead. I could have wept at his grave, not for my personal loss, but for the greater loss to the worlds of theatre and politics, perishing slowly from grief and malnutrition like Greyfriar's Bobby. God, life is so unfair.

11 p.m.
Tonight's show marginally less fraught with crapness, i.e. no one got glued to anything, got things stuck in orifices,

562

or fell off the stage. Although at one point three Year Eight Criminals and Retards climbed on it to try to stop the Nazis storming up the staircase. Sad Ed had to use his bulk to intervene. Which was successful, but confusing storyline-wise. Mr Pringle was over the moon though. He said it showed that the play was so powerful it moved the audience to intervene in history. It did not. It moved some fist-happy mentalists who know a good opportunity for a fight when they see one.

. . . .

Saturday 13

4 p.m.
Thank God it is the last night tonight. Have decided am not even going to after-show party. It will only compound my frustrations—artistic and forbidden-love-wise.

4.30 p.m.
Oh my God. Think may not be frustrated after all. Have just bumped into Mr Pringle at fridge. He said, 'Listen, Rachel. I know the show isn't how we planned it, but I just wanted to say thanks. Your commitment is unquestionable. You ARE Anne.' At which point coughed milk on his Che Guavara T-shirt as was in shock from *a*) being caught in act of proscribed drinking from carton and *b*) use of 'we' to indicate our shared theatrical vision. But he obviously did not care, or possibly notice due to potent love (or presence of dog trying to reach cold meat

container), because then he said, 'You are coming to the party, aren't you?' Said yes. He said, 'Good. I really want you to meet Henry.' Then he went back to his room with two rich teas and a Müller Fruit Corner. He flies in the face of Mum's 'food only at the table and to be consumed with cutlery' rules. We are united in our artistic dream, our disregard for authority, and our forbidden love! Oh it is so obvious now. He wants me to meet his best friend so he can get official approval. And possibly an audition to their guerrilla theatre company. Hurrah! I will not need to apply to college after all. I will be travelling the world in a camper van, fuelled only by creativity and love. And lead replacement petrol. Am going to confess all to Scarlet immediately. Can leave her out of loop no longer. She must share in my joy.

5 p.m.
Scarlet says it is no surprise as her bat-like powers had detected my fatal attraction to Mr Pringle weeks ago, but she was waiting for me to come to her, rather than scare me with her supernatural abilities. (Being Head Goth clearly imbues holder with over-inflated sense of power. It is like when Trevor Pledger actually thought he was a vampire and tried to fly off bike shed roof.) Anyway, she is all for it, as, being an older man, he will tutor me in the 'art of love-making'. Said will be nice just to snog him first, before any penises get involved. Ick. Although will have to get used to penis potential as he is older man

and unlike Sad Ed's his will be utterly worldly. Oh my God. Maybe tonight will be night, i.e. will not only be in love with older man but will finally do 'It'. Will be utter meeting of minds and bodies. As opposed to twenty seconds on a bag of potatoes at the back of the Co-Op (Fat Kylie). Yes will do it. Must think of Anne Frank, i.e. cannot turn down opportunity in case tomorrow I am imprisoned in an annexe and then sent to concentration camp and certain death. (Which is exactly what will happen if Mum finds out. Although will not be concentration camp. Will be Auntie Joyless, who makes Mum look lenient.) Anyway, I am a grown-up, after all. And grown-up love is not about romance and happy endings. It is about the facts of life. And I'm pretty sure I know all of them now.

11.30 p.m.
Some facts I did not know:
1. Henry is short for Henrietta.
2. She is not working-class left-wing anarchist. She is daughter of evil Tory MP for Saffron Walden and environs Hugo Thorndyke.
3. She does not work on *Newsnight*. Or even *One Show*. She is runner on *Masterchef*.
4. She is Mr Pringle's fiancée.

On the plus side, at least he does not know that I was in love with him.

11.35 p.m.
Scarlet has texted to say she has told Mr Pringle he is a menace to young hearts and minds and that he had better keep his evil, dream-shattering penis away from me in future.

Oh God. Wish was dead. In fact am going to beg God to strike me down in my sleep. Preferably with a plague of frogs. As that would be utterly literary. Though do not know how frogs could actually kill you. Unless they are those poisonous blue ones. Although James's Ninja ones were quite perilous. Maybe a bolt of lightning would be better. Yes, will pray to be burned alive by electrical storm.

11.40 p.m.
In non-painful way.

11.45 p.m.
That does not singe bedding, or Mum will be extra minty.

. . . .

Sunday 14
9 a.m.
Am still utterly alive. And utterly depressed. What is the point of God if he (or she, or the laser-eyed dog) will not smite you down in your hour of need. On the plusside Mr Pringle did not come home last night. According to Mum he stayed at the Thorndykes' mock Georgian

mansion in Steeple Bumpstead. I hope he chokes to death on his class betrayal. Or at least on one of Mrs Thorndyke's overly chewy macaroons.

3 p.m.
Mr Pringle did not choke to death either on own hypocrisy or almond-based biscuits. He is very much alive and is moving out. He is going to stay at Thorndyke Towers aka enemy lair instead. He told Mum it is because Henry finished filming early, and he would rather respect Mum's 'not under my roof' wishes. It is not. It is because he is horrified at my 'definitely under my roof' wishes. Am praying for death again. Will sob on bed until the Lord hears me in my hour of need.

3.15 p.m.
Ooh. Is knock on door. Maybe it is grim reaper.

3.30 p.m.
Was James. So fairly grim. He demanded to know why I was so depressed. I said it is credit crunch, i.e. we will be destitute now that Mr Pringle has gone with his rent cheques and it is only Mum I am sorry for. James says *au contraire* Mum is quite happy as she was getting quite tired of the heated anti-John Humphrys atmosphere at the Shreddies table plus Mr Pringle has paid up through the whole of January anyway. Said cheque will bounce as he is impoverished teacher and Mum has been defrauded.

James said that is unlikely given that his great-great-grandfather invented diamond-based golf knitwear. Said why did I not know this essential fact. James said it is because I am not a fact-based person. Said he is wrong, I am utterly fact-friendly. And anyway why is he so cheery. He said it is because he 'got some' at the after-show party last night. It is with Wendy Shoebridge who is in Year Nine and is leader of the Forget-Me-Not Patrol at Fifth Guides (Baptist). This is typical. I am being out grown-upped by an eleven year old. My life is officially over.

. . . .

Monday 15

8 a.m.

Except that, typically, it isn't. It goes on in all its predictability, i.e. Mum is refusing to let Dad have a third slice of toast in case it redistributes more leg fat to his waistline, James is singing 'Up Where We Belong' and the dog is wandering aimlessly around the hallway with what looks like a toothbrush in its mouth. All of which only emphasizes the huge Mr Pringle-shaped fact-based left-wing hole at the Shreddies table.

4 p.m.

School is unbearable. Had to spend most of day lying on saggy sofa being fed reviving Maltesers by Sad Ed. Every corridor is replete with the possibility of bumping into

Mr Pringle. Scarlet says it does not help that I spent most of first break lurking by the drama studio. I said it does not help that she was the one who had gone there in the first place to get shouty at him and I was only there to arbitrate. Think I may have very slightly overplayed the exact nature of my relationship with Mr Pringle to Scarlet as she is definitely under impression that bodily fluids of some sort have been exchanged and that he is a two-timing pervert-in-school pseudo-socialist love menace (her words, not mine). Sad Ed is in agreement. But it is hollow support. He is only doing it to lure Scarlet towards his bodily fluids.

Thank God school is over in four days and with it my daily torment of being so close and yet so far from my older man dream.

5 p.m.
It is also good for Mr Pringle as I do not rate his chances against Scarlet. She has just texted to say she is thinking of reporting him to the *Guardian* as this is the sort of scandal that could being down the entire Tory party. Have texted her to hold off until David Cameron's poll ratings go up in order to achieve maximum effect (I learned this off Suzy). She has agreed. Thank God.

6 p.m.
Have just seen Gordon Brown on News. Think it may have been a mistake to pin my happiness on the reviving

fortunes of a man with no neck, giant head, and Vosene-compromised hair.

. . . .

Tuesday 16

There is good news on the David Cameron/Mr Pringle downfall front. It is utterly bat-related, i.e. the film of *Twilight* comes out on Friday and Scarlet is too consumed with potential vampire-lust to bring down the Tory party. Goth corner was awash with excitement. In a sort of subdued, corpse-like way.

The mathletes table was also awash with lust. It was James, who spent the whole of lunch with his mouth full of Wendy Shoebridge's tongue instead of his ham and tomato sandwiches. Have pointed out to him that he is in danger of compromising himself nutritionally but he said he does not need food, he and Wendy will subsist on each other's love (he is wrong, I have tried it, you just get dizzy). Plus they shared a packet of yoghurt-coated blueberries in the computer room at first break. It is a match made in heaven. Or PC World.

Did not see Mr Pringle. But it is only temporary relief. Tomorrow it is drama and will have to share airspace with his treacherous Tory-snogging lips once again. May have to plead illness. The dog is looking a bit peaky at the moment. Will claim I have what it has got.

. . . .

Wednesday 17

8 a.m.

Mum says I do not have what the dog has got, unless I
have also swallowed a tube of Aquafresh and a dozen
organic eggs (large), and I have to go to school as I
am collecting Jesus from the Camilla Parker Bowles
Memorial Crèche as Grandpa and Treena have got
Christmas lunch at the Twilight Years Day Centre and will
be too compromised by Linda Ronstadt and sherry trifle
to be in charge of a minor.

4 p.m.

Oh God. It was worse than I could have possibly imagined. Even the scenario in which Mr Pringle shot me with
Mark Lambert's air rifle and then opened fire on rest of
drama class. It started off OK, i.e. was merely pale and
shaky when Mr Pringle came into room, but that could
have been low blood sugar because I had given half my
turkey roll to Sad Ed out of pity because Scarlet had just
told him he is waste of head boy space and makes Mr
Wilmott look effectual. But then Mr Pringle revealed devastating news, i.e. that he is leaving school totally. And
instead of realizing this is probably a good thing, as *a*) it
will alleviate my pain and *b*) it will alleviate his pain, and
potentially David Cameron's because there is less chance
Scarlet will remember to bring about their downfall, I
stood up and, before I could stop it, my mouth had said
something like 'No, but you can't. Not because of me.

It was pathetic. I'm totally over it.' And Mr Pringle said, 'Er . . . actually, Rachel, this isn't about you. This is because I've got a part in *EastEnders*. That's where I was on Friday—at an audition.' And yet still mouth did not shut up, it said, 'Oh my God. You are an utter charlatan. You said soap operas are the opiate of the masses, even though Scarlet says it is religion, but whatever. I thought it was about facts, not fiction, about raw, political, life-changing conflict, not whether or not Peggy should marry Archie.' And Sad Ed said, 'She shouldn't, because he is much better in *Gavin and Stacey* and should leave and concentrate on edgy BBC3-based comedy.' Mr Pringle said, 'It *is* about the facts, Rachel. But it's also about following your heart.' So I said, 'What, and your heart lies in playing a cockney wide boy with a heart of gold who gets his girlfriend's best friend pregnant only she turns out to be his long-lost sister?' And he said, 'Actually I'm going to be a market inspector but the point is, I'll get paid four times what I do here and then I can fund me and Henry to make real, political stuff.' At which point thank God regained control of mouth and legs and stormed out, which was utterly dramatic, except when I had to storm back in to remind Sad Ed that he should be storming too.

So now am not only not snogging older man, but entire drama A-level knows about my torment. (Although Sad Ed says that to be honest, half the class were trying to unstick Caris from the fire exit and Reuben Tull was stoned and at that point thought he was an albatross so

my secret is still fairly safe.) But, worse, Mr Pringle has let down fact-based fans everywhere. He has no staying power and has fallen prey to the lure of money, and a fairytale happy ending. Or a grim one involving an explosion at the Queen Vic. But it is utterly not real. I will show him. I will remain strong in my political convictions. And be happy to work for less-than-minimum wage at Woolworth's.

5 p.m.
Mum is writing to Mr Wilmott to complain about the standard of teaching in the Camilla Parker Bowles Memorial Crèche. It is because Jesus is very sad about his namesake's having to sleep in a manger because there were 'no crisps for a bed'. It is Fat Kylie, she has Wotsits on the brain. And 99s in the pants. It is lucky Mum did not also hear Jesus's version of 'Jingle Bells' involving a 'one-whore open sleigh'. The mind boggles.

* *

Thursday 18
8.30 a.m.
Woolworth's is closing. Mum informed me over my Shreddies, having been informed by John Humphrys, from whom she has also acquired an irritating smug tone. She is not at all sympathetic and says it is just 'winnowing the wheat from the chaff' and leaves room for potential expansion of quality establishments like John Lewis.

Pointed out that now she will have to fund me or no one will get any Christmas presents at all and the house will be utterly like Bob Cratchit's with James as the crippled one and her as Scrooge. She said she will think about it. She will not. Being compared to Scrooge is not an insult in her book. God, there is no end to my misery. It is so unfair. Everyone else is basking in festive spirit and I am condemned to walk in perpetual misery, with nothing but cold, hard truth flowing through my veins. Even Sad Ed is uncharacteristically merry. It is because Scarlet has agreed that he can go to see *Twilight* with her. But only on condition that he does not do the eyebrow thing, or the hair, or attempts at brooding sexuality, which in fact only make him look mental.

4 p.m.
Oh my God. Am not alone after all. Someone else is about to get injection of cold hard truth, i.e. James. Have just witnessed treachery first-hand and it is a double betrayal, i.e. his best friend and girlfriend. Mad Harry and Wendy were locked in lust outside the mobile science lab (they are locust monitors). James is going to be devastated. Is Mumtaz all over again. Will break grave news to him gently. Have got emergency reviving Marmite sandwich and a Glade Plug-in (could not find smelling salts).

4.15 p.m.
James has eaten the sandwich and his room smells of

pine forests. But he is not in slightest devastated. He says he is fully aware of nature of Mad Harry's and Wendy's relationship and they are conjugating with his full blessing. Said why is he not mourning the loss of his older woman computer-based geek love? He said, *au contraire*, he has not lost love, he and Mad Harry are sharing Wendy on a one day on/one day off basis. It is a grown-up modern arrangement and I couldn't possibly understand. He is right. She is mental. One of them is bad enough, but two. She has strong tonsils.

. . . .

Friday 19

Thank God it is the last day of school for two weeks. The sooner this term, and this year, is over the better. It is utterly not the season to be jolly. Christmas is for children, not grown-ups. Am beyond wearing tinsel headbands or lingering under Mrs Leech's mistletoe. And if Thin Kylie puts 'Hallelujah' (crap Alexandra Burke version) on the common room CD player again then will break Middle East peace accord, storm the Um Bongo cushion and overthrow the government myself. May well spend day in library instead ingesting facts. That way will also avoid Mr Pringle. By the time I emerge at quarter past three, like boffiny butterfly, he will be gone from my life for ever.

1 p.m.

Except that did not anticipate Mr Pringle would be in

library having argument with Mr Knox about suspicious
bitemarks in a copy of *Mother Courage*. It is the dog. It does
not like books. Especially ones with ugly old women on
the cover. Tried to hide behind revolving Jacqueline
Wilson display but it got whizzed by a Year Seven (still at
age when revolving doors, display cases, and chairs are
open invitation to spin mentally) so was revealed every
few seconds behind whirling Tracey Beakers. He said,
'Can I have a word, Rach?' Said, 'No, this is library. Is illegal. Shush.' He said, 'Outside, in private.' Said OK. Then
ensued utterly humiliating monologue, i.e. 'Rachel, I just
wanted to say that I'm sorry if I somehow gave you the
impression that I was in any way interested. I mean, you
must realize that it was just never on the cards. I'm too
old for you. You need someone your own age. You see
that, don't you?' Except that I didn't, because at that
point Sad Ed whizzed past pushing Scarlet on the Davros
throne (festive version, i.e. with battery controlled fairy
lights around base) and singing 'Bat Out of Hell'. But I
didn't say anything. I just shrugged and walked away.
Because am grown-up. And do not cry in front other people. Or hit them.

3 p.m.
Unlike Scarlet. According to Sad Ed Mr Pringle is in Mrs
Leech's office nursing a black eye and bruised genitals.
Scarlet claims it was an accident and that she lost control
of the Davros throne. She did not. She never loses control

of anything. She is like Stalin. Sad Ed says on plus side he found out (through judicious use of a finger of Twix) who is taking over drama next term. It is Mr Vaughan. According to Mrs Leech, Sophie Microwave Muffins has left him for her Natural Sciences professor and he is utterly heartbroken. So it is one in, one out, on the pervert front.

4 p.m.
Not that Mr Pringle was pervert after all.

4.15 p.m.
Which is typical.

. . . .

Saturday 20
11 a.m.
Am still in bed. What is point of getting up when you have no job to go to. Now I know how long-term unemployed feel.

11.15 a.m.
Am up. Is not Mum and her anti-malingering/prolaundry stance. Is hideous sound of James and Wendy through wall next door. It is obviously his day on. Have no idea what they are doing but there is a lot of 'Oooh'ing and 'Oh my God'ing. Ick. Am going to see Sad Ed instead to beg for sublet trolley work, i.e. he can pay

me to mind the herd while he spends quality time pestering Scarlet. Is mutually beneficial grown-up arrangement. Hurrah.

4 p.m.
Sad Ed not in agreement at all about arrangement. He says it is utterly against company rules and he could face the sack or prison and anyway he is seeing Scarlet tonight at the cinema where it will be dark, and she will be utterly in the mood for love having eaten aphrodisiac pick-and-mix and got all clammy over Robert Pattinson. Said *a*) since when did he care about rules, he is utterly against The Man, even though The Man is actually a woman, i.e. Mrs Noakes and *b*) cherry cola bottles are not aphrodisiac. He said *a*) it is utterly rock starrish and anti-The Man to do menial labour as a youth so that you can then rebel against it and write about it on critically acclaimed albums before killing yourself and *b*) it is the sugar, it makes you lick your lips, which makes you think about sex. He is going to empty some Silver Spoon into bag for good measure. Said is good thing am too broke to go as would not want to be luring random goths with my liking for Jelly Tots. Then Reuben said if I was looking for work then he would give me £2 to deliver Christmas 'present' to Wizard Weeks. Said what is in present? He said is herbally organic thing. Declined. I may be desperate, but I am not being his drugs mule.

9 p.m.
Being fact-based is utterly detrimental to love gone bad, as what I need right now is twinkly vampires and white-toothed werewolf boys. Or at very least Colin Firth in a wet shirt. Plus no one else understands my plight. They are all too busy engrossed in festive *Casualty*. Even dog is glued to screen. (It is the ITU. It likes the bleeping.) If only Jack was here.

11 p.m.
Sad Ed has texted. He did not get to snog Scarlet by the power of Silver Spoon and pick-and-mix. But she did fall asleep on him in sick-smelling Volvo and he has her sugary spit on his shoulder so he is happy. He says he will never wash it. He doesn't anyway. It still has Turkish Delight residue on it from October.

· ·

Sunday 21
Predictably 'Hallelujah', the tedious Alexandra Burke, Thin Kylie-endorsed version, as opposed to utterly brilliant untimely death Sad Ed-endorsed Jeff Buckley version, is Christmas Number One. James is jubilant. It is because the mathletes will rake in at least £87 in profit next term, as they had somehow managed to convince most of Year Seven that Golden Wonder would triumph, despite not actually having a single out. Or being a real band.

Am also in the money. Ish. Mum has agreed to my request for emergency funds. Though she is not issuing credit due to my subprime tendencies. Am going to have to earn it instead by helping with festive chores. Asked how much she was offering an hour. She said £2.50, including a 15-minute juice and biscuit break and an hour for lunch. All meals provided. Tried to bargain her up to £2.75 but she has clearly been watching *The Apprentice* as she immediately dropped her offer to £2.25 and I can buy my own health-giving snacks. Have accepted first offer. At very least it will take my mind off the utterly Eliotian wasteland that is my world.

Monday 22

Is torture. My hands are raw and have Cillit-Bang-induced headache. Am like prisoner of war. But with endless Radio 4 in background. Which is tantamount to mental cruelty. Meanwhile James is up in his bedroom with Wendy *and* Mad Harry. Mum is mental. They are probably having some hideous three-way love orgy.

3 p.m.

They are not having hideous three-way love orgy. They are playing Warhammer, in full costume, i.e cloaks and random hats (one Harry Potter pointy wizard, one cycle helmet, and a swimming cap). Which is possibly worse.

5 p.m.

Cannot go on any longer. Have now: hoovered under beds, hoovered in beds, made twenty metres of paper chains and decorated (environmentally-, carpet- and dog-friendly) tree—TWICE—because apparently my eclectic, inspired 'place decorations in any available gap' method does not fit in with Mum's rigid 'only green and blue baubles, no tinsel and for heaven's sake don't clump them at the top the weight ratio is all wrong, Rachel' method. Have informed Mum that am leaving her employ forthwith due to artistic differences. She threatened to withhold pay as am breaking terms of contract. Pointed out that had not signed contract so therefore she owed me £20. Mum said *au contraire, a*) I had signed contract several years ago pertaining to household chores, which was still valid until my eighteenth birthday and *b*) no one gets paid for their lunch hour so technically she only owed me £17.50. Have agreed compromise. Am doing hour of babysitting this evening while Mum and Dad go to Terry and Cherie's festive warm Baileys and prawn ring party and will get full £20 and no-blame redundancy. Is bargain as they will be back within twenty minutes feigning headaches. There is no way Mum will consume prawn rings. It breaks rules pertaining to seafood, overambition, and Coleen Nolan.

11 p.m.

Mum and Dad are still not back from the Britchers'. Am

torn between keeping quiet so can amass fortune as babysitting pay will go into time and half past midnight (have checked original contract) or going over road to rescue parents from potential hostage situation. There can be no other explanation as to why they can have been detained so long except under duress.

11.30 p.m.

Except 'accidental' consumption of eight Tia Marias (Dad) and heated debate as to whether or not Tia Maria is actual person (Mum and Cherie). For once am in agreement with Thin Kylie, i.e. 'Your mum is, like, worse than that winking woman.' (i.e Ann Robinson. At least assume it is. Not Mrs Dyer (fat feet, smells of Yardley, nervous tic).) Have removed parents and sent them to bed, but not without securing agreement of extra £5 for duties beyond scope of contract. So now have £35. Am rich beyond compare and will be able to buy family and friends utterly luxurious Christmas gifts. Hurrah!

Tuesday 23

9 a.m.

Except that Scarlet has just texted to demand presence in Duke tonight for wobbly toilet table pre-Christmas celebration. And will need at least £20 for purchasing of beverages and snacks and another £5 for jukebox in order to prevent Reuben torturing pub with the entire

Tangerine Dream back catalogue. Which only leaves £10 (am excellent at maths, is Riley family gift, like Redknapps with football) but have run out of hair products and cannot possibly go to pub resembling puffa-fish head so in fact have exactly no money for presents. Need Plan B.

9.15 a.m.
Have got Plan B. Am going to blackmail James into handing over his mathlete money by threatening to tell Mum that he is having inappropriate relations with Wendy Shoebridge in at least one proscribed area (bust, pants, and back of neck all banned until at least age 18).

9.20 a.m.
James says I will have to do better as *a*) in fact he has not technically breached any proscribed areas due to double vest protection and *b*) in any case he will match my threat and raise me a 'But Rachel got naked in bed with Justin Statham' (thus breaching several areas, including snogging people who live in mock tudor mansions). Need Plan C. And possibly Plan D as well.

10 a.m.
Have got it. Am going to utilize talents and write everyone fact-based festive-themed personal poems. Then when am famous they will be able to sell them on eBay for fortune so is utterly gift that keeps on giving. Will

start with Mum as she is notoriously hard to please, poetry-wise (she does not like limericks, religious iconography, or whimsical robins playing in snow).

1 p.m.
Mire of gloom is compromising, talent-wise. Am giving up on Mum and trying Sad Ed instead. He likes anything that rhymes. Will be a cinch.

Hmm. Will just possibly watch bit of *Ice Age* with James and dog though. Is for cheering up purposes, to aid poetry. And full of mammoth facts, so legal.

3 p.m.
Ooh. And *Brave Little Toaster*.

6 p.m.
Am not cheered. Am devastated and weepy at scale of braveness of toaster. Am going to pub. Will write when get back later. Hopefully mire of gloom will be ousted by festive spirit instead (though not actual spirit, as that would be illegal).

11.30 p.m.
Mire of gloom not entirely ousted despite consumption of several spirits. Is because Scarlet discovered brilliant method of confusing Shorty McNulty, i.e. purchasing two tonic waters and one double Malibu (retro drink thus utterly cool and tastes like liquid Bounty bars, i.e.

coconut, i.e. utterly health-giving). And then pouring Malibu into tonics thus creating two alcoholic drinks from one. Is brilliant. And am completely inspired to write poem, despite ongoing misery. Am like Coleridge, racked by depression and writing by candlelight (or John Lewis angle poise, but with energy saving bulb so fairly gloomy and underpowered) under influence of narcotics. Perhaps will do 'Rime of Ancient Mariner' style thing and be youngest ever Poet Laureate.

. . . .

Wednesday 24

Christmas Eve

10 a.m.

Ow. Why does head hurt? Malibu is sneaky drink and not at all conducive to health arrangements.

10.15 a.m.

Or poetry. Have read last night's work back and is not 'Rime of Ancient Mariner' literary genius. Though is definitely under influence of narcotics, and inexplicably written in Tippex:

Festive Feast

> *Christmas is coming.*
> *The goose is getting fat.*
> *So we can eat it.*
> *Except Scarlet who is vegetarian.*

> *And Sad Ed because they are having duck because*
> *Aled likes duck.*

But it will have to do as think may be sick if try to use brain this morning. Will put in envelopes with instructions to read in secret as is personal. No one will ever know.

2 p.m.
Am marginally revived after not-at-all festive lunch of salad. It is because Dad is in charge of catering temporarily while Mum and James go shopping for a present for Wendy. And he is not allowed to use the cooker, toaster, freezer or microwave.

3 p.m.
Granny Clegg has rung to say Happy Christmas. Dad pointed out she was a day early (unprecedented, usually she is three days late) but she said she had a full social calendar tomorrow and so would be unable to spend time gassing on the phone (also unprecedented as there is nothing Granny Clegg likes more than gassing on the phone: favourite topics—Why are oranges round? and Why don't bees develop gluier bottoms to keep the stings in?). Dad asked what wonderment was compromising her ability to pick up phone. She said she had fifteen people for lunch including Pig, Denzil, Hester Trelowarren, Maureen from the Spar and Auntie Joyless (she actually

586

called her this) and her puritanical offspring Boaz and Mary. Dad asked what she was cooking. Granny said Turkey Twizzlers with Smash and a choice of Viennetta or Butterscotch Angel Delight for pudding.

3.30 p.m.
Mum and James are back from shops (with Warhammer figurines and a GCSE maths textbook for Wendy) and Dad has recounted latest Clegg mentalism. Mum said on plus side at least her idiotic relatives (she actually said this) are at least 300 miles away this year, and have no means of transport now that Hilary (one l, penis, future black Prime Minister)'s environmentally friendly Nissan Micra has a broken gasket, so there can be no surprise visits. That way we can have a brisk lunch and it will all be back to normal (i.e. decorations down, Quality Street consumed, and crap Clegg presents in recycling) by Boxing Day. For once am utterly in agreement with Mum. The sooner this charade of childish cheerfulness is over the better. Am going to watch News 24 instead to fill self with facts and combat Christmas creep.

8 p.m.
Oooh. There is potential terrorist situation at Stansted airport. Apparently bearded man has been arrested for carrying inflammatory material (though is unclear if they actually mean violence-inciting or just packet of firelighters). Mum says it is definitely Osama Bin Laden.

Although James has pointed out that chances of him arriving in Essex on an easyJet flight from Sciathos are slim to say the least. Mum says that's what he wants us to think which is why it is utterly cunning. Only not so cunning now the police have seen through his plan and have the world's most notorious madman in custody in Bishop's Stortford.

9.15 p.m.
The police do not have the world's most notorious madman in custody in Bishop's Stortford. PC Doone just rang to ask if we knew of a James Riley. Mum said yes indeed and he is at this very minute doing advanced Sudoku with the dog. PC Doone said no he isn't he is at this very minute locked in a cell talking about marigolds and rocking gently. Mum said is not James, is Osama, pretending to be James. At which point a confusing argument went on for three minutes while Mum and PC Doone argued over how Osama would know James, and the implications of the marigolds (Mum's theory: gloves, to hide fingerprints) until James came to phone to assert his official nature and managed to deduce identity of criminal suspect. Is not Osama Bin Laden. Is Uncle Jim, i.e. Dad's brother (full genetic match one, as opposed to soon to be three-year-old baby Jesus who is half Riley, half Boltoner) who has been living in Tibet for several years with his girlfriend Marigold (and who we had all forgotten about). Anyway he is not being charged with terrorism after all as

588

the inflammatory material turned out to be 'inflammable', only it wasn't. It was a bottle of rank alcohol. PC Doone said the sooner he is out of the station the better as he is annoying everyone with his sitar, and clearly needs mental help. Mum said PC Doone should call emergency psychiatric care. But apparently they are at their office party at TGI Friday's. Dad has gone to fetch him. Mum is mad with crossness. Not only was she sorely off the mark with her marigold glove theory, but she is being invaded by an idiotic relative after all, i.e. the black sheep of the family. Pointed out that black sheep is racist and anti-ovine but at that point she made her lips disappear so went for situation-diffusing wee instead.

9.30 p.m.
James has rung Grandpa to inform him of impending return of Prodigal Son. He said 'Who?' No wonder Uncle Jim has issues.

11.45 p.m.
Uncle Jim is in house. But is out of bounds to all contact with impressionable members of family, i.e. me and James. Pointed out I was utterly grown-up and in fact used to dealing with drug-addled mentalists, i.e. Reuben Tull. But Mum said I can wait until breakfast when he will have slept off the ouzo (Mum's forensic breath test) and been washed and shaved. (Mum does not allow beards in house on grounds of being untrustworthy and

589

unhygienic. How she puts up with dog is miracle.) James says Uncle Jim has definitely come to right place and Mum's diet of tough love and high fibre will sort him out in no time. She is better than Prozac any day. Said he has not come to right place. He will be begging for prescription drugs within minutes when he finds out Mum's regime is more restrictive than *Celebrity Fat Camp*.

. . . .

Thursday 25

Christmas Day

Is Christmas Day, i.e. season of goodwill and forgiveness (possibly) to all men. Yet instead Riley household is imbued with mintyness. Is not over credit crunch nature of presents. (Although James has already broken his hole puncher and is blaming Mum for purchasing from Gayhomes instead of superior WHSmith. Mum is blaming James for trying to punch holes in trousers, brussels sprout, and dog.) Or personal poems, which received high praise, e.g. 'Gosh' (Dad) and 'It is the thought that counts' (Mum). It is over impromptu presence of Uncle Jim. On plus side, he no longer looks like fundamentalist, i.e. beardy, in robes, with rabid expression in eyes. Instead is relatively fresh-faced and wearing pair of Dad's corduroys. Although freshness does not extend to breath which is definitely still of ouzo variety. But as only words uttered so far are 'please God no' when Mum tried to

clean out his ears, is hard to tell for sure. James says it will all be fine when Grandpa comes over with Treena and Baby Jesus for birthday tea and Uncle Jim will be moved with love for his infant brother, and estranged father. Said *a*) do not think Jesus and his health- and brain-compromising antics will move anyone except Mum and her bottle of Cillit Bang, *b*) Grandpa Riley is not estranged, just strange, and *c*) oh shit, had utterly forgotten that is birthday of other Jesus (i.e. not at all spiritual and with no ability to turn water into wine) and have not got him present. Oooh. Maybe will write him poem. He can put in box of treasures until he can read, i.e. in about ten years.

3.15 p.m.
Ugh. Brain obviously being sapped by atmosphere of non-festive gloom, and possibly excessively brandy-soaked Christmas pudding (due to slippage of wrist according to Dad, and latent alcoholism, according to Mum) as have utter writer's block. Will listen to soothing music for inspiration.

3.20 p.m.
Have had utter Newton moment (i.e. pain of apple falling on head eased by discovery of gravity) i.e. put on CD player, and realized had accidentally left in nausea-inducing Christmas Crackers album (dog likes East 17 'Stay'—it finds it soothing) BUT first song was 'Mary's

Boy Child', i.e. all about Baby Jesus, so have basically stolen it and rejigged lyrics, i.e:

*Now Ernest and his wife Treena came to Addenbrooke's
    Hospital that night,*
*They found no place to bear her child, not a single bed
    was in sight.* (Due to ward closures following
    outbreak of Norovirus)

*And then they found a little nook on a trolley all forlorn,
And in the dermatology wing cold and dark* (actually
    heated to standard twenty-one degrees but
    that doesn't scan), *Treena's little boy was born.*

*Hark now hear Beastly Boys sing, Jesus was born today,
Yes, Treena's boy child Jesus Riley was born on
    Christmas Day.*

Hurrah. Is not plagiarism, is cunning satire. And is just in time as can hear unmistakable sound of small child trailing feet through pea gravel in utterly banned manner (even coverage needed for maximum security effect).

5 p.m.
As predicted, presence of Baby Jesus did not move Uncle Jim to wordy confession. Particularly given that Jesus seemed convinced he was Craig Revel Horwood and the whole John Sergeant thing reared its ugly head again

until Mum put on CBeebies. On plus side, he did seem to bond with Grandpa, particularly over their mutual (if silent) appreciation of Pinky Dinky Doo. Jesus's birthday poem did not go down as well as hoped either. Gave Treena envelope. She said, 'Christ on a bike, it's not bloody book tokens is it?' Said 'No' (although you can never have enough book tokens). Treena said 'Thank flamin' 'eck. Your mam gave him a tenner's worth last year and we still an't spent them yet, I mean how many books does a kid need?' Did not answer. Let poem speak for itself. Though not sure what it said to Treena as she was stunned into silence.

6 p.m.
Prodigal relation returning thing is spreading like wildfire. Scarlet rang to say she has got email from Jack. Apparently he is coming home for New Year. Suzy is mental with excitement and says it is best Christmas present ever, except possibly for when she got a bottle of House of Commons whisky from Charles Clarke. Said yeah, is brilliant present. Scarlet said why do you sound so minty about it then? Said was not Jack. Was that dog had just eaten my Quality Street golden penny.

But was not dog (although he had eaten seven golden pennies and four purple nut things). It is Jack. Why hasn't he emailed me to tell me he is coming home?

6 p.m.
Not that I care. Because I'm grown-up and I know there are no happy endings and knights in shining anything.

6.30 p.m.
But the thing is. Maybe I do. Care I mean.

7.10 p.m.
Oh God. Maybe should email him and tell him.

7.30 p.m.
No will not email him. Am grown-up and fact based and above all affairs of the heart. Or pants.

7.35 p.m.
Oooh. Will email him and tell him that instead. Then is like am getting cake and eating it, i.e. contacting Jack, but also reasserting my commitment to adulthood.

7.40 p.m.
Have sent email as follows:

> I hear that you are coming back for New Year. Which was shock as in fact had utterly forgotten you even existed, have been so busy with my studies of economic crisis etc. Am utterly changed person, you probably won't even recognize me.

PS Although hair is still mental.

Is completely nonchalant, i.e. he will think have not been thinking about him at all. Which have not.

7.50 p.m.
Well, not often anyway.

8 p.m.
Until now. Is like he is camping out in brain. With fully secured guy ropes and a week's worth of calor gas. All can think about is Jack. Nothing can move him.

8.30 p.m.
Except James. There is nothing like sight of idiotic eleven year old in a hole-punched swimming cap trying to do splits to banish thoughts of former lover from head.

8.35 p.m.
Except that am now thinking about not thinking about him which means am actually thinking about him. Damn.

8.40 p.m.
Maybe will just check email to see if he has replied. In nonchalant way.

8.45 p.m.
No email. But am utterly nonchalant.

9 p.m.

Will just check again.

9.10 p.m.

No email. And Mum says to stop turning computer on as is non-festive anti-family activity and if I want something to do I can watch *The Vicar of Dibley* with everyone else.

. . . .

Friday 26

Boxing Day

Have checked email (Christmas officially over in Riley household, i.e. tree may still be up but fairy lights are off, chocolate boxes in recycling, and last of turkey has been chopped, curried, and frozen in meal-sized portions, to avoid waste and poisoning issues) but there is no reply. Think it is because Christmas clogs up ether and my email possibly still hovering somewhere mid-Atlantic waiting to get through cloggy cloud of round robins and online sale shopping transactions.

2 p.m.

James says emails do not hover above oceans and I am sounding more like Granny Clegg every day. Said that was unfair as Granny Clegg thinks the internet works by giant invisible cables but James said, 'How *does* the internet work, Einstein?' and had to admit did not know

596

unless it is by microwaves. Although maybe Granny Clegg does know actual answer now. Maybe bang on head has knocked sense into her.

3 p.m.
Granny Clegg rang. Asked her how internet worked. She said giant invisible cables. On plus side, she said Christmas at Pasty Manor was utter success, despite Hester's pet chicken Dale mysteriously disappearing in 'Bermuda Triangle' in scullery, leaving only three ginger feathers behind as reminder of his trusting eyes. Eyes not trusting. Eyes beady and menacing. But did not say that. Instead asked her if Bruce had eaten much today. She said no he has been mysteriously off his food and she is taking him to vet in case he is also being affected by the Bermuda Triangle forces, sapping his appetite.

Told her about Uncle Jim coming home. She went mental with excitement. But it turns out she thought I meant her Uncle Jimmy who died of syphilis in 1936. She is not so excited about Uncle Jim. It is because he is embracer of alternative culture. And Cleggs are very much anti-alternative or indeed any culture. They do not even buy olive oil as is too left-wing.

I feel sorry for Uncle Jim. No wonder he is not talking to anyone when they all think he is a criminal or mental or a 'filthy commie'. He is utter non-racist black sheep of family.

. . . .

Saturday 27

Both Jack and Uncle Jim are resolute in their silence, i.e. there is no email from Chichicastenango and Uncle Jim is mute on sofa watching *Tom and Jerry* with dog on his lap and bottle of Waitrose Belgian lager in hand. Said was amazed Mum was letting him consume alcohol in house, and at eleven in morning, but she says it is minimal alcohol by volume and is clever ruse to make him need to wee so that she can commandeer sofa and turn off TV without plaintive wailing (both Jim and dog).

2.10 p.m.

Oh my God. Have had complete revelation. I am also (non-racist) black sheep of family. Uncle Jim and I are at one. We are both depressed. We are both misunderstood. And we both have compromising hairdos (he has freakishly low hairline which gives him slight air of Cro-Magnon man/O'Grady). Am going to show solidarity by sitting on sofa and watching cartoons.

2.15 p.m.

But without the bottle of Belgian lager. I did try but Mum says I am not Amy Winehouse, much as I like to think I am, and I can have a glass of water or a small orange juice. She is wrong. I do not think I am Amy Winehouse.

2.20 p.m.
Although we do share poetic talent, cheating ex-boyfriends, and voluminous hair.

3 p.m.
Cartoons are off now. It was not the weeing. It was the falling asleep. Mum is now panicked that overfull bladder will give way during sleep and he will seep onto sofa. That will teach her. Or more probably mean we have reinstatement of plastic sofa covering (usually only brought out during presence of Bruce and Grandpa Clegg, neither of whom have complete control of urinary tract).

. . . .

Sunday 28

Still no email from Jack. It is good thing he is 5,466 miles away as Mum has decided enough is enough when it comes to silence and she is determined to break Uncle Jim. It is like Guantanamo Bay with Mum and James (who is assisting her in matter) as evil CIA agents. I do not rate Uncle Jim's chances. They are using the dining room as their torture chamber. James is already inside researching tactics on the internet.

10 a.m.
Mum has rejected waterboarding, sleep deprivation, and slapping. But is allowing mild threat (sectioning, or

withdrawal of all alcohol) and menacing stares. They are starting after lunch, and Dad and I are under instructions to leave table subtly after consumption of pudding course. As pudding is banana split asked if could leave before but Mum said would arouse too much suspicion. She is wrong. Is more convincing. Who voluntarily eats warm bananas?

5 p.m.
Uncle Jim has caved. It took two hours and forty-three minutes. And six bottles of Belgian lager. It turns out he has been in a trauma- (and possibly drug-) induced catatonic stupor after the love of his life, i.e. Marigold, left him halfway up a Himalaya for an accountant from Chipping Sodbury. Apparently she says he is a grown-up. Said Uncle Jim is a grown-up, i.e. he is 37. But Mum is utterly on Marigold's side, despite her being *a*) hippy and *b*) called Marigold. She said *a*) an accountant is a sound financial bet for the future and *b*) no man who still reads *Asterix* and *Tintin* can be classed as a grown-up.

Poor Uncle Jim. We are both victims of anti-fiction ageist policies. It is further proof that there are no happy endings. In fact do not know why I am wasting my time waiting for Jack to email. Love is utter charade and cold hard facts (and BBC) are only dependable constant in life. It is utterly depressing. In fact may join Uncle Jim in drowning sorrows in dining room.

6 p.m.

Mum has barred way to dining room. She says I do not need any alcohol to loosen my already overactive imagination or voicebox. Am going to drown sorrows down Duke instead. Although admittedly in non-alcoholic beverages. And possibly not in drowning quantities due to funding issues. Have traded book token with James on a crippling twenty per cent interest deal, i.e. I got £4 in return. Pointed out that interest rates were currently in fact languishing around the one per cent mark, but he said not for the likes of me they're not and went into a lecture on credit risk, so snatched money before he either changed mind or bored me to death. On plus side, Sad Ed will be there and will totally understand my plight. Plus hopefully he has had colossally awful Christmas so will feel somewhat smug. Scarlet is not coming. She says she is too busy preparing for return of Jack, i.e. repainting his bedroom walls black and getting his drum kit out of attic. Apparently Suzy had boxed everything up and Farrow and Balled everything off-white during mental premature nesting phase. Asked where baby will go if they ever get one? Scarlet said it is going to share with Bob and Suzy so they can fully bond as a family. It is baby I feel sorry for. I have seen what goes on in that bedroom and it is not savoury. Or even legal.

11 p.m.

At least in scheme of things I am not as sad as Sad Ed

(who actually got a packet of vests for Christmas, which he says just accentuates his non-worldly penis issues). Or as Uncle Jim. Whose penis, it turns out, is very much worldly. In fact it is possibly worldly penis, and its straying too close to someone called India Britt-Dullforce, that caused Marigold to fling self into arms of accountant. (Have just overheard him telling Mum ins and outs (literally) of relationship.) On plus side, at least he is still talking. It is over six hours of ceaseless confession now. Mum must be jubilant.

. . . .

Monday 29

Islamic New Year

Mum is not at all jubilant. In fact she is very minty, due to lack of sleep and abundance of talking. Apparently Uncle Jim kept her up until three banging on about Marigold's golden aura and how India Britt-Dullforce had bad 'chi'. She says she is like boy with finger in dyke (dam thing, not butch lesbian person) and she should have jolly well kept it in instead of letting in flood of psychobabble and unsavoury sexploits. He is back at it already this morning, only James is taking role of sympathetic listener. Said this was risk given James is underage and already quite cult-based (Lord of the Rings, Warhammer, Ninja Turtles) but she says it is better than Dad as James is utterly moral when it comes to adultery, and Dad is still in doghouse for siding with Camilla

602

in Princess Diana debacle. Did not tell her about the James/Mad Harry/Wendy Shoebridge love triangle. They are all meeting up later at Mad Harry's to swap presents. I dread to think what he will come home with. Possibly 'cooties' (definitely real, as Googled by James).

5 p.m.
James got a book of Greek myths and a keyring spirit level. Which is marginally better than cooties. But only marginally.

. . . .

Tuesday 30
There is yet more prodigal child 'good' news Chez Stone. Scarlet has rung to say Suzy and Bob have been allocated a baby. They got a letter this morning telling them it is being despatched within weeks. Asked what kind. Scarlet said it is mainly white, with a hint of exotic, i.e. its mother is Irish. Said actually meant is it boy or girl. Scarlet said it is a girl, called Aoife. But they are definitely going to rename her Obama. And that tomorrow's fancy dress New Year's Eve party is utterly in her honour. Asked what theme was. Scarlet says it is heroes and heroines, as Obama is modern hero. She is going as Bella Swan, obviously. Said am not coming as am me, i.e. my own hero except that am utterly non-heroic. And am peed off. Scarlet said does not have to be fictional. Suzy is coming

as Harriet Harman and Bob as Nelson Mandela. Said do not let him near boot polish. Scarlet said as if, that is utterly racist. He is going to just hold symbolic copy of *Economist*. Am still not going. New Year's Eve parties are just childish excuses to drink dubious punch and snog dubious guests.

· ·

Wednesday 31

New Year's Eve

Thank God it is New Year's Eve. The sooner 2008 is over the better. It has been utterly the worst year ever. Both the world and my life have been racked by ill-fortune and economic mismanagement. Plus am still one centimetre down on last year (millimetre gain was blip caused by rogue hair matting). The only consolation is that next year cannot possibly get any worse.

Am utterly resolute in decision not to partake in Scarlet's hero-themed welcome home Jack and Obama New Year's Eve party. Sad Ed has already been round to reveal his outfit of choice. It is Batman. Pointed out that this is mistake on several grounds, i.e. *a*) is utter lie as his heroes are all miserable/dead musicians, e.g. Jim Morrison/Morrisey etc. and *b*) tight and shiny bat suit is very revealing of bulges, including non-worldly penis and bingo wings. Sad Ed said am right on both counts but is all ploy to win over Scarlet as Batman is ultimate goth superhero, plus he knows for fact she is going as

Catwoman, who everyone knows was doing Batman on the side. Plus on positive side, lycra is girdle-like and he has lost several inches off waist. He is mistaken if he thinks that outfit will win Scarlet over. He does not look at all batly. He looks like a crap transvestite. Sad Ed has begged me to go with him, preferably dressed as Robin, but said it would compromise all my anti-hero ideals. Plus am needed at home to babysit Jesus and Uncle Jim. Grandpa and Treena are getting drunk in Queen Lizzie, Mum and Dad are going to play Jenga at Clive and Marjory's and James is at a Warhammer mathletes ner-dathon with Mad Harry and Wendy. They are mental with potential debauchery. Apparently Damon Parker is bringing a can of shandy and Ali Hassan has a Kanye West CD. They are morons. Sad Ed says I will regret it later when he is doing utterly grown-up things like putting his penis to good use and I am watching *Lark Rise to Candleford*. Said *a*) ick and *b*) it is *Road Runner* actually. Jesus does not like Julia Sawalha. Nor does the dog. It is static hair issues again. Yet it is not afraid of meep-meep-ing emu creature. Anyway, he is wrong, I will not regret my decision.

10 p.m.
Oh God. If have to watch idiot Wile E. Coyote blow himself up again am going to potentially steal Sad Ed's thunder and engage in untimely death. Why does he not learn? Even Jesus has fallen asleep. May just go upstairs

and text Sad Ed to check on progress. Is just being caring. Am not actually interested in gossip.

10.05 p.m.
Have got reply. He is all minty as there are three Batmen, and both of them have proper suits as opposed to leotards borrowed off their mums and cardboard masks. Plus they do not have tails. Have pointed out that did think tail was mistake as do not recall bats actually having them.

10.10 p.m.
He says he has removed tail but it has left gaping hole on buttock, revealing birthmark shaped like Gary Lineker's head. Have told him to get felt tip and colour buttock black and no one will be any the wiser.

10.15 p.m.
Sad Ed says cannot find felt tip but has stolen goth eyeliner from Scarlet's bedroom. Said that is good.

10.20 p.m.
Sad Ed says he is now in trouble for leaving black bottom prints all over Habitat sofa. Have texted back to say am losing interest in his buttocks and what else is happening please.

10.30 p.m.
Oooh text beep. Will be gossip from Sad Ed. Not that

need gossip. Is purely philanthropical, i.e. making sure all friends have not drowned in eggnog punch.

10.31 p.m.
Was not Sad Ed. Unbelievably was Justin Statham asking if had changed mind about his grown-up pants area. Said NO. AM ANTI-PANTS. KEEP CONTENTS TO SELF. ICK.

10.32 p.m.
Ugh. Text beep. Is probably Justin again. When will he get message that am utterly not interested in content of his pants.

10.35 p.m.
Was not Justin. Apparently he got pants message after all. Was Sad Ed. Whose pants content I have seen and rejected outright. Anyway, he says no one drowned in punch, but that is not eggnog, is new experimental gin, pineapple juice, and chocolate sauce variety. Which is all very interesting. But notice that Jack is not mentioned. Not that care about him. Or contents of his pants. Am just concerned that he has made it home safely and is not caught up in actual Osama Bin Laden Al Qaeda bomb plot at airport (as opposed to drunk beardy uncle plot).

10.40 p.m.
Although would be good if he was caught up. I could steal the Fiesta, drive to airport and infiltrate aircraft and talk

terrorists down with my negotiating skills, and utterly rescue Jack. Hurrah. Will text Sad Ed to check if Jack in peril.

10.45 p.m.
Sad Ed says he not at party but not in peril. He stuck in traffic on A11 in Nelson Mandela's sick-smelling Volvo. Never mind. Is probably good thing. Do not want to rescue ungrateful Jack, who has not even told me he is coming home yet. Plus rescuing only works in fiction. In real fact-based life I would crash Fiesta on mini round-about and end up in hospital with gear stick where gear-stick should not be. Will check on Uncle Jim and moronic coyote (dog, not Wile E) instead.

11 p.m.
Oh God. Uncle Jim is having sobbing breakdown due to turning off of *Road Runner* and reading of *Tintin in Tibet*, which just reminds him of Marigold. Is all my fault. I should have followed Mum's instructions (A4, magneted to fridge) and monitored him at all times. Will check list to see what have to do in this situation.

11.15 p.m.
List has no instructions for weeping uncles. Although it does tell me how to relight the boiler pilot, make an emergency escape rope from bedsheets, and perform Heimlich manoeuvre on dog. Will use initiative and tell

608

him some simple facts of life, i.e. there are no happy endings, love does not exist, and the sooner he grows up the better.

11.20 p.m.
Uncle Jim is not at all in agreement with fact-based stance. Said he of all people should understand, given utterly non-happy ending of love life halfway up a Himalaya. He said *au contraire*, it has only fuelled his conviction that love is everything, and that if you don't believe in happy endings then there is no point to universe. Told him if he had any Riley sense, he would grow up, and read some Stephen Hawking instead of the *Asterix* and *Tintin*. He said where's the fun in that? Said life isn't meant to be fun and stormed out before he could baffle me with any more yoghurt-knitting alternative nonsense.

11.25 p.m.
Oh. Have got text. Is probably Sad Ed with more buttock-related hoo-ha.

11.26 p.m.
Was not Sad Ed. Was Jack. It said, 'Just got email. Must have got clogged in Christmas ether. Where are you, Riley? Want to see the new you!' Have not texted back. Cannot even be bothered to reply. Especially as the new me is wearing no make-up, is all red-faced from getting minty, and is in perpetually vile mood.

11.27 p.m.
Actually, is true. Am always in vile mood these days. Why is that?

11.30 p.m.
Oh God. Have had revelation. Is thanks to yoghurt-knitting Uncle Jim. He sat outside bedroom door (refused to let him in as was all red-faced from mintyness) and said 'Do you know who you sound like, Rach?' Said 'Sensible grown-up.' He said, 'Yeah. Like your mum.' And then stomach did hideous enormous heave thing. And realized do sound exactly like Mum. Although with slightly less use of phrase 'I told you so'. But none the less, have utterly morphed into low-fun, permanently minty Janet Riley. Was about to utter strangulated cry but Uncle Jim clearly on one of his confessional rants and got in first with 'Don't grow up yet, Rach. In fact don't grow up ever. Happy endings aren't just in books. You just need to believe in yourself. And in love.' And then he started going on about believing in rainbows and pots of gold so switched off at that bit because James spent a year trying to deduce the possibility of pot of gold and has established beyond reasonable doubt that it does not exist. But he is right about happy endings. That they're worth aiming for. Because even if you fall down, half the fun is in trying.

I want my happy ending. I want to be a princess. I want my knight in shining whatever.

And I don't need rescuing. But maybe I can rescue him

instead. And tell him that I might not be grown-up. And I might make mistakes. Colossal ones involving magic mushrooms and naked ex-boyfriends. But that it doesn't mean I don't love him.

11.35 p.m.
Because I do. I love him.

11.45 p.m.
Oh. I really love him. I have to go and tell him. I have to rescue him right now. Jesus will be fine. He is asleep on dog and dog is asleep on washing machine. What can possibly go wrong there? And anyway, Uncle Jim is here. And he might not be grown-up in Mum's eyes. But he's clever. And sober, for once (Belgian lager out of bounds now floodgates opened). And he knows more about life than anyone else I know. Oh God, have only got quarter of an hour of year left. Why, oh why did I wish it away. I have to get there before midnight. I have to tell him before he snogs Hillary Clinton or the Invisible Woman.

11.46 p.m.
OK. This is it. I'm going to get my happy ending. Not as a heroine. Mostly because I don't have the time to make authentic Sylvia Plath costume. Instead am going as me. Because Jack was right about one thing. Being me is enough. In fact, it's utterly brilliant.

Or at least it will be. In about fourteen minutes . . .

Joanna Nadin was born in Northampton and moved to Saffron Walden in Essex when she was three. She did well at school (being a terrible swot) and then went to Hull University to study Drama. Three years of pretending to be a toaster and pretending to like Fellini films put her off the theatre for life. She moved to London to study for an MA in Political Communications and after a few years as an autocue girl and a radio newsreader got a job with the Labour Party as a campaigns writer and Special Adviser. She now lives in Bath with her daughter and is a freelance government speech writer and TV scriptwriter. She has written many books including six about Rachel Riley, and has been shortlisted twice for the Queen of Teen Award.